Praise for *New York Times* bestselling author Diana Palmer

"Palmer proves that love and passion can be found even in the most dangerous situations."
—*Publishers Weekly* on *Untamed*

"You just can't do better than a Diana Palmer story to make your heart lighter and smile brighter."
—*Fresh Fiction* on *Wyoming Rugged*

"Diana Palmer is a mesmerizing storyteller who captures the essence of what a romance should be."
—*Affaire de Coeur*

"The popular Palmer has penned another winning novel, a perfect blend of romance and suspense."
—*Booklist* on *Lawman*

"Diana Palmer's characters leap off the page. She captures their emotions and scars beautifully and makes them come alive for readers."
—*RT Book Reviews* on *Lawless*

Dear Reader,

I can't believe that it has been thirty years since my first Long, Tall Texan book, *Calhoun*, debuted! The series was suggested by my former editor Tara Gavin, who asked if I might like to set stories in a fictional town of my own design. Would I! And the rest is history.

As the years went by, I found more and more sexy ranchers and cowboys to add to the collection. My readers (especially Amy!) found time to gift me with a notebook listing every single one of them, wives and kids and connections to other families in my own Texas town of Jacobsville. Eventually the town got a little too big for me, so I added another smaller town called Comanche Wells and began to fill it up, too.

You can't imagine how much pleasure this series has given me. I continue to add to the population of Jacobs County, Texas, and I have no plans to stop. Ever.

I hope all of you enjoy reading the Long, Tall Texans as much as I enjoy writing them. Thank you all for your kindness and loyalty and friendship. I am your biggest fan!

Love,

Diana Palmer

NEW YORK TIMES BESTSELLING AUTHOR

DIANA PALMER

LONG, TALL TEXANS:

Alexander

—

J.B.

Previously published as *Man in Control* and *Heartbreaker*

◆ **HARLEQUIN** SPECIAL RELEASE

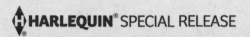 HARLEQUIN® SPECIAL RELEASE

ISBN-13: 978-1-335-62403-1

Long, Tall Texans: Alexander/J.B.

Copyright © 2020 by Harlequin Books S.A.

Alexander
First published as Man in Control in 2003.
This edition published in 2020.
Copyright © 2003 by Diana Palmer

J.B.
First published as Heartbreaker in 2006.
This edition published in 2020.
Copyright © 2006 by Diana Palmer

Recycling programs
for this product may
not exist in your area.

This edition published by arrangement with Harlequin Books S.A.

For questions and comments about the quality of this book,
please contact us at CustomerService@Harlequin.com.

Harlequin Enterprises ULC
22 Adelaide St. West, 40th Floor
Toronto, Ontario M5H 4E3, Canada
www.Harlequin.com

Printed in U.S.A.

CONTENTS

A prolific author of more than one hundred books, **Diana Palmer** got her start as a newspaper reporter. A *New York Times* bestselling author and voted one of the top ten romance writers in America, she has a gift for telling the most sensual tales with charm and humor. Diana lives with her family in Cornelia, Georgia. Visit her website at www.dianapalmer.com.

Books by Diana Palmer

Long, Tall Texans

Fearless
Heartless
Dangerous
Merciless
Courageous
Protector
Invincible
Untamed
Defender
Undaunted

The Wyoming Men

Wyoming Tough
Wyoming Fierce
Wyoming Bold
Wyoming Strong
Wyoming Rugged
Wyoming Brave

Morcai Battalion

The Morcai Battalion
The Morcai Battalion: The Recruit
The Morcai Battalion: Invictus
The Morcai Battalion: The Rescue

Visit the Author Profile page
at Harlequin.com for more titles.

ALEXANDER

In loving memory of Diana Galloway

PROLOGUE

ALEXANDER TYRELL COBB glared at his desk in the Houston Drug Enforcement Administration office with barely contained frustration. There was a photograph of a lovely woman in a ball gown in an expensive frame, the only visible sign of any emotional connections. Like the conservative clothes he wore to work, the photograph gave away little of the private man.

The photograph was misleading. The woman in it wasn't a close friend. She was a casual date, when he was between assignments. The frame had been given to him with the photo in it. He'd never put a woman's photo in a frame. Well, except for Jodie Clayburn. She and his sister, Margie, were best friends from years past. Most of the family photos he had included Jodie. She wasn't really family, of course. But there was no other Cobb family left, just as there was no other Clayburn family left. The three survivors of the two families were a forced mixture of different lifestyles.

Jodie was in love with Alexander. He knew it, and tried not to acknowledge it. She was totally wrong for him. He had no desire to marry and have a family. On the other hand, if he'd been seriously interested in children and a home life, Jodie would have been at the top of his list of potential mates. She had wonderful qualities. He wasn't about to tell her so. She'd been hung up on him in the past to a disturbing degree. He'd managed to keep her at arm's length, and he had no plans to lessen the space between them. He was married to his job.

Jodie, on the other hand, was an employee at a local oil corporation which was being used in an international drug smuggling operation. Alexander was almost certain of it. But he couldn't prove it. He was going to have to find some way to investigate one of Jodie's acquaintances without letting anyone realize they were being watched.

In the meantime, there was a party planned at the Cobb ranch in Jacobsville, Texas, on Saturday. He dreaded it already. He hated parties. Margie had already invited Jodie, probably because their housekeeper, Jessie, refused to work that weekend. Jodie cooked with a masterful hand, and she could make canapés. Kirry had been invited, too, because Margie was a budding dress designer who needed a friend in the business. Kirry was senior buyer for the department store where she worked. She was pretty and capable, but Alexander found her good company and not much more. Their relationship had always been lukewarm and even now, it was slowly fizzling out. She was demanding. He had enough demands on the job.

He put the picture facedown on his desk and pulled a file folder closer, opening it to the photograph of a suspected drug smuggler who was working out of Houston. He had his work cut out for him. He wished he could avoid going home for the party, but Margie would never forgive him. If he didn't show up, neither would Kirry, and Alexander would never hear the end of it. He put the weekend to the back of his mind and concentrated on the job at hand.

CHAPTER ONE

THERE WAS NO way out of it. Margie Cobb had invited her to a party on the family ranch in Jacobsville, Texas. Jodie Clayburn had gone through her entire repertoire of excuses. Her favorite was that, given the right incentive, Margie's big brother, Alexander Tyrell Cobb, would feed her to his cattle. Not even that one had worked.

"He hates me, Margie," she groaned over the phone from her apartment in Houston, Texas. "You know he does. He'd be perfectly happy if I stayed away from him for the rest of my natural life and he never had to see me again."

"That's not true," Margie defended. "Lex really likes you, I know he does," she added with forced conviction, using the nickname that only a handful of people on earth were allowed to use. Jodie wasn't one of them.

"Right. He just hides his affection for me in bouts of bad temper laced with sarcasm," came the dry reply.

"Sure," Margie replied with failing humor.

Jodie lay back on her sofa with the freedom phone at her ear and pushed back her long blond hair. It was getting too long. She really needed to have it cut, but she liked the feel of it. Her gray eyes smiled as she remembered how much Brody Vance liked long hair. He worked at the Ritter Oil Corporation branch office in Houston with her, and was on the management fast track.

As Jody was. She was administrative assistant to Brody, and if Brody had his way, she'd take his job as Human Resources generalist when he moved up to Human Resources manager. He liked her. She liked him, too. Of course he had a knockout girlfriend who was a Marketing Division manager in Houston, but she was always on the road somewhere. He was lonely. So he had lunch frequently with Jodie. She was trying very hard to develop a crush on him. He was beginning to notice her. Alexander had accused her of trying to sleep her way to the executive washroom…

"I was not!" she exclaimed, remembering his unexpected visit to her office with an executive of the company who was a personal friend. It had played havoc with her nerves and her heart. Seeing Alexander unexpectedly melted her from the neck down, despite her best efforts not to let him affect her.

"Excuse me?" Margie replied, aghast.

Jodie sat up quickly. "Nothing!" she said. "Sorry. I was just thinking. Did you know that Alexander has a friend who works for my company?"

There was a long pause. "He does?"

"Jasper Duncan, the Human Resources manager for our division."

"Oh. Yes. Jasper!" There was another pause. "How do you know about that?"

"Because Mr. Duncan brought him right to my desk while I was talking to a…well, to a good friend of mine, my boss."

"Right, the one he thinks you're sleeping with."

"Margie!" she exploded.

There was an embarrassed laugh. "Sorry. I know

there's nothing going on. Alexander always thinks the worst of people. You know about Rachel."

"Everybody knows about Rachel," she muttered. "It was six years ago and he still throws her up to us."

"We did introduce him," Margie said defensively.

"Well, how were we to know she was a female gigolo who was only interested in marrying a rich man? She should have had better sense than to think Alexander would play that sort of game, anyway!"

"You do know him pretty well, don't you?" Margie murmured.

"We all grew up together in Jacobsville, Texas," Jodie reminded her. "Sort of," she added pensively. "Alexander was eight years ahead of us in school, and then he moved to Houston to work for the DEA when he got out of college."

"He's still eight years ahead of us," Margie chuckled. "Come on. You know you'll hate yourself if you miss this party. We're having a houseful of people. Derek will be there," she added sweetly, trying to inject a lure.

Derek was Margie's distant cousin, a dream of a man with some peculiar habits and a really weird sense of humor.

"You know what happened the last time Derek and I were together," Jodie said with a sense of foreboding.

"Oh, I'm sure Alexander has forgotten about *that* by now," she was assured.

"He has a long memory. And Derek can talk me into anything," Jodie added worriedly.

"I'll hang out with both of you and protect you from dangerous impulses. Come on. Say yes. I've got an opportunity to show my designs. It depends on this party going smoothly. And I've made up this marvelous dress pattern I want to try out on you. For someone with the body of a clotheshorse, you have no sense of style at all!"

"You have enough for both of us. You're a budding fashion designer. I'm a lady executive. I have to dress the part."

"Baloney. When was the last time your boss wore a black dress to a party?"

Jodie was remembering a commercial she'd seen on television with men in black dresses. She howled, thinking of Alexander's hairy legs in a short skirt. Then she tried to imagine where he'd keep his sidearm in a short skirt, and she really howled.

She told Margie what she was thinking, and they both collapsed into laughter.

"Okay," she capitulated at last. "I'll come. But if I break a tree limb over your brother's thick skull, you can't say you weren't forewarned."

"I swear, I won't say a word."

"Then I'll see you Friday afternoon about four," Jodie said with resignation. "I'll rent a car and drive over."

"Uh, Jodie…"

She groaned. "All right, Margie, all right, I'll fly to the Jacobsville airport and you can pick me up there."

"Great!"

"Just because I had two little bitty fender benders," she muttered.

"You totaled two cars, Jodie, and Alexander had to bail you out of jail after the last one…"

"Well, that stupid thickheaded barbarian deserved to be hit! He called me a…well, never mind, but he asked for a punch in the mouth!" Jodie fumed.

Margie was trying not to laugh. Again.

"Anyway, it was only a small fine and the judge took

my side when he heard the whole story," she said, ignoring Margie's quick reminder that Alexander had talked to the judge first. "Not that your brother ever let me forget it! Just because he works for the Justice Department is no reason for him to lecture me on law!"

"We just want you to arrive alive, darling," Margie drawled. "Now throw a few things into a suitcase, tell your boss you have a sick cousin you have to take care of before rush hour, and we'll... *I'll*...meet you at the airport Friday afternoon. You phone and tell me your flight number, okay?"

"Okay," Jodie replied, missing the slip.

"See you then! We're going to have a ball."

"Sure we are," Jodie told her. But when she hung up, she was calling herself all sorts of names for being such a weakling. Alexander was going to cut her up, she just knew it. He didn't like her. He never had. He'd gotten more antagonistic since she moved to Houston, where he worked, too. Further, it would probably mean a lot of work for Jodie, because she usually had to prepare meals if she showed up. The family cook, Jessie, hated being around Alexander when he was home, so she ran for the hills. Margie couldn't cook at all, so Jodie usually ended up with KP. Not that she minded. It was just that she felt used from time to time.

And despite Margie's assurances, she knew she was in for the fight of her life once she set foot on the Cobb ranch. At least Margie hadn't said anything about inviting Alexander's sometimes girlfriend, Kirry Dane. A weekend with the elegant buyer for an exclusive Houston department store would be too much.

The thing was, she had to go when Margie asked her. She owed the Cobbs so much. When her parents, small

Jacobsville ranchers, had been drowned in a riptide during a modest Florida vacation at the beach, it had been Alexander who flew down to take care of all the arrangements and comfort a devastated seventeen-year-old Jodie. When she entered business college, Alexander had gone with her to register and paid the fees himself. She spent every holiday with Margie. Since the death of the Cobbs' father, and their inheritance of the Jacobsville ranch property, she'd spent her vacation every summer there with Margie. Her life was so intertwined with that of the Cobbs that she couldn't even imagine life without them.

But Alexander had a very ambiguous relationship with Jodie. From time to time he was affectionate, in his gruff way. But he also seemed to resent her presence and he picked at her constantly. He had for the past year.

She got up and went to pack, putting the antagonism to the back of her mind. It did no good to dwell on her confrontations with Alexander. He was like a force of nature which had to be accepted, since it couldn't be controlled.

THE JACOBSVILLE AIRPORT was crowded for a Friday afternoon. It was a tiny airport compared to those in larger cities, but a lot of people in south Texas used it for commuter flights to San Antonio and Houston. There was a restaurant and two concourses, and the halls were lined with beautiful paintings of traditional Texas scenery.

Jodie almost bowed under the weight of her oversize handbag and the unruly carry-on bag whose wheels didn't quite work. She looked around for Margie. The brunette wouldn't be hard to spot because she was tall for a woman, and always wore something striking—usually one of her own flamboyant designs.

But she didn't see any tall brunettes. What she did see, and what stopped her dead in her tracks, was a tall and striking dark-haired man in a gray vested business suit. A man with broad shoulders and narrow hips and big feet in hand-tooled leather boots. He turned, looking around, and spotted her. Even at the distance, those deep-set, cold green eyes were formidable. So was he. He looked absolutely furious.

She stood very still, like a woman confronted with a spitting cobra, and waited while he approached her with the long, quick stride she remembered from years of painful confrontations. Her chin lifted and her eyes narrowed. She drew in a quick breath, and geared up for combat.

Alexander Tyrell Cobb was thirty-three. He was a senior agent for the Drug Enforcement Administration. Usually, he worked out of Houston, but he was on vacation for a week. That meant he was at the family ranch in Jacobsville. He'd grown up there, with Margie, but their mother had taken them from their father after the divorce and had them live with her in Houston. It hadn't been until her death that they'd finally been allowed to return home to their father's ranch. The old man had loved them dearly. It had broken his heart when he'd lost them to their mother.

Alexander lived on the ranch sporadically even now, when he wasn't away on business. He also had an apartment in Houston. Margie lived at the ranch all the time, and kept things running smoothly while her big brother was out shutting down drug smugglers.

He looked like a man who could do that single-handed. He had big fists, like his big feet, and Jodie had seen him use them once on a man who slapped Margie. He rarely smiled. He had a temper like a scalded snake, and he was all business when he tucked that big .45 automatic into its hand-tooled leather holster and went out looking for trouble.

In the past two years, he'd been helping to shut down an international drug lord, Manuel Lopez, who'd died mysteriously in an explosion in the Bahamas. Now he was after the dead drug lord's latest successor, a Central American national who was reputed to have business connections in the port city of Houston.

She'd developed a feverish crush on him when she was in her teens. She'd written him a love poem. Alexander, with typical efficiency, had circled the grammatical and spelling errors and bought her a supplemental English book to help her correct the mistakes. Her self-esteem had taken a serious nosedive, and after that, she kept her deepest feelings carefully hidden.

She'd seen him only a few times since her move to Houston when she began attending business college. When she visited Margie these days, Alexander never seemed to be around except at Christmas. It was as if he'd been avoiding her. Then, just a couple of weeks ago, he'd dropped by her office to see Jasper. It had been a shock to see him unexpectedly, and her hands had trembled on her file folders, despite her best efforts to play it cool. She wanted to think she'd outgrown her flaming crush on him. Sadly, it had only gotten worse. It was easier on her nerves when she didn't have to see him. Fortunately it was a big city and they didn't travel in the same circles. But she didn't know where Alexander's office or apartment were, and she didn't ask.

In fact, her nerves were already on edge right now, just from the level, intent stare of those green eyes across a crowded concourse. She clutched the handle of her wheeled suitcase with a taut grip. Alexander made her knees weak.

He strode toward her. He never looked right or left. His gaze was right on her the whole way. She wondered if he was like that on the job, so intent on what he was doing that he seemed relentless.

He was a sexy beast, too. There was a tightly controlled sensuality in every movement of those long, powerful legs, in the way he carried himself. He was elegant, arrogant. Jodie couldn't remember a time in her life when she hadn't been fascinated by him. She hoped it didn't show. She worked hard at pretending to be his enemy.

He stopped in front of her and looked down his nose into her wide eyes. His were green, clear as water, with dark rims that made them seem even more piercing. He had thick black eyelashes and black eyebrows that were as black as his neatly cut, thick, straight hair.

"You're late," he said in his deep, gravelly voice, throwing down the gauntlet at once. He looked annoyed, half out of humor and wanting someone to bite.

"I can't fly the plane," she replied sarcastically. "I had to depend on *men* for that."

He gave her a speaking glance and turned. "The car's in the parking lot. Let's go."

"Margie was supposed to meet me," she muttered, dragging her case behind her.

"Margie knew I had to be here anyway, so she had me wait for you," he said enigmatically. "I never knew a woman who could keep an appointment, anyway."

The carry-on bag fell over for the tenth time. She muttered and finally just picked the heavy thing up. "You might offer to help me," she said, glowering at her companion.

His eyebrows arched. "Help a woman carry a heavy load? My God, I'd be stripped, lashed to a rail and carried through Houston by torchlight!"

She gave him a seething glance. "Manners don't go out of style!"

"Pity I never had any to begin with." He watched her struggle with the luggage, green eyes dancing with pure venom.

She was sweating already. "I hate you," she said through her teeth as she followed along with him.

"That's a change," he said with a shrug, pushing back his jacket as he dug into his slacks pocket for his car keys.

A security guard spotted the pistol on his belt and came forward menacingly. With meticulous patience, and very carefully, Alexander reached into the inside pocket of his suit coat and produced his badge and ID. He had it out before the guard reached them.

The man took it. "Wait a minute," he said, and moved aside to check it out over the radio.

"Maybe you're on a wanted list somewhere," Jodie said enthusiastically. "Maybe they'll put you in jail while they check out your ID!"

"If they do," he replied nonchalantly, "rent-a-cop over there will be looking for another job by morning."

He didn't smile as he said it, and Jodie knew he meant what he was saying. Alexander had a vindictive streak a mile wide. There was a saying among law enforcement people that Cobb would follow you all the way to hell to get you if you crossed him. From their years of uneasy acquaintance, she knew it was more than myth.

The security guard came back and handed Alexander his ID. "Sorry, sir, but it's my job to check out suspicious people."

Alexander glared at him. "Then why haven't you checked out the gentleman in the silk suit over there with the bulge in his hatband? He's terrified that you're going to notice him."

The security guard frowned and glanced toward the elegant man, who tugged at his collar. "Thanks for the tip," he murmured, and started toward the man.

"You might have offered to lend him your gun," she told Alexander.

"He's got one. Of a sort," he added with disgust at the pearl-handled sidearm the security guard was carrying.

"Men have to have their weapons, don't they?" she chided.

He gave her a quick glance. "With a mouth like yours, you don't need a weapon. Careful you don't cut your chin with that tongue."

She aimed a kick at his shin and missed, almost losing her balance.

"Assault on a law enforcement officer is a felony," he pointed out without even breaking stride.

She recovered her balance and went out the door after him without another word. If they ever suspended the rules for one day, she knew who she was going after!

ONCE THEY REACHED his car, an elegant white Jaguar S-type, he did put her bags in the trunk—but he left her to open her own door and get in. It wasn't surprising to find him driving such a car, on a federal agent's salary, because he and Margie were independently wealthy. Their late mother had left them both well-off, but unlike Margie, who loved the social life, Alexander refused to live on an inheritance. He enjoyed working for his living. It was one of many things Jodie admired about him.

The admiration didn't last long. He threw down the gauntlet again without hesitation. "How's your boyfriend?" he asked as he pulled out into traffic.

"I don't have a boyfriend!" she snapped, still wiping away sweat. It was hot for August, even in south Texas.

"No? You'd like to have one, though, wouldn't you?" He adjusted the rearview mirror as he stopped at a traffic light.

"He's my boss. That's all."

"Pity. You could hardly take your eyes off him, that day I stopped by your office."

"*He's* handsome," she said with deliberate emphasis.

His eyebrow jerked. "Looks don't get you promoted in the Drug Enforcement Administration," he told her.

"You'd know. You've worked for it half your life."

"Not quite half. I'm only thirty-three."

"One foot in the grave…"

He glanced at her. "You're twenty-five, I believe? And never been engaged?"

He knew that would hurt. She averted her gaze to the window. Until a few months ago, she'd been about fifty pounds overweight and not very careful about her clothing or makeup. She was still clueless about how to dress. She dressed like an overweight woman, with loose clothing that showed nothing of her pretty figure. She folded her arms over her breasts defensively.

"I can't go through with this," she said through her teeth. "Three days of you will put me in therapy!"

He actually smiled. "That would be worth putting up with three days of you to see."

She crossed her legs under her full skirt and concentrated on the road. Her eyes caressed the silky brown bird's-eye maple that graced the car's dash and steering wheel.

"Margie promised she'd meet me," she muttered, repeating herself.

"She told me you'd be thrilled if I did," he replied with a searing glance. "You're still hung up on me, aren't you?" he asked with faint sarcasm.

Her jaw fell. "She lied! I did not say I'd be thrilled for you to meet me!" she raged. "I only came because she promised that she'd be here when I landed. I wanted to rent a car and drive!"

His green eyes narrowed on her flushed face. "That would have been suicide," he murmured. "Or homicide, depending on your point of view."

"I can drive!"

"You and the demolition derby guys," he agreed. He accelerated around a slow-moving car and the powerful Jaguar growled like the big cat it was named for. She glanced at him and saw the pure joy of the car's performance in his face as he slid effortlessly back into the lane ahead of the slow car. He enjoyed fast cars and, gossip said, faster women. But that side of his life had always been concealed from Jodie. It was as if he'd placed her permanently off-limits and planned to keep her there.

"At least I don't humiliate other drivers by streaking past them at jet fighter speed!" she raged. She was all but babbling, and after only ten minutes of his company. Seething inwardly, she turned toward the window so that she wouldn't have to look at him.

"I wasn't streaking. I'm doing the speed limit," he said. He glanced at the speedometer, smiled faintly and eased up on the accelerator. His eyes slid over Jodie curiously.

"You've lost so much weight, I hardly recognized you when I stopped by to talk to Jasper."

"Right. I looked different when I was fat."

"You were never fat," he shot back angrily. "You were voluptuous. There's a difference."

She glanced at him. "I was terribly overweight."

"And you think men like to run their hands over bones, do you?"

She shifted in her seat. "I wouldn't know."

"You had a low self-image. You still have it. There's nothing wrong with you. Except for that sharp tongue," he added.

"Look who's complaining!"

"If I don't yell, nobody listens."

"You never yell," she corrected. "You can look at people and make them run for cover."

He smiled without malice. "I practice in my bathroom mirror."

She couldn't believe she'd heard that.

"You need to start thinking about a Halloween costume," he murmured as he made a turn.

"For what? Are you going to hire me out for parties?" she muttered.

"For our annual Halloween party next month," he said with muted disgust. "Margie's invited half of Jacobsville to come over in silly clothes and masks to eat candy apples."

"What are you coming as?"

He gave her a careless glance. "A Drug Enforcement Agency field agent."

She rolled her eyes toward the ceiling of the car.

"I make a convincing DEA field agent," he persisted.

"I wouldn't argue with that," she had to agree. "I hear

that Manuel Lopez mysteriously blew up in the Bahamas the year before last, and nobody's replaced him yet," she added. "Did you have anything to do with his sudden demise?"

"DEA agents don't blow up drug lords. Not even one as bad as Lopez."

"Somebody did."

He glanced at her with a faint smile. "In a manner of speaking."

"One of the former mercs from Jacobsville, I heard."

"Micah Steele was somewhere around when it happened. He's never been actually connected with Lopez's death."

"He moved back here and married Callie Kirby, didn't he? They have a little girl now."

He nodded. "He's practicing medicine at Jacobsville General as a resident, hoping to go into private practice when he finishes his last semester of study."

"Lucky Callie," she murmured absently, staring out the window. "She always wanted to get married and have kids, and she was crazy about Micah most of her life."

He watched her curiously. "Didn't you want to get married, too?"

She didn't answer. "So now that Lopez is out of the way, and nobody's replaced him, you don't have a lot to do, do you?"

He laughed shortly. "Lopez has a new successor, a Peruvian national living in Mexico on an open-ended visa. He's got colleagues in Houston helping him smuggle his product into the United States."

"Do you know who they are?" she asked excitedly.

He gave her a cold glare. "Oh, sure, I'm going to tell you their names right now."

"You don't have to be sarcastic, Cobb," she said icily.

One thick eyebrow jerked. "You're the only person I know, outside work, who uses my last name as if it were my first name."

"You don't use my real name, either."

"Don't I?" He seemed surprised. He glanced at her. "You don't look like a Jordana."

"I never thought I looked like a Jordana, either," she said with a sigh. "My mother loved odd names. She even gave them to the cats."

Remembering her mother made her sad. She'd lost both parents in a freak accident during a modest vacation in Florida after her high school graduation. Her parents had gone swimming in the ocean, having no idea that the pretty red flags on the beach warned of treacherous riptides that could drown even experienced swimmers. Which her mother and father were not. She could still remember the horror of it. Alexander had come to take care of the details, and to get her back home. Odd how many tragedies and crises he'd seen her through over the years.

"Your mother was a sweet woman," he recalled. "I'm sorry you lost her. And your father."

"He was a sweet man, too," she recalled. It had been eight years ago, and she could remember happy times now, but it still made her sad to think of them.

"Strange, isn't it, that you don't take after either of them?" he asked caustically. "No man in his right mind could call you 'sweet.'"

"Stop right there, Cobb," she threatened, using his last name again. It was much more comfortable than getting personal with the nickname Margie used for him. "I could say things about you, too."

"What? That I'm dashing and intelligent and the

answer to a maiden's prayer?" He pursed his lips and glanced her way as he pulled into the road that led to the ranch. "Which brings up another question. Are you sleeping with that airheaded boss of yours at work yet?"

"He is not airheaded!" she exclaimed, offended.

"He eats tofu and quiche, he drives a red convertible of uncertain age, he plays tennis and he doesn't know how to program a computer without crashing the system."

That was far too knowledgeable to have come from a dossier. Her eyes narrowed. "You've had him checked out!" she accused with certainty.

He only smiled. It wasn't a nice smile.

CHAPTER TWO

"YOU CAN'T GO around snooping into people's private lives like that," Jodie exclaimed heatedly. "It's not right!"

"I'm looking for a high-level divisional manager who works for the new drug lord in his Houston territory," he replied calmly. "I check out everybody who might have an inkling of what's going on." He turned his head slightly. "I even checked you out."

"Me?" she exclaimed.

He gave her a speaking look. "I should have known better. If I had a social life like yours, I'd join a convent."

"I can see you now, in long skirts…"

"It was a figure of speech," he said curtly. "You haven't been on a date in two years. Amazing, considering how many eligible bachelors there are in your building alone, much less the whole of Houston." He gave her a penetrating stare. "Are you sure you aren't still stuck on me?"

She drew in a short breath. "Oh, sure, I am," she muttered. "I only come down here so that I can sit and moon over you and think of ways to poison all your girlfriends."

He chuckled in spite of himself. "Okay. I get the idea."

"Who in my building do you suspect, exactly?" she persisted.

He hesitated. His dark brows drew together in a frown as the ranch house came into view down the long, dusty road. "I can't tell you that," he said. "Right now it's only a suspicion."

"I could help you trap him," she volunteered. "If I get a gun, that is. I won't help you if I have to be unarmed."

He chuckled again. "You shoot like you drive, Jodie."

She made an angry sound in her throat. "I could shoot just fine if I got enough practice. Is it my fault that my landlord doesn't like us busting targets in my apartment building?"

"Have Margie invite you down just to shoot. She can teach you as well as I can."

It was an unpleasant reminder that he wasn't keen on being with her.

"I don't remember asking you to teach me anything," she returned.

He pulled up in front of the house. "Well, not lately, at least," he had to agree.

Margie heard the car drive up and came barreling out onto the porch. She was tall, like Alexander, and she had green eyes, too, but her dark hair had faint undertones of auburn. She was pretty, unlike poor Jodie, and she wore anything with flair. She designed and made her own clothes, and they were beautiful.

She ran to Jodie and hugged her, laughing. "I'm so glad you came!"

"I thought you were going to pick me up at the airport, Margie," came the droll reply.

Margie looked blank for an instant. "Oh, gosh, I was, wasn't I? I got busy with a design and just lost all track of time. Besides, Lex had already gone to the airport to pick up Kirry, but she couldn't get his cell phone, so she phoned me and said she was delayed until tomorrow afternoon. He was right there already, so I just phoned him and had him bring you home."

Kirry was Alexander's current girlfriend. The fashion buyer had just returned home recently from a buying trip to Paris. It didn't occur to Margie that it would have been pure torture to have to ride to the ranch with Alexander and his girlfriend. But, then, Margie didn't think things through. And to give her credit, she didn't realize that Jodie was still crazy about Alexander Cobb.

"She's coming down tomorrow to look at some of my new designs," Margie continued, unabashed, "and, of course, for the party in her honor that we're giving here. She leads a very busy life."

Jodie felt her heart crashing at her feet, and she didn't dare show it. A weekend with Kirry Dane drooling over Alexander, and vice versa. Why hadn't she argued harder and stayed home?

Alexander checked his watch. "I've got to make a few phone calls, then I'm going to drive into town and see about that fencing I ordered."

"That's what we have a foreman for," Margie informed him.

"Chayce went home to Georgia for the weekend. His father's in the hospital."

"You didn't tell me that!"

"Did you need to know?" he shot right back.

Margie shook her head, exasperated, as he just walked away without a backward glance. "I do live here, too," she muttered, but it was too late. He'd already gone into the house.

"I'm going to be in the way if the party's for Kirry," Jodie said worriedly. "Honestly, Margie, you shouldn't have invited me. No wonder Alexander's so angry!"

"It's my house, too, and I can invite who I like," Margie replied curtly, intimating that she and Alexander had argued about Jodie's inclusion at the party. That hurt even more. "You're my best friend, Jodie, and I need an ego boost," Margie continued unabashed. "Kirry is so worldly and sophisticated. She hates it here and she makes me feel insecure. But I need her help to get my designs shown at the store where she works. So, you're my security blanket." She linked her arm with Jodie's. "Besides, Kirry and Lex together get on my nerves."

What about my nerves? Jodie was wondering. And my heart, having to see Alexander with Kirry all weekend? But she only smiled and pretended that it didn't matter. She was Margie's friend, and she owed her a lot. Even if it was going to mean eating her heart out watching the man she loved hang on to that beautiful woman, Kirry Dane.

Margie stopped just before they went into the house. She looked worried. "You have gotten over that crush you had on my brother…?" she asked quickly.

"You and your brother!" Jodie gasped. "Honestly, I'm too old for schoolgirl crushes," she lied through her teeth, "and besides, there's this wonderful guy at the office that I like a lot. It's just that he's going with someone."

Margie grimaced. "You poor kid. It's always like that with you, isn't it?"

"Go right ahead and step on my ego, don't mind me," Jodie retorted.

Margie flushed. "I'm a pig," she said. "Sorry, Jodie. I don't know what's the matter with me. Yes, I do," she added at once. "Cousin Derek arrived unexpectedly this morning. Jessie's already threatened to cook him up with a pan of eggs, and one of the cowboys ran a tractor through a fence trying to get away from him. In fact, Jessie remembered that she could have a weekend off whenever she wanted, so she's gone to Dallas for the weekend to see her brother. And here I am with no cook and a party tomorrow night!"

"Except me?" Jodie ventured, and her heart sank again when she saw Margie's face. No wonder she'd been insistent. There wouldn't be any food without someone to cook it, and Margie couldn't cook.

"You don't mind, do you, dear?" Margie asked quickly. "After all, you do make the most scrumptious little canapés, and you're a great cook. Even Jessie asks you for recipes."

"No," Jodie lied. "I don't mind."

"And you can help me keep Derek out of Alexander's way."

"Derek." Jodie's eyes lit up. She loved the Cobbs' renegade cousin from Oklahoma. He was a rodeo cowboy who won belts at every competition, six foot two of pure lithe muscle, with a handsome face and a modest demeanor— when he wasn't up to some horrible devilment. He drove housekeepers and cowboys crazy with his antics, and Alexander barely tolerated him. He was Margie's favorite of their few cousins. Not that he was really a cousin. He was only related by marriage. Of course, Margie didn't know that. Derek had told Jodie once, but asked her not to tell. She wondered why.

"Don't even think about helping him do anything crazy while you're here," Margie cautioned. "Lex doesn't know he's here yet. I, uh, haven't told him."

"Margie!" came a thunderous roar from the general direction of Alexander's office.

Margie groaned. "Oh, dear, Lex does seem to know about Derek."

"My suitcase," Jodie said, halting, hoping to get out of the line of fire in time.

"Lex will bring it in, dear, come along." She almost dragged her best friend into the house.

Derek was leaning against the staircase banister, handsome as a devil, with dancing brown eyes and a lean, good-looking face under jet-black hair. In front of him, Alexander was holding up a rubber chicken by the neck.

"I thought you liked chicken," Derek drawled.

"Cooked," Alexander replied tersely. "Not in my desk chair pretending to be a cushion!"

"You could cook that, but the fumes would clear out the kitchen for sure," Derek chuckled.

Cobb threw it at the man, turned, went back into his office and slammed the door. Muttered curses came right through two inches of solid mahogany.

"Derek, how could you?" Margie wailed.

He tossed her the chicken and came forward to lift her up and kiss her saucily on the nose. "Now, now, you can't expect me to be dignified. It isn't in my nature. Hi, sprout!" he added, putting Margie down only to pick up Jodie and swing her around in a bear hug. "How's my best girl?"

"I'm just fine, Derek," she replied, kissing his cheek. "You look great."

"So do you." He let her dangle from his hands and his keen dark eyes scanned her flushed face. "Has Cobb been picking on you all the way home?" he asked lazily.

"Why can't you two call him Lex, like I do?" Margie wanted to know.

"He doesn't look like a Lex," Derek replied.

"He always picks on me," Jodie said heavily as Derek

let her slide back onto her feet. "If he had a list of people he doesn't like, I'd lead it."

"We'd tie for that spot, I reckon," Derek replied. He gave Margie a slow, steady appraisal. "New duds? I like that skirt."

Margie grinned up at him. "I made it."

"Good for you. When are you going to have a show of all those pretty things you make?"

"That's what I'm working on. Lex's girlfriend Kirry is trying to get her store to let me do a parade of my designs."

"Kirry." Derek wrinkled his straight nose. "Talk about slow poison. And he thought Rachel was bad!"

"Don't mention Rachel!" Margie cautioned quickly.

"Kirry makes her look like a church mouse," Derek said flatly. "She's a social climber with dollar signs for eyes. Mark my words, it isn't his body she's after."

"He likes her," Margie replied.

"He likes liver and onions, too," Derek said, and made a horrible face.

Jodie laughed at the byplay.

Derek glanced at her. "Why doesn't he ever look at you, sprout? You'd be perfect for him."

"Don't be silly," Jodie said with a forced smile. "I'm not his type at all."

"You're not mercenary. You're a sucker for anyone in trouble. You like cats and dogs and children, and you don't like nightlife. You're perfect."

"He likes opera and theater," she returned.

"And you don't?" Derek asked.

Margie grabbed him by the arm. "Come on and let's have coffee while you tell us about your latest rodeo triumph."

"How do you know it was?" he teased.

"When have you ever lost a belt?" she replied with a grin.

Jodie followed along behind them, already uneasy about the weekend. She had a feeling that it wasn't going to be the best one of her life.

LATER, JODIE ESCAPED from the banter between Margie and her cousin and went out to the corral near the barn to look at the new calves. One of the older ranch hands, Johnny, came out to join her. He was missing a tooth in front from a bull's hooves and a finger from a too-tight rope that slipped. His chaps and hat and boots were worn and dirty from hard work. But he had a heart of pure gold, and Jodie loved him. He reminded her of her late father.

"Hey, Johnny!" she greeted, standing on the top rung of the wooden fence in old jeans, boots, and a long-sleeved blue checked shirt. Her hair was up in a pony-tail. She looked about twelve.

He grinned back. "Hey, Jodie! Come to see my babies?"

"Sure have!"

"Ain't they purty?" he drawled, joining her at the fence, where she was feeding her eyes on the pretty lit-tle white-faced, red-coated calves.

"Yes, they are," she agreed with a sigh. "I miss this up in Houston. The closest I get to cattle is the rodeo when it comes to town."

He winced. "You poor kid," he said. "You lost every-thing at once, all them years ago."

That was true. She'd lost her parents and her home, all at once. If Alexander hadn't gotten her into business college, where she could live on campus, she'd have been homeless.

She smiled down at him. "Time heals even the worst wounds, Johnny. Besides, I still get to come down here and visit once in a while."

He looked irritated. "Wish you came more than that Dane woman," he said under his breath. "Can't stand cattle and dust, don't like cowboys, looks at us like we'd get her dirty just by speaking to her."

She reached over and patted him gently on the shoulder. "We all have our burdens to bear."

He sighed. "I reckon so. Why don't you move back down here?" he added. "Plenty of jobs going in Jacobsville right now. I hear tell the police chief needs a new secretary."

She chuckled. "I'm not going to work for Cash Grier," she assured him. "They said his last secretary emptied the trash can over his head, and it was full of half-empty coffee cups and coffee grounds."

"Well, some folks don't take to police work," he said, but he chuckled.

"Nothing to do, Johnny?" came a deep, terse voice from behind Jodie.

Johnny straightened immediately. "Just started mucking out the stable, boss. I only came over to say howdy to Miss Jodie."

"Good to see you again, Johnny," she said.

"Same here, miss."

He tipped his hat and went slowly back into the barn.

"Don't divert the hired help," Alexander said curtly.

She got down from the fence. It was a long way up to his eyes in her flat shoes. "He was a friend of my father's," she reminded him. "I was being polite."

She turned and started back to the house.

"Running away?"

She stopped and faced him. "I'm not going to be your whipping boy," she said.

His eyebrows arched. "Wrong gender."

"You know what I mean. You're furious that Derek's here, and Kirry's not, and you want somebody to take it out on."

He moved restlessly at the accusation. His scowl was suddenly darker. "Don't do that."

She knew what he meant. She could always see through his bad temper to the reason for it, something his own sister had never been able to do.

"Derek will leave in the morning and Kirry will be here by afternoon," she said. "Derek can't do that much damage in a night. Besides, you know how close he and Margie are."

"He's too flighty for her, distant relation or not," he muttered.

She sighed, looking up at him with quiet, soft eyes full of memories. "Like me," she said under her breath.

He frowned. "What?"

"That's always been your main argument against me—that I'm too flighty. That's why you didn't like it when Derek was trying to get me to go out with him three years ago," she reminded him.

He stared at her for a few seconds, still scowling. "Did I say that?"

She nodded then turned away. "I've got to go help Margie organize the food and drinks," she added. "Left to her own devices, we'll be eating turkey and bacon roll-ups and drinking spring water."

"What did you have in mind?" he asked amusedly.

"A nice baked chicken with garlic-and-chives mashed potatoes, fruit salad, homemade rolls and biscuits, gravy, fresh asparagus and a chocolate pound cake for dessert," she said absently.

"You can cook?" he asked, astonished.

She glared at him over one shoulder. "You didn't notice? Margie hasn't cooked a meal any time I've been down here for the weekend, except for one barbecue that the cowboys roasted a side of beef for."

He didn't say another word, but he looked unusually thoughtful.

THE MEAL CAME out beautifully. By the time she had it on the table, Jodie was flushed from the heat of the kitchen and her hair was disheveled, but she'd produced a perfect meal.

Margie enthused over the results with every dish she tasted, and so did Derek. Alexander was unusually quiet. He finished his chocolate pound cake and a second cup of coffee before he gave his sister a dark look.

"You told me you'd been doing all the cooking when Jessie wasn't here and Jodie was," he said flatly.

Margie actually flushed. She dropped her fork and couldn't meet Jodie's surprised glance.

"You always made such a fuss of extra company when Jessie was gone," she protested without realizing she was only making things worse.

Alexander's teeth ground together when he saw the look on Jodie's face. He threw down his napkin and got noisily to his feet. "You're as insensitive as a cactus plant, Margie," he said angrily.

"You're better?" she retorted, with her eyebrows reaching for her hairline. "You're the one who always complains when I invite Jodie, even though she hasn't got any family except us…oh, dear."

Jodie had already gotten to her own feet and was collecting dirty dishes. She didn't respond to the bickering. She felt it, though. It hurt to know that Alexander barely tolerated her; almost as much as it hurt to know Margie had taken credit for her cooking all these years.

"I'll help you clear, darlin'," Derek offered with a meaningful look at the Cobbs. "Both of you could use some sensitivity training. You just step all over Jodie's feelings without the least notice. Some 'second family' you turned out to be!"

He propelled Jodie ahead of him into the kitchen and closed the door. For once, he looked angry.

She smiled at him. "Don't take it so personally, Derek," she said. "Insults just bounce off me. I'm so used to Alexander by now that I hardly listen."

He tilted her chin up and read the pain in her soft eyes. "He walks on your heart every time he speaks to you," he said bluntly. "He doesn't even know how you feel, when a blind man could see it."

She patted his cheek. "You're a nice man, Derek."

He shrugged. "I've always been a nice man, for all the good it does me. Women flock to hang all over Cobb while he glowers and insults them."

"Someday a nice, sweet woman will come along and take you in hand, and thank God every day for you," she told him.

He chuckled. "Want to take me on?"

She wrinkled her nose at him. "You're very sweet, but I've got my eye on a rather nice man at my office. He's sweet, too, and his girlfriend treats him like dirt. He deserves someone better."

"He'd be lucky to get you," Derek said.

She smiled.

They were frozen in that affectionate tableau when the door opened and Alexander exploded into the room. He stopped short, obviously unsettled by what he thought he was seeing. Especially when Jodie jerked her hand down from Derek's cheek, and he let go of her chin.

"Something you forgot to say about Jodie's unwanted presence in your life?" Derek drawled, and for an instant, the smiling, gentle man Jodie knew became a threatening presence.

Alexander scowled. "Margie didn't mean that the way it sounded," he returned.

"Margie never means things the way they sound," Derek said coldly, "but she never stops to think how much words can hurt, either. She walks around in a perpetual Margie-haze of self-absorption. Even now, Jodie's only here because she can make canapés for the party tomorrow night—or didn't you know?" he added with absolute venom.

Margie came into the room behind her brother, downcast and quiet. She winced as she met Derek's accusing eyes.

"I'm a pig," she confessed. "I really don't mean to hurt people. I love Jodie. She knows it, even if you don't."

"You have a great way of showing it, honey," Derek replied, a little less antagonistic to her than to her brother. "Inviting Jodie down just to cook for a party is pretty thoughtless."

Margie's eyes fell. "You can go home if you want to, Jodie, and I'm really sorry," she offered.

"Oh, for heaven's sake, I don't mind cooking!" Jodie went to Margie and hugged her hard. "I could always say no if I didn't want to do it! Derek's just being kind, that's all."

Margie glared at her cousin. "Kind."

Derek glared back. "Sure I am. It runs in the family. Glad you could come, Jodie, want to wash and wax my car when you finish doing the dishes?" he added sarcastically.

"You stop that!" Margie raged at him.

"Then get in here and help her do the dishes," Derek drawled. "Or do your hands melt in hot water?"

"We do have a dishwasher," Alexander said tersely.

"Gosh! You've actually seen it, then?" Derek exclaimed.

Alexander said a nasty word and stormed out of the kitchen.

"One down," Derek said with twinkling eyes and looking at Margie. "One to go."

"Quit that, or she'll toss you out and I'll be stuck here with them and Kirry all weekend," Jodie said softly.

"Kirry?" He gaped at Margie. "You invited Kirry?"

Margie ground her teeth together and clenched her small hands. "She's the guest of honor!"

"Lord, give me a bus ticket!" He moved toward the door. "Sorry, honey, I'm not into masochism, and a night of unadulterated Kirry would put me in a mental ward. I'm leaving."

"But you just got here!" Margie wailed.

He turned at the door. "You should have told me who was coming to the party. I'd still be in San Antonio. Want to come with me, Jodie?" he offered. "I'll take you to a fiesta!"

Margie looked murderous. "She's my friend."

"She's not, or you wouldn't have forced her down here to suffer Kirry all weekend," he added.

"Give me a minute to get out of the line of fire, will you?" Jodie held up her hands and went back to the dining room to scoop up dirty dishes, forcibly smiling.

Derek glanced at the closed door, and moved closer to Margie. "Don't try to convince me that you don't know how Jodie feels about your brother."

"She got over that old crush years ago, she said so!" Margie returned.

"She lied," he said shortly. "She's as much in love with him as she ever was, not that either of you ever notice! It's killing her just to be around him, and you stick her with Kirry. How do you think she's going to feel, watching Kirry slither all over Cobb for a whole night?"

Margie bit her lower lip and looked hunted. "She said…"

"Oh, sure, she's going to tell you that she's in love with Cobb." He nodded. "Great instincts, Marge."

"Don't call me Marge!"

He bent and brushed an insolent kiss across her parted lips, making her gasp. His dark eyes narrowed as he assayed the unwilling response. "Never thought of me like that, either, huh?" he drawled.

"You're…my…cousin," she choked.

"I'm no close relation to you at all, despite Cobb's antagonism. One day I'm going to walk out the door with you over my shoulder, and Cobb can do his worst." He winked at her. "See you, sweetheart."

He turned and ambled out the door. Margie was still staring after him helplessly and holding her hand to her lips when Jodie came in with another stack of dishes.

"What's wrong with you?" Jodie asked.

"Derek kissed me," she said in a husky tone.

"He's always kissing you."

Margie swallowed hard. "Not like this."

Jodie's eyebrows went up and she grinned. "I thought it was about time."

"What?"

"Nothing," Jodie said at once. "Here, can you open the dishwasher for me? My hands are full."

Margie broke out of her trance and went to help, shell-shocked and quiet.

"Don't let Derek upset you," Jodie said gently. "He thinks he's doing me a favor, but he's not. I don't mind helping out, in any way I can. I owe you and Cobb so much…"

"You don't owe us a thing," Margie said at once. "Oh, Jodie, you shouldn't let me make use of you like this. You should speak up for yourself. You don't do that enough."

"I know. It's why I haven't advanced in the company," she had to admit. "I just don't like confrontations."

"You had enough of them as a kid, didn't you?" Margie asked.

Jodie flushed. "I loved my parents. I really did."

"But they fought, too. Just like ours. Our mother hated our father, even after he was dead. She drank and drank, trying to forget him, just the same. She soured my brother on women, you know. She picked on him from the time he was six, and every year it got worse. He had a roaring inferiority complex when he was in high school."

"Yes? Well, he's obviously got over it now," Jodie said waspishly.

Margie shook her head. "Not really. If he had, he'd know he could do better than Kirry."

"I thought you liked her!"

Margie looked shamefaced. "I do, sort of. Well, she's got an important job and she could really help me get my foot in the door at Weston's, the exclusive department store where she works."

"Oh, Margie," Jodie said wearily, shaking her head.

"I use people," Margie admitted. "But," she added brightly, "I try to do it in a nice way, and I always send flowers or presents or something afterward, don't I?"

Jodie laughed helplessly. "Yes, you do," she admitted. "Here, help me load up the dishes, and then you can tell me what sort of canapés you want me to make for tomorrow."

She didn't add that she knew she'd spend the whole day tomorrow making them, because the party was for almost forty people, and lunch had to be provided, as well. It was a logistical nightmare. But she could cope. She'd done it before. And Margie was her best friend.

CHAPTER THREE

JODIE WAS UP at dawn making biscuits and dough for the canapés. She'd only just taken up breakfast when Alexander came into the kitchen, wearing jeans and boots and a long-sleeved chambray shirt. He looked freshly showered and clean-shaven, his dark hair still damp.

"I've got breakfast," Jodie offered without looking too closely at him. He was overpowering in tight jeans and a shirt unbuttoned to his collarbone, where thick curling black hair peeked out. She had to fight not to throw herself at him.

"Coffee?" he murmured.

"In the pot."

He poured himself a cup, watching the deft motions of her hands as she buttered biscuits and scooped eggs onto a platter already brimming over with bacon and sausages.

"Aren't you eating?" he asked as he seated himself at the table.

"Haven't time," she said, arranging a layer of canapés on a baking sheet. "Most of your guests are coming in time for lunch, so these have to be done now, before I get too busy."

His sensuous lips made a thin line. "I can't stand him, but Derek is right about one thing. You do let Margie use you."

"You and Margie were there when I had nobody else,"

she said without seeing the flinch of his eyelids. "I consider that she's entitled to anything I can ever do for her."

"You sell yourself short."

"I appreciate it when people do things for me without being asked," she replied. She put the canapés in the oven and set the timer, pushing back sweaty hair that had escaped from her bun.

His eyes went over her figure in baggy pants and an oversize T-shirt. "You dress like a bag lady," he muttered.

She glanced at him, surprised. "I dress very nicely at work."

"Like a dowager bag lady," he corrected. "You wear the same sort of clothes you favored when you were overweight. You're not anymore. Why don't you wear things that fit?"

It was surprising that he noticed her enough to even know what she was wearing. "Margie's the fashion model, not me," she reminded him. "Besides, I'm not the type for trendy stuff. I'm just ordinary."

He frowned. She had a real ego problem. He and Margie hadn't done much for it, either. She accepted anything that was thrown at her, as if she deserved it. He was surprised how much it bothered him, to see her so undervalued even by herself. Not that he was interested in her, he added silently. She wasn't his type at all.

"Kirry's coming this morning," he added. "I have to pick her up at the airport at noon."

Jodie only smiled. "Margie's hoping she'll help her with a market for her designs."

"I think she'll try," he said conservatively. "Eat breakfast," he said. "You can't go all day without food."

"I don't have time," she repeated, starting on another batch of canapés. "Unless you want to sacrifice yourself in a bowl of dough?" she offered, extending the bowl with a mischievous smile.

His green eyes twinkled affectionately in spite of himself. "No, thanks."

"I didn't think so."

He watched her work while he ate, nebulous thoughts racing through his mind. Jodie was so much a part of his life that he never felt discomfort when they were together. He had a hard time with strangers. He appeared to be stoic and aloof, but in fact he was an introvert who didn't quite know how to mix with people who weren't in law enforcement. Like Jodie herself, he considered. She was almost painfully shy around people she didn't know—and tonight, she was going to be thrown in headfirst with a crowd she probably wouldn't even like.

Kirry's friends were social climbers, high society. Alexander himself wasn't comfortable with them, and Jodie certainly wouldn't be. They were into expensive cars, European vacations, diamonds, investments, and they traveled in circles that included some of the most famous people alive, from movie stars to Formula 1 race car drivers, to financial geniuses, playwrights and authors. They classified their friends by wealth and status, not by character. In their world, right and wrong didn't even exist.

"You're not going to like this crowd," he said aloud.

She glanced at him. "I'll be in the kitchen most of the time," she said easily, "or helping serve."

He looked outraged. "You're a guest, not the kitchen help!"

"Don't be absurd," she murmured absently, "I haven't even got the right clothes to wear to Kirry's sort of party. I'd be an embarrassment."

He set his coffee cup down with muted force. "Then why the hell did you come in the first place?" he asked.

"Margie asked me to," she said simply.

He got up and went out without another word. Jodie was going to regret this visit. He was sorry Margie had insisted that she come.

THE PARTY WAS in full swing. Alexander had picked up Kirry at the airport and lugged her suitcases up to the second guest room, down the hall from Jodie's. Kirry, blonde and svelte and from a wealthy background, was like the Cobbs, old money and family ties. She looked at Jodie without seeing her, and talked only to Margie and Alexander during lunch. Fortunately there were plenty of other people there who didn't mind talking to Jodie, especially an elderly couple apparently rolling in wealth to judge by the diamonds the matron was decked out in.

After lunch, Kirry had Alexander drive her into town and Jodie silently excused herself and escaped to the kitchen.

She had a nice little black dress, off the rack at a local department store, and high heels to match, which she wore to the party. But it was hidden under the big apron she wore most of the evening, heating and arranging canapés and washing dishes and crystal glasses in between uses.

It was almost ten o'clock before she was able to join Margie and her friends. But by then, Margie was hanging on to Kirry like a bat, with Alexander nearby, and Jodie couldn't get near her.

She stood in a corner by herself, wishing that Derek hadn't run from this weekend, so that she'd at least have someone to talk to. But that wasn't happening. She started talking to the elderly matron she'd sat beside at lunch, but another couple joined them and mentioned their week in Paris, and a mutual friend, and Jodie was out of her depth. She moved to another circle, but they were discussing annuities and investments, and she knew nothing to contribute to that discussion, either.

Alexander noticed, seething, that she was alone most of the evening. He started to get up, but Kirry moved closer and clung to his sleeve while Margie talked about her latest collection and offered to show it to Kirry in the morning. Kirry was very possessive. They weren't involved, as he'd been with other women. Perhaps that was why she was reluctant to let him move away. She hated the very thought of any other woman looking at him. That possessiveness was wearing thin. She was beautiful and she carried herself well, but she had an attitude he didn't like, and she was positively rude to any of his colleagues that spoke to him when they were together. Not that she had any idea what Alexander actually did for a living. He was independently wealthy and people in his and Margie's circle of friends assumed that the ranch was his full-time occupation. He'd taught Jodie and Margie never to mention that he worked in Drug Enforcement. They could say that he dabbled in security work, if they liked, but nothing more. When he'd started out with the DEA, he'd done a lot of undercover work. It wasn't politic to let people know that.

Jodie, meanwhile, had discovered champagne. She'd never let herself drink at any of the Cobb parties in the past, but she was feeling particularly isolated tonight, and it was painful. She liked the bubbles, the fragrance of flowers that clung to the exquisite beverage and the delicious taste. So she had three glasses, one after the other, and pretty soon she didn't mind at all that Margie and Alexander's guests were treating her like a barmaid who'd tried to insert herself into their exalted circles.

She noticed that she'd had too much to drink when she walked toward a doorway and ran headfirst into the door facing. She began to giggle softly. Her hair was coming down from its high coiffure, but she didn't care. She took out the circular comb that had held it in place and shook her head, letting the thick, waving wealth of hair fall to her shoulders.

The action caught the eye of a man nearby, a bored race car driver who'd been dragged to this hick party by his wife. He sized up Jodie, and despite the dress that did absolutely nothing for her, he was intrigued.

He moved close, leaning against the door facing she'd hit so unexpectedly.

"Hurt yourself?" he asked in a pleasant deep drawl, faintly accented.

Jodie looked up at the newcomer curiously and managed a lopsided grin. He was a dish, with curly black hair and dancing black eyes, an olive complexion and the body of an athlete.

"Only my hard head," she replied with a chuckle. "Who are you?"

"Francisco," he replied lazily. He lifted his glass to her in a toast. "You're the first person tonight who even asked." He leaned down so that he was eye to eye with her. "I'm a foreigner, you see."

"Are you, really?"

He was enchanted. He laughed, and it wasn't a polite social laugh at all. "I'm from Madrid," he said. "Didn't you notice my accent?"

"I don't speak any foreign languages," she confessed

sadly, sipping what was left of her champagne. "I don't understand high finance or read popular novels or know any movie stars, and I've never been on a holiday abroad. So I thought I'd go sit in the kitchen."

He laughed again. "May I join you, then?" he asked.

She looked pointedly at his left hand. There was no ring.

He took a ring out of his slacks pocket and dangled it in front of her. "We don't advertise our commitment at parties. My wife likes it that way. That's my wife," he added with pure disdain, nodding toward a blonde woman in a skintight red dress that looked sprayed on. She was leaning against a very handsome blond man.

"She's beautiful," she remarked.

"She's anybody's," he returned coldly. "The man she's stalking is a rising motion picture star. He's poor. She's rich. She's financing his career in return for the occasional loan of his body."

Her eyes almost popped out of her eyelids.

He shook his head. "You're not worldly, are you?" he mused. "I have an open marriage. She does what she pleases. So do I."

"Don't you love her?" she asked curiously.

"One marries for love, you think." He sighed. "What a child you are. I married her because her father owned the company. As his son-in-law, I get to drive the car in competition."

"You're the race car driver!" she exclaimed softly. "Kirry mentioned you were coming."

"Kirry." His lips curled distastefully and he glanced across the room into a pair of cold, angry green eyes above the head of Kirry Dane. "She was last year's diversion," he murmured. "She wanted to be seen at Monaco."

Jodie was surprised by his lack of inhibition. She wondered if Alexander knew about this relationship, or if he cared. She'd never thought whether he bothered asking about his date's previous entanglements.

"Her boyfriend doesn't like me," he murmured absently, and smiled icily, lifting his glass.

Jodie looked behind her. Kirry had turned away, but Alexander was suddenly making a beeline across the room toward them.

Francisco made a face. "There's one man you don't want to make an enemy of," he confided. "Are you a relation of his, by any chance?"

Jodie laughed a little too loudly. "Good Lord, no." She chuckled. "I'm the cook!"

"I beg your pardon?" he asked.

By that time, Alexander was facing her. He took the crystal champagne flute from her hands and put it gingerly on a nearby table.

"I wasn't going to break it, Alexander," she muttered. "I do know it's Waterford crystal!"

"How many glasses have you had?" he demanded.

"I don't like your tone," she retorted, moving clumsily, so that Francisco had to grab her arm to keep her upright. "I had three glasses. It's not that strong, and I'm not drunk!"

"And ducks don't have feathers," Alexander replied tersely. He caught her other arm and pulled her none too gently from Francisco's grasp. "I'll take care of Jodie. Hadn't you better reacquire your wife?" he added pointedly to the younger man.

Francisco sighed, with a long, wistful appraisal of Jodie. "It seems so," he replied. "Nice to have met you— Jodie, is it?"

Jodie grinned woozily. "It's Jordana, actually, but most people call me Jodie. And I was glad to meet you, too, Francisco! I never met a real race car driver before!"

He started to speak, but it was too late, because Alexander was already marching her out of the room and down the hall.

"Will you stop dragging me around?" she demanded, stumbling on her high heels.

He pulled her into the dark-paneled library and closed the door with a muted thud. He let go of her arm and glared down at her. "Will you stop trying to seduce married men?" he shot back. "Gomez and his wife are on the cover of half the tabloids in Texas right now," he added bluntly.

"Why?"

"Her father just died and she inherited the car company. She's trying to sell it and her husband is fighting her in court, tooth and nail."

"And they're still married?"

"Apparently, in name, at least. She's pregnant, I hear, with another man's child."

She looked up at him coldly. "Some circles you and Margie travel in," she said with contempt.

"Circles you'd never fit into," he agreed.

"Not hardly," she drawled ungrammatically. "And I wouldn't want to. In my world, people get married and have kids and build a home together." She nodded her head toward the closed door. "Those people in there wouldn't know what a home was if you drew it for them!"

His green eyes narrowed on her face. "You're smashed. Why don't you go to bed?"

She lifted her chin and smiled mistily. "Why don't you come with me?" she purred.

The look on his face would have amused her, if she'd been sober. He just stared, shocked.

She arched her shoulders and made a husky little sound in her throat. She parted her lips and ran her tongue slowly around them, the way she'd read in a magazine article that said men were turned on by it.

Apparently they were. Alexander was staring at her mouth with an odd expression. His chest was rising and falling very quickly. She could see the motion of it through his white shirt and dinner jacket.

She moved closer, draping herself against him as she'd seen that slinky blonde woman in the red dress do it. She moved her leg against his and felt his whole body stiffen abruptly.

Her hands went to the front of his shirt under the jacket. She drew her fingers down it, feeling the ripple of muscle. His big hands caught her shoulders, but he wasn't pushing.

"You look at me, but you never see me," she murmured. Her lips brushed against his throat. He smelled of expensive cologne and soap. "I'm not pretty. I'm not sexy. But I would die for you…!"

His hard mouth cut off the words. He curled her into his body with a rigid arm at her back, and his mouth opened against her moist, full, parted lips with the fury of a summer storm.

It wasn't premeditated. The feel of her against him had triggered a raging arousal in his muscular body. He went in headfirst, without thinking of the consequences.

If he was helpless, so was she. As he enveloped her against him, her arms slid around his warm body under the jacket and her mouth answered the hunger of his. She made a husky little moan that apparently made matters worse. His mouth became suddenly insistent, as if he heard the need in her soft cry and was doing his best to satisfy the hunger it betrayed.

Her hands lifted to the back of his head and her fingers dug into his scalp as she arched her body upward in a hopeless plea.

He whispered something that she couldn't understand before he bent and lifted her, with her mouth still trapped under his demanding lips, and carried her to the sofa.

He spread her body onto the cold leather and slid over it, one powerful leg inserting itself between both of hers in a frantic, furious exchange of passion. He'd never known such raging need, not only in himself, but in Jodie. She was liquid in his embrace, yielding to everything he asked without a word being spoken.

He moved slightly, just enough to get his hand in between them. It smoothed over her collarbone and down into the soft dip of her dress, over the lacy bra she was wearing underneath. He felt the hard little nipple in his palm as he increased the insistent pressure of the caress and heard her cry of delight go into his open mouth.

Her hands were on the buttons of his shirt. It was dangerous. It was reckless. She'd incited him to madness. When he felt the buttons give, and her hands speared into the thick hair over his chest, he groaned harshly. His body shivered with desire.

His mouth ground into hers as his leg moved between hers. One lean hand went under her hips and gathered her up against the fierce arousal of his body, moving her against him in a blatant physical statement of intent.

Jodie's head was spinning. All her dreams of love were coming true. Alexander wanted her! She could feel the insistent pressure of his body over hers. He was kissing

her as if he'd die to have her, and she gloried in the fury
of his hunger. She relaxed with a husky little laugh and
kissed him back languidly, feeling her body melt under
him, melt into him. She was on fire, burning with unfamiliar needs, drowning in unfamiliar sensations that
made her whole body tingle with pleasure. She lifted her
hips against his and gasped at the blatant contact.

Alexander lifted his head and looked at her. His face
was a rigid mask. Only his green eyes were alive in it,
glittering down at her in a rasping, unsteady silence of
merged breathing.

"Don't stop," she whispered, moving her hips again.

He was tempted. It showed. But that iron control
wouldn't let him slip into carelessness. She'd been drinking. In fact, she was smashed. He had his own suspicions
about her innocence, and they wouldn't shut up. His body
was begging him to forget her lack of experience and
give it relief. But his will was too strong. He was the
man in control. It was his responsibility to protect her,
even from himself.

"You're drunk, Jodie," he said. His voice was faintly
unsteady, but it was terse and firm.

"Does it matter?" she asked lazily.

"Don't be ridiculous."

He moved away, getting to his feet. He looked down
at her sprawled body in its disheveled dress and he ached
all the way to his toes. But he couldn't do this. Not when
she was so vulnerable.

She sighed and closed her eyes. It had been so sweet,
lying in his arms. She smiled dreamily. Was she dreaming?

"Get up, for God's sake!" he snapped.

When her eyes opened, he was standing her firmly

on her feet. "You're going to bed, right now, before you make an utter fool of yourself!"

She blinked, staring up at him. "I can't go to bed. Who'll do the dishes?"

"Jodie!"

She giggled, trying to lean against him. He thrust her away and took her arm, moving her toward the door. "I told Francisco I was the cook. That's me," she drawled cheerfully. "Cook, bottle-washer, best friend and household slave." She laughed louder.

He propelled her out the door, back down the hall toward the staircase, and urged her up it. She was still giggling a little too loudly for comfort, but the noise of the music from the living room covered it nicely.

He got her to the guest room she was occupying and put her inside. "Go to bed," he said through his teeth.

She leaned against the door facing, totally at sea. "You could come inside," she murmured wickedly. "There's a bed."

"You need one," he agreed tersely. "Go get in it."

"Always bossing me around," she sighed. "Don't you like kissing me, Alexander?"

"You're going to hate yourself in the morning," he assured her.

She yawned, her mind going around in circles, like the room. "I think I'll go to bed now."

"Great idea."

He started to walk out.

"Could you send Francisco up, please?" she taunted. "I'd like to lie down and discuss race cars with him."

"In your dreams!" he said coldly.

He actually slammed the door, totally out of patience, self-control and tact. He waited a minute, to make sure she didn't try to come back out. But there was only the sound of slow progress toward the bed and a sudden loud whoosh. When he opened the door again and peeked in, she was lying facedown in her dress on the covers, sound asleep. He closed the door again, determined not to get close to her a second time. He went back to the party, feeling as if he'd had his stomach punched. He couldn't imagine what had possessed him to let Jodie tempt him into indiscretion. His lack of control worried him so much that he was twice as attentive to Kirry as he usually was.

When he saw her up to her room, after the party was over, he kissed her with intent. She was perfectly willing, but his body let him down. He couldn't manage any interest at all.

"You're just tired," she assured him with a worldly smile. "We have all the time in the world. Sleep tight."

"Sure. You, too."

He left her and went back downstairs. He was restless, angry at his attack of impotence with the one woman who was capable of curing it. Or, at least, he imagined she was. He and Kirry had never been lovers, although they'd come close at one time. Now she was a pleasant companion from time to time, a bauble to show off, to take around town. It infuriated him that he could be whole with Jodie, who was almost certainly a virgin, and he couldn't even function with a sophisticated woman like Kirry. Maybe it was his age.

The rattle of plates caught his attention. He moved toward the sound and found a distressed Margie in the kitchen trying to put dishes in the dishwasher.

"That doesn't look right," he commented with a frown when he noticed the lack of conformity in the way she was tossing plates and bowls and cups and crystal all together. "You'll break the crystal."

She glared at him. "Well, what do I know about washing dishes?" she exclaimed. "That's why we have Jessie!"

He cocked his head. "You're out of sorts."

She pushed back her red-tinged dark hair angrily. "Yes, I'm out of sorts! Kirry said she doesn't think I'm ready to show my collection yet. She said her store had shows booked for the rest of the year, and she couldn't help me!"

"All that buttering up and dragging Jodie down here to work, for nothing," he said sarcastically.

"Where is Jodie?" she demanded. "I haven't seen her for two hours, and here's all this work that isn't getting done except by me!"

He leaned back against the half-open door and stared at his sister. "She's passed out on her bed, dead drunk," he said distastefully. "After trying to seduce the world's number one race car driver, and then me."

Margie stood up and stared back. "You?"

"I wish I could impress on you how tired I am of finding Jodie underfoot every time I walk into my own house," he said coldly. "We can't have a party without her, we can't have a holiday without her. My own birthday means an invitation! Why can't you just hire a cook when you need one instead of landing me with your erstwhile best friend?"

"I thought you liked Jodie, a little," Margie stammered.

"She's blue collar, Margie," he persisted, still smarting under his loss of control and furious that Jodie was responsible for it. "She'll never fit in our circles, no matter how much you try to force her into them. She was telling people tonight that she was the cook, and it's not far wrong. She's a social disaster with legs. She knows nothing about our sort of lifestyle, she can't carry on a decent conversation and she dresses like a homeless person. It's an embarrassment to have her here!"

Margie sighed miserably. "I hope you haven't said things like that to her, Lex," she worried. "She may not be an upper class sort of person, but she's sweet and kind, and she doesn't gossip. She's the only real friend I've ever had. Not that I've behaved much like one," she added sadly.

"You should have friends in your own class," he said coldly. "I don't want Jodie invited down here again," he added firmly, holding up a hand when Margie tried to speak. "I mean it. You find some excuse, but you keep her away from here. I'm not going to be stalked by your bag lady of a friend. I don't want her underfoot at any more holidays, and God forbid, at my birthday party! If you want to see her, drive to Houston, fly to Houston, stay in Houston! But don't bring her here anymore."

"Did she really try to seduce you?" Margie wondered aloud.

"I don't want to talk about it," he said flatly. "It was embarrassing."

"She'll probably be horrified when she wakes up and remembers what happened. Whatever did," Margie added, fishing.

"I'll be horrified for months myself. Kirry is my steady girl," he added deliberately. "I'm not hitting on some other woman behind her back, and Jodie should have known it. Not that it seemed to matter to her, about me or the married racer."

"She's never had a drink, as far as I know," Margie ventured gently. "She's not like our mother, Lex."

His face closed up. Jodie's behavior had aroused painful memories of his mother, who drank often, and to excess. She was a constant embarrassment anytime people came to the house, and she delighted in embarrassing her son any way possible. Jodie's unmanageable silliness brought back nightmares.

"There's nothing in the world more disgusting than a drunk woman," he said aloud. "Nothing that makes me sicker to my stomach."

Margie closed the dishwasher and started it. There was a terrible cracking sound. The crystal! She winced. "I don't care what's broken. I'm not a cook. I can't wash dishes. I'm a dress designer!"

"Hire help for Jessie," he said.

"Okay," she said, giving in. "I won't invite Jodie back again. But how do I tell her, Lex? She's never going to understand. And it will hurt her."

He knew that. He couldn't bear to know it. His face hardened. "Just keep her away from me. I don't care how."

"I'll think of something," Margie said weakly.

Outside in the hall, a white-faced Jodie was stealthily making her way back to the staircase. She'd come down belatedly to do the dishes, still tingling hours after Alexander's feverish lovemaking. She'd been floating, delirious with hope that he might have started to see her in a different light. And then she'd heard what he said. She'd heard every single word. She disgusted him. She was such a social disaster, in fact, that he never wanted her to come to the house again. She'd embarrassed him and made a fool of herself.

He was right. She'd behaved stupidly, and now she was

going to pay for it by being an outcast. The only family she had no longer wanted her.

She went back to her room, closed the door quietly, and picked up the telephone. She changed her airplane ticket for an early-morning flight.

THE NEXT MORNING, she went to Margie's room at day-break. She hadn't slept a wink. She'd packed and changed her clothes, and now she was ready to go.

"Will you drive me to the airport?" she asked her sleepy friend. "Or do you want me to ask Johnny?"

Margie sat up, blinking. Then she remembered Lex's odd comments and her own shame at how she'd treated her best friend. She flushed.

"I'll drive you," Margie said at once. "But don't you want to wait until after breakfast?" She flushed again, remembering that Jodie would have had to cook it.

"I'm not hungry. There's leftover sausage and bacon in the fridge, along with some biscuits. You can just heat them up. Alexander can cook eggs to go with them," she added, almost choking on his name.

Margie felt guilty. "You're upset," she ventured.

Keeping quiet was the hardest thing Jodie had ever done. "I got drunk last night and did some…really stupid things," she summarized. "I'd just like to go home, Margie. Okay?"

Margie tried not to let her relief show. Jodie was leaving without a fuss. Lex would be pleased, and she'd be off the hook. She smiled. "Okay. I'll just get dressed, and then we'll go!"

CHAPTER FOUR

IF RUNNING AWAY seemed the right thing to do, actually doing it became complicated the minute Jodie went down the staircase with her suitcase.

The last thing she'd expected was to find the cause of her flight standing in the hall watching her. She ground her teeth together to keep from speaking.

Alexander was leaning against the banister, and he looked both uncomfortable and concerned when he saw Jodie's pale complexion and swollen eyelids.

He stood upright, scowling. "I'm driving Kirry back to Houston this afternoon," he said at once, noting Jodie's suitcase. "You can ride with us."

Jodie forced a quiet smile. Her eyes didn't quite meet his. "Thanks for the offer, Alexander, but I have an airplane ticket."

"Then I'll drive you to the airport," he added quietly.

Her face tightened. She swallowed down her hurt. "Thanks, but Margie's already dressed and ready to go. And we have some things to talk about on the way," she added before he could offer again.

He watched her uneasily. Jodie was acting like a fugitive evading the police. She wouldn't meet his eyes, or let him near her. He'd had all night to regret his behavior, and he was still blaming her for it. He'd overreacted. He knew she'd had a crush on him at one time. He'd hurt her with his cold rejection. She'd been drinking. It hadn't been her fault, but he'd blamed her for the whole fiasco. He felt guilty because of the way she looked.

Before he could say anything else, Margie came bouncing down the steps. "Okay, I'm ready! Let's go," she told Jodie.

"I'm right behind you. So long, Alexander," she told him without looking up past his top shirt button.

He didn't reply. He stood watching until the front door closed behind her. He still didn't understand his own conflicting emotions. He'd hoped to have some time alone with Jodie while he explored this suddenly changed relationship between them. But she was clearly embarrassed about her behavior the night before, and she was running scared. Probably letting her go was the best way to handle it. After a few days, he'd go to see her at the office and smooth things over. He couldn't bear having her look that way and knowing he was responsible for it. Regardless of his burst of bad temper, he cared about Jodie. He didn't want her to be hurt.

"YOU LOOK VERY PALE, Jodie," Margie commented when she walked her best friend to the security checkpoint. "Are you sure you're all right?"

"I'm embarrassed about how I acted last night, that's all," she assured her best friend. "How did you luck out with Kirry, by the way?"

"Not too well," she replied with a sigh. "And I think I broke all the crystal by putting it in the dishwasher."

"I'm sorry I wasn't able to do that for you," Jodie apologized.

"It's not your fault. Nothing is your fault." Margie

looked tormented. "I was going to ask you down to Lex's birthday party next month…"

"Margie, I can't really face Alexander right now, okay?" she interrupted gently, and saw the relief plain on the taller woman's face. "So I'm going to make myself scarce for a little while."

"That might be best," Margie had to admit.

Jodie smiled. "Thanks for asking me to the party," she managed. "I had a good time."

That was a lie, and they both knew it.

"I'll make all this up to you one day, I promise I will," Margie said unexpectedly, and hugged Jodie, hard. "I'm not much of a friend, Jodie, but I'm going to change. I am. You'll see."

"I wouldn't be much of a friend if I wanted to remake you," Jodie replied, smiling. "I'll see you around, Margie," she added enigmatically, and left before Margie could ask what she meant.

It was a short trip back to Houston. Jodie fought tears all the way. She couldn't remember anything hurting so much in all her life. Alexander couldn't bear the sight of her. He didn't want her around. She made him sick. She…disgusted him.

Most of her memories of love swirled around Alexander Cobb. She'd daydreamed about him even before she realized her feelings had deepened into love. She treasured unexpected meetings with him, she tingled just from having him smile at her. But all that had been a lie. She was a responsibility he took seriously, like his job. She meant nothing more than that to him. It was a painful realization, and it was going to take time for the hurt to lessen.

But for the moment it was too painful to bear. She drew the air carrier's magazine out of its pocket in the back of the seat ahead of her and settled back to read it. By the time she finished, the plane was landing. She walked through the Houston concourse with a new resolution. She was going to forget Alexander. It was time to put away the past and start fresh.

ALEXANDER WAS ALONE in the library when his sister came back from the airport.

He went out into the hall to meet her. "Did she say anything to you?" he asked at once.

Surprised by the question, and his faint anxiety, she hesitated. "About what?"

He glowered down at her. "About why she was leaving abruptly. I know her ticket was for late this afternoon. She must have changed it."

"She said she was too embarrassed to face you," Margie replied.

"Anything else?" he persisted.

"Not really." She felt uneasy herself. "You know Jodie. She's painfully shy, Lex. She doesn't drink, ever. I guess whatever happened made her ashamed of herself and uncomfortable around you. She'll get over it in time."

"Do you think so?" he wondered aloud.

"What are you both doing down here?" Kirry asked petulantly with a yawn. She came down the staircase in a red silk gown and black silk robe and slippers, her long blond hair sweeping around her shoulders. "I feel as if I haven't even slept. Is breakfast ready?"

Margie started. "Well, Jessie isn't here," she began.

"Where's that little cook who was at the party last

night?" she asked carelessly. "Why can't she make break-fast?"

"Jodie's not a cook," Alexander said tersely. "She's Margie's best friend."

Kirry's eyebrows arched. "She looked like a lush to me," Kirry said unkindly. "People like that should never drink. Is she too hung over to cook, then?"

"She's gone home," Margie said, resenting Kirry's remarks.

"Then who's going to make toast and coffee for me?" Kirry demanded. "I have to have breakfast."

"I can make toast," Margie said, turning. She wanted Kirry's help with her collection, but she disliked the woman intensely.

"Then I'll get dressed. Want to come up and do my zip, Lex?" Kirry drawled.

"No," he said flatly. "I'll make coffee." He went into the kitchen behind Margie.

Kirry stared after him blankly. He'd never spoken to her in such a way before, and Margie had been positively rude. They shouldn't drink, either, she was thinking as she went back upstairs to dress. Obviously it was hang-overs and bad tempers all around this morning.

TWO WEEKS LATER, Jodie sat in on a meeting between Brody and an employee of their information systems sec-tion who had been rude and insulting to a fellow worker. It was Brody's job as Human Resources generalist to oversee personnel matters, and he was a diplomat. It gave Jodie the chance to see what sort of duties she would be expected to perform if she moved up from administra-tive assistant to manager.

"Mr. Koswalski, this is Ms. Clayburn, my administrative assistant. She's here to take notes," he added.

Jodie was surprised, because she thought she was there to learn the job. But she smiled and pulled out her small pad and pen, perching it on her knee.

"You've had a complaint about me, haven't you?" Koswalski asked with a sigh.

Brody's eyebrows arched. "Well, yes…"

"One of our executives hired a systems specialist with no practical experience in oil exploration," Koswalski told him. "I was preparing an article for inclusion in our quarterly magazine and the system went down. She was sent to repair it. She saw my article and made some comments about the terms I used, and how unprofessional they sounded. Obviously she didn't understand the difference between a rigger and a roughneck. When I tried to explain, she accused me of talking down to her and walked out." He threw up his hands. "Sir, I wasn't rude, and I wasn't uncooperative. I was trying to teach her the language of the industry."

Brody looked as if he meant to say something, but he glanced at Jodie and cleared his throat instead. "You didn't call her names, Mr. Koswalski?"

"No, sir, I did not," the young man replied courteously. "But she did call me several. Besides that, quite frankly, she had a glazed look in her eyes and a red nose." His face tautened. "Mr. Vance, I've seen too many people who use drugs to mistake signs of drug use. She didn't repair the system, she made matters worse. I had to call in another specialist to undo her damage. I have his name, and his assignment," he added, producing a slip of paper, which he handed to Brody. "I'm sorry to make a countercharge of incompetence against another employee, but my integrity is at stake."

Brody took the slip of paper and read the name. He looked at the younger man again. "I know this technician. He's the best we have. He'll confirm what you just told me?"

"He will, Mr. Vance."

Brody nodded. "I'll check with him and make some investigation of your charges. You'll be notified when we have a resolution. Thank you, Mr. Koswalski."

"Thank you, Mr. Vance," the young man replied, standing. "I enjoy my job very much. If I lose it, it should be on merit, not lies."

"I quite agree," Brody replied. "Good day."

"Good day." Koswalski left, very dignified.

Brody turned to Jodie. "How would you characterize our Mr. Koswalski?"

"He seems sincere, honest, and hardworking."

He nodded. "He's here on time every morning, never takes longer than he has for lunch, does any task he's given willingly and without protest, even if it means working late hours."

He picked up a file folder. "On the other hand, the systems specialist, a Ms. Burgen, has been late four out of five mornings she's worked here. She misses work on Mondays every other week. She complains if she's asked to do overtime, and her work is unsatisfactory." He looked up. "Your course of action, in my place?"

"I would fire her," she said.

He smiled slowly. "She has an invalid mother and a two-year-old son," he said surprisingly. "She was fired from her last job. If she loses this one, she faces an uncertain future."

She bit her lower lip. It was one thing to condone firing an incompetent employee, but given the woman's home life the decision was uncomfortable.

"If you take my place, you'll be required to make such recommendations. In fact, you'll be required to make them to me," he added. "You can't wear your heart on your sleeve. You work for a business that depends on its income. Incompetent employees will cost us time, money, and possibly even clients. No business can exist that way for long."

She looked up at him with sad eyes. "It's not a nice job, Brody."

He nodded. "It's like gardening. You have to separate the weeds from the vegetables. Too many weeds, no more vegetables."

"I understand." She looked at her pad. "So what will you recommend?" she added.

"That our security section make a thorough investigation of her job performance," he said. "If she has a drug problem that relates to it, she'll be given the choice of counseling and treatment or separation. Unless she's caught using drugs on the job, of course," he added coolly. "In that case, she'll be arrested."

She knew she was growing cold inside. What had sounded like a wonderful position was weighing on her like a rock.

"Jodie, is this really what you want to do?" he asked gently, smiling. "Forgive me, but you're not a hardhearted person, and you're forever making excuses for people. It isn't the mark of a manager."

"I'm beginning to realize that," she said quietly. She searched his eyes. "Doesn't it bother you, recommending that people lose their jobs?"

"No," he said simply. "I'm sorry for them, but not sorry enough to risk my paycheck and yours keeping them on a job they're not qualified to perform. That's business, Jodie."

"I suppose so." She toyed with her pad. "I was a whiz with computers in business college," she mused. "I didn't want to be a systems specialist because I'm not mechanically-minded, but I could do anything with software." She glanced at him. "Maybe I'm in the wrong job to begin with. Maybe I should have been a software specialist."

He grinned. "If you decide, eventually, that you'd like to do that, write a job description, give it to your Human Resources manager, and apply for the job," he counseled.

"You're kidding!"

"I'm not. It's how I got my job," he confided.

"Well!"

"You don't have to fire software," he reminded her. "And if it doesn't work, it won't worry your conscience to toss it out. But all this is premature. You don't have to decide right now what you want to do. Besides," he added with a sigh, "I may not even get that promotion I'm hoping for."

"You'll get it," she assured him. "You're terrific at what you do, Brody."

"Do you really think so?" he asked, and seemed to care about her reply.

"I certainly do."

He smiled. "Thanks. Cara doesn't think much of my abilities, I'm afraid. I suppose it's because she's so good at marketing. She gets promotions all the time. And the travel…! She's out of town more than she's in, but she loves it. She was in Mexico last week and in Peru the week before that. Imagine! I'd love to go to Mexico and see Chichen Itza." He sighed.

"So would I. You like archaeology?" she fished.

He grinned. "Love it. You?"

"Oh, yes!"

"There's a museum exhibit of Mayan pottery at the art museum," he said enthusiastically. "Cara hates that sort of thing. I don't suppose you'd like to go with me to see it next Saturday?"

Next Saturday. Alexander's birthday. She'd mourned for the past two weeks since she'd come back from the Cobbs' party, miserable and hurting. But she wouldn't be invited to his birthday party, and she wouldn't go even if she was.

"I'd love to," she said with a beaming smile. "But… won't your girlfriend mind?"

He frowned. "I don't know." He looked down at her. "We, uh, don't have to advertise it, do we?"

She understood. It was a little uncomfortable going out with a committed man, but it wasn't as if he were married or anything. Besides, his girlfriend treated him like dirt. She wouldn't.

"No, we don't," she agreed. "I'll look forward to it."

"Great!" He beamed, too. "I'll phone you Friday night and we'll decide where and when to meet, okay?"

"Okay!"

SHE WAS ON a new track, a new life, and she felt like a new person. She'd started going to a retro coffeehouse in the evenings, where they served good coffee and people read poetry onstage or played folk music with guitars. Jodie fit right in with the artsy crowd. She'd even gotten up for the first time and read one of her poems, a sad one about rejected love that Alexander had inspired. Everyone applauded, even the owner, a man named Johnny. The boost of confidence she felt made her less inhibited, and the next time she read her poetry, she wasn't afraid of the crowd. She was reborn. She was the new, improved Jodie, who could conquer the world. And now Brody wanted to date her. She was delighted.

That feeling lasted precisely two hours. She came back in after lunch to find Alexander Cobb perched on her desk, in her small cubicle, waiting for her.

She hadn't had enough time to get over her disastrous last meeting with him. She wanted to turn and run, but that wasn't going to work. He'd already spotted her.

She walked calmly to her desk—although her heart was doing cartwheels—and put her purse in her lower desk drawer.

"Hello, Alexander," she said somberly. "What can I do for you?"

Her attitude sent him reeling. Jodie had always been unsettled and full of joy when she came upon him unexpectedly. He didn't realize how much he'd enjoyed the headlong reaction until it wasn't there anymore.

He stared at her across the desk, puzzled and disturbed. "What happened wasn't anybody's fault," he said stiffly. "Don't wear yourself out regretting it."

She relaxed a little, but only a little. "I drank too much. I won't do it a second time," she assured him. "How's Margie?"

"Quiet," he said. The one word was alarming. Margie was never quiet.

"Why?" she asked.

Shrugging, he picked up a paper clip from her desk and studied it. "She can't get anywhere with her designs.

She expected immediate success, and she can't even get a foot in the door."

"I'm sorry. She's really good."

He nodded and his green eyes met hers narrowly. "I need to talk to you," he said. "Can you meet me downstairs at the coffee bar when you get off from work?"

She didn't want to, and it was obvious. "Couldn't you just phone me at home?" she countered.

He scowled. "No. I can't discuss this over the phone." She was still hesitating. "Do you have other plans?" he asked.

She shook her head. "No. I don't want to miss my bus."

"I can drive you…"

"No! I mean—" she lowered her voice "—no, I won't put you to any trouble. There are two buses. The second runs an hour after the first one."

"It won't take an hour," he assured her. But he felt as if something was missing from their conversation. She didn't tease him, taunt him, antagonize him. In fact, she looked very much as if she wanted to avoid him altogether.

"All right, then," she said, sitting down at her desk. "I'll see you there about five after five."

He nodded, pausing at the opening of the cubicle to look back at her. It was a bad time to remember the taste of her full, soft mouth under his. But he couldn't help it. She was wearing a very businesslike dark suit with a pale pink blouse, her long hair up in a bun. She should have looked like a businesswoman, but she was much too vulnerable, too insecure, to give that image. She didn't have the self-confidence to rate a higher job, but he couldn't tell her that. Jodie had a massive inferiority complex. The least thing hurt her. As he'd hurt her.

The muscles in his jaw tautened. "This doesn't suit you," he said abruptly, nodding around the sterile little glass and wood cage they kept her in. "Won't they even let you have a potted plant?"

She was aghast at the comment. He never made personal remarks. She shifted restlessly in her chair. "It isn't dignified," she stammered.

He moved a step closer. "Jodie, a job shouldn't mimic jail. If you don't like what you do, where you do it, you're wasting the major part of your life."

She knew that. She tasted panic when she swallowed. But jobs were thin on the ground and she had the chance for advancement in this one. She put to the back of her mind Brody's comments on her shortcomings as a manager.

"I like my job very much," she lied.

His eyes slid over her with something like possession. "No, you don't. Pity. You have a gift for computer programming. I'll bet you haven't written a single routine since you've been here."

Her face clenched. "Don't you have something to do? Because I'm busy."

"Suit yourself. As soon after five as you can make it, please," he said, adding deliberately, "I have a dinner date."

With Kirry. Always with Kirry. She knew it. She hated Kirry. She hated him, too. But she smiled. "No problem. See you." She turned on her computer and pulled up her memo file to see what tasks were upcoming. She ignored Alexander, who gave her another long, curious appraisal before he left her alone.

She felt the sting of his presence all the way to her poor heart. He was so much a part of her life that it was like being amputated when she thought of a lifetime without his complicated presence.

For the first time, she thought about moving to another city. Ritter Oil Corporation had a headquarters office in Tulsa, Oklahoma. Perhaps she could get a transfer there… and do what, she asked herself? She was barely qualified for the predominantly clerical job she was doing now, and painfully unqualified for firing people, even if they deserved it. She'd let her pride force her into taking this job, because Alexander kept asking when she was going to start working after her graduation from business college. He probably hadn't meant that he thought she was taking advantage of his financial help—but she took it that way. So she went to work for the first company that offered her a job, just to shut him up.

In retrospect, she should have looked a little harder. She'd been under consideration for a job with the local police department, as a computer specialist. She had the skills to write programs, to restructure software. She was a whiz at opening protected files, finding lost documents, tracking down suspicious emails and finding ways to circumvent write-protected software. Her professor had recommended her for a career in law enforcement as a cyber crime specialist, but she'd jumped at the first post-college job that came her way.

Now here she was, stuck in a dead-end job that she didn't even like, kept in a cubicle like a box of printer paper and only taken out when some higher-up needed her to take a letter or organize a schedule, or compile his notes…

She had a vision of herself as a cardboard box full of supplies and started giggling.

Another administrative assistant stuck her head in

the cubicle. "Better keep it down," she advised softly. "They've had a complaint about the noise levels in here."

"I'm only laughing to myself," Jodie protested, shocked.

"They want us quiet while we're working. No personal phone calls, no talking to ourselves—and there's a new memo about the length of time people are taking in the bathroom..."

"Oh, good God!" Jodie burst out furiously.

The other woman put a feverish hand to her lips and looked around nervously. "Shhh!" she cautioned.

Jodie stood up and gave the woman her best military salute.

Sadly the vice president in charge of personnel was walking by her cubicle at the time. He stopped, eyeing both women suspiciously.

Already in trouble, and not giving a damn anymore, Jodie saluted him, too.

Surprisingly he had to suppress a smile. He wiped it off quickly. "Back to work, girls," he cautioned and kept walking.

The other woman moved closer. "Now see what you've done!" she hissed. "We'll both be on report!"

"If he tries to put me on report, I'll put him on report, as well," Jodie replied coolly. "Nobody calls me a 'girl' in a working office!"

The other woman threw up her hands and walked out.

Jodie turned her attention back to her chores and put the incident out of her mind. But it was very disturbing to realize how much authority the company had over her working life, and she didn't like it. She wondered if old man Ritter, the head of the corporation, encouraged such office politics. From what she'd heard about him, he was something of a renegade. He didn't seem to like rules and regulations very much, but, then, he couldn't be everywhere. Maybe he didn't even know the suppressive tactics his executives used to keep employees under control here.

Being cautioned never to speak was bad enough, and personalization of cubicles was strictly forbidden by company policy. But to have executives complain about the time employees spent in the bathroom made Jodie furious. She had a girlfriend who was a diabetic, and made frequent trips to the restroom in school. Some teachers had made it very difficult for her until her parents had requested a teacher conference to explain their daughter's health problem. She had a feeling no sort of conference would help at this job.

She went back to work, but the day had been disturbing in more ways than one.

AT EXACTLY FIVE minutes past quitting time, she walked into the little coffee shop downstairs. Alexander had a table, and he was waiting for her. He'd already ordered the French Vanilla cappuccino she liked so much, along with chocolate biscotti.

She was surprised by his memory of her preferences. She draped her old coat over the empty chair at the corner table and sat down. Fortunately the shop wasn't crowded, as it was early in the evening, and there were no customers anywhere near them.

"Right on time," Alexander noted, checking his expensive wristwatch.

"I usually am," she said absently, sipping her cappuccino. "This is wonderful," she added with a tiny smile.

He seemed puzzled. "Don't you come here often?"

"Actually, it's not something I can fit into my budget," she confessed.

Now it was shock that claimed his features. "You make a good salary," he commented.

"If you want to rent someplace with good security, it costs more," she told him. "I have to dress nicely for work, and that costs, too. By the time I add in utilities and food and bus fare, there isn't a lot left. We aren't all in your income tax bracket, Alexander," she added without rancor.

He let his attention wander to his own cappuccino. He sipped it quietly.

"I never think of you as being in a different economic class," he said.

"Don't you?" She knew better, and her thoughts were bitter. She couldn't forget what she'd overheard him say to his sister, that she was only blue collar and she didn't fit in with them.

He sat up straight. "Something's worrying you," he said flatly. "You're not the same. You haven't been since the party."

Her face felt numb. She couldn't lower her pride enough to tell him what she'd overheard. It was just too much, on top of everything else that had gone haywire lately.

"Why can't you talk to me?" he persisted.

She looked up at him with buried resentments, hurt pride, and outraged sentiment plain in her cold eyes. "It would be like talking to the floor," she said. "If you're here, it's because you want something. So, what is it?"

His expression was eloquent. He sipped cappuccino carefully and then put the delicate cup in its saucer with precision.

"Why do you think I want something?"

She felt ancient. "Margie invites me to parties so that I can cook and clean up the kitchen, if Jessie isn't available," she said in a tone without inflection. "Or if she's sick and needs nursing. You come to see me if you need something typed, or a computer program tweaked, or some clue traced back to an ISP online. Neither of you ever come near me unless I'm useful."

His breath caught. "Jodie, it's not like that!"

She looked at him steadily. "Yes, it is. It always has been. I'm not complaining," she added at once. "I don't know what I would have done if it hadn't been for you and Margie. I owe you more than I can ever repay in my lifetime. It's just that since you're here, there's something you need done, and I know it. No problem. Tell me what you want me to do."

His eyes closed and opened again, on a pained expression. It was true. He and Margie had used her shamelessly, but without realizing they were so obvious. He hated the thought.

"It's a little late to develop a conscience," she added with a faint smile. "It's out of character, anyway. Come on. What is it?"

He toyed with his biscotti. "I told you that we're tracking a link to the drug cartel."

She nodded.

"In your company," he added.

"You said I couldn't help," she reminded him.

"Well, I was wrong. In fact, you're the only one who can help me with this."

A few weeks ago, she'd have joked about getting a badge or a gun. Now she just waited for answers. The days of friendly teasing were long gone.

He met her searching gaze. "I want you to pretend that we're developing a relationship," he said, "so that I have a reason to hang around your division."

She didn't react. She was proud of herself. It would have been painfully easy to dump the thick, creamy cappuccino all over his immaculate trousers and anoint him with the cream.

His eyebrow jerked. "Yes, you're right, I'm using you. It's the only way I can find to do surveillance. I can't hang around Jasper or people will think I'm keen on him!"

That thought provoked a faint smile. "His wife wouldn't like it."

He shrugged. "Will you do it?"

She hesitated.

He anticipated that. He took out a photograph and slid it across the table to her.

She picked it up. It was of two young boys, about five or six, both smiling broadly. They had thick, straight black hair and black eyes and dark complexions. They looked Latin. She looked back up at Alexander with a question in her eyes.

"Their mother was tired of having drug users in her neighborhood. They met in an abandoned house next door to her. There were frequent disputes, usually followed by running gun battles. The dealer who made the house his headquarters got ambitious. He decided to double-cross the new drug leadership that came in after Manuel Lopez's old territory was finally divided," he said carelessly. "Mama Garcia kept a close eye on what was going on and kept the police informed. She made the fatal error of telling her infrequent neighbor that his days in her neighborhood were numbered. He told his supplier.

"All this got back to the new dealer network. So when

they came to take out the double-crossing dealer, they were quite particular about where they placed the shots. They knew where Mama Garcia lived, and they targeted her along with their rival. Miguel and Juan were hit almost twenty times with automatic weapon fire. They died in the firefight, along with the rebellious dealer. Their mother was wounded and will probably never walk again."

She winced as she looked at the photograph of the two little boys, so happy and smiling. Both dead, over drugs.

He saw her discomfort and nodded. "The local distributor I'm after ordered the hit. He works in this building, in this corporation, in this division." He leaned forward, and she'd never seen him look so menacing. "I'm going to take him out. So, I'll ask you one more time, Jodie. Will you help me?"

CHAPTER FIVE

JODIE GROANED INWARDLY. She knew as she looked one last time at the photograph that she couldn't let a child killer walk the streets, no matter what the sacrifice to herself.

She handed him back the photograph. "Yes, I'll do it," she said in a subdued tone. "When do I start?"

"Tomorrow at lunch. We'll go out to eat. You can give me the grand tour on the way."

"Okay."

"You still look reluctant," he said with narrowed eyes.

"Brody just asked me out, for the first time," she confessed, trying to sound more despondent than she actually was. It wouldn't hurt to let Alexander know that she wasn't pining over him.

His expression was not easily read. "I thought he was engaged."

She grimaced. "Well, things are cooling off," she defended herself. "His girlfriend travels all over the world. She just came back from trips to Mexico and Peru, and she doesn't pay Brody much attention even when she's here!" she muttered.

"Peru?" He seemed thoughtful. He studied her quietly for a long moment before he spoke. "They're still engaged, Jodie."

And he thought less of her because she was ignoring another woman's rights. Of course he did. She didn't like the idea, either, and she knew she wasn't going to go out with Brody a week from Saturday. Not now. Alexander made her feel too guilty.

She traced the rim of her china coffee cup. "You're right," she had to admit. "It's just that she treats him so badly," she added with a wistful smile. "He's a sweet man. He's always encouraging me in my job, telling me I can do things, believing in me."

"Which is no damned reason to have an affair with a man," he said furiously. It made him angry to think that another man was trying to uplift Jodie's ego when he'd done nothing but damage to it.

She lowered her voice. "I am not having an affair with him!"

"But you would, if he asked," he said, his eyes as cold as green glass.

She started to argue, then stopped. It would do no good to argue. Besides, it was her life, and he had no business telling her how to live it.

"How do you want me to act while we're pretending to get involved?" she countered sourly. "Do you want me to throw myself at you and start kissing you when you walk into my cubicle?"

His eyes dilated. "I beg your pardon?"

"Never mind," she said, ruffled. "I'll play it by ear."

He really did seem different, she thought, watching him hesitate uncharacteristically. He drew a USB flash drive out of his inside jacket pocket and handed it to her.

"Another chore," he added, glancing around to make sure they weren't being observed. "I want you to check out these websites, and the email addresses, without leaving footprints. I want to know if they're legitimate and who owns them. They're password protected and in code."

"No problem," she said easily. "I can get behind any firewall they put up."

"Don't leave an address they can trace back to you," he emphasized. "These people won't hesitate to kill children. They wouldn't mind wasting you."

"I get the point. I'm not sloppy." She slipped the USB flash drive into her purse and finished her coffee. "Anything else?"

"Yes. Margie said to tell you that she's sorry."

Her eyebrows arched. "For what?"

"For everything." He searched her eyes. "And for the record, you don't owe us endless favors, debt or no debt."

She got to her feet. "I know that. I'll have this information for you tomorrow by the time you get here."

He got up, too, catching the bill before she had time to grab it. "My conference, my treat," he said. He stared down at her with an intensity that was disturbing. "You're still keeping something back," he said in a deep, low tone.

"Nothing of any importance," she replied. It was disconcerting that he could read her expressions that well.

His eyes narrowed. "Do you really like working here, Jodie?"

"You're the one who said I needed to stop loafing and get a job," she accused with more bitterness than she realized. "So I got one."

He actually winced. "I said you needed to get your priorities straight," he countered. "Not that you needed to jump into a job you hate."

"I like Brody."

"Brody isn't the damned job," he replied tersely. "You're not cut out for monotony. It will kill your soul."

She knew that; she didn't want to admit it. "Don't you have a hot date?" she asked sarcastically, out of patience with his meddling.

He sighed heavily. "Yes. Why don't you?"

"Men aren't worth the trouble they cause," she lied, turning.

"Oh, you'd know?" he drawled sarcastically. "With your hectic social life?"

She turned, furious. "When Brody's free, look out," she said.

He didn't reply. But he watched her all the way down the hall.

SHE FUMED ALL the way home. Alexander had such a nerve, she thought angrily. He could taunt her with his conquests, use her to do his decryption work, force her into becoming his accomplice in an investigation…!

Wait a minute, she thought suddenly, her hand resting on her purse over the USB flash drive he'd entrusted her with. He had some of the best cyber crime experts in the country on his payroll. Why was he farming out work to an amateur who didn't even work for him?

The answer came in slowly, as she recalled bits and pieces of information she'd heard during the Lopez investigation. She knew people in Jacobsville who kept in touch with her after her move to Houston. Someone had mentioned that there were suspicions of a mole in the law enforcement community, a shadowy figure who'd funneled information to Lopez so that he could escape capture.

Then Alexander's unusual request made sense. He suspected somebody in his organization of working with the drug dealers, and he wanted someone he could trust to do this investigation for him.

She felt oddly touched by his confidence, not only in her ability, but also in her character. He'd refused to let her help him before, but now he was trusting her with explosive information. He was letting her into his life, even on a limited basis. He had to care about her, a little.

Sure he did, she told herself glumly. She was a computer whiz, and he knew it. Hadn't he paid for the college education that had honed those skills? He trusted her ability to manipulate software and track criminal activity through cyberspace. That didn't amount to a declaration of love. She had to stop living in dreams. There was no hope of a future with Alexander. She wasn't even his type. He liked highly intelligent, confident women. He liked professionals. Jodie was more like a mouse. She kept in her little corner, avoiding confrontation, hiding her abilities, speaking only when spoken to, never demanding anything.

She traced the outline of the USB flash drive through the soft leather of her purse, bought almost new at a yard sale. She pursed her lips. Well, maybe it was time she stopped being everybody's lackey and started standing up for herself. She was smart. She was capable. She could do any job she really wanted to do.

She thought about firing a woman with a dependent elderly mother and child and ground her teeth together. It was becoming obvious that she was never going to enjoy that sort of job.

On the other hand, tracking down criminals was exciting. It made her face flush as she considered how valuable she could be to Alexander in this investigation. She thought of the two little Garcia boys and their poor mother, and her eyes narrowed angrily. She was going to help Alexander catch the animal who'd ordered that depraved execution. And she was just the woman with the skills to do it.

JODIE SPENT MOST of the evening and the wee hours of the morning tracking down the information Alexander had asked her to find for him. She despaired a time or two, because she ran into one dead end after another. The drug dealers must have cyber experts of their own, and of a high caliber, if they could do this sort of thing.

She finally found a website that listed information which was, on the surface, nothing more than advisories about the best sites to find UFO information. But one of the addresses coincided with the material she'd printed out from Alexander's USB flash drive, as a possible link to the drug network. She opened site after site, but she found nothing more than double-talk about possible landing sites and dates. Most covered pages and pages of data, but the last one had only one page of information. It was oddly concise, and the sites were all in a defined area—Texas and Mexico and Peru. Strange, she thought. But, then, Peru was right next door to Colombia. And while drugs and Colombia went together like apples and pie, few people outside law enforcement would connect Peru with drug smuggling.

It was two in the morning, and she was so sleepy that she began to laugh at her own inadequacy. But as she looked at the last site she made sudden sense of the numbers and landing sites. Quickly she printed out the single page of UFO landing sites.

There was a pattern in the listings. It was so obvious that it hit her in the face. She grabbed a pencil and pad and began writing down the numbers. From there, it was a quick move to transpose them with letters. They spelled an email address.

She plugged back into her ISP and changed identities to avoid leaving digital footprints. Then she used a hacker's device to find the source of the email. It originated from a foreign server, and linked directly to a city in Peru. Moreover, a city in Peru near the border with Colombia. She copied down the information without risking leaving it in her hard drive and got out fast.

She folded the sheets of paper covered with her information—because she hadn't wanted to leave anything on her computer that could be accessed if she were online—and placed them in her purse. She smiled sleepily as she climbed into bed with a huge yawn. Alexander, she thought, was going to be impressed.

IN FACT, HE was speechless. He went over the figures in his car in the parking lot on the way to lunch. His eyes met Jodie's and he shook his head.

"This is ingenious," he murmured.

"They did do a good job of hiding information..." she agreed.

"No! Your work," he corrected instantly. "This is quality work, Jodie. Quality work. I can't think of anyone who could have done it better."

"Thanks," she said.

"And you're taking notes for Brody Vance," he said with veiled contempt. "He should be working for you."

She chuckled at the thought of Brody with a pad and pen sitting with his legs crossed under a skirt, in front of her desk. "He wouldn't suit."

"You don't suit the job you're doing," he replied.

"When this case is solved, I want you to consider switching vocations. Any law enforcement agency with a cyber crime unit would be proud to have you."

Except his, she was thinking, but she didn't say it. A compliment from Alexander was worth something. "I might do that," she said noncommittally.

"I'll put this to good use," he said, sliding the folded sheets into his inside suit pocket. "Where do you want to eat?" he added.

"I usually eat downstairs in the cafeteria. They have a blue plate special…"

"Where does your boss have lunch?"

"Brody?" She blinked. "When his girlfriend's in town, he usually goes to a Mexican restaurant, La Rancheria. It's three blocks over near the north expressway," she added.

"I know where it is. What's his girlfriend like?"

She shrugged. "Very dark, very beautiful, very chic. She's District Marketing manager for the whole southwest. She oversees our sales force for the gas and propane distribution network. We sell all over the world, of course, not just in Texas."

"But she travels to Mexico and Peru," he murmured as he turned the Jaguar into traffic.

"She has family in both places," she said disinterestedly. "Her mother was moving from a town in Peru near the Colombian border down to Mexico City, and Cara had to help organize it. That's what she told Brody." She frowned. "Odd, I thought Brody said her mother was dead. But, then, I didn't really pay attention. I've only seen her a couple of times. She leads Brody around by the nose. He's not very forceful."

"Do you like Mexican food?"

"The real thing, yes," she said with a sigh. "I usually get my chili fix from cans or TV dinners. It's not the same."

"No, it's not."

"You used to love eggs ranchero for breakfast," she commented, and then could have bitten her tongue out for admitting that she remembered his food preferences.

"Yes. You made them for me at four in the morning, the day my father died. Jessie was in tears, so was Margie. Nobody was awake. I'd come from overseas and didn't even have supper. You heard me rattling around in the kitchen trying to make a sandwich," he recalled with a strangely tender smile. "You got up and started cooking. Never said a word, either," he added. "You put the plate in front of me, poured coffee, and went away." He shrugged. "I couldn't have talked to save my life. I was too broken up at losing Dad. You knew that. I never understood how."

"Neither did I," she confessed. She looked out the window. It was a cold day, misting rain. The city looked smoggy. That wasn't surprising. It usually did.

"What is it about Vance that attracts you?" he asked abruptly.

"Brody? Well, he's kind and encouraging, he always makes people feel good about themselves. I like being with him. He's... I don't know...comfortable."

"Comfortable." He made the word sound insulting. He turned into the parking lot of the Mexican restaurant.

"You asked," she pointed out.

He cut off the engine and glanced at her. "God forbid that a woman should ever find me comfortable!"

"That would take a miracle," she said sweetly and unfastened her seat belt.

He only laughed.

THEY HAD A quiet lunch. Brody wasn't there, but Alexander kept looking around as if he expected the man to materialize right beside the table.

"Are you looking for someone?" she asked finally.

He glanced at her over his dessert, a caramel flan. "I'm always looking for someone," he returned. "It's my job."

She didn't think about what he did for a living most of the time. Of course, the bulge under his jacket where he carried his gun was a dead giveaway, and sometimes he mentioned a case he was working on. Today, their combined efforts on the computer tracking brought it up. But she could go whole days without realizing that he put himself at risk to do the job. In his position, it was inevitable that he would make enemies. Some of them must have been dangerous, but he'd never been wounded.

"Thinking deep thoughts?" he asked her as he registered her expression.

"Not really. This flan is delicious."

"No wonder your boss frequents the place. The food is good, too."

"I really like the way they make coffee…"

"Kennedy!" Alexander called to a man just entering the restaurant, interrupting Jodie's comment.

An older man glanced his way, hesitated, and then smiled broadly as he joined them. "Cobb!" he greeted. "Good to see you!"

"I thought you were in New Orleans," Alexander commented.

"I was. Got through quicker than I thought I would. Who's this?" he added with a curious glance at Jodie.

"Jodie's my girl," Alexander said carelessly. "Jodie, this is Bert Kennedy, one of my senior agents."

They shook hands.

"Glad to meet you, Mr. Kennedy."

"Same here, Miss…?"

Alexander ignored the question. Jodie just smiled at him.

"Uh, any luck on the shipyard tip?" Kennedy asked.

Alexander shook his head. "Didn't pan out." He didn't meet the older man's eyes. "We may put a man at Thorn Oil next week," he said in a quiet tone, glancing around to make sure they weren't subject to eavesdroppers. "I'll tell you about it later."

Kennedy had been nervous, but now he relaxed and began to grin. "Great! I'd love to be in on the surveillance," he added. "Unless you have something bigger?"

"We'll talk about it later. See you."

Kennedy nodded, and walked on to a table by the window.

"Is he one of your best men?" she asked Alexander.

"Kennedy is a renegade," he murmured coolly, watching the man from a distance. "He's the bird who brought mercenaries into my drug bust in Jacobsville the year before last, without warning mc first. One of their undercover guys almost got killed because we didn't know who he was."

"Eb Scott's men," she ventured.

He nodded. "I was already upset because Manuel Lopez had killed my undercover officer, Walt Monroe. He was my newest agent. I sent him to infiltrate Lopez's organization." His eyes were bleak. "I wanted Lopez. I wanted him badly. The night of the raid, I had no idea that Scott and his gang were even on the place. They werc running a Mexican national undercover. If Kennedy knew, he didn't tell me. We could have killed him,

or Scott, or any of his men. They weren't supposed to
be there."

"I expect Mr. Kennedy lived to regret that decision."

He gave her a cool look. "Oh, he regretted it, all right."

She wasn't surprised that Mr. Kennedy was intimidated by Alexander. Most people were, herself included.

She finished her coffee. "Thanks for lunch," she said.
"I really enjoyed it."

He studied her with real interest. "You have exquisite manners," he commented. "Your mother did, too."

She felt her cheeks go hot. "She was a stickler for
courtesy," she replied.

"So was your father. They were good people."

"Like your own father."

"I loved him. My mother never forgave him for leaving her for a younger woman," he commented in a rare
lapse. "She drank like a fish. Margie and I were stuck
with her, because she put on such a good front in court
that nobody believed she was a raging alcoholic. She
got custody and made us pay for my father's infidelities
until she finally died. By then, we were almost grown.
We still loved him, though."

She hadn't known the Cobbs' mother very well. Margie had been reluctant to invite her to their home while
the older woman was still alive, although Margie spent a
lot of time at Jodie's home. Margie and Alexander were
very fond of Mr. and Mrs. Clayburn, and they brought
wonderful Christmas presents to them every year. Jodie
had often wondered just how much damage his mother
had done to Alexander in his younger, formative years. It
might explain a lot about his behavior from time to time.

"Did you love your mother?" she asked.

He glared at her. "I hated her."

She swallowed. She thought back to the party, to her uninhibited behavior when she'd had those glasses of champagne. She'd brought back terrible memories for Alexander, of his mother, his childhood. Only now did she understand why he'd reacted so violently. No wonder she'd made him sick. He identified her behavior with his mother's. But he'd said other things, as well, things she couldn't forget. Things that hurt.

She dropped her eyes and looked at her watch. "I really have to get back," she began.

His hand went across the table to cover hers. "Don't," he said roughly. "Don't look like that! You don't drink normally, not ever. That's why the champagne hit you so hard. I overreacted. Don't let it ruin things between us, Jodie."

She took a slow breath to calm herself. She couldn't meet his eyes. She looked at his mouth instead, and that was worse. It was a chiseled, sensuous mouth and she couldn't stop remembering how it felt to be kissed by it. He was expert. He was overwhelming. She wanted him to drag her into his arms and kiss her blind, and that would never do.

She withdrew her hand with a slow smile. "I'm not holding grudges, Alexander," she reassured him. "Listen, I really have to get back. I've got a USB flash drive full of letters to get out by quitting time."

"All right," he said. "Let's go."

Kennedy raised his hand and waved as they went out. Alexander returned the salute, sliding his hand around Jodie's waist as they left the building. But she noticed that he dropped it the minute they entered the parking lot. He was putting on an act, and she'd better remember it. She'd already been hurt once. There was no sense in inviting more pain from the same source.

He left her at the front door of her building with a curious, narrow-eyed gaze that stayed with her the rest of the day.

THE PHONE ON her desk rang early the following morning and she answered it absently while she typed.

"Do you still like symphony concerts?" came a deep voice in reply.

Alexander! Her fingers flew across the keys, making errors. "Uh, yes."

"There's a special performance of Debussy tomorrow night."

"I read about it in the entertainment section of the newspaper," she said. "They're doing 'Afternoon of a Faun' and 'La Mer,' my two favorites."

He chuckled. "I know."

"I'd love to see it," she admitted.

"I've got tickets. I'll pick you up at seven. Will you have time to eat supper by then?" he added, implying that he was asking her to the concert only, not to dinner.

"Of course," she replied.

"I have to work late, or I'd include dinner," he said softly.

"No problem. I have leftovers that have to be eaten," she said.

"Then I'll see you at seven."

"At seven." She hung up. Her hands were ice cold and shaking. She felt her insides shake. Alexander was taking her to a concert. Mentally her thoughts flew to her closet. She only had one good dress, a black one. She could pair it with her winter coat and a small strand of pearls that Margie and Alexander had given her when she graduated from college. She could put her hair up. She wouldn't look too bad.

She felt like a teenager on her first date until she realized why they were going out together. Alexander hadn't just discovered love eternal. He was putting on an act. But why put it on at a concert?

The answer came in an unexpected way. Brody stopped by her office a few minutes after Alexander's call. He came into the cubicle, looking nervous.

"Is something wrong?" she asked.

He drew in a long breath. "About next Saturday..." he began.

"I can't go," she blurted out.

His relief was patent. "I'm so glad you said that," he replied, relief making him limp. "Cara's going to be home and she wants to spend the day with me."

"Alexander's having a birthday party that day," she replied, painfully aware that she wouldn't be invited, although Alexander would surely want her coworkers to think that she was.

"I, uh, couldn't help but notice that he took you out to lunch yesterday," he said. "You've known him for a long time."

"A very long time," she confessed. "He just phoned, in fact, to invite me to a concert of Debussy..."

"Debussy?" he exclaimed.

"Well, yes...?"

"I'll see you there," he said. "Cara and I are going, too. Isn't *that* a coincidence?"

She laughed, as he did. "I can't believe it! I didn't even know you liked Debussy!"

He grimaced. "Actually, I don't," he had to confess. "Cara does."

She smiled wickedly. "I don't think Alexander's very keen on him, either, but he'll pretend to be."

He smiled back. "Forgive me, but he doesn't seem quite your type," he began slowly, flushing a little. "He's a rather tough sort of man, isn't he? And I think he was wearing a gun yesterday, too… Jodie?" he added when she burst out laughing.

"He's sort of in security work, part-time," she told him, without adding where he worked or what he did. Alexander had always made a point of keeping his exact job secret, even among his friends, for reasons Jodie was only beginning to understand.

"Oh. Oh!" He laughed with sheer relief. "And here I thought maybe you were getting involved with a mobster!"

She'd have to remember to tell Alexander that. Not that it would impress him.

"No, he's not quite that bad," she assured him. "About next Saturday, Brody, I would have canceled anyway. It didn't feel right."

"No, it didn't," he seconded. "You and I are too conventional, Jodie. Neither of us is comfortable stepping out of bounds. I'll bet you never had a speeding ticket."

"Never," she agreed. "Not that I drive very much anymore. It's so convenient to take buses," she added, without mentioning that she'd had to sell her car months ago. The repair bills, because it was an older model, were eating her alive.

"I suppose so. Uh, I did notice that your friend drives a new Jaguar."

She smiled sedately. "He and his sister are independently wealthy," she told him. "They own a ranch and breed some of the finest cattle in south Texas. That's how he can afford to run a Jaguar."

"I see." He stuck his hands in his pockets and watched her. "Debussy. Somehow I never thought of you as a classical concert-goer."

"But I am. I love ballet and theater, too. Not that I get the opportunity to see much of them these days."

"Does your friend like them, too?"

"He's the one who taught me about them," she confided. "He was forever taking me and his sister to performances when we were in our teens. He said that we needed to learn culture, because it was important. We weren't keen at the time, but we learned to love it as he did. Except for Debussy," she added on a chuckle. "And I sometimes think I like that composer just to spite him."

"It's a beautiful piece, if you like modern. I'm a Beethoven man myself."

"And I don't like Beethoven, except for the Ninth Symphony."

"That figures. Well, thanks for understanding. I, uh, I guess we'll see you at the concert tonight, then!"

"I guess so."

They exchanged smiles and then he left. She turned her attention back to her computer, curious about the coincidence.

Had Alexander known that Brody and his girlfriend Cara were going to the same performance? Or had it really been one of those inexplicable things?

Then another thought popped into her mind. What if Alexander was staking out her company because he suspected Brody of being in the drug lord's organization?

CHAPTER SIX

THE SUSPICION THAT Alexander was after Brody kept Jodie brooding for the rest of the day. Brody was a gentle, sweet man. Surely he couldn't be involved in anything as unsavory as drug smuggling!

If someone at the corporation was under investigation, she couldn't blow Alexander's cover by mentioning anything to her boss. But, wait, hadn't Alexander told his agent, Kennedy, that they were investigating a case at Thorn Oil Corporation? Then she remembered why Alexander wanted to pretend to be interested in Jodie. Something was crazy here. Why would he lie to Kennedy?

She shook her head and put the questions away. She wasn't going to find any answers on her own.

She'd been dressed and ready for an hour when she buzzed Alexander into her apartment building. By the time he got to her room and knocked at the door, she was a nervous wreck.

She opened the door, and he gave her a not very flattering scrutiny. She thought she looked nice in her sedate black dress and high heels, with her hair in a bun. Obviously he didn't. He was dashing, though, in a dinner jacket and slacks and highly polished black shoes. His black tie was perfectly straight against the expensive white cotton of his shirt.

"You never wear your hair down," Alexander said

curtly. "And you've worn that same dress to two out of three parties at our house."

She flushed. "It's the only good dress I have, Alexander," she said tightly.

He sighed angrily. "Margie would love to make you something, if you'd let her."

She turned to lock her door. Her hands were cold and numb. He couldn't let her enjoy one single evening without criticizing something about her. She felt near tears…

She gasped as he suddenly whipped her around and bent to kiss her with grinding, passionate fervor. She didn't have time to respond. It was over as soon as it had begun, despite her rubbery legs and wispy breathing. She stood looking up at him with wide, misty, shocked eyes in a pale face.

His own green eyes glittered into hers as he studied her reaction. "Stop letting me put you down," he said unexpectedly. "I know I don't do much for your ego, but you have to stand up for yourself. You're not a carpet, Jodie, stop letting people walk on you."

She was still trying to breathe and think at the same time.

"And now you look like an accident victim," he murmured. He pulled out a handkerchief, his eyes on her mouth. "I suppose I'm covered with pink lipstick," he added, pressing the handkerchief into her hand. "Clean me up."

"It…doesn't come off," she stammered.

He cocked an eyebrow and waited for an explanation.

"It's that new kind they advertise. You put it on and it lasts all day. It won't come off on coffee cups or even linen." She handed him back the handkerchief.

He put it up, but he didn't move. His hands went to

the pert bun on the top of her head and before she could stop him, he loosed her hair from the circular comb that held the wealth of hair in placc. It fell softly, in waves, to her shoulders.

Alexander caught his breath. "Beautiful," he whispered, the comb held absently in one hand while he ran the other through the soft strands of hair.

"It took forever...to get it put up," she protested weakly.

"I love long hair," he said gruffly. He bent, tilting her chin up, to kiss her with exquisite tenderness. "Leave it like that."

He put the comb in her hand and waited while she stuck it into her purse. Her hands shook. He saw that, too, and he smiled.

When she finished, he linked her fingers into his and they started off down the hall.

THE CONCERT HALL was full. Apparently quite a few people in Houston liked Debussy, Jodie thought mischievously as they walked down the aisle to their seats. She knew that Alexander didn't like it at all, but it was nice of him to suffer through it, considering her own affection for the pieces the orchestra was playing.

Of course, he might only be here because he was spying on Brody, she thought, and then worried about that. She couldn't believe Brody would ever deal in anything dishonest. He was too much like Jodie herself. But why would Alexander be spending so much time at her place of work if he didn't suspect Brody?

It was all very puzzling. She sat down in the reserved seat next to Alexander and waited for the curtain to go up. They'd gotten into a traffic jam on the way and had arrived just in the nick of time. The lights went out almost the minute they sat down.

In the darkness, lit comfortably by the lights from the stage where the orchestra was placed, she felt Alexander's big, warm hand curl into hers. She sighed helplessly, loving the exciting, electric contact of his touch.

He heard the soft sound, and his fingers tightened. He didn't let go until intermission.

"Want to stretch your legs?" he invited, standing.

"Yes, I think so," she agreed. She got up, still excited by his proximity, and walked out with him. He didn't hold her hand this time, she noticed, and wondered why.

When they were in the lobby, Brody spotted them and moved quickly toward them, his girlfriend in tow.

She was pretty, Jodie noted, very elegant and dark-haired and long-legged. She wished she was half as pretty. Brody's girlfriend looked Hispanic. She was certainly striking.

"Well, hello!" Brody said with genuine warmth. "Sweetheart, this is my secretary, Jodie Clayburn... excuse me," he added quickly, with an embarrassed smile at Jodie's tight-lipped glance, "I mean, my administrative assistant. And this is Jodie's date, Mr., uh, Mr...."

"Cobb," Alexander prompted.

"Mr. Cobb," Brody parroted. "This is my girlfriend, Cara Dominguez," he introduced.

"Pleased to meet you," Cara said in a bored tone.

"Same here," Jodie replied.

"Cara's in marketing," Brody said, trying to force the conversation to ignite. "She works for Bradford Marketing Associates, down the street. They're a subsidiary of Ritter Oil Corporation. They sell drilling equipment and machine parts for oil equipment all over the United States. Cara is over the southwestern division."

"And what do you do, Mr. Cobb?" Cara asked Alexander, who was simply watching her, without commenting.

"Oh, he's in security work," Brody volunteered.

Cara's eyebrows arched. "Really!" she asked, but without much real interest.

"I work for the Drug Enforcement Administration," Alexander said with a faint smile, his eyes acknowledging Jodie's shock. "I'm undercover and out of the country a lot of the time," he added with the straightest face Jodie had ever seen. "I don't have to work at all, of course," he added with a cool smile, "but I like the cachet of law enforcement duties."

Jodie was trying not to look at him or react. It was difficult.

"How nice," Cara said after a minute, and she seemed disconcerted by his honesty. "You are working on a case now?" she fished.

One of the first things Jodie and Margie had learned from Alexander when he went with the DEA was not to mention what he did for a living, past the fact that he did "security work." She'd always assumed it had something to do with his infrequent undercover assignments. And here he was spilling all the beans!

"Sort of," Alexander said lazily. "We're investigating a company with Houston connections," he added deliberately.

Cara was all ears. "That would not be Thorn Oil Corporation?"

Alexander gave her a very nice shocked look.

She laughed. "One hears things," she mused. "Don't worry, I never tell what I know."

"Right," Brody chuckled, making a joke of it. He hadn't known what Alexander did for a living until now.

Alexander laughed, too. "I have to have the occasional diversion," he confessed. "My father was wealthy. My sister and I were his only beneficiaries."

Cara was eyeing him with increased interest. "You live in Houston, Mr. Cobb?"

He nodded.

"Are you enjoying the concert?" Brody broke in, uncomfortable at the way his girlfriend was looking at Alexander.

"It's wonderful," Jodie said.

"I understand the Houston ballet is doing *The Nutcracker* starting in November," Cara purred, smiling at Alexander. "If you like ballet, perhaps we will meet again."

"Perhaps we will," Alexander replied. "Do you live in Houston, also, Miss Dominguez?"

"Yes, but I travel a great deal," she said with careless detachment. "My contacts are far reaching."

"She's only just come back from Mexico," Brody said with a nervous laugh.

"Yes, I've been helping my mother move," Cara said tightly. "After my father…died, she lost her home and had nowhere to go."

"I'm very sorry," Jodie told her. "I lost my parents some years ago. I know how it feels."

Cara turned back to Brody. "We need to get back to our seats. Nice to have met you both," she added with a social smile as she took Brody's hand and drew him along with her. He barely had time to say goodbye.

Alexander glanced down at Jodie. "Your boss looked shocked when I told him what I did."

She shook her head. "You told me never to do that, but you told them everything!"

"I told them nothing Cara didn't know already," he said enigmatically. He slid his hand into hers and smiled secretively. "Let's go back."

"It's a very nice concert," she commented.

"Is it? I hate Debussy," he murmured unsurprisingly.

The comment kept her quiet until they were out of the theater and on their way back to her apartment in his car.

"Why did you ask me out if you don't like concerts?" she asked.

He glanced at her. "I had my reasons. What do you think of your boss's girlfriend?"

"She's nice enough. She leads Brody around like a child, though."

"Most women would," he said lazily. "He's not assertive."

"He certainly is," she defended him. "He has to fire people."

"He's not for you, Jodie, girlfriend or not," he said surprisingly. "You'd stagnate in a relationship with him."

"It's my life," she pointed out.

"So it is."

They went the rest of the way in silence. He walked her to her apartment door and stood staring down at her for a long moment. "Buy a new dress."

"Why?" she asked, surprised.

"I'll take you to see *The Nutcracker* next month. As I recall, it was one of your favorite ballets."

"Yes," she stammered.

"So I'll take you," he said. He checked his watch. "I've got a late call to make, and meetings the first of the week. But I'll take you to lunch next Wednesday."

"Okay," she replied.

He reached out suddenly and drew her against him, hard. He held her there, probing her eyes with his until her lips parted. Then he bent and kissed her hungrily, twisting his mouth against hers until she yielded and gave him what he wanted. A long, breathless moment later, he lifted his head.

"Not bad," he murmured softly. "But you could use a little practice. Sleep well."

He let her go and walked away while she tried to find her voice. He never looked back once. Jodie stood at her door watching until he stepped into the elevator and the doors closed.

SHE USUALLY LEFT at eleven-thirty to go to lunch, and Alexander knew it. But he was late the following Wednesday. She'd chewed off three of her long fingernails by the time he showed up. She was in the lobby where clients were met, along with several of her colleagues who were just leaving for lunch. Alexander came in, looking windblown and half out of humor.

"I can't make it for lunch," he said at once. "I'm sorry. Something came up."

"That's all right," she said, trying not to let her disappointment show. "Another time."

"I'll be out of town for the next couple of days," he continued, not lowering his voice, "but don't you forget my birthday party on Saturday. Call me from the airport and I'll pick you up. If I'm not back by then, Margie will. All right?"

Amazing how much he sounded as if he really wanted her to come. But she knew he was only putting on an act for the employees who were listening to him.

"All right," she agreed. "Have a safe trip. I'll see you Saturday."

He reached out and touched her cheek tenderly. "So long," he said, smiling. He walked away slowly, as if he hated to leave her, and she watched him go with equal reluctance. There were smiling faces all around. It was working. People believed they were involved, which was just what he wanted.

Later, while Brody was signing the letters he'd dictated earlier, she wondered where Alexander was going that would keep him out of town for so long.

"You look pensive," Brody said curiously. "Something worrying you?"

"Nothing, really," she lied. "I was just thinking about Alexander's birthday party on Saturday."

He sighed as he signed the last letter. "It must be nice to have a party," he murmured. "I stopped having them years ago."

"Cara could throw one for you," she suggested.

He grimaced. "She's not the least bit sentimental. She's all business, most of the time, and she never seems to stop working. She's on a trip to Arizona this week to try to land a new client."

"You'll miss her, I'm sure," Jodie said.

He shrugged. "I'll try to." He flushed. "Sorry, that just popped out."

She smiled. "We all have our problems, Brody."

"Yes, I noticed that your friend, Cobb, hardly touches you, except when he thinks someone is watching. He must be one cold fish," he added with disgust.

Jodie flushed then, remembering Alexander's ardor.

He cleared his throat and changed the subject, and not a minute too soon.

JODIE WAS DOING housework in her apartment when the phone rang Saturday morning.

"Jodie?" Margie asked gently.

"Yes. How are you, Margie?" she asked, but not with her usual cheerful friendliness.

"You're still angry at me, aren't you?" She sighed. "I'm so sorry for making you do all the cooking…"

"I'm not angry," Jodie replied.

There was a long sigh. "I thought Kirry would help me arrange a showing of my designs at her department store," she confessed miserably. "But that's never going to happen. She only pretended to be my friend so that she could get to Alexander. I guess you know she's furious because he's been seen with you?"

"She has nothing to be jealous about," Jodie said coldly. "You can tell her so, for me. Was that all you wanted?"

"Jodie, that's not why I called!" Margie exclaimed. She hesitated. "Alexander wanted me to phone you and make sure you were coming to his birthday party."

"There's no chance of that," Jodie replied firmly.

"But…but he's expecting you," Margie stammered. "He said you promised to come, but that I had to call you and make sure you showed up."

"Kirry's invited, of course?" Jodie asked.

"Well…well, yes, I assumed he'd want her to come so I invited her, too."

"I'm invited to make her jealous, I suppose."

There was a static pause. "Jodie, what's going on? You won't return my calls, you won't meet me for lunch, you don't answer notes. If you're not mad at me, what's wrong?"

Jodie looked down at the floor. It needed mopping,

she thought absently. "Alexander told you that he was sick of tripping over me every time he came back to the ranch, and that you were especially not to ask me to his birthday party."

There was a terrible stillness on the end of the line for several seconds. "Oh, my God," Margie groaned. "You heard what he said that night!"

"I heard every single word, Margie," Jodie said tightly. "He thinks I'm still crazy about him, and it…disgusts him. He said I'm not in your social set and you should make friends among your own social circle." She took a deep, steadying breath. "Maybe he's right, Margie. The two of you took care of me when I had nobody else, but I've been taking advantage of it all these years, making believe that you were my family. In a way I'm grateful that Alexander opened my eyes. I've been an idiot."

"Jodie, he didn't mean it, I know he didn't! Sometimes he just says things without thinking them through. I know he wouldn't hurt you deliberately."

"He didn't know I could hear him," she said. "I drank too much and behaved like an idiot. We both know how Alexander feels about women who get drunk. But I've come to my senses now. I'm not going to impose on your hospitality…"

"But Alexander wants you to come!" Margie argued. "He said so!"

"No, he doesn't, Margie," Jodie said wistfully. "You don't understand what's going on, but I'm helping Alexander with a case. He's using me as a blind while he's surveilling a suspect, and don't you dare let on that you know it. It's not personal between us. It couldn't be. I'm not his sort of woman and we both know it."

Margie's intake of breath was audible. "What am I going to tell him when you don't show up?"

"You won't need to tell him anything," Jodie said easily. "He isn't expecting me. It was just for show. He'll tell you all about it one day. Now I have to go, Margie. I'm working in the kitchen, and things are going to burn," she added, lying through her teeth.

"We could have lunch next week," the other woman offered.

"No. You need to find friends in your class, Margie. I'm not part of your family, and you don't owe me anything. Now, goodbye!"

She hung up and unplugged the phone in case Margie tried to call back. She felt sick. But severing ties with Margie was the right thing to do. Once Alexander was through with her, once he'd caught his criminal, he'd leave her strictly alone. She was going to get out of his life, and Margie's, right now. It was the only sensible way to get over her feelings for Alexander.

The house was full of people when Alexander went inside, carrying his bag on a shoulder strap.

Margie met him at the door. "I'll bet you're tired, but at least you got here." She chuckled, trying not to show her worry. "Leave your bag by the door and come on in. Everybody's in the dining room with the cake."

He walked beside her toward the spacious dining room, where about twenty people were waiting near a table set with china and crystal, punch and coffee and cake. He searched the crowd and began to scowl.

"I don't see Jodie," he said at once. "Where is she? Didn't you phone her?"

"Yes," she groaned, "but she wouldn't come. Please, Lex, can't we talk about it later? Look, Kirry's here!"

"Damn Kirry," he said through his teeth, glaring down at his sister. "Why didn't she come?"

She drew in a miserable breath. "Because she heard us talking the last time she was here," she replied slowly. "She said you were right about her not being in our social class, and that she heard you say that the last thing you wanted was to trip over her at your birthday party." She winced, because the look on his face was so full of pain.

"She heard me," he said, almost choking on the words. "Good God, no wonder she looked at me the way she did. No wonder she's been acting so strangely!"

"She won't go out to lunch with me, she won't come here, she doesn't even want me to call her anymore," Margie said sadly. "I feel as if I've lost my own sister."

His own loss was much worse. He felt sick to his soul. He'd never meant for Jodie to hear those harsh, terrible words. He'd been reacting to his own helpless loss of control with her, not her hesitant ardor. It was himself he'd been angry at. Now he understood why Jodie was so reluctant to be around him lately. It was ironic that he found himself thinking about her around the clock, and she was as standoffish as a woman who found him bad company when they were alone. If only he could turn the clock back, make everything right. Jodie, so sweet and tender and loving, Jodie who had loved him once, hearing him tell Margie that Jodie disgusted him…!

"I should be shot," he ground out. "Shot!"

"Don't. It's your birthday," Margie reminded him. "Please. All these people came just to wish you well."

He didn't say another word. He simply walked into the room and let the congratulations flow over him. But he didn't feel happy. He felt as if his heart had withered and died in his chest.

That night, he slipped into his office while Kirry was talking to Margie, and he phoned Jodie. He'd had two straight malt whiskeys with no water, and he wasn't quite sober. It had taken that much to dull the sharp edge of pain.

"You didn't come," he said when she answered.

She hadn't expected him to notice. She swallowed, hard. "The invitation was all for show," she said, her voice husky. "You didn't expect me."

There was a pause. "Did you go out with Brody after all?" he drawled sarcastically. "Is that why you didn't show up?"

"No, I didn't," she muttered. "I'm not spending another minute of my life trying to fit into your exalted social class," she added hotly. "Cheating wives, consciousless husbands, social climbing friends…that's not my idea of a party!"

He sat back in his chair. "You might not believe it, but it's not mine, either," he said flatly. "I'd rather get a fast food hamburger and talk shop with the guys."

That was surprising. But she didn't quite trust him. "That isn't Kirry's style," she pointed out.

He laughed coldly. "It would become her style in minutes if she thought it would make me propose. I'm rich. Haven't you noticed?"

"It's hard to miss," she replied.

"Kirry likes life in the fast lane. She wants to be decked out in diamonds and taken to all the most expensive places four nights a week. Five on holidays."

"I'm sure she wants you, too."

"Are you?"

"I'm folding clothes, Alexander. Was there anything else?" she added formally, trying to get him to hang up. The conversation was getting painful.

"I never knew that you heard me the night of our last party, Jodie," he said in a deep, husky, pained sort of voice. "I'm more sorry than I can say. You don't know what it was like when my mother had parties. She drank like a fish…"

So Margie had told him. It wasn't really a surprise. "I had some champagne," she interrupted. "I don't drink, so it overwhelmed me. I'm very sorry for the way I behaved."

There was another pause. "I loved it," he said gruffly.

Now she couldn't even manage a reply. She just stared at the receiver, waiting for him to say something else.

"Talk to me!" he growled.

"What do you want me to say?" she asked unsteadily. "You were right. I don't belong in your class. I never will. You said I was a nuisance, and you were ri—"

"Jodie!" Her name sounded as if it were torn from his throat. "Jodie, don't! I didn't mean what I said. You've never been a nuisance!"

"It's too late," she said heavily. "I won't come back to the ranch again, ever, Alexander, not for you or even for Margie. I'm going to live my own life, make my own way in the world."

"By pushing us out of it?" he queried.

She sighed. "I suppose so."

"But not until I solve this case," he added after a minute. "Right?"

She wanted to argue, but she kept seeing the little boys' faces in that photograph he'd shown her. "Not until then," she said.

There was a rough sound, as if he'd been holding his breath and suddenly let it out. "All right."

"Alexander, where are you?" That was Kirry's voice, very loud.

"In a minute, Kirry! I'm on the phone!"

"We're going to open the presents. Come on!"

Jodie heard the sound Alexander made, and she laughed softly in spite of herself. "I thought it was your birthday?" she mused.

"It started to be, but my best present is back in Houston folding clothes," he said vehemently.

Her heart jumped. She had to fight not to react. "I'm nobody's present, Alexander," she informed him. "And now I really do have to go. Happy birthday."

"I'm thirty-four," he said. "Margie is the only family I have. Two of my colleagues just had babies," he remarked, his voice just slightly slurred. "Their desks are full of photographs of the kids and their wives. Know what I've got in a frame on my desk, Jodie? Kirry, in a ball gown."

"I guess the married guys would switch places with you…"

"That's not what I mean! I didn't put it there, she did. Instead of a wife and kids, I've got a would-be debutante who wants to own Paris."

"That was your choice," she pointed out.

"That's what you think. She gave me the framed picture." There was a pause. "Why don't you give me a photo?"

"Sure. Why not? Who would you like a photo of, and I'll see if I can find one for you."

"You, idiot!"

"I don't have any photos of myself."

"Why not?"

"Who'd take them?" she asked. "I don't even own a camera."

"We'll have to do something about that," he murmured. "Do you like parks? We could go jogging early Monday in that one near where you live. The one with the goofy sculpture."

"It's modern art. It isn't goofy."

"You're entitled to your opinion. Do you jog?"

"Not really."

"Do you have sweats and sneakers?"

She sighed irritably. "Well, yes, but…"

"No buts. I'll see you bright and early Monday." There was a pause. "I'll even apologize."

"That would be a media event."

"I'm serious," he added quietly. "I've never regretted anything in my life more than knowing you heard what I said to Margie that night."

For an apology, it was fairly headlong. Alexander never made apologies. It was a red letter event.

"Okay," she said after a few seconds.

He sighed, hard. "We can start over," he said firmly.

"Alexander, are you coming out of there?" came Kirry's petulant voice in the background.

"Better tell Kirry first," she chided.

"I'll tell her…get the hell out of my study!" he raged abruptly, and there was the sound of something heavy hitting the wall. Then there was the sound of a door closing with a quick snap.

"What did you do?" Jodie exclaimed.

"I threw a book in her general direction. Don't worry. It wasn't a book I liked. It was something on Colombian politics."

"You could have hit her!"

"In pistol competition, I hit one hundred targets out of a hundred shots. The book hit ten feet from where she was standing."

"You shouldn't throw things at people."

"But I'm uncivilized," he reminded her. "I need someone to mellow me out."

"Kirry's already there."

"Not for long, if she opens that damned door again. I'll see you Monday. Okay?"

There was a long hesitation. But finally she said, "Okay."

She put down the receiver and stared at it blankly. Her life had just shifted ten degrees and she had no idea why. At least, not right then.

CHAPTER SEVEN

JODIE HAD JUST changed into her sweats and was making breakfast in her sock feet when Alexander knocked on the door.

He was wearing gray sweats, like hers, with gray running shoes. He gave her a long, thorough appraisal. "I don't like your hair in a bun," he commented.

"I can't run with it down," she told him. "It tangles."

He sniffed the air. "Breakfast?" he asked hopefully.

"Just bacon and eggs and biscuits."

"Just! I had a granola bar," he said with absolute disdain.

She laughed nervously. It was new to have him in her apartment, to have him wanting to be with her. She didn't understand his change of attitude, and she didn't really trust it. But she was too enchanted to question it too closely.

"If you'll feed me," he began, "I'll let you keep up with me while we jog."

"That sounds suspiciously like a bribe," she teased, moving toward the table. "What *would* your bosses say?"

"You're not a client," he pointed out, seating himself at the table. "Or a perpetrator. So it doesn't count."

She poured him a mug of coffee and put it next to his plate, frowning as she noted the lack of matching dishes and even silverware. The table—a prize from a yard sale—had noticeable scratches and she didn't even have a tablecloth.

"What a comedown this must be," she muttered to herself as she fetched the blackberry jam and put it on the table, along with another teaspoon that didn't match the forks.

He gave her an odd look. "I'm not making comparisons, Jodie," he said softly, and his eyes were as soft as his deep voice. "You live within your means, and you do extremely well at it. You'd be surprised how many people are mortgaged right down to the fillings in their teeth trying to put on a show for their acquaintances. Which is, incidentally, why a lot of them end up in prison, trying to make a quick buck by selling drugs."

She made a face. "I'd rather starve than live like that."

"So would I," he confessed. He bit into a biscuit and moaned softly. "If only Jessie could make these the way you do," he said.

She smiled, pleased at the compliment, because Jessie was a wonderful cook. "They're the only thing I do well."

"No, they aren't." He tasted the jam and frowned. "I didn't know they made blackberry jam," he noted.

"You can buy it, but I like to make my own and put it up," she said. "That came from blackberries I picked last summer, on the ranch. They're actually your own blackberries," she added sheepishly.

"You can have as many as you like, if you'll keep me supplied with this jam," he said, helping himself to more biscuits.

"I'm glad you like it."

They ate in a companionable silence. When she poured their second cups of strong coffee, there weren't any biscuits left.

"Now I need to jog," he teased, "to work off the weight I've just put on. Coffee's good, too, Jodie. Everything was good."

"You were just hungry."

He sat back holding his coffee and stared at her. "You've never learned how to take a compliment," he said gently. "You do a lot of things better than other people, but you're modest to the point of self-abasement."

She moved a shoulder. "I like cooking."

He sipped coffee, still watching her. She was pretty early in the morning, he mused, with her face blooming like a rose, her skin clean and free of makeup. Her lips had a natural blush, and they had a shape that was arousing. He remembered how it felt to kiss her, and he ached to do it again. But this was new territory for her. He had to take his time. If he rushed her, he was going to lose her. That thought, once indifferent, took on supreme importance now. He was only beginning to see how much a part of him Jodie already was. He could have kicked himself for what he'd said about her at the ill-fated party.

"The party was a bust," he said abruptly.

Her eyes widened. "Pardon?"

"Kirry opened the presents and commented on their value and usefulness until the guests turned to strong drink," he said with a twinkle in his green eyes. "Then she took offense when a former friend of hers turned up with her ex-boyfriend and made a scene. She left in a trail of flames by cab before we even got to the live band."

She was trying not to smile. It was hard not to be amused at Kirry's situation. The woman was trying, even to people like Margie, who wanted to be friends with her.

"I guess there went Margie's shot at fashion fame," she said sadly.

"Kirry would never have helped her," he said carelessly, and finished his coffee. "She never had any intention of risking her job on a new designer's reputation. She was stringing Margie along so that she could hang out with us. She was wearing thin even before Saturday night."

"Sorry," she said, not knowing what else to say.

"We weren't lovers," he offered blatantly.

She blushed and then caught her breath. "Alexander…!"

"I wanted you to know that, in case anything is ever said about my relationship with her," he added, very seriously. "It was never more than a surface attraction. I can't abide a woman who wears makeup to bed."

She wouldn't ask, she wouldn't ask, she wouldn't…! "How do you know she does?" she blurted out.

He grinned at her. "Margie told me. She asked Kirry why, and Kirry said you never knew when a gentleman might knock on your door after midnight." He leaned forward. "I never did."

"I wasn't going to ask!"

"Sure you were." His eyes slid over her pretty breasts, nicely but not blatantly outlined under the gray jersey top she was wearing. "You're possessive about me. You don't want to be, but you are."

She was losing ground. She got to her feet and made a big thing of checking to see that her shoelaces were tied. "Shouldn't we go?"

He got up, stretched lazily, and started to clear the table. She was shocked to watch him.

"You've never done that," she remarked.

He glanced at her. "If I get married, and I might, I think marriage should be a fifty-fifty proposition. There's nothing romantic about a man lying around the apartment in a dirty T-shirt watching football while his wife slaves in the kitchen." He frowned thoughtfully. "Come to think of it, I don't like football."

"You don't wear dirty T-shirts, either," she replied, feeling sad because he'd mentioned marrying. Maybe there was another woman in his life, besides Kirry.

He chuckled. "Not unless I'm working in the garage." He came around the table after he'd put the dishes in the sink and took her gently by the shoulders, his expression somber. "We've never discussed personal issues. I know less about you than a stranger does. Do you like children? Do you want to have them? Or is a career primary in your life right now?"

The questions were vaguely terrifying. He was going from total indifference to intent scrutiny, and it was too soon. Her face took on a hunted look.

"Never mind," he said quickly, when he saw that. "Don't worry about the question. It isn't important."

She relaxed, but only a little. "I...love children," she faltered. "I like working, or I would if I had a challenging job. But that doesn't mean I'd want to put off having a family if I got married. My mother worked while I was growing up, but she was always there when I needed her, and she never put her job before her family. Neither would I." She searched his eyes, thinking how beautiful a shade of green they were, and about little children with them. Her expression went dreamy. "Fame and fortune may sound enticing, but they wouldn't make up for having people love you." She shrugged. "I guess that sounds corny."

"Actually, it sounds very mature." He bent and drew his mouth gently over her lips, a whisper of contact that didn't demand anything. "I feel the same way."

"You do?" She was unconsciously reaching up to him, trying to prolong the contact. It was unsettling that his lightest touch could send her reeling like this. She wanted more. She wanted him to crush her in his arms and kiss her blind.

He nibbled her upper lip slowly. "It isn't enough, is it?"

"Well...no..."

His arms drew her up, against the steely length of his body, and his mouth opened her lips to a kiss that was consuming with its heat. She moaned helplessly, clinging to him.

He lifted his mouth a breath away. His voice was strained when he spoke. "Do you have any idea what those little noises do to me?" he groaned.

"Noises?" she asked, oblivious, as she stared at his mouth.

"Never mind." He kissed her again, devouring her soft lips. The sounds she made drugged him. He was measuring the distance from the kitchen to her bedroom when he realized how fast things were progressing.

He drew back, and held her away from him, his jaw taut with an attempt at control.

"Alexander," she whispered, her voice pleading as she looked up at him with misty soft eyes.

"I almost never get women pregnant on Monday, but this could be an exception," he said in a choked tone.

Her eyes widened like saucers as she realized what he was saying.

He burst out laughing at her expression. He moved back even more. "I only carry identification and twenty dollars on me when I jog," he confessed. "The other things I keep in my wallet are still in it, at my apartment," he added, his tone blatantly expressive.

She divined what he was intimating and she flushed. She pushed back straggly hair from her face as she searched for her composure.

"Of course, a lot of modern women keep their own supply," he drawled. "I expect you have a box full in your medicine cabinet."

She flushed even more, and now she was glaring at him.

He chuckled, amused. "Your parents were very strict," he recalled. "And deeply religious. You still have those old attitudes about premarital sex, don't you?"

She nodded, grimacing.

"Don't apologize," he said wistfully. "In ten minutes or so, the ache will ease and I can actually stand up straight... God, Jodie!" he burst out laughing at her horrified expression. "I'm kidding!"

"You're a terrible man," she moaned.

"No, I'm just normal," he replied. "I'd love nothing better than a few hours in bed with you, but I'm not enough of a scoundrel to seduce you. Besides all that—" he sighed "—your conscience would kill both of us."

"Rub it in."

He shrugged. "You'd be surprised how many women at my office abstain, and make no bones about it to eligible bachelors who want to take them out," he said, and he smiled tenderly at her. "We tend to think of them as rugged individualists with the good sense not to take chances." He leaned forward. "And there are actually a couple of the younger male agents who feel the same way!"

"You're kidding!"

He shook his head, smiling. "Maybe it's a trend. You know, back in the early twentieth century, most women and men went to their weddings chaste. A man with a bad reputation was as untouchable as a woman with one."

"I'll bet you never told a woman in your life that you were going to abstain," she murmured wickedly.

He didn't smile back. He studied her for a long moment. "I'm telling you that I am. For the foreseeable future."

She didn't know how to take that, and it showed.

"I'm not in your class as a novice," he confessed, "but I'm no rake, either. I don't find other women desirable lately. Just you." He shrugged. "Careful, it may be contagious."

She laughed. Her whole face lit up. She was beautiful.

He drew her against him and kissed her, very briefly, before he moved away again. "We should go," he said. "I have a meeting at the office at ten. Then we could have lunch."

"Okay," she said. She felt lighthearted. Overwhelmed. She started toward the door and then stopped. "Can I ask you a question?"

"Shoot."

"Are you staking out my company because you're investigating Brody for drug smuggling?"

He gave her an old, wise look. "You're sharp, Jodie. I'll have to watch what I say around you."

"That means you're not going to tell me. Right?"

He chuckled. "Right." He led the way into the hall and then waited for her to lock her door behind them.

She slipped the key into her pocket.

"No ID?" he mused as they went downstairs and started jogging down the sparsely occupied sidewalk.

"Just the key and five dollars, in case I need money for a bottle of water or something," she confessed.

He sighed, not even showing the strain as they moved quickly along. "One of our forensic reconstruction artists is always lecturing us on carrying identification. She says that it's easier to have something on you that will identify you, so that she doesn't have to take your skull and model clay to do a reconstruction of your face. She helps solve a lot of murder victims' identities, but she has plenty that she can't identify. The faces haunt her, she says."

"I watched a program about forensic reconstruction on educational television two weeks ago."

"I know the one you mean. I saw it, too. That was our artist," he said with traces of pride in his deep voice. "She's a wonder."

"I guess it wouldn't hurt to carry my driver's license around with me," she murmured.

He didn't say another word, but he grinned to himself.

THE MEETING WAS a drug task force formed of a special agent from the Houston FBI office, a Houston police detective who specialized in local gangs, a Texas Ranger from Company A, an agent from the US Customs Service and a sheriff's deputy from Harris County who headed her department's drug unit.

They sat down in a conference room in the nearest Houston police station to discuss intelligence.

"We've got a good lead on the new division chief of the Culebra cartel in Mexico," Alexander announced when it was his turn to speak. "We know that he has somebody on his payroll from Ritter Oil Corporation, and that he's funneling drugs through a warehouse where oil regulators and drilling equipment are kept before they're shipped out all over the southwest. Since the parking lot of that warehouse is locked by a key code, the division chief has to have someone on the inside."

"Do we know how it's being moved and when?" the FBI agent asked.

Alexander had suspicions, but no concrete evidence. "Waiting for final word on when. But we do have an informant, a young man who got cold feet and came to US Customs with information about the drug smuggling. I interviewed the young man, with help from Customs," he added, nodding with a smile at the petite brunette customs official at the table with them.

"That would be me," she said with a grin.

"The informant says that a shipment of processed cocaine is on the way here, one of the biggest in several years. It was shipped from the Guajira Peninsula in Colombia to Central America and transshipped by plane to an isolated landing site in rural Mexico. From there it was carried to a warehouse in Mexico City owned by a subsidiary of an oil company here in Houston. It was reboxed with legitimate oil processing equipment manufactured in Europe, in boxes with false bottoms. It was shipped legally to the oil company's district office in Galveston where it was inspected briefly and passed through customs."

"The oil company is one that's never been involved in any illegal activity," the customs representative said wistfully, "so the agent didn't look for hidden contraband."

"To continue," Alexander said, "it's going to be shipped into the Houston warehouse via the Houston Ship Canal as domestic inventory from Galveston."

"Which means, no more customs inspections," the Texas Ranger said.

"Exactly," Alexander agreed.

The brunette customs agent shook her head. "A few shipments get by our inspectors, but not many. We have contacts everywhere, too, and one of those tipped us off about the young man who was willing to inform on the perpetrators of an incoming cocaine shipment," she told the others. "So we saved our bacon."

"You had the contacts I gave you, don't forget," the blonde lieutenant of detectives from Houston reminded her with a smile, as she adjusted her collar.

"Do we even have a suspect?" the customs agent asked.

Alexander nodded. "I've got someone on the inside at Ritter Oil, and I'm watching a potential suspect. I don't have enough evidence yet to make an accusation, but I hope to get it, and soon. I'm doing this undercover, so this information is to be kept in this room. I've put it out that we have another company, Thorn Oil, under surveillance, as a cover story. Under no circumstances are any of you to discuss any of this meeting, even with another DEA agent—*especially* with another DEA agent—until further notice. That's essential."

The police lieutenant gave him a pointed look. "Can I ask why?"

"Because the oil corporation isn't the only entity that's harboring an inside informant," Alexander replied flatly. "And that's all I feel comfortable saying."

"You can count on us," the Texas Ranger assured him. "We won't blow your cover. The person you're watching, can you tell us why you're watching him?"

"In order to use that warehouse for storage purposes, the drug lord has to have access to it," Alexander explained. "I'm betting he has some sort of access to the locked gate and that he's paying the night watchman to look the other way."

"That would make sense," the customs agent agreed grimly. "These people know how little law enforcement personnel make. They can easily afford to offer a poorly paid night watchman a six figure 'donation' to just turn his head at the appropriate time."

"That much money would tempt even a law-abiding citizen," Alexander agreed. "But more than that, very often there's a need that compromises integrity. A sheriff in another state had a wife dying of cancer and no insurance. He got fifty thousand dollars for not noticing a shipment of drugs coming into his county."

"They catch him?" the policewoman asked.

"Yes. He wasn't very good at being a crook. He confessed, before he was even suspected of being involved."

"How many people in your agency know about this?" the deputy sheriff asked Alexander.

"Nobody, at the moment," he replied. "It has to stay that way, until we make the bust. I'll depend on all of you to back me up. The mules working for the new drug lord carry automatic weapons and they've killed so many people down in Mexico that they won't hesitate to waste anyone who gets in their way."

"Good thing the president of Mexico isn't intimidated by them," the customs agent said with a grin. "He's done more to attack drug trafficking than any president before him."

"He's a good egg," Alexander agreed. "Let's hope we can shut down this operation before any more kids go down."

"Amen to that," the FBI agent said solemnly.

ALEXANDER SHOWED UP at Jodie's office feeling more optimistic than he had for weeks. He was close to an arrest, but the next few days would be critical. After their meeting, the task force had gleaned information from the informant that the drug shipment was coming into Houston the following week. He had to be alert, and he had to spend a lot of time at Jodie's office so that he didn't miss anything.

He took her out to lunch, but he was preoccupied.

"You're onto something," she guessed.

He nodded, smiling. "Something big. How would you like to be part of a surveillance?"

"Me? Wow. Can I have a gun?"

He glared at her. "No."

She shrugged. "Okay. But don't expect me to save your life without one."

"Not giving you one might save my life," he said pointedly.

She ignored the gibe. "Surveillance?" she prodded. "Of what?"

"You'll find out when we go, and not a word to anybody."

"Okay," she agreed. "How do you do surveillance?"

"We sit in a parked car and drink coffee and wish we were watching television," he said honestly. "It gets incredibly boring. Not so much if we have a companion. That's where you come in," he added with a grin. "We can sit in the car and neck and nobody will guess we're spying on them."

"In a Jaguar," she murmured. "Sure, nobody will notice us in one of those!"

He gave her a long look. "We'll be in a law enforcement vehicle, undercover."

"Right. In a car with government license plates, four antennae and those little round hubcaps…"

"Will you stop?" he groaned.

"Sorry!" She grinned at him over her coffee. "But I like the necking part."

He pursed his lips and gave her a wicked grin. "So do I."

She laughed a little self-consciously and finished her lunch.

They were on the way back to his Jaguar when his DEA agent, Kennedy, drove up. He got out of his car and approached them with a big smile.

"Hi, Cobb! How's it going?" he asked.

"Couldn't be better," Alexander told him complacently. "What's new?"

"Oh, nothing, I'm still working on that smuggling ring." He glanced at Alexander curiously. "Heard anything about a new drug task force?"

"Just rumors," Alexander assured him, and noticed a faint reaction from the other man. "Nothing definite. I'll let you know if I hear anything."

"Thanks." Kennedy shrugged. "There are always rumors."

"Do you have anybody at Thorn Oil, just in case?" Alexander asked him pointedly.

Kennedy cleared his throat and laughed. "Nobody at all. Why?"

"No reason. No reason at all. Enjoy your lunch."

"Sure. I never see you at staff meetings lately," he added. "You got something undercover going on?"

Alexander deliberately tugged Jodie close against his side and gave her a look that could have warmed coffee.

"Something," he said, with a smile in Kennedy's direction. "See you."

"Yeah. See you!"

Kennedy walked on toward the restaurant, a little distracted.

Jodie waited until they were closed up in Alexander's car before she spoke. "You didn't tell him anything truthful," she remarked.

"Kennedy's got a loose tongue," he told her as he cranked the car. "You don't tell him anything you don't want repeated. Honest to God, he's worse than Margie!"

"So that's it," she said, laughing. "I just wondered. Isn't it odd that he seems to show up at places where we eat a lot?"

"Plenty of the guys eat where we do," he replied lazily. "We know where the good food is."

"You really do," she had to admit. "That steak was wonderful!"

"Glad you liked it."

"I could cook for you, sometime," she offered, and then flushed at her own boldness.

"After I wind up this case, I'll let you," he said, with a warm smile. "Meanwhile, I've got a lot of work to do."

She wondered about that statement after he left her at the office. She was still puzzling over it when she walked right into Brody when she got off the elevator at her floor.

"Oh, sorry!" she exclaimed, only then noticing that Cara was with him. "Hello," she greeted the woman as she stopped to punch her time card before entering the cubicle area.

Cara wasn't inclined to be polite. She gave Jodie a cold look and turned back to Brody. "I don't understand why you can't do me this one little favor," she muttered. "It isn't as if I ask you often for anything."

"Yes, but dear, it's an odd place to leave your car. There arc garages…"

"My car is very cxpensive," she pointed out, her faint accent growing in intensity, like the anger in her black eyes. "All I require is for you to let me in, only that."

Jodie's ears perked up. She pretended to have trouble getting her card into the time clock, and hummed deliberately to herself, although not so loudly that she couldn't hear what the other two people were saying.

"Company rules…" he began.

"Rules, rules! You are to be an executive, are you not? Do you have to ask permission for such a small thing? Or are you not man enough to make such decisions for yourself?" she added cannily.

"Nice to see you both," Jodie said, and moved away— but not quickly. She fumbled in her purse and walked very slowly as she did. She was curious to know what Cara wanted.

"I suppose I could, just this once," Brody capitulated. "But you know, dear, a warehouse isn't as safe as a parking garage, strictly speaking."

Jodie's heart leaped.

"Yours certainly is, you have an armed guard, do you not? Besides, I work for a subsidiary of Ritter Oil. It is not as if I had no right to leave my car there when I go out of town for the company."

"All right, all right," Brody said. "Tomorrow night then. What time?"

"At six-thirty," she told him. "It will be dark, so you must flash your lights twice to let me know it is you."

They spoke at length, but Jodie was already out of

earshot. She'd heard enough of the suspicious conversation to wonder about it. But she was much too cautious to phone Alexander from her work station.

She would have to wait until the end of the day, even if it drove her crazy. Meanwhile she pretended that she'd noticed nothing.

Brody came by her cubicle later that afternoon, just before quitting time, while she was finishing a letter he'd dictated.

"Can I help you?" she asked automatically, and smiled.

He smiled back and looked uncomfortable. "No, not really. I just wondered what you thought about what Cara asked me?"

She gave him a blank look. "What she asked you?" she said. "I'm sorry, I'd just come from having lunch with Alexander." She smiled and sighed and lowered her eyes demurely. "To tell you the truth, I wasn't paying attention to anything except the time clock. What did she ask you?" She opened her eyes very wide and looked blank.

"Never mind. She phoned and made a comment about your being there. It's nothing. Nothing at all."

She smiled up at him. "Did you enjoy the concert that night?"

"Yes, actually I did, despite the fact that Cara went out to the powder room and didn't show up again for an hour." He shook his head. "Honestly, that woman is so mysterious! I never know what she's thinking."

"She's very crisp, isn't she?" she mused. "I mean, she's assertive and aggressive. I guess she's a good marketer."

"She is," he sighed. "At least, I guess she is. I haven't heard much from the big boss about her work. In fact, there was some talk about letting her go a month or two ago, because she lost a contract. Funny, it was one she was supposedly out of town negotiating at the time, but the client said he'd never seen her. Mr. Ritter talked him into staying, but he had words with Cara about the affair."

"Could that have been when her mother was ill?" she asked.

"Her mother hasn't ever been ill, as far as I know," he murmured. "She did move from Peru to Mexico, but you know about that." He put his hands in his pockets. "She wants me to do something that isn't quite acceptable, and I'm nervous about it. I'm due for a promotion. I don't want to get mixed up in anything the least bit suspicious."

"Why, Brody, what does she want you to do?" she asked innocently.

He glanced at her, started to speak, and then smiled sheepishly. "Well, it's nothing, really. Just a favor." He shrugged. "I'm sure I'm making a big deal out of nothing. You never told me that your boyfriend works for the Drug Enforcement Administration."

"He doesn't advertise it," she stammered. "He does a lot of undercover work at night," she added.

Brody sighed. "I see. Well, I'll let you finish. You and Cobb seem to get along very well," he added.

"I've known him a long time."

"So you have. You've known me a long time, too, though," he added with a slow smile.

"Not really. Only three years."

"Is it? I thought it was longer." He toyed with his tie. "You and Cobb seem to spend a lot of time together."

"Not as much as we'd like," she said, seeing a chance to help Alexander and throw Cara off the track. "And I have a cousin staying with me for a few days, so we spend a lot of time in parked cars necking," she added.

Brody actually flushed. "Oh." He glanced at his watch

and grimaced. "I've got a meeting with our vice president in charge of human resources at four, I'd better get going. See you later."

"See you, Brody."

She was very glad that she'd learned to keep what she knew to herself. What Brody's girlfriend had let slip was potentially explosive information, even if it was only circumstantial. She'd have a lot to tell Alexander when she saw him. Furthermore, she'd already given Alexander some cover by telling Brody about the company car, and the fact that they spent time at night necking in one. He was going to be proud of her, she just knew it!

CHAPTER EIGHT

THE MINUTE SHE got to her apartment, Jodie grabbed the phone and called Alexander.

"Can you come by right away?" Jodie asked him quickly.

He hesitated. "To your apartment? Why?"

She didn't know if her phone might be bugged. She couldn't risk it. She sighed theatrically. "Because I'm wearing a see-through gown with a row of prophylactics pinned to the hem…!"

"Jodie!" He sounded shocked.

"Listen, I have something to tell you," she said firmly.

He hesitated again and then he groaned. "I can't right now…"

"Who's on the phone, Alex?" came a sultry voice from somewhere in the background.

Jodie didn't need to ask who the voice belonged to. Her heart began to race with impotent fury. "Sorry I interrupted," she said flatly. "I'm sure you and Kirry have lots to talk about."

She hung up and then unplugged the phone. So much for any feelings Alexander had for her. He was already seeing Kirry again, alone and at his apartment. No doubt he was only seeing Jodie to avert suspicion at Ritter Oil. The sweet talk was to allay any suspicion that he was using her. Why hadn't she realized that? The Cobbs were always using her, for one reason or another. She was being a fool again. Despite what he'd said, it was obvious now that Alexander had no interest in her except as a pawn.

She fought down tears and went to her computer. She might as well use some of her expertise to check out Miss Cara Dominguez and see if the woman had a rap sheet. With a silent apology to the local law enforcement departments, she hacked into criminal files and checked her out.

What she found was interesting enough to take her mind off Alexander. It seemed that Cara didn't have a lily-white past at all. In fact, she'd once been arrested for possession with intent to distribute cocaine and had managed to get the charges dropped. Besides that, she had some very odd connections internationally. It was hinted in the records of an international law enforcement agency—whose files gave way to her expertise also— that her uncle was one of the Colombian drug lords. She wondered if Alexander knew that.

Would he care? He was with Kirry. Damn Kirry! She threw a plastic coffee cup at the wall in impotent rage.

Just as it hit, there was a buzz at the intercom. She glowered at it, but the caller was insistent. She pushed the button.

"Yes?" she asked angrily.

"Let me in," Alexander said tersely.

"Are you alone?" she asked with barely contained sarcasm.

"In more ways than you might realize," he replied, his voice deep and subdued. "Let me in, Jodie."

She buzzed him in with helpless reluctance and waited at her opened door for him to come out of the elevator.

He was still in his suit. He looked elegant, expensive,

and very irritated. He walked into the apartment ahead of her and went straight to the kitchen.

"I was going to take you out to eat when Kirry showed up, in tears, and begged to talk to me," he said heavily, examining pots until he found one that contained a nice beef stew. He got a bowl out of the cupboard and proceeded to fill it. "Any corn bread?" he asked wistfully, having sniffed it when he entered the apartment.

"It's only just getting done," she said, reaching around him for a pot holder. She opened the oven and produced a pone of corn bread.

"I'm hungry," he said.

"You're always hungry," she accused, but she was feeling better.

He caught her by the shoulders and pulled her against him, tilting her chin up so that he could see into her mutinous eyes. "I don't want Kirry. I said that, and I meant it."

"Even if you didn't, you couldn't say so," she muttered. "You need me to help you smoke out your drug smuggler."

He scowled. "Do you really think I'm that sort of man?" he asked, and sounded wounded. "I'll admit that Margie and I don't have a good track record with you, but I'd draw the line at pretending an emotion I didn't feel, just to catch crooks."

She shifted restlessly and didn't speak.

He shook his head. "No ego," he mused, watching her. "None at all. You can't see what's right under your nose."

"My chin, and no, I can't see it…"

He chuckled, bending to kiss her briefly, fiercely. "Feed me. Then we might watch television together for a while. I'll be working most evenings during the week, but Friday night we could go see a movie or something."

Her heart skipped. "A movie?"

"Or we could go bowling. I used to like it."

Her mind was spinning. He actually wanted to be with her! But cold reality worked its way between them again. "You haven't asked why I wanted you to come over," she began as he started for the table with his bowl of stew.

"No, I haven't. Why?" he asked, pouring himself a cup of freshly brewed coffee and accepting a dish of corn bread from her.

She put coffee and corn bread at her place at the table and put butter next to it before she sat down and gave Alexander a mischievous smile. "Cara talked Brody into letting her into the warehouse parking lot after hours tomorrow— about six-thirty in the evening. She said she wanted to park her car there, but it sounded thin to me."

He caught his breath. "Jodie, you're a wonder."

"That's not all," she added, sipping coffee and adding more cream to it. "She was arrested at the age of seventeen for possession with intent to distribute cocaine, and she got off because the charges were dropped. There's an unconfirmed suspicion that her uncle is one of the top Colombian drug lords."

"Where did you get that?"

She flushed. "I can't tell you. Sorry."

"You've hacked into some poor soul's protected files, haven't you?" he asked sternly, but with twinkling eyes.

"I can't tell you," she repeated.

"Okay, I give up." He ate stew and corn bread with obvious enthusiasm. "Then I guess you and I will go on a stakeout tomorrow night."

She smiled smugly. "Yes, in your boss's borrowed security car, because my cousin is visiting and we can't neck in the apartment. I told Brody that, and he'll tell

Cara that, so if we're seen near my office, they won't think a thing of it."

"Sheer genius," he mused, studying her. "Like I said, you're a natural for law enforcement work. You've got to get your expert computer certification and change professions, Jodie. You're wasted in personnel work."

"Human resources work," she reminded him.

"New label, same job."

She wrinkled her nose. "Maybe so."

They finished their supper in pleasant silence, and she produced a small loaf of pound cake for dessert, with peaches and whipped cream.

"If I ate here often, I'd get fat," he murmured.

She laughed. "Not likely. The cake was made with margarine and reduced-fat milk. I make rolls the same way, except with light olive oil in place of margarine. I don't want clogged arteries before I'm thirty," she added. "And I especially don't want to look like I used to."

He smiled at her warmly. "I like the way you used to look," he said surprisingly. "I like you any way at all, Jodie," he continued softly. "That hasn't changed."

She didn't know whether or not to trust him, and it showed in her face.

He sighed. "It's going to be a long siege," he said enigmatically.

Later, they curled up together on the couch to watch the evening news. There was a brief allusion to a drug smuggling catch by US Customs in the Gulf of Mexico, showing the helicopters they used to catch the fast little boats used in smuggling.

"Those boats go like the wind," Jodie remarked.

He yawned. "They do, indeed. The Colombian National Police busted an operation that was building a submarine for drug smuggling a couple of years ago."

"That's incredible!"

"Some of the smuggling methods are, too, like the tunnel under the Mexican border that was discovered, and having little children swallow balloons filled with cocaine to get them through customs."

"That's barbaric," she said.

He nodded. "It's a profitable business. Greed makes animals of men sometimes, and of women, too."

She cuddled close to him. "It isn't Brody you were after, is it? It's his girlfriend."

He chuckled and wrapped her up in his arms. "You're too sharp for me."

"I learned from an expert," she said, lifting her eyes to his handsome face.

He looked down at her intently for a few seconds before he bent to her mouth and began to kiss her hungrily. Her arms slid up around his neck and she held on for dear life as the kiss devoured her.

Finally he lifted his head and put her away from him, with visible effort. "No more of that tonight," he said huskily.

"Spoilsport," she muttered.

"You're the one with the conscience, honey," he drawled meaningfully. "I'm willing, but you'd never live it down."

"I probably wouldn't," she confessed, but her eyes were misty and wistful.

He pushed back her hair. "Don't look like that," he chided. "It isn't the end of the world. I like you the way you are, Jodie, hang-ups and all. Okay?"

She smiled. "Okay."

"And I'm not sleeping with Kirry!"

The smile grew larger.

He kissed the tip of her nose and got up. "I've got some preparations to make. I'll pick you up tomorrow at 6:20 sharp and we'll park at the warehouse in the undercover car." He hesitated. "It might be better if I had a female agent in the car with me…"

"No, you don't," she said firmly, getting to her feet. "This is my stakeout. You wouldn't even know where to go, or when, if it wasn't for me."

"True. But it could be very dangerous," he added grimly.

"I'm not afraid."

"All right," he said finally. "But you'll stay in the car and out of the line of fire."

"Whatever you say," she agreed at once.

THE WAREHOUSE PARKING lot was deserted. The night watchman was visible in the doorway of the warehouse as he opened the door to look out. He did that twice.

"He's in on it," Alexander said coldly, folding Jodie closer in his arms. "He knows they're coming, and he's watching for them."

"No doubt. Ouch." She reached under her rib cage and touched a small hard object in his coat pocket. "What is that, another gun?"

"Another cell phone," he said. "I have two. I'm leaving one with you, in case you see something I don't while I'm inside," he added, indicating a cell phone he'd placed on the dash.

"You do have backup?" she worried.

"Yes. My whole team. They're well concealed, but they're in place."

"Thank goodness!"

He shifted her in his arms so that he could look to his left at the warehouse while he was apparently kissing her.

"Your heart is going very fast," she murmured under his cool lips.

"Adrenaline," he murmured. "I live on rushes of it. I could never settle for a nine-to-five desk job."

She smiled against his mouth. "I don't like it much, either."

He nuzzled her cheek with his just as a car drove past them toward the warehouse. It hesitated for a few seconds and then sped on.

"That's Brody's car," she murmured.

"And that one, following it?" he asked, indicating a small red hardtop convertible of some expensive foreign make.

"Cara."

"Amazing that she can afford a Ferrari on thirty-five thousand a year," he mused, "and considering that her mother is poor."

"I was thinking the same thing," she murmured. "Kiss me again."

"No time, honey." He pulled out a two-way radio and spoke into it. "All units, stand by. Target in motion. Repeat, target in motion. Stand by."

Several voices took turns asserting their readiness. Alexander watched as Brody's car suddenly reappeared and he drove away. The gates of the warehouse closed behind his car. He paused near Alexander's car again, and then drove off down the road.

As soon as he was out of sight, a van came into sight. Cara appeared at the parking lot entrance, inserted a card key into the lock, opened the gate and motioned the van forward. The gate didn't close again, but remained open.

Alexander gave it time to get to a loading dock and its occupants to exit the cab and begin opening the rear doors before he took out the walkie-talkie again.

"All units, move in. I repeat, all units, move in. We are good to go!"

He took the cell phone from the dash and put it into Jodie's hands. "You sit right here, with the doors locked, and don't move until I call you on that phone and tell you it's safe. Under no circumstances are you to come into the parking lot. Okay?"

She nodded. "Okay. Don't get shot," she added.

He kissed her. "I don't plan to. See you later."

He got out of the car and went toward a building next door to the warehouse. He was joined by another figure in black. They went down an alley together, out of sight.

Jodie slid down into her seat, so that only her eyes and the top of her head were visible in the concealing darkness, barely lit by a nearby streetlight. She waited with her heart pounding in her chest for several minutes, until she heard a single gunshot. There was pandemonium in the parking lot. Dark figures ran to and fro. More shots were fired. Her heart jumped into her throat. She gritted her teeth, praying that Alexander wasn't in the line of fire.

Then, suddenly, she spotted him, with another dark figure. They had two people in custody, a man and a woman. They were standing near another loading dock, apparently conversing with the men, when Jodie spotted a solitary figure outside the gates, on the sidewalk, moving toward the open gate. The figure was slight, and it held what looked like an automatic weapon. She'd seen

Alexander with one of those, a rare time when he'd been arming himself for a drug bust.

She had a single button to push to make Alexander's cell phone ring, but when she pressed in the number, nothing happened. The phone went dead in her hand.

The man with the machine gun was moving closer to where Alexander and the other man stood with their prisoners, their backs to the gate.

The key was in the car. She only saw one way to save Alexander. She got behind the wheel, cranked the car, put it in gear and aimed it right for the armed man, who was now framed in the gate.

She ran the car at him. He whirled at the sudden noise of an approaching vehicle and started spraying it with machine gun fire.

Jodie ducked down behind the wheel, praying that the weapon didn't have bullets that would penetrate the engine block as easily as they shattered the windshield of the car she was driving. There was a loud thud.

She had to stop the car, because she couldn't see where she was going, but the windshield didn't catch any more bullets. Now she heard gunshots that didn't sound like that of the small automatic her assailant was carrying.

The door of the car was suddenly jerked open, and she looked up, wide-eyed and panicky, into Alexander's white face.

"Jodie!" he ground out. "Put the car out of gear!"

She put it into Park with trembling hands and cut off the ignition.

Alexander dragged her out of it and began going over her with his hands, feeling for blood. She was covered with little shards of glass. Her face was bleeding. So were her hands. She'd put them over her face the instant the man started firing.

Slowly she became aware that Alexander's hands had a faint tremor as they searched her body.

"I'm okay," she said in a thin voice. "Are you?"

"Yes."

But he was rattled, and it showed.

"He was going to shoot you in the back," she began.

"I told you to use the cell phone!" he raged.

"It wouldn't work!"

He reached beside her and picked it up. His eyes closed. The battery was dead.

"And you stop yelling at me," she raged back at him. "I couldn't let him kill you!"

He caught her up in his arms, bruisingly close, and kissed her furiously. Then he just held her, rocked her, riveted her to his hard body with fierce hunger. "You crazy woman," he bit off at her ear. "You brave, crazy, wonderful woman!"

She held him, too, content now, safe now. Her eyes closed. It was over, and he was alive. Thank God.

He let her go reluctantly as two other men came up, giving them curious looks.

"She's all right," he told them, moving back a little. "Just a few cuts from the broken windshield."

"That was one of the bravest things I've ever seen a woman do," one of the men, an older man with jet-black hair and eyes, murmured. "She drove right into the bullets."

"We'd be dead if she hadn't," the other man, equally dark-haired and dark-eyed, said with a grin. "Thanks!"

"You're welcome," she said with a sheepish smile as she moved closer to Alexander.

"The car's a total write-off," the older man mused.

"Like you've never totaled a car in a gun battle, Hunter," Alexander said with a chuckle.

The other man shrugged. "Maybe one or two. What the hell. The government has all that money we confiscate from drug smugglers to replace cars. You might ask your boss for that cute little Ferrari, Cobb."

"I already drive a Jaguar," he said, laughing. "With all due respect to Ferrari, I wouldn't trade it for anything else."

"I helped make the bust," Jodie complained. "They should give it to me!"

"I wouldn't be too optimistic about that," came a droll remark from the second of the two men. "I think Cobb's boss is partial to Italian sports cars, and he can't afford a Ferrari on his salary."

"Darn," Jodie said on a sigh. "Just my luck."

"You should take her to the hospital and have her checked," Hunter told Alexander. "She's bleeding."

"She could be dead, pulling a stunt like that," Alexander said with renewed anger as he looked at her.

"That's no way to thank a person for saving your life," Jodie pointed out, still riding an adrenaline high.

"You're probably right, but you took a chance you shouldn't have," Alexander said grimly. "Come on. We'll hitch a ride with one of my men."

"Your car might still be drivable," she said, looking at it. The windshield was shattered but still clinging to the frame. She winced. "Or maybe not."

"Maybe not," Alexander agreed. "See you, Hunter. Lane. Thanks for the help."

"Any time," Hunter replied, and they walked back toward the warehouse with Alexander and Jodie. "Colby

Lane was in town overnight and bored to death, so I brought him along for the fun."

"Fun!" Jodie exclaimed.

The older man chuckled. "He leads a mundane nine-to-five life. I've talked him into giving it up for international intrigue at Ritter Oil."

"I was just convinced," the man named Colby Lane said with a chuckle.

"Good. Tomorrow you can tell Ritter you'll take the job. See you, Cobb."

"Sure thing."

"Who were those two guys you were talking to?" Jodie asked when the hospital had treated her cuts and Alexander had commandeered another car to take her home in.

"Phillip Hunter and Colby Lane. You've surely heard of Hunter."

"He's a local legend," she replied with a smile, "but I didn't recognize him in that black garb. He's our security chief."

"Lane's doing the same job for the Hutton corporation, but they're moving overseas and he isn't keen on going. So Hunter's trying to get him to come down here as his second-in-command at Ritter Oil."

"Why was Mr. Lane here tonight?"

"Probably just as Phillip said—Lane just got into town, and Hunter volunteered him to help out. He and Hunter are old friends."

"He looked very dark," she commented.

"They're both Apache," he said easily. "Hunter's married to a knockout blonde geologist who works for Ritter. They have a young daughter. Lane's not married."

"They seem to know each other very well."

Alexander chuckled. "They have similar backgrounds in black ops. Highest level covert operations," he clarified. "They used to work for the 'company.'"

"Not Ritter's company," she guessed.

He chuckled. "No. Not Ritter's."

"Did you arrest Cara?"

"Our Houston policewoman made the actual arrest, so that Cara wouldn't know I headed the operation. Cara was arrested along with two men she swears she doesn't know," he replied. "We had probable cause to do a search anyway, but I had a search warrant in my pocket, and I had to use it. We found enough cocaine in there to get a city high, and the two men in the truck had some on them."

"How about Cara?"

He sighed. "She was clean. Now we have to connect her." He glanced at her apologetically. "That will mean getting your boss involved. However innocently, he did let her into a locked parking lot."

"But wasn't the night watchman working for them? Couldn't he have let them in?"

"He could have. But I have a feeling Cara wanted Brody involved, so that he'd be willing to do what she asked so that she didn't give him away for breaking a strict company rule," he replied. He saw her expression and he smiled. "Don't worry. I won't let him be prosecuted."

"Thanks, Alexander."

He moved closer and studied the cuts on her face and arms. He winced. "You poor baby," he said gently. "I wouldn't have had you hurt for the world."

"You'd have been dead if I hadn't done something," she said matter-of-factly. "The phone went dead and you were too far away to hear me if I yelled. Besides," she added with a chuckle, "I hate going to funerals."

"Me, too." He swept her close and kissed the breath out of her. "I have to go back to work, tie up loose ends. You'll need to come with me to the nearest police precinct and give a statement, as well. You're a material witness." He hesitated, frowning.

"What's wrong?" she asked.

"Cara knows who you are, and she can find out where you live," he said. "She's a vengeful witch. Chances are very good that she's going to make bond. I'm going to arrange some security for you."

"Do you think that's necessary?"

He nodded grimly. "I'm afraid it is. Would you like to know the estimated street value of the cocaine we've just confiscated?"

"Yes."

"From thirty to thirty-five million dollars."

She whistled softly. "Now I understand why they're willing to kill people. And that's just one shipment, right?"

"Just one, although it's unusually large. There's another drug smuggling investigation going on right now involving Colombian rebels, but I can't tell you about that one. It's top secret." He smoothed back her hair and looked at her as if she were a treasure trove. "Thank you for what you did," he said after a minute. "Even if it was crazy, it saved my life, not to mention Lane's and Hunter's."

She reached up a soft hand to smooth over his cheek, where it was slightly rough from a day's growth of beard. "You're welcome. But you would have done the same thing, if it had been me or Margie."

"Yes, I'm afraid I would have."

He still looked worried. She tugged his head down and kissed him warmly, her body exploding inside when he half lifted her against him and kissed her until her lips were sore.

"I could have lost you tonight," he said curtly.

"Oh, I'm a weed," she murmured into his throat. "We're very hard to uproot."

His arms tightened. "Just the same, you watch your back. If Brody asks what you know, and he will, you tell him nothing," he added. "You were with me when things started happening, you didn't even know what was going on until bullets started flying. Right?"

"Right."

He sighed heavily and kissed her one last time before he put her back onto her own feet. "I've got to go help the guys with the paperwork," he said reluctantly. "I'd much rather be with you. For tonight, lock your doors and keep your freedom phone handy. If you need me, I'm a phone call away. Tomorrow, you'll have security."

"I've got a nice, big, heavy flashlight like the one you keep in your car," she told him pertly. "If anybody tries to get in, they'll get a headache."

Unless they had guns, he added silently, but he didn't say that. "Don't be overconfident," he cautioned. "Never underestimate the enemy."

She saluted him.

He tugged her face up and kissed her, hard. "Incorrigible," he pronounced her. "But I can't imagine life without you, so be cautious!"

"I will. I promise. You have to promise, too," she added.

He gave her a warm smile. "Oh, I have my eye on the future, too," he assured her. "I don't plan to cash in my chips right now. I'll phone you tomorrow."

"Okay. Good night."

"Good night. Lock this," he added when he went out the door.

She did, loudly, and heard him chuckle as he went down the hall. Once he was gone, she sank down into her single easy chair and shivered as she recalled the feverish events of the evening. She was alive. He was alive. But she could still hear the bullets, feel the shattering of the windshield followed by dozens of tiny, painful cuts on her skin even through the sweater she'd been wearing. It was amazing that she'd come out of a firefight with so few wounds.

She went to bed, but she didn't sleep well. Alexander phoned very early the next morning to check on her and tell her that he'd see her at lunch.

She put on her coat and went to work, prepared for some comments from her coworkers, despite the fact that she was wearing a long-sleeved, high-necked blouse. Nothing was going to hide the tiny cuts that lined her cheeks and chin. She knew better than to mention where she got them, so she made up a nasty fall down the steps at her apartment building.

It worked with everyone except Brody. He came in as soon as she'd turned on her computer, looking worried and sad.

"Are you all right?" he asked abruptly. "I was worried sick all night."

Her wide-eyed look wasn't feigned. "How did you know?" she faltered.

"I had to go and bail Cara out of jail early this morning," he said coolly. "She's been accused of drug smuggling, can you imagine it? She was only parking her car when those lunatics opened fire!"

CHAPTER NINE

REMEMBERING WHAT ALEXANDER had cautioned her about, Jodie managed not to laugh out loud at Brody. How could a man be so naive?

"Drug smuggling?" she exclaimed, playing her part. "Cara?"

"That's what they said," he replied. "Apparently some of Ritter's security people had the warehouse staked out. When the shooting started, they returned fire, and I guess they called in the police. In fact, your friend Cobb was there when they arrested Cara."

"Yes, I know. He heard the shooting and walked right into it," she said, choosing her words carefully. "We were parked across the street..."

"I saw you when I let Cara into the parking lot," Brody said, embarrassed. "One of the gang came in with a machine gun and they say you aimed Cobb's car right at him and drove into a hail of bullets to save his life. I guess you really do care about him."

"Yes," she confessed. "I do."

"It was a courageous thing to do. Cara said you must be crazy about the guy to do that."

"Poor Cara," she replied, sidestepping the question. "I'm so sorry for the trouble she's in. Why in the world do they think she was involved? She was just in the wrong place at the wrong time."

Brody seemed to relax. "That's what Cara said. Uh, Cobb wasn't in on that bust deliberately, was he?"

"We were in a parked car outside the gate. We didn't know about any bust," she replied.

"So that's why he was there," he murmured absently, nodding. "I thought it must be something of the sort. Cara didn't know any of the others, but one was a female detective and another was a female deputy sheriff. The policewoman arrested her."

"Don't mess with Texas women," Jodie said, adding on a word to the well-known Texas motto.

He laughed. "So it seems. Uh, there was supposed to be a DEA agent there, as well. Cara has a friend who works out of the Houston office, but he's been out of town a lot lately and she hasn't been able to contact him. She says it's funny, but he seems to actually be avoiding her." He gave her an odd look. "I gather that it wasn't Cobb. But do you know anything about who the agent was?"

"No," she said straight-faced. "And Alexander didn't mention it, either. He tells me everything, so I'd know if it was him."

"I see."

She wondered if Cara's friend at the DEA was named Kennedy, but she pretended to know nothing. "What's Cara going to do?" she asked, sounding concerned.

"Get a good lawyer, I suppose," he said heavily.

"I wish her well. I'm so sorry, Brody."

He sighed heavily. "I seem to have a knack for getting myself into tight corners, but I think Cara's easily superior to me in that respect. Well, I'd better phone the attorney whose name she gave me. You're sure you're all right?"

"I'm fine, Brody, honestly." She smiled at him.

He smiled back. "See you."

She watched him go with relief. She'd been impro-
vising widely to make sure he didn't connect Alexander
with the surveillance of the warehouse.

WHEN ALEXANDER PHONED HER, she arranged to meet him
briefly at the café downstairs for coffee. He was pushed
for time, having been in meetings with his drug unit most
of the day planning strategy.

"You've become a local legend," he told her with a
mischievous smile when they were drinking cappuccino.

"Me?" she exclaimed.

He grinned at her. "The oil clerk who drove through
a hail of bullets to save her lover."

She flushed and glared at him. "Point one, I am not
a clerk, I'm an administrative assistant. And point two,
I am not your—!"

"I didn't say I started the rumor." He chuckled. His
eyes became solemn as he studied her across the table.
"But the part about being a heroine, I endorse enthusiastically. That being said, would you like to add to your
legend?"

She paid attention. "Are you kidding? What do you
want me to do?"

"Cara made bond this afternoon," he told her. "We've
got a tail on her, but she's sure to suspect that. She'll make
contact with one of her subordinates, in some public place
where she thinks we won't be able to tape her. When she
does, I'm going to want you to accidentally happen upon
her and plant a microphone under her table."

"Wow! 'Jane Bond' stuff!"

"Jane?" he wondered.

She shrugged. "A woman named James would be a novelty."

"Point taken. Are you game?"

"Of course. But why wouldn't you let one of your own people do it?"

His face was revealing. "The last hearty professional we sent to do that little task stumbled over his own feet and pitched headfirst into the table our target was occupying. In the process he overturned a carafe of scalding coffee, also on the target, who had to be taken to the hospital for treatment."

"What if I do the same thing?" she worried.

He smiled gently. "You don't have a clumsy bone in your body, Jodie. But even if you did, Cara knows you. She might suspect me, but she won't suspect you."

"When do I start?"

"I'll let you know," he promised. "In the meantime, keep your eyes and ears open, and don't..."

Just as he spoke, there was a commotion outside the coffee shop. A young woman with long blond hair was trailing away a dark-haired little girl with a shocked face. Behind them, one of the men Jodie recognized from the drug bust—one of Alexander's friends—was waving his arms and talking loudly in a language Jodie had never heard before, his expression furious.

The trio passed out of sight, but not before Jodie finally recognized the man Alexander had called Colby Lane.

"What in the world...?" she wondered.

"It's a long story," Alexander told her. "And I'm not at liberty to repeat it. Let's just say that Colby has been rather suddenly introduced to a previously unknown member of his family."

"Was he cursing—and in what language?" she persisted.

"You can't curse in Apache," he assured her. "It's like Japanese—if you really want to tick somebody off in Japan, you say something about their mother's belly button. But giving them the finger doesn't have any meaning."

"Really?" She was fascinated.

He chuckled. "Anyway, Native Americans—whose origins are also suspected to be Asian—don't use curse words in their own language."

"Mr. Lane looked very upset. And I thought I recognized that blonde woman. She was transferred here from their Arizona office just a few weeks ago. She has a little girl, about the same age as Mr. Hunter's daughter."

"Let it lie," Alexander advised. "We have problems of our own. I meant to mention that we've located one of Cara's known associates serving as a waiter in a little coffeehouse off Alameda called The Beat…"

"I go there!" she exclaimed. "I go there a lot! You can get all sorts of fancy coffees and it's like a retro 'beatnik' joint. They play bongos and wear all black and customers get up and read their poetry." She flushed. "I actually did that myself, just last week."

He was impressed. "You, getting up in front of people to read poetry? I didn't know you still wrote poetry, Jodie."

"It's very personal stuff," she said, uneasy.

He began to look arrogant. "About me?"

She glared at him. "At the time I wrote it, you were my least favorite person on the planet," she informed him.

"Ouch!" He was thinking again. "But if they already know you there, it's even less of a stretch if you show up when Cara does—assuming she even uses the café for her purposes. We'll have to wait and see. I don't expect her to arrange a rendezvous with a colleague just to suit me."

"Nice of you," she teased.

He chuckled. He reached across the table and linked her fingers with his. His green eyes probed hers for a long moment. "Those cuts are noticeable on your face," he said quietly. "Do they hurt?"

"Not nearly as much as having you gunned down in front of me would have," she replied.

His eyes began to glitter with feeling. His fingers contracted around hers. "Which is just how I felt when I saw those bullets slamming into the windshield of my car, with you at the wheel."

Her breath caught. He'd never admitted so much in the past.

He laughed self-consciously and released her hand. "We're getting morose. A miss is as good as a mile, and I still have paperwork to finish that I haven't even started on." He glanced at his watch. "I can't promise anything, but we might see a movie this weekend."

"That would be nice," she said. "You'll let me know…?"

He frowned. "I don't like putting you in the line of fire a second time."

"I go to the coffee shop all the time," she reminded him. "I'm not risking anything." Except my heart, again, she thought.

He sighed. "I suppose so. Just the same, don't let down your guard. I hope you can tell if someone's tailing you?"

"I get goose bumps on the back of my neck," she assured him. "I'll be careful. You do the same," she added firmly.

He smiled gently. "I'll do my best."

HAVING SETTLED DOWN with a good book the following day after a sandwich and soup supper, it was a surprise to have Alexander phone her and ask her to go down to the coffee shop on the double.

"I'll meet you in the parking lot with the equipment," he said. "Get a cab and have it drop you off. I'll reimburse you. Hurry, Jodie."

"Okay. I'm on my way," she promised, lounging in pajamas and a robe.

She dashed into the bedroom, threw on a long black velvet skirt, a black sweater, loafers, and ran a quick brush through her loose hair before perching her little black beret on top of her head. She grabbed her coat and rushed out the door, barely pausing except to lock it. She was at the elevator before she remembered her purse, lying on the couch. She dashed back to get it, cursing her own lack of preparedness in an emergency.

MINUTES LATER, SHE got out of the cab at the side door of The Beat coffeehouse.

Alexander waited by his company car while Jodie paid the cab. She joined him, careful to notice that she was unobserved.

He straightened at her approach. In the well-lit parking lot, she could see his eyes. They were troubled.

"I'm here," she said, just for something to say. "What do you want me to do?"

"I'm not sure I want you to do anything," he said honestly. "This is dangerous. Right now, she has no reason to suspect you. But if you bug her table for me, and she finds out that you did, your life could be in danger."

"Hey, listen, you were the one who told me about the

little boys being shot by her henchmen," she reminded him. "I know the risk, Alexander. I'm willing to take it."

"Your knees are knocking," he murmured.

She laughed, a little unsteadily. "I guess they are. And my heart's pounding. But I'm still willing to do it. Now what exactly do I do?"

He opened the passenger door for her. "Get in. I'll brief you."

"Is she here?" she asked when they were inside.

"Yes. She's at the table nearest the kitchen door, at the left side of the stage. Here." He handed her a fountain pen.

"No, thanks," she said, waving it away. "I've got two in my purse…"

He opened her hand and placed the capped pen in it. She looked at it, surprised by its heaviness. "It's a miniature receiver," he told her. He produced a small black box with an antenna, and what looked like an earplug with a tiny wire sticking out the fat end. "The box is a receiver, linked to a tape recorder. The earplug is also a receiver, which we use when we're in close quarters and don't want to attract attention. Since the box has a range of several hundred feet, I'll be able to hear what comes into the pen from my car."

"Do you want me to accidentally leave the pen on her table?"

"I want you to accidentally drop it under her table," he said. "If she sees it, the game's up. We're not the only people who deal in counterespionage."

She sucked in her breath. She was getting the picture. Cara was no dummy. "Okay. I'll lean over her table to say hello and make sure I put it where she won't feel it with her foot. How will that do?"

"Yes. But you have to make sure she doesn't see you do it."

"I'll be very careful."

He was having second thoughts. She was brave, but courage wasn't the only requirement for such an assignment. He remembered her driving through gunfire to save him. She could have died then. He'd thought about little else, and he hadn't slept well. Jodie was like a silver thread that ran through his life. In recent weeks, he'd been considering, seriously, how hard it would be to go on without her. He wasn't certain that he could.

"Why are you watching me like that?" she wanted to know, smiling curiously. "I'm not a dummy. I won't let you down, honest."

"It wasn't that." He closed her fingers around the pen. "Are you sure you want to go through with this?"

"Very sure."

"Okay." He hesitated. "What are you going to give as an excuse for being there?"

She gave him a bright smile. "I phoned Johnny—the owner—earlier, just after you phoned me and told him I had a new poem, but I was a little nervous about getting up in front of a big crowd. He said there was only a small crowd and I'd do fine."

"You improvise very well."

"I've been observing you for years," she teased. "But it's true. I do have a poem to read, which should throw Cara off the track."

He tugged her chin up and kissed her, hard. "You're going to be fine."

She smiled at him. "Which one of us are you supposed to be reassuring?"

"Both of us," he said tenderly. He kissed her again. "Go to work."

"What do I do when she leaves?"

"Get a cab back to your apartment. I'll meet you there. If anything goes wrong," he added firmly, "or if she acts suspicious, you stay in the coffeehouse and phone my cell number. Got that?" He handed her a card with his mobile phone number on it.

"I've got it."

She opened the car door and stepped out into the cool night air. With a subdued wave, she turned, pulled her coat closer around her and walked purposefully toward the coffeehouse. What she didn't tell Alexander was that her new poem was about him.

She didn't look around noticeably as she made her way through the sparse crowd to the table where she usually sat on her evenings here. She held the pen carefully in her hand, behind a long fold of her coat. As she pulled out a chair at the table, her eyes swept the room and she spotted Cara at a table with another woman. She smiled and Cara frowned.

Uh-oh, she thought, but she pinned the smile firmly to her face and moved to Cara's table.

"I thought it was you," she said cheerily. "I didn't know you ever came here! Brody never mentioned it to me."

Cara gave her a very suspicious look. "This is not your normal evening entertainment, surely?"

"But I come here all the time," Jodie replied honestly. "Johnny's one of my fans."

"Fans." Cara turned the word over on her tongue as if she'd never heard it.

"Aficionados," Jodie persisted. "I write poetry."

"You?"

The other woman made it sound like an insult. The woman beside her, an even older woman with a face like plate steel, only looked.

Jodie felt a chill of fear and worked to hide it. Her palm sweated against the weight of the pen hidden in her hand. As she hesitated, Johnny came walking over in his apron.

"Hey, Jodie!" he greeted. "Now don't worry, there's only these two unfamiliar ladies in here, you know everybody else. You just get up there and give it your best. It'll be great!"

"Johnny, you make me feel so much better," she told the man.

"These ladies friends of yours?" he asked, noticing them—especially Cara—with interested dark eyes.

"Cara's boyfriend is my boss at work," Jodie said.

"Lucky boyfriend," Johnny murmured, his voice dropping an octave.

Cara relaxed and smiled. "I am Cara Dominguez," she introduced herself. "This is my *amiga*, Chiva."

Johnny leaned over the table to shake hands and Jodie pretended to be overbalanced by him. In the process of righting herself and accepting his apology, she managed to let the pen drop under the table where it lay unnoticed several inches from either woman's foot.

"Sorry, Jodie, meeting two such lovely ladies made me clumsy." He chuckled.

She grinned at him. "No harm done. I'm not hurt."

"Okay, then, you go get on that stage. Want your usual French Vanilla cappuccino?"

"You bet. Make it a large one, with a croissant, please."

"It'll be on the house," he informed her. "That's incentive for you."

"Gee, thanks!" she exclaimed.

"My treat. Nice to meet you ladies."

"It is for us the same," Cara purred. She glanced at Jodie, much less suspicious now. "So you write poetry. I will enjoy listening to it."

Jodie chuckled. "I'm not great, but people here are generally kind. Good to see you."

Cara shrugged. The other woman said nothing.

Jodie pulled off her coat and went up onto the stage, trying to ignore her shaking knees. Meanwhile she prayed that Alexander could hear what the two women were saying. Because the minute she pulled the microphone closer, introduced herself, and pulled out the folded sheet of paper that contained her poem, Cara leaned toward the other woman and started speaking urgently.

Probably exchanging fashion tips, or some such thing, Jodie thought dismally, but she smiled at the crowd, unfolded the paper, and began to read.

Apparently her efforts weren't too bad, because the small crowd paid attention to every line of the poem. And when she finished reading it, there was enthusiastic applause.

Cara and her friend, however, were much too intent on conversation to pay Jodie any attention. She went back to her seat, ate her croissant and drank her cappuccino with her back to the table where Cara and the other woman were sitting, just to make sure they knew she wasn't watching them.

A few minutes later, Johnny came by her table and patted her on the back. "That was some good work, girl!" he exclaimed. "I'm sorry your friend didn't seem to care enough to listen to it."

"She's not into poetry," she confided.

"I guess not. She and that odd-looking friend of hers didn't even finish their coffee."

"They're gone?" she asked without turning.

He nodded. "About five minutes ago, I guess. No great loss, if you ask me."

"Thanks for the treat, Johnny, and for the encouragement," she added.

"Um, I sure would like to have a copy of that poem."

Her eyes widened. "You would? Honestly?"

He shrugged. "It was really good. I know this guy. He works for a small press. They publish poetry. I'd like to show it to him. If you don't mind."

"Mind!" She handed him the folded paper. "I don't mind! Thanks, Johnny!"

"No problem. I'll be in touch." He turned, and then paused, digging into his apron pocket. "Say, is this yours? I'm afraid I may have stepped on it. It was under that table where your friend was sitting."

"Yes, it's mine," she said, taking it from him. "Thanks a lot."

He winced. "If I broke it, I'll buy you a new one, okay?"

"It's just a pen," she said with determined carelessness. "No problem."

"You wait, I'll call you a cab."

"That would be great!"

She settled back to wait, her head full of hopeful success, and not only for Alexander.

"Is it broken?" she asked Alexander when she was back at her apartment, and he was examining his listening device.

"I'll have the lab guys check it out," he told her.

"Could you hear anything?"

He grinned hugely. "Not only did I hear plenty, I taped it. We've got a lead we'd never have had without you. There's just one bad thing."

"Oh?"

"Cara thinks your poetry stinks," he said with a twinkle in his eyes.

"She can think what she likes, but Johnny's showing it to a publisher friend of his. He thought it was wonderful."

He searched her face. "So did I, Jodie."

She felt a little nervous, but certainly he couldn't have known that he was the subject of it, so she just thanked him offhandedly.

"Now I'm sure I'm cut out for espionage," she murmured.

"You may be, but I don't know if my nerves could take it."

"You thought I'd mess up," she guessed.

He shook his head, holding her hand firmly in his. "It wasn't that. I don't like having you at risk, Jodie. I don't want you on the firing line ever again, even if you did save my skin last night."

She searched his green eyes hungrily. "I wouldn't want to live in a world that didn't contain you, too," she said. Then, backtracking out of embarrassment, she laughed and added, "I really couldn't live without the aggravation."

He laughed, as he was meant to. "Same here." He checked his watch. "I don't want to go," he said unexpectedly, "but I've got to get back to my office and go through this tape. Tomorrow, I'll be in conference with my drug unit. You pretend that nothing at all was amiss, except you saw Cara at your favorite evening haunt. Right?"

"Right," she assured him.

"I'll call you."

"That's what they all say," she said drily.

He paused at the door and looked at her. "Who?"

"Excuse me?"

"Who else is promising to call you?" he persisted.

"The president, for my advice on his foreign policy, of course," she informed him.

He laughed warmly. "Incorrigible," he said to himself, winked at her, and let himself out. "Lock it!" he called through it.

She snicked the lock audibly and heard him chuckle again. She leaned back against the door with a relieved sigh. It was over. She'd done what he asked her, and she hadn't fouled it up. Most of all, he was pleased with her.

She was amazed at the smiles she got from him in recent weeks. He'd always been reserved, taciturn, with most other people. But he enjoyed her company and it showed.

THE NEXT DAY, Brody seemed very preoccupied. She took dictation, which he gave haltingly, and almost absently.

"Are you okay?" she wanted to know.

He moved restively around his office. He turned to stare at her curiously. "Are you involved in some sort of top secret operation or something?"

Her eyes popped. "Pardon?"

He cleared his throat. "I know you were at a coffee-house where Cara went last night with a friend. I wondered if you were spying on her…?"

"I go to The Beat all the time, Brody," she told him, surprised. "Alexander's idea of an evening out is a concert or the theater, but my tastes run to bad poetry and bongos. I've been going there for weeks. It's no secret. The owner knows me very well."

He relaxed suddenly and smiled. "Thank goodness! That's what Cara told me, of course, but it seemed odd that you'd be there when she was. I mean, like you and your boyfriend showed up at the restaurant where we had lunch that day, and then you were at the concert, too. And your friend does work for the DEA…"

"Coincidences," she said lazily. "That's all. Unless you think I've been following you," she added with deliberate emphasis, demurely lowering her eyes.

There was a long, shocked pause. "Why, I never thought…considered…really?"

She crossed her legs. "I think you're very nice, Brody, and Cara treats you like a pet dog," she said with appropriate indignation. She peered at him covertly. "You're too good for her."

He was obviously embarrassed, flattered, and uncertain. "My gosh… I'm sorry, but I knew about Cobb working for the DEA, and then the drug bust came so unexpectedly. Well, it seemed logical that he might be spying on Cara with your help…"

"I never dreamed that I looked like a secret agent!" she exclaimed, and then she chuckled. "As if Alexander would ever trust me with something so dangerous," she added, lowering her eyes so that he couldn't see them.

He sighed. "Forgive me. I've had these crazy theories. Cara thought I was nuts, especially after she told me the owner of that coffeehouse knew you very well and encouraged you to read…well…very bad poetry. She thought maybe he had a case on you."

"It was not bad poetry! And he had a case on Cara, not me," she replied with just the right amount of pique.

"Did he!"

"I told him she was your girlfriend, don't worry," she said, and managed to sound regretful.

"Jodie, I'm very flattered," he faltered.

She held up a hand. "Let's not talk about it, Brody, okay? You just dictate, and I'll write."

He sighed, studying her closely. After a minute, he shrugged, and began dictating. This time, he was concise and relaxed. Jodie felt like collapsing with relief, herself. It had been a close call, and not even because Cara was suspicious. It was Brody who seemed to sense problems.

CHAPTER TEN

IT WAS A relief that Cara didn't suspect Jodie of spying, but it was worrying that Brody did. He was an intelligent man, and it wouldn't be easy to fool him. She'd have to mention that to Alexander when she saw him.

He came by the apartment that evening, soon after Jodie got home from work, taciturn and worried.

"Something happened," she guessed uneasily.

He nodded. "Got any coffee?"

"Sure. Come on into the kitchen."

He sat down and she poured him a cup from the potful she'd just made. He sipped it and studied her across the table. "Kennedy came back to town today. He's Cara's contact."

"Oh, dear," she murmured, sensing that something was very wrong.

He nodded. "I called him into my office and told him I was firing him, and why. I have sworn statements from two witnesses who are willing to testify against him in return for reduced sentences." He sighed. "He said that he knew you were involved, that you'd helped me finger Cara, and that he'd tell her if I didn't back down."

"Don't feel bad about it," she said, mentally panicking while trying not to show it. "You couldn't let him stay, after what he did."

He looked at her blankly. "You're a constant surprise to me, Jodie. How did you know I wouldn't back down?"

She smiled gently. "You wouldn't be Alexander if you let people bluff you."

"Yes, baby, but he's not bluffing."

The endearment caught her off guard, made her feel warm inside, warm all over. "So what do we do now?" she asked, a little disconcerted.

He noted her warm color and smiled tenderly. "You go live with Margie for a few days, until I wrap up this case. Our cover's blown now for sure."

"Margie can shoot a gun, but she's not all that great at it, Alexander," she pointed out.

"Our foreman, Chayce, is, and so is cousin Derek," he replied. "He was involved in national security work when he was just out of college. He's a dead shot, and he'll be bringing his two brothers with him." He chuckled. "Funny. All I had to say was that Margie might be in danger along with you, and he volunteered at once."

"You don't like him," she recalled.

He shrugged. "I don't like the idea of Margie getting involved with a cousin. But Derek seemed to know that, too, and he told me something I didn't know before when I phoned him. He wasn't my uncle's son. His mother had an affair with an old beau and he was the result. It was a family secret until last night. Which means," he added, "that he's only related to us by marriage, not by blood."

"He told you himself?" she asked.

"He told me. Apparently, he told you, too. But he didn't tell Margie."

"Have you?" she wondered.

"That's for him to do," he replied. "I've interfered enough." He checked his watch. "I've got to go. I have a man watching the apartment," he added. "The one I told you about. But tomorrow, you tell Brody you're taking a few days off to look after a sick relative and you go to Margic. Got that?"

"But my job…!"

"It's your life!" he shot back, eyes blazing. "This is no game. These people will kill you as surely as they killed those children. I am not going to watch you die, Jodie. Least of all for something I got you into!"

She caught her breath. This was far more serious than she'd realized.

"I told you," he emphasized, "Cara knows you were involved. The secret's out. You leave town. Period."

She stared at him and knew she was trapped. Her job was going to be an afterthought. They'd fire her. She was even afraid to take a day off when she was sick, because the company policy in her department was so strict.

"If you lose that job, it will be a blessing," Alexander told her flatly. "You're too good to waste your life taking somebody else's dictation. When this is over, I'll help you find something better. I'll take you to classes so that you can get your expert computer certification, then I'll get an employment agency busy to find you a better job."

That was a little disappointing. Obviously he didn't have a future with her in mind, or he wouldn't be interested in getting her a job.

He leaned back in his chair, sipping coffee. "Although," he added suddenly, his gaze intent, "there might be an alternative."

"An alternative?"

"We'll talk about that later," he said. He finished his coffee. "I have to go."

She got up and walked him to the door. "You be careful, too," she chided.

He opened his jacket and indicated the .45 automatic in its hand-tooled leather holster.

"It won't shoot itself," she reminded him pertly.

He chuckled, drew her into his arms, and kissed her until her young body ached with deep, secret longings.

He lifted his head finally, and he wasn't breathing normally. She felt the intensity of his gaze all the way to her toes as he looked at her. "All these years," he murmured, "and I wasted them sniping at you."

"You seemed to enjoy it at the time," she remarked absently, watching his mouth hover over hers.

"I didn't want a marriage like my parents had. I played the field, to keep women from getting serious about me," he confessed. He traced her upper lip with his mouth, with breathless tenderness. "Especially you," he added roughly. "No one else posed the threat you did, with your old-fashioned ideals and your sterling character. But I couldn't let you see how attracted to you I was. I did a pretty good job. And then you had too much champagne at a party and did what I'd been afraid you'd do since you graduated from high school."

"You were afraid…?"

He nibbled her upper lip. "I knew that if you ever got close, I'd never be able to let you go," he whispered sensuously. "What I spouted to Margie was a lot of hot air. I ached from head to toe after what we did together. I wanted you so badly, honey. I didn't sleep all night thinking about how easy it would have been."

"I didn't sleep thinking that you hated me," she confessed.

He sighed regretfully. "I didn't know you'd overheard

me, but I said enough when I left you at your bedroom. I felt guilty when I went downstairs and saw your face. You were shamed and humiliated, and it was my fault. I only wanted a chance to make amends, but you started backing away and you wouldn't stop. That was when I knew what a mistake I'd made."

She toyed with his shirt button. "And then you needed help to catch a drug smuggler," she mused.

There was a pause long enough to make her look up. "You're good, Jodie, and I did need somebody out of the agency to dig out that information for me. But…"

"But?"

He smiled sheepishly. "Houston PD owes me a favor. They'd have been glad to get the information for me. So would the Texas Rangers, or the county sheriff."

"Then why did you ask me to do it?" she exclaimed.

His hands went to frame her face. They felt warm and strong against her soft skin. "I was losing you," he whispered as he bent again to rub his lips tenderly over her mouth. "You wouldn't let me near you any other way."

His mouth was making pudding of her brain. She slid her arms up around his neck and her hands tangled in the thick hair above his nape. "But there was Kirry…"

"Window dressing. I didn't even like her, especially by the time my birthday rolled around. I gave Margie hell for inviting her to my birthday party, did she tell you?"

She shook her head, dazed.

He caught her upper lip in his mouth and toyed with it. His breathing grew unsteady. His hands on her face became insistent. "I got drunk when Margie told me you'd overheard us," he whispered. "It took two neat whiskeys for me to even phone you. Too much was riding on my ability to make an apology. And frankly, baby, I don't make a habit of giving them."

She melted into his body, hungry for closer contact. "I was so ashamed of what I'd done…"

His mouth crushed down onto hers with passionate intent. "I loved what you did," he ground out. "I wasn't kidding when I told you that. I could taste you long after I went to bed. I dreamed about it all night."

"So did I," she whispered.

His lips parted hers ardently. "I thought you were hung up on damned Brody," he murmured, "until you aimed that car at the gunman. I prayed for all I was worth until I got to you and knew that you were all right. I could have lost you forever. It haunts me!"

"I'm tougher than old cowboy boots," she whispered, elated beyond belief at what he was saying to her.

"And softer than silk, in all the right places. Come here." He moved her against the wall. His body pressed hers gently against it while he kissed her with all the pent-up longing he'd been suppressing for weeks. When she moaned, he felt his body tremble with aching need.

"You're killing me," he ground out.

"Wh…what?"

He lifted his head and looked down into soft, curious gray eyes. "You haven't got a clue," he muttered. "Can't you tell when a man's dying of lust?"

Her eyebrows arched as he rested his weight on his hands next to her ears on the wall and suddenly pressed his hips into hers, emphatically demonstrating the question.

She swallowed hard. "Alexander, I was really only kidding about having a dress with prophylactics pinned to the hem…"

He burst out laughing and forced his aching body away

from hers. "I've never laughed as much in my life as I do with you," he said on a long sigh. "But I really would give half an arm to lay you down on the carpet right now, Jodie."

She flushed with more delight than fear. "One of us could run to the drugstore, I guess," she murmured drily.

"Not now," he whispered wickedly. "But hold that thought until I wind up this case."

She laughed. "Okay."

He nibbled her upper lip. "I'll pick you up at work about nine in the morning," he murmured as he lifted his head. "And I'll drive you down to Jacobsville."

"You're really worried," she realized, when she saw the somber expression.

"Yes, Jodie. I'm really worried. Keep your doors locked and don't answer the phone."

"What if it's you?" she worried.

"Do you still have the cell phone I loaned you?"

"Yes."

She produced it. He opened it, turned it on, and checked the battery. "It's fully charged. Leave it on. If I need to call you, I'll use this number. You can call me if you're afraid. Okay?"

"Okay."

He kissed her one last time, gave her a soulful, enigmatic look, and went out the door. She bolted it behind him and stood there for several long seconds, her head whirling with the changes that were suddenly upsetting her life and career. Alexander was trying to tell her something, but she couldn't quite decide what. Did he want an affair? He certainly couldn't be thinking about marriage, he hated the whole thought of it. But, what did he want? She worried the question until morning, and still had no answers.

"You're going to leave for three days, just like that?"
Brody exploded at work the next morning, his face harder
than Jodie had ever seen it. "How the hell am I going to
manage without a secretary?" he blustered. "I can't type
my own letters!"

The real man, under the facade, Jodie thought, fascinated with her first glimpse of Brody's dark side. She'd
never seen him really angry.

"I'm not just a secretary," she reminded him.

"Oh, hell, you do mail and requisition forms," he said
coldly. "Call it what you like, it's donkey work." His eyes
narrowed. "It's because of what you did to Cara, isn't it?
You're scared, so you're running away!"

Her face flamed with temper. She stood up from her
desk and gave him a look that would have melted steel.
"Would you be keen to hang around if they were gunning
for you? You listen to me, Brody, these drug lords don't
care who dies as long as they get their money. There are
two dead little children who didn't do a thing wrong, except stand between a drug dealer and their mother, who
was trying to shut down drug dealing in her neighborhood. Cara is part of that sick trade, and if you defend
her, so are you!"

He gaped at her. In the years they'd worked together,
Jodie had never talked back to him.

She grabbed up her purse and got the few personal
belongings out of her desk. "Never mind holding my
job open for me. I quit!" she told him flatly. "There must
be more to life than pandering to the ego of a man who
thinks I'm a donkey. One more thing, Brody," she added,
facing him with her arms full of her belongings. "You
and your drug-dealing girlfriend can both go to hell,
with my blessing!"

She turned and stalked out of her cubicle. She imagined a trail of fire behind her. Brody's incredulous gasp had been music to her ears. Alexander was right. She was wasted here. She'd find something better, she knew it.

On her way out the door, she almost collided with Phillip Hunter. He righted her, his black eyebrows arching.

"You're leaving, Miss Clayburn?" he asked.

"I'm leaving, Mr. Hunter," she said, still bristling from her encounter with Brody.

"Great. Come with me."

He motioned with his chin. She followed him, puzzled, because he'd never spoken to her before except in a cordial, impersonal way.

He led her into the boardroom and closed the door. Inside was the other dark man she'd met briefly during the drug bust at the warehouse, Colby Lane, and the owner of the corporation himself, Eugene Ritter.

"Sit down, Ms. Clayburn," Ritter said with a warm smile, his blue eyes twinkling under a lock of silver hair.

She dropped into a chair, with her sack full of possessions clutched close to her chest.

"Mr. Ritter," she began, wondering what in the world she was going to do now. "I can explain..."

"You don't have to," he said gently. "I already know everything. When this drug case is wrapped up—and Cobb assures me it will be soon—how would you like to come back and work for me in an area where your skills won't be wasted?"

She was speechless. She just stared at him over her bulging carry-all.

"Phillip wants to go home to Arizona to work in our branch office there, and Colby Lane here—" he indicated the other dark man "—is going to replace him. He knows about your computer skills and Cobb's already told him that you're a whiz with investigations. How would you like to work for Lane as a computer security consultant? It will pay well and you'll have autonomy within the corporation. The downside," he added slowly, "is that you may have to do some traveling eventually, to our various branch offices, to work with Hunter and our other troubleshooters. Is that a problem?"

She shook her head, still grasping for a hold on the situation.

"Good!" He rubbed his hands together. "Then we'll draw up a contract for you, and you can have your attorney read and approve it when you come back." He was suddenly solemn. "There are going to be a lot of changes here in the near future. I've been coasting along in our headquarters office in Oklahoma and letting the outlying divisions take care of themselves, with near-disastrous results. If Hunter hadn't been tipped off by Cobb about the warehouse being used as a drug drop, we could have been facing federal charges, with no intentional involvement whatsoever on our part, on international drug smuggling. Tell Cobb we owe him one for that."

She grinned. "I will. And, Mr. Ritter, thank you very much for the opportunity. I won't let you down."

"I know that, Ms. Clayburn," he told her, smiling back. "Hunter will walk you outside. Just in case. Not that I think you need too much protection," he added, tongue-in-cheek. "There aren't a lot of people who'll drive into gunfire to save another person."

She laughed. "If I'd had time to think about it, I probably wouldn't have done it. Just the same, I won't mind having an escort to the front entrance," she confessed, standing. "I'm getting a cab to my apartment."

"We'll talk again," Ritter assured her, standing. He was tall and very elegant in a gray business suit. "All right, come on, Lane. We'll inspect the warehouse one last time."

"Yes, sir," Lane agreed.

"I'm just stunned," Jodie murmured when they reached the street, where the cab she'd called was waiting. She'd also phoned Cobb to meet her at her apartment.

"Ritter sees more than people think he does," Hunter told her, chuckling. "He's sharp, and he doesn't miss much. Tell Cobb I owe him one, too. My wife and I have been a little preoccupied lately—we just found out that we're expecting again. My mind hasn't been as much on the job as it should have been."

"Congratulations!"

He shrugged. "I wouldn't mind another girl, but Jennifer wants a son this time, a matched set, she calls it. She wants to be near her cousin Danetta, who's also expecting a second child. She and Cabe Ritter, the old man's son, have a son but they want a daughter." He chuckled. "We'll see what we both get. Meanwhile, you go straight to your apartment with no stops," he directed, becoming solemn. He looked over the top of the cab, saw something, and nodded approvingly. "Cobb's having you tailed. No, don't look back. If anyone makes a try for you, dive for cover and let your escort handle it, okay?"

"Okay. But I'm not really nervous about it now."

"So I saw the other night," he replied. "You've got guts, Ms. Clayburn. You'll be a welcome addition to security here."

She beamed. "I'll do my best. Thanks again."

"No problem. Be safe."

He closed the door and watched the taxi pull away.

Her escort, in a dark unmarked car, pulled right out behind the cab. She found herself wishing that Cara and
her group would make a try for her. It wouldn't bother
her one bit to have the woman land in jail for a long time.

ALEXANDER WAS WAITING for her at her apartment. He
picked up the suitcase she'd packed and then he drove
her down to the Jacobsville ranch. She didn't have time
to tell him about the changes in her life. She was saving that for a surprise. She was feeling good about her
own abilities, and her confidence in herself had a surprising effect on her friend Margie, who met her at the
door with faint shock.

Margie hugged her, but her eyes were wary. "There's
something different about you," she murmured sedately.

"I've been exercising," she assured the other woman
amusedly.

"Sure she has." Alexander chuckled. "By aiming cars
at men armed with automatic weapons."

"What!" Margie exclaimed, gasping.

"Well, they were shooting at Alexander," Jodie told
her. "What else could I do?"

Margie and her brother exchanged a long, serious look.
He nodded slowly, and then he smiled. Margie beamed.

"What's that all about?" Jodie wondered aloud.

"We're passing along mental messages," Margie told
her with wicked eyes. "Never mind. You're just in time
to try on the flamenco dress I made you for our Halloween party."

"Halloween party." Jodie nodded blankly.

"It's this Saturday," Margie said, exasperated. "We always have it the weekend before Halloween, remember?"

"I didn't realize it was that far along in the month," Jodie said. "I guess I've been busier than I realized."

"She writes poetry about me," Alexander said as he went up the staircase with Jodie's bag.

"I do not write poetry about you!" Jodie called after him.

He only laughed. "And she reads it onstage in a retro beatnik coffeehouse."

"For real?" Margie asked. "Jodie, I have to come stay with you in Houston so you can take me there. I love coffeehouses and poetry!" She shook her head. "I can't imagine you reading poetry on a stage. Or driving a car into bullets, for that matter." She looked shocked. "Jodie, you've changed."

Jodie nodded. "I guess I have."

Margie hugged her impulsively. "Are we still friends?" she wondered. "I haven't been a good one, but I'm going to try. I can actually make canapés!" she added. "I took lessons. So now you can come to parties when Jessie's not here, and I won't even ask you to do any of the work!"

Jodie burst out laughing. "This I have to see."

"You can, Friday. I expect it will take all day, what with the decorating, and I'm doing all that myself, too. Derek thinks I'm improving madly," she added, and a faint flush came to her cheeks.

"Cousin Derek's here already?" she asked.

"He's not actually my cousin at all, except by marriage, although I only just found out," Margie said, drawing Jodie along with her into the living room. "He's got two brothers and they're on the way here. One of them is a cattle rancher and the other is a divorced grizzly bear."

"A what?"

Margie looked worried. "He's a Bureau of Land Management enforcement agent," she said. "He tracks down poachers and people who deal in illegal hunting and such. He's the one whose wife left him for a car salesman. He's very bitter."

"Is Derek close to them?"

"To the rancher one," Margie said. "He doesn't see the grizzly bear too often, thank goodness."

"Thank goodness?" Jodie probed delicately.

Margie flushed. "I think Cousin Derek wants to be much more than my cousin."

"It's about time," Jodie said with a wicked smile. "He's just your type."

Margie made a face. "Come on into the kitchen and we'll see what there is to eat. I don't know about you, but I'm hungry." She stopped suddenly. "Don't take this the wrong way, but why are Derek and his brothers moving in and why are you and Alexander here in the middle of the week?"

"Oh, somebody's just going to try to kill me, that's all," Jodie said matter-of-factly. "But Alexander's more than able to handle them, with Cousin Derek's help and some hard work by the DEA and Alexander's drug unit."

"Trying to kill you." Margie nodded. "Right."

"That's no joke," Alexander said from the doorway. He came into the room and pulled Jodie to his side, bending to kiss her gently. "I have to go. Derek's on the job, and his brothers will be here within an hour or two. Nothing to worry about."

"Except you getting shot," Jodie replied worriedly.

He opened his jacket and showed her his gun.

"I know. You're indestructible. But come back in one piece, okay?" she asked softly.

He searched her eyes and smiled tenderly. "That's a

deal. See you later." He winked at Margie and took one last look at Jodie before he left.

"How people change," Margie murmured drily.

But Jodie wasn't really listening. Her eyes were still on Alexander's broad back as he went out the door.

ALEXANDER AND HIS group met somberly that evening to compare notes and plan strategy. They knew by now where Cara Dominguez was, who her cohorts were and just how much Brody Vance knew about her operation. The security guard on the job at the Ritter warehouse was linked to the organization, as well, but thought he was home free. What he didn't know was that Alexander had a court order to wiretap his office, and the agent overseeing that job had some interesting information to impart about a drug shipment that was still concealed in Ritter's warehouse. It was one that no one knew about until the wiretap. And it was a much bigger load than the one the drug unit had just busted.

The trick was going to be catching the thieves with the merchandise. It wasn't enough to know they were connected with it. They had to have hard evidence, facts that would stand up in court. They had to have a chain of evidence that would definitively link Cara to the drug shipment.

Just when Alexander thought he was ready to spring the trap, Cara Dominguez disappeared off the face of the earth. The security guard was immediately arrested, before he could flee, but he had nothing to say under advice of counsel.

When they went to the Ritter warehouse, with Colby Lane and Phillip Hunter, to appropriate the drug shipment, they found cartons of drilling equipment parts.

Even with drug-sniffing dogs, they found no trace of the missing shipment. And everybody connected with Cara Dominguez suddenly developed amnesia and couldn't remember anything about her.

The only good thing about it was that the operation had obviously changed locations, and there was no further reason for anyone to target Jodie. Where it had moved was a job for the DEA to follow up on. Alexander was sure that Kennedy had something to do with the sudden disappearance of Cara, and the shipment, but he couldn't prove a thing. The only move he had left was to prosecute Kennedy for giving secret information to a known drug dealer, and that he could prove. He had Kennedy arraigned on charges of conspiracy to distribute controlled substances, which effectively removed the man from any chance of a future job in law enforcement— even if he managed to weasel out of a long jail term for what he'd already done.

ALEXANDER RETURNED TO the Jacobsville ranch on Friday, to find Margie and Jodie in the kitchen making canapés while Cousin Derek and two other men sat at the kitchen table. Derek was sampling the sausage rolls while a taller dark-eyed man with jet-black hair oiled his handgun and a second dark-haired man with eyes as green as Alexander's sat glaring at his two companions.

"She's gone," Alexander said heavily. "Took a powder. We can't find a trace of her, so far, and the drug shipment vanished into thin air. Needless to say, I'm relieved on your behalf," he told a radiant Jodie. "But it's not what I wanted to happen."

"Your inside man slipped up," the green-eyed stranger said in a deep bass voice.

"I didn't have an inside man, Zeke," Alexander said, dropping into a chair with the other men. "More's the pity."

"Don't mind him," the other stranger said easily. "He's perfect. He never loses a case or misses a shot. And he can cook."

Zeke glared at him. "You could do with a few lessons in marksmanship, Josiah," he returned curtly. "You can't even hit a target."

"That's a fact," Derek agreed at once, dark eyes dancing. "He tried to shoot a snake once and took the mailbox down with a shotgun."

"I can hit what I aim at when I want to," Josiah said huffily. "I hated that damned mailbox. I shot it on purpose."

His brothers almost rolled on the floor laughing. Josiah sighed and poured himself another cup of coffee. "Then I guess I'm on a plane back to Oklahoma."

"And I'm on one to Wyoming." Zeke nodded.

Derek glared at them. "And I'm booked for a rodeo in Arizona. Listen, why don't we sell up and move down here? Texas has lots of ranches. In fact, I expect we could find one near here without a lot of trouble."

"You might at that," Alexander told them as he poured his own cup of coffee, taking the opportunity to ruffle Jodie's blond hair and smile tenderly down at her. "I hear the old Jacobs place is up for sale again. That eastern dude who took it over lost his shirt in the stock market. It's just as well. He didn't know much about horses anyway."

"It's a horse farm?" Josiah asked, interested.

Alexander nodded. "A seed herd of Arabians and a couple of foals they bred from racing stock. He had pipe dreams about entering a horse in the Kentucky Derby one day."

"Why'd he give it up?"

"Well, for one thing, he didn't know anything about horses. He wouldn't ask for advice from anybody who did, but he'd read this book. He figured he could do it himself. That was before he got kicked out of the barn the first time," he added in a droll tone.

Zeke made a rough sound. "I'm not keen on horses. And I work in Wyoming."

"You're a little too late, anyway," Margie interrupted, but she was watching Derek with new intensity. "We heard that one of Cash Grier's brothers came down here to look at it. Apparently, they're interested."

"Grier has brothers?" Jodie exclaimed. "What a horrifying thought! How many?"

"Three. They've been on the outs for a long time, but they're making overtures. It seems the ranch would get them close enough to Cash to try and heal the breach."

"That's one mean hombre," Derek ventured.

"He keeps the peace," Alexander defended him. "And he makes life interesting in town. Especially just lately."

"What's going on lately?" Derek wanted to know.

Alexander, Jodie and Margie exchanged secretive smiles. "Never mind," Alexander said. "There are other properties, if you're really interested. You might stop by one of the real estate agencies and stock up on brochures."

"He'll never leave Oklahoma," Derek said, nodding toward Josiah. "And Wyoming's the only place left that's sparsely populated enough to appeal to our family grizzly." He glanced at Margie and grinned. "However, I only need a temporary base of operations since I'm on the road so much. I might buy me a little cabin nearby and come serenade Margie on weekends when I'm in town."

Margie laughed, but she was flushed with excitement. "Might you, now?"

"Of course, you're set on a designing career," he mused.

"And you're hooked on breaking bones and spraining muscles in the rodeo circuit."

"We might find some common ground one day," Derek replied.

Margie only smiled. "Are you all staying for my Halloween party?" she asked the brothers.

Zeke finished his coffee and got up. "I don't do parties. Excuse me. I have to call the airline."

"I'm right behind you," Josiah said, following his brother with an apologetic smile.

"Well, I guess it's just me," Derek said. "What do you think, Marge, how about if I borrow one of Alex's suits and come as a college professor?"

She burst out laughing.

Alexander caught Jodie by the hand and pulled her out of the kitchen with him.

"Where are we going?" she asked.

"For a walk, now that nobody's shooting at us," he said, linking her fingers into his.

He led her out the front door and around to the side of the house, by the long fences that kept the cattle in.

"When do you have to go back to work?" he asked Jodie reluctantly.

"That wasn't exactly discussed," she confessed, with a secret smile, because he didn't know which job she was returning to take. "But I suppose next week will do nicely."

"I still think Brody Vance is involved in this somehow," he said flatly, turning to her. "I can't prove it yet, but I'm certain he's not as innocent as he's pretending to be."

"That's exactly what I think," she agreed, surprising him. "By the way," she added, "I quit my job before we came down here."

"You quit...good for you!" he exclaimed, hugging her close. "I'm proud of you, Jodie!"

She laughed, holding on tight. "Don't be too proud. I'm still working for Mr. Ritter. But it's going to be in a totally different capacity."

"Doing what?" he asked flatly.

"I'm going to be working with Colby Lane as a computer security consultant," she told him.

"What about Hunter?" he asked.

"He's going back to Arizona with his wife. They're expecting a second child, and I think they want a little less excitement in their life right now," she confided with a grin. "So Colby Lane is taking over security. Mr. Ritter said I might have to do some traveling later on as a troubleshooter, but it wouldn't be often."

He was studying her with soft, quiet eyes. "As long as it's sporadic and not for too long, that's fine. You'll do well in security," he said. "Old man Ritter isn't as dense as I thought he was. I'm glad he's still keeping an eye on the company. Colby Lane will keep his security people on their toes just as well as Hunter did."

"I think Mr. Hunter is irritated that Cara managed to get into that warehouse parking lot," she ventured.

"He is. But it could have happened to anyone. Brody Vance is our wild card. He's going to need watching. And no, you can't offer to do it," he added firmly. "Let Lane set up his own surveillance. You stick to the job you're given and stop sticking your neck out."

"I like that!" she exclaimed. "And who was it who encouraged me to stick my neck out in the first place planting bugs near people in coffeehouses?"

He searched her eyes quietly. "You did a great job. I was proud of you. I always thought we might work well together."

"We did, didn't we?" she mused.

He pushed back wispy strands of loose hair from her cheek and studied her hungrily. "I have in mind another opportunity for mutual cooperation," he said, bending to her mouth.

CHAPTER ELEVEN

"WHAT SORT OF mutual cooperation?" she whispered against his searching lips. "Does it involve guns and bugs?"

He smiled against her soft mouth. "I was thinking more of prophylactics…"

While Jodie was trying to let the extraordinary statement filter into her brain, and trying to decide whether to slug him or kiss him back, a loud voice penetrated their oblivion.

"Jodie!" Margie yelled. "Where are you?"

Alexander lifted his head. He seemed as dazed as she felt.

"Jodie!" Margie yelled more insistently.

"On my way!" Jodie yelled back.

"Sisters are a pain," he murmured on a long sigh.

She smiled at him. "I'm sure it's a minor disaster that only I can cope with," she assured him.

He chuckled. "Go ahead. But tonight," he added in a deep, husky tone, "you're mine."

She flushed at the way he said it. She started to argue, but Margie was yelling again, so she ran toward the house instead.

ALEXANDER STARED HUNGRILY at Jodie when she came down the stairs just before the first party guest arrived the next evening. They'd spent the day together, riding around the ranch and talking. There hadn't been any more physical encounters, but there was a new closeness between them that everyone noticed.

Jodie's blond hair was long and wavy. She was wearing a red dress with a long, ruffled hem, an elasticized neckline that was pushed off the shoulders, leaving her creamy skin visible. She was wearing high heels and more makeup than she usually put on. And she was breathtaking. He just shook his head, his eyes eating her as she came down the staircase, holding on to the banister.

"You could be dessert," he murmured when she reached him.

"So could you," she replied, adoring him with her eyes. "But you aren't even wearing a costume."

"I am so," he argued with a wry smile. "I'm disguised as a government agent."

"Alexander!" she wailed.

He chuckled and caught her fingers in his. "I look better than Derek does. He's coming as a rodeo cowboy, complete with banged-up chaps, worn-out boots, and a championship belt buckle the size of my foot."

"He'll look authentic," she replied.

He smiled. "So do I. Don't I?"

She sighed, loving the way he looked. "I suppose you do, at that. There's going to be a big crowd, Margie says."

He tilted her chin up to his eyes. "There won't be anyone here except the two of us, Jodie," he said quietly.

The way he was looking at her, she could almost believe it.

"I think Margie feels that way with Derek," she murmured absently. "Too bad his brothers wouldn't stay."

"They aren't the partying type," he said. "Neither are we, really."

She nodded. Her eyes searched his and she felt giddy all over at the shift in their relationship. It was as if all the arguments of years past were blown away like sand. She felt new, young, on top of the world. And if his expression was anything to go by, he felt the same way.

He traced her face with his eyes. "How do you feel about short engagements?" he asked out of the blue.

She was sure that it was a rhetorical question. "I suppose it depends on the people involved. If they knew each other well…"

"I've known you longer than any other woman in my life except my sister," he interrupted. His face tightened as he stared down at her with narrow, hungry eyes. "I want to marry you, Jodie."

She opened her mouth to speak and couldn't even manage words. The shock robbed her of speech.

He grimaced. "I thought it might come as a shock. You don't have to answer me this minute," he said easily, taking her hand. "You think about it for a while. Let's go mingle with the guests as they come in and spend the night dancing. Then I'll ask you again."

She went along with him unprotesting, but she was certain she was hearing things. Alexander wasn't a marrying man. He must be temporarily out of his mind with worry over his unsolved case. But he didn't look like the product of a deranged mind, and the way he held Jodie's hand tight in his, and the way he watched her, were convincing.

Not only that, but he had eyes for her alone. Kirry didn't come, but there were plenty of other attractive women at the party. None of them attracted so much as a glance from Alexander. He danced only with Jodie, and held her so closely that people who knew both of them started to speculate openly on their changed relationship.

"People are watching us," Jodie murmured as they finished one dance only to start right into another one.

"Let them watch," he said huskily. His eyes fell to her soft mouth. "I'm glad you work in Houston, Jodie. I won't have to find excuses to commute to Jacobsville to see you."

"You never liked me before," she murmured out loud.

"I never got this close to you before," he countered. "I've lived my whole life trying to forget the way my mother was, Jodie," he confessed. "She gave me emotional scars that I still carry. I kept women at a safe distance. I actually thought I had you at a safe distance, too," he added on a chuckle. "And then I started taking you around for business reasons and got caught in my own web."

"Did you, really?" she murmured with wonder.

"Careful," he whispered. "I'm dead serious." He bent and brushed his mouth beside hers, nuzzling her cheek with his nose. "It's too late to go back, Jodie. I can't let go."

His arm contracted. She gasped softly at the increased intimacy of the contact. She could feel the hunger in him. Her own body began to vibrate faintly as she realized how susceptible she was.

"You be careful," she countered breathlessly. "I'm on fire! You could find yourself on the floor in a closet, being ravished, if you keep this up."

"If that's a promise, lead me to a closet," he said, only half joking.

She laughed. He didn't.

In fact, his arm contracted even more and he groaned softly at her ear. "Jodie," he said in a choked tone, "how do you feel about runaway marriages?"

"Excuse me?"

He lifted his head and looked down into her eyes with dark intensity. "Runaway marriage. You get in a car, run away to Mexico in the middle of somebody's Halloween party and get married." His arm brought her closer. "They're binding even in this country. We could get to the airport in about six minutes, and onto a plane in less than an hour."

"To where?" she burst out, aghast.

"Anywhere in Mexico," he groaned, his eyes biting into hers as he lifted his head. "We can be married again in Jacobsville whenever you like."

"Then why go to Mexico tonight?" she asked, flustered.

His hand slid low on her spine and pulled her hips into his with a look that made her blush.

"That is not a good reason to go to Mexico on the spur of the moment," she said, while her body told her brain to shut up.

"That's what you think." His expression was eloquent.

"But what if I said yes?" she burst out. "You could end up tied to me for life, when all you want is immediate relief! And speaking of relief, there's a bedroom right up the stairs…!"

He stopped dancing. His face was solemn. "Tell me you wouldn't mind a quick fling in my bed, Jodie," he challenged. "Tell me your conscience wouldn't bother you at all."

She sighed. "I'd like to," she began.

"But your parents didn't raise you that way," he concluded for her. "In fact, my father was like that," he added quietly. "He was old-fashioned and I'm like him. There haven't even been that many women, if you'd like to know, Jodie," he confessed. "And right now, I wish there hadn't been even one."

"That is the sweetest thing to say," she whispered, and pulled his face down so that she could kiss him.

"As it happens, I mean it." He kissed her back, very lightly. "Run away with me," he challenged. "Right now!"

It was crazy. He had to be out of his mind. But the temptation to get him to a minister before he changed his mind was all-consuming. She was suddenly caught up in the same excitement she saw in his face. "But you're so conventional!"

"I'll be very conventional again first thing tomorrow," he promised. "Tonight, I'm going for broke. Grab a coat. Don't tell anybody where we're going. I'll think up something to say to Margie."

She glanced toward the back of the room, where Margie was watching them excitedly and whispering something to Derek that made him laugh.

"All right. We're both crazy, but I'm not arguing with you. Tell her whatever you like. Make it good," she told him, and dashed up the staircase.

HE WAS WAITING for her at the front door. He looked irritated.

"What's wrong?" Jodie asked when she reached him. Her heart plummeted. "Changed your mind?"

"Not on your life!" He caught her arm and pulled her out the door, closing it quickly behind them. "Margie's too smart for her own good. Or Derek is."

"You can't put anything past Margie," she said, laughing with relief as they ran down the steps and toward the garage, where he kept his Jaguar.

"Or Derek," he murmured, chuckling.

He unlocked the door with his keyless entry and popped out the laser key with his thumb on the button. He looked down at her hesitantly. "I'm game if you are," he told her. "But you can still back out if you want to."

She shook her head, her eyes full of dreams. "You might never be in the mood again."

"That's a laugh." He put her inside and minutes later, they were en route to the airport.

Holding hands all the way during the flight, making plans, they arrived in El Paso with bated breath. Alexander rented a car at the airport and they drove across the border, stopping at customs and looking so radiant that the guard guessed their purpose immediately.

"You're going over to get married, I'd bet," the man said with a huge grin. *"Buena suerte,"* he added, handing back their identification. "And drive carefully!"

"You bet!" Alexander told him as he drove off.

THEY FOUND A small chapel and a minister willing to perform the ceremony after a short conversation with a police officer near a traffic light.

Jodie borrowed a peso from the minister's wife for luck and was handed a small bouquet of silk flowers to hold while the words were spoken, in Spanish, that would make them man and wife.

Alexander translated for her, his eyes soft and warm and possessive as the minister pronounced them man and wife at last. He drew a ring out of his pocket, a beautiful embossed gold band, which he slid onto her finger. It was a perfect fit. She recognized it as one she'd sighed over years ago in a jewelry shop she'd gone to with Margie when they were dreaming about marriage in the distant future. She'd been back to the shop over the years to make sure it was still there. Apparently Margie had told Alexander about it.

They signed the necessary documents, Alexander paid the minister, and they got back into the car with a marriage license.

Jodie stared at her ring and her new husband with wide-eyed wonder. "We must be crazy," she commented.

He laughed. "We're not crazy. We're very sensible. First we have an elopement, then we have a honeymoon, then we have a normal wedding with Margie and our friends." He glanced at her with twinkling eyes. "You said you didn't have to be back at work until next week. We'll have our honeymoon before you go back."

"Where, exactly, did you have in mind for a honeymoon?" she asked.

THREE HOURS LATER, tangled with Alexander in a big king-size bed with waves pounding the shore outside the window, she lay in the shadows of the moonlit Gulf of Mexico. The hotel was first class, the food was supposed to be the best in Galveston, the beach was like sugar sand. But all she saw was Alexander's face above hers as her body throbbed in the molasses slow rhythm of his kisses on her breasts on cool, crisp sheets.

"You taste like candy," he whispered against her belly.

"You never said I was sweet before," she teased breathlessly.

"You always were. I didn't know how to say it. You gave me the shakes every time I got near you." His mouth opened on her diaphragm and pressed down, hard.

She gasped at the warm pleasure of it. Her hands tangled in his thick, dark hair. "That was mutual, too." She drew his face to her breasts and coaxed his mouth onto them. "This is very nice," she murmured unsteadily.

"It gets better." His hands found her in a new and invasive way. She started to protest, only to find his mouth crushing down over her parted lips about the same time that his movements lifted her completely off the bed in a throbbing wave of unexpected pleasure.

"Oh, you like that, do you?" he murmured against her mouth. "How about this...?"

She cried out. His lips stifled the sound and his leg moved between both of hers. He kissed her passionately while his lean hips shifted and she felt him in an intimacy they hadn't yet shared.

He felt her body jerk as she tried to reject the shock of invasion, but his mouth gentled hers, his hands soothed her, teased her, coaxed her into allowing the slow merging of their bodies.

She gasped, her hands biting into his back in mingled fear and excitement.

"It won't hurt long," he whispered reassuringly, and his tongue probed her lips as he began a slow, steady rhythm that rippled down her nerves like pure joy on a roller coaster of pleasure.

"That's it," he murmured against her eager lips. "Come up against me and find the pressure and the rhythm that you need. That's it. That's...it!"

She was amazed that he didn't mind letting her experiment, that he was willing to help her experience him. She'd heard some horror stories about wedding nights from former friends. This wasn't one. She'd found a man who wanted eager participation, not passive acceptance.

She moved and shifted and he laughed roughly, his deep voice throbbing with pleasure, as her seeking body kindled waves of delight in his own.

She was on fire with power. She moved under him, invited him, challenged him, provoked him. And he went with her, every step of the way up the ladder to a mutual climax that groaned out at her ear in ripples of satiation. She clung to him, shivering in the explosive aftermath of an experience that exceeded her wildest hopes.

"And now you know," he whispered, kissing her eyelids closed.

"Now I know." She nose-dived into his damp throat and clung while they slowly settled back to earth again.

"I love you, baby," he whispered tenderly.

Joy flooded through her. "I love you, too!" she whispered breathlessly.

He curled her into his body with a long yawn and with the ocean purring like a wet kitten outside the windows, they drifted off into a warm, soft sleep.

"Hey."

She heard his voice at her ear. Then there was an aroma, a delicious smell of fresh coffee, rich and dark and delicious.

Her eyes didn't even open, but her head followed the retreat of the coffee.

"I thought that would do it. Breakfast," Alexander coaxed. "We've got your favorite, pecan waffles with bacon."

Her eyes opened. "You remembered!"

He grinned at her. "I know what you like." His lips pursed. "Especially after last night."

She laughed, dragging herself out of bed in the slip

she'd worn to bed, because it was still too soon to sleep in nothing at all. She was shy with him.

He was completely dressed, right down to his shoes. He gave her an appreciative sweep of his green eyes that took in her bare feet and her disheveled hair.

"You look wonderful like that," he said. "I always knew you would."

"When was that, exactly?" she chided, taking a seat at the table facing the window. "Before or after you accused me of being a layabout?"

"Ouch!" he groaned.

"It's okay. I forgive you," she said with a wicked glance. "I could never hold a grudge against a man who was that good in bed."

"And just think, I was very subdued last night, in deference to your first time."

She gasped. "Well!"

His eyebrows arched. "Think of the possibilities. If you aren't too delicate after last night, we could explore some of them later."

"Later?"

"I had in mind taking you around town and showing you off," he said, flipping open a napkin. "They have all sorts of interesting things to see here."

She sipped coffee, trying to ignore her body, which was making emphatic statements about what *it* wanted to do with the day.

He was watching her with covert, wise eyes. "On the other hand," he murmured as he nibbled a pancake, "if you were feeling lazy, we could just lie around in the bed and listen to the ocean, while we…"

Her hand poised over the waffle. "While we…?"

He began to smile. She laughed. The intimacy was

new and secret, and exciting. She rushed through the waffle and part of the bacon, and then pushed herself away from the table and literally threw herself into his arms across the chair. He prided himself on his control, because they actually almost made it to the bed...

TWO DAYS LATER, worn-out, and not because of any sight-seeing trip, they dragged themselves into the ranch house with a bag full of peace offerings for Margie which included seashells, baskets, a pretty ruffled sundress and some taffy.

Margie gave them a long, amused look. "There is going to have to be a wedding here," she informed them. "It won't do to run off to Mexico and get married, you have to do it in Jacobsville before anybody will believe you're really man and wife."

"I don't mind," Alexander said complacently, "but I'm not making the arrangements."

"Jodie and I can do that."

"But I have to go back to work," she told Margie, and went forward to hand her the bag and hug her. "And I haven't even told you about my new job!"

"What about your new husband?" Alexander groaned. "Are you going to desert me?"

She gave him a wicked glance. "Don't you have to talk to somebody about ranch business? Margie doesn't even know that I'm changing jobs!"

He sighed. "That's all husbands are good for," he murmured to himself. "You marry a woman, and she runs off and leaves you to gossip with a girlfriend."

"My sister-in-law, if you please," Jodie corrected him with a grin. "I'll cook you a nice apple pie for later, Alexander," she promised.

"Okay, I do take bribes," he had to confess. He grinned at her. "But now that we're married, couldn't you find something else to call me? Something a little less formal?"

She thought about it for a minute. "Darling," she said.

He looked at her with an odd expression, smiled as if he couldn't help himself, and made a noise like a tiger. He went out the back door while they were still laughing.

JODIE MOVED INTO her new job with a little apprehension, because of what she'd said to Brody Vance, but he was as genial as if no cross words had ever been spoken between them. Cara Dominguez still hadn't been heard from or seen, neither had her accomplice. There was still a shipment of drugs missing, that had to be in the warehouse somewhere, but guards and stepped-up surveillance assured that the drug dealers couldn't get near the warehouse to search for it.

One of Cara's rivals in the business was arrested in a guns-for-drugs deal in Houston that made national and international headlines. Alexander told Jodie about it just before the wire services broke the story, and assured her that Cara's organization was going to be next on the list of objectives for his department.

Meanwhile, Jodie learned the ropes of computer security and went back to school to finish her certification, with Alexander's blessing. Margie came up to see her while she was arranging a showing of her new designs with a local modeling agency and a department store that Kirry didn't work for.

Alexander kept shorter hours and did more delegating of chores, so that he could be at home when Jodie was. They bought a small house on the outskirts of Houston. Margie arranged to help Jodie with the decorating scheme. She was still amazed at the change in her best friend, who was now independent, strong-willed, hardworking and nobody's doormat.

There was still the retro coffeehouse, of course, and one night Jodie had a phone call from the owner, Johnny. She listened, exploded with delight, and ran to tell Alexander the news.

"The publisher wants to buy my poems!" she exclaimed. "He wants to include them in an anthology of Texas poetry! Isn't it exciting?"

"It's exciting," he agreed, bending to kiss her warmly. "Now tell the truth. They're about me, aren't they?"

She sighed. "Yes, they're about you. But I'm afraid this will be the only volume of poetry I ever create."

"Really? Why?"

She nibbled his chin. "Because misery is what makes good poetry. And just between us two," she added as her fingers went to his shirt buttons, "I'm far too happy to write good poetry ever again."

He guided her fingers down his shirt, smiling secretively. "I have plans to keep you that way, too," he murmured deeply.

And he did.

* * * * *

J.B.

To Tara Gavin and Melissa Jeglinski, with love

CHAPTER ONE

IT HAD BEEN a grueling semester. Tellie Maddox had her history degree, but she was feeling betrayed. He hadn't shown up for her graduation exercises. Marge had, along with Dawn and Brandi, her two daughters. None of them were related to Tellie, who was orphaned many years ago, but they were as close to her as sisters. They'd cared enough to be here for her special day. J.B. hadn't. It was one more heartbreak in a whole series of them in Tellie's life that J.B. was responsible for.

She looked around her dorm room sadly, remembering how happy she'd been here for four years, sharing with Sandy Melton, a fellow history major. Sandy had already gone, off to England to continue her studies in medieval history. Tellie pushed back her short, wavy dark hair and sighed. Her pale green eyes searched for the last of her textbooks. She should take them to the campus bookstore, she supposed, and resell them. She was going to need every penny she could get to make it through the summer. When the fall semester began, in August, she was going to have to pay tuition again as she worked on her master's degree. She wanted to teach at college level. No chance of that, with just a bachelor's degree, unless she taught adult education as an adjunct member of staff.

Once she'd thought that one day J.B. might fall in love

with her and want to marry her. Those hopeless dreams grew dimmer every day.

J. B. Hammock was Marge's brother. He'd rescued Tellie from a boy in the foster home where she'd been staying since her mother's death. Her mother had been the estranged wife of J.B.'s top horse wrangler, who'd later moved out of state and vanished. Tellie had gone to a foster home, despite Marge's objections, because J.B. said that a widow with two children to raise didn't need the complication of a teenager.

All that had changed with the attempted assault by another foster child in care with the same family. J.B. heard about it from a policeman who was one of his best friends. He swore out a warrant himself and had Tellie give a statement about what had happened. The boy, only thirteen at the time, was arrested and subsequently sent to juvenile hall. Tellie had slugged the boy when he tried to remove her blouse and sat on him until the family heard her yelling. Even at such a young age, Tellie was fearless. It had helped that the boy was half her size and half-drunk.

J.B. had jerked Tellie right out of the foster home the night the boy was arrested. He'd taken her straight to Marge for sanctuary. Marge had loved her almost at once. Most people did love Tellie. She was honest and sweet and generous with her time, and she wasn't afraid of hard work. Even at the age of fourteen, she'd taken charge of the kitchen and Dawn and Brandi. The sisters were nine and ten at the time respectively. They'd loved having an older girl in the house. Marge's job as a Realtor kept her on the road at all sorts of odd hours. But she could depend on Tellie to keep the girls in school clothes and help with their homework. She was a born babysitter.

Tellie had doted on J.B. He was very rich, and very temperamental. He owned hundreds of acres of prime ranch land near Jacobsville, where he raised purebred Santa Gertrudis cattle and entertained the rich and famous at his hundred-year-old rancho. He had a fabulous French chef in residence, along with a housekeeper named Nell who could singe the feathers off a duck with her temper at ten paces. Nell ran the house, and J.B., to an extent. He knew famous politicians, and movie stars, and foreign royalty from his days as a rodeo champion. He had impeccable manners, a legacy from his Spanish grandmother, and wealth from his British grandfather, who had been a peer of the realm. J.B.'s roots were European, despite his very American cattle operation.

But he did intimidate people. Locally he was known more for chasing Ralph Barrows off his place on foot, wielding a replica fantasy sword from the Lord of the Rings movie trilogy. Barrows had gotten drunk and shot J.B.'s favorite German shepherd for growling at him and barking when he tried to sneak into the bunkhouse in the small hours of the morning during roundup. Drinking wasn't allowed on the ranch. And nobody hurt an animal there. J.B. couldn't get to the key to his gun cabinet fast enough, so he grabbed the sword from its wall display and struck out for the bunkhouse the minute his foreman told him what was going on. The dog recovered, although it limped badly. Barrows hadn't been seen since.

J.B. wasn't really a social animal, despite the grand parties he threw at the ranch. He kept to himself, except for the numerous gorgeous women he squired around in his private jet. He had a nasty temper and the arrogance of position and wealth. Tellie was closer to him than almost anyone, even Marge, because she'd taken charge

of him when she was fourteen and he went on a legend-
ary drunk after his father died. It was Tellie who'd made
Marge drive her to J.B.'s place when Nell called in a panic
and said that J.B. was wrecking the den and the computers. It was Tellie who'd set him down, calmed him and
made cinnamon coffee for him to help sober him up.

J.B. tolerated her interventions over the years. He was
like her property, her private male. Nobody dared to say
that, of course, not even Tellie. But she was possessive
of him and, as she grew older, she became jealous of the
women who passed through his life in such numbers. She
tried not to let it show. Invariably, though, it did.

When she was eighteen, one of his girlfriends had
made an unkind remark to Tellie, who'd flared back at
her that J.B. wouldn't keep *her* around for much longer
if she was going to be rude to his family! After the girl
left, J.B. had it out with Tellie, his green eyes flaming like
emeralds, his thick black hair almost standing up straight
on his head with bad temper. Tellie didn't own him, he
reminded her, and if she didn't stop trying to possess
him, she'd be out on her ear. She wasn't even part of his
family, he'd added cruelly. She had no right whatsoever
to make any claims on his life.

She'd shot back that his girlfriends were all alike—
long-legged, big-breasted, pretty girls with the brains of
bats! He'd looked at her small breasts and remarked that
she certainly wouldn't fit that description.

She'd slapped him. It was involuntary and she was immediately sorry. But before she could take it back, he'd
jerked her against his tall, lean body and kissed her in a
way that still made her knees weak four years later. But
her mouth had opened weakly under his, and the tiny

movement had kindled a shudder in the muscular body so close to hers.

He'd backed her up against the sofa and crushed her down on it, under the length of him. The kiss had grown hard, insistent, passionate. His big, lean hand had found her breast under her blouse, and she'd panicked. The sensations he caused made her push at him and fight to get free.

She jerked her mind back to the present. J.B. had torn himself away from her, in an even worse temper than before. His eyes had blazed down at her, as if she'd done something unforgivable. Furious, he'd told her to get out of his life and stay out. She was due to leave for college the same week, and he hadn't even said goodbye. He'd ignored her from that day onward.

Holidays had come and gone. Slowly tensions had lessened between them, but J.B. had made sure that they were never alone again. He'd given her presents for her birthday and Christmas, but they were always impersonal ones, like computer hardware or software, or biography and history books that he knew she liked. She'd given him ties. In fact, she'd given him the same exact tie for every birthday and every Christmas present. She'd found a closeout special and bought two boxes of identical ties. She was set for life, she reasoned, for presents for J.B. Marge had remarked on the odd and monotonous present, but J.B. himself said nothing at all. Well, he said thank-you every time he opened a present from Tellie, but he said nothing more. Presumably he'd given the ties away. He never wore one. Tellie hadn't expected that he would. They were incredibly ugly. Yellow, with a putrid green dragon with red eyes. She still had enough left for ten more years…

"Are you ready, Tellie?" Marge called from the door.

She was like her brother, tall and dark-haired, but her eyes were brown where J.B.'s were green. Marge had a sweet nature, and she wasn't violent. She had a live-wire personality. Everybody loved her. She was long widowed and had never looked at another man. Love, she often told Tellie, for some people was undying, even if one lost the partner. She would never find anyone else as wonderful as her late husband. She had no interest in trying.

"I just have a couple more blouses to pack," Tellie said with a smile.

Dawn and Brandi wandered around her dorm room curiously.

"You'll do this one day, yourselves," Tellie assured them.

"Not me," Dawn, the youngest, at sixteen, replied with a grin. "I'm going to be a cattle baron like Uncle J.B. when I get through agricultural college."

"I'm going to be an attorney," Brandi, who would be a senior in the fall at seventeen, said with a smile. "I want to help poor people."

"She can already bargain me into anything," Marge said with an amused wink at Tellie.

"Me, too," Tellie had to admit. "She's still got my favorite jacket, and I never even got to wear it once."

"It looks much better on me," Brandi assured her. "Red just isn't your color."

A lot she knew, Tellie thought, because every time she thought about J.B., she saw red.

Marge watched Tellie pack her suitcase with a somber expression. "He really did have an emergency at the ranch," she told Tellie gently. "The big barn caught fire.

They had fire departments from all over Jacobs County out there putting it out."

"I'm sure he would have come, if he'd been able," Tellie replied politely. She didn't believe it. J.B. hadn't shown any interest in her at all in recent years. He'd avoided her whenever possible. Perhaps the ties had driven him nuts and he'd torched the barn himself, thinking of it as a giant yellow dragon tie. The thought amused her, and she laughed.

"What are you laughing about?" Marge teased.

"I was thinking maybe J.B.'s gone off his rocker and started seeing yellow dragon ties everywhere…"

Marge chuckled. "It wouldn't surprise me. Those ties are just awful, Tellie, really!"

"I think they suit him," Tellie said with irrepressible humor. "I'm sure that he's going to wear one eventually."

Marge started to speak and apparently thought better of it. "Well, I wouldn't hold my breath waiting," she said instead.

"Who's the flavor of the month?" Tellie wondered aloud.

Marge lifted an eyebrow. She knew what Tellie meant, all too well. She despaired of her brother ever getting serious about a woman again. "He's dating one of the Kingstons' cousins, from Fort Worth. She was a runner-up for Miss Texas."

Tellie wasn't surprised. J.B. had a passion for beautiful blondes. Over the years, he'd escorted his share of movie starlets. Tellie, with her ordinary face and figure, was hardly on a par to compete with such beauties.

"They're just display models," Marge whispered wickedly, so that her daughters didn't hear her.

Tellie burst out laughing. "Oh, Marge, what would I do without you?"

Marge shrugged. "It's us against the men of the world," she pointed out. "Even my brother qualifies as the enemy from time to time." She paused. "Don't they give you a recording of the graduation exercises?"

"Yes, along with my diploma," Tellie agreed. "Why?"

"I say we get the boys to rope J.B. to his easy chair in the den and make him watch the recording for twenty-four straight hours," she suggested. "Revenge is sweet!"

"He'd just go to sleep during the commencement speech," Tellie sighed. "And I wouldn't blame him. I almost did myself."

"Shame on you! The speaker was a famous politician!"

"Famously boring," Brandi remarked with a wicked grin.

"Notice how furiously everybody applauded when he stopped speaking," Dawn agreed.

"You two have been hanging out with me for too long," Tellie observed. "You're picking up all my bad habits."

They both hugged her. "We love you, bad habits and all," they said. "Congratulations on your degree!"

"You did very well indeed," Marge echoed. "Magna cum laude, no less! I'm proud of you."

"Honor graduates don't have social lives, Mother," Brandi pointed out. "No wonder she made such good grades. She spent every weekend in the dorm, studying!"

"Not every weekend," Tellie muttered. "There was that archaeology field trip…"

"With the geek squad." Dawn yawned.

"They weren't all geeks," she reminded them. "Anyway, I like digging up old things."

"Then you should have gotten your degree in archaeology instead of history," Brandi said.

She chuckled. "I'll be digging up old documents instead of old relics," she said. "It will be a cleaner job, at least."

"When do you start your master's degree work?" Marge asked.

"Fall semester," she replied, smiling. "I thought I'd take the summer off and spend a little time with you guys. I've already lined up a job working for the Ballenger brothers at their feedlot while Calhoun and Abby take a cruise to Greece with the boys. I guess all those summers following J.B. and his veterinarian around the ranch finally paid off. At least I know enough about feeding out cattle to handle the paperwork!"

"Lucky Calhoun and Abby. Wow," Dawn said on a sigh. "I'd love to get a three-month vacation!"

"Wouldn't we all," Tellie agreed wistfully. "In my case, a job is a vacation from all the studying! Biology was so hard!"

"We don't get to dissect things anymore at our school," Brandi said. "Everybody's afraid of blood these days."

"With good reason, I'm sorry to say," Marge mused.

"We don't get to do dissections, either," Tellie told her with a smile. "We had a rat on a dissecting board and we all got to use it for identification purposes. It was so nice that we had an air-conditioned lab!"

The girls made faces.

"Speaking of labs," Marge interrupted, "who wants a nice hamburger?"

"Nobody dissects cows, Mom," Brandi informed her.

"We can dissect the hamburger," Tellie suggested, "and identify the part of the cow it came from."

"It came from a steer, not a cow," Marge said wryly. "You could use a refresher course in Ranching 101, Tellie."

They all knew who'd be teaching it at home, and that was a sore spot. Tellie's smile faded. "I expect I'll get all the information I need working from Justin at the feedlot."

"They've got some handsome new cowboys working for them," Marge said with sparkling eyes. "One's an ex–Green Beret who grew up on a ranch in West Texas."

Tellie shrugged one shoulder. "I'm not sure I want to meet any men. I've still got three years of study to get my master's degree so that I can start teaching history in college."

"You can teach now, can't you?" Dawn asked.

"I can teach adult education," Tellie replied. "But I have to have at least a master's degree to teach at the college level, and a PhD is preferred."

"Why don't you want to teach little kids?" Brandi asked curiously.

Tellie grinned. "Because you two hooligans destroyed all my illusions about sweet little kids," she replied, and ducked when Brandi threw a pillow at her.

"We were such sweet little kids," Dawn said belligerently. "You better say we were, or else, Tellie!"

"Or else what?" she replied.

Dawn wiggled her eyebrows. "Or else I'll burn the potatoes. It's my night to cook supper at home."

"Don't pay any attention to her, dear," Marge said. "She always burns the potatoes."

"Oh, Mom!" the teenager wailed.

Tellie just laughed. But her heart wasn't in the word-play. She was miserable because J.B. had missed her graduation, and nothing was going to make up for that.

MARGE'S HOUSE WAS on the outskirts of Jacobsville, about six miles from the big ranch that had been in her and J.B.'s family for three generations. It was a friendly little house with a bay window out front and a small front porch with a white swing. All around it were the flowers that Marge planted obsessively. It was May, and everything was blooming. Every color in the rainbow graced the small yard, including a small rose garden with an arch that was Marge's pride and joy. These were antique roses, not hybrids, and they had scents that were like perfume.

"I'd forgotten all over again how beautiful it was," Tellie said on a sigh.

"Howard loved it, too," Marge said, her dark eyes soft with memories for an instant as she looked around the lush, clipped lawn that led to the stepping stone walkway that led to the front porch.

"I never met him," Tellie said. "But he must have been a lovely person."

"He was," Marge agreed, her eyes sad as she recalled her husband.

"Look, it's Uncle J.B.!" Dawn cried, pointing to the narrow paved road that led up to the dirt driveway of Marge's house.

Tellie felt every muscle in her body contract. She turned around as the sporty red Jaguar slid to a halt, throwing up clouds of yellow dust. The door opened and J.B. climbed out.

He was tall and lean, with jet-black hair and dark green eyes. His cheekbones were high, his mouth thin. He had big ears and big feet. But he was so masculine that women were drawn to him like magnets. He had a sensuality in his walk that made Tellie's heart skip.

"Where the hell have you been?" he growled as he joined them. "I looked everywhere for you until I finally gave up and drove back home!"

"What do you mean, where were we?" Marge exclaimed. "We were at Tellie's graduation. Not that you could be bothered to show up…!"

"I was across the stadium from you," J.B. said harshly. "I didn't see you until it was over. By the time I got through the crowd and out of the parking lot, you'd left the dorm and headed down here."

"You came to my graduation?" Tellie asked, in a husky, soft tone.

He turned, glaring at her. His eyes were large, framed by thick black lashes, deep set and biting. "We had a fire at the barn. I was late. Do you think I'd miss something so important as your college graduation?" he added angrily, although his eyes evaded hers.

Her heart lifted, against her will. He didn't want her. She was like a second sister to him. But any contact with him made her tingle with delight. She couldn't help the radiance that lit up her plain face and made it pretty.

He glanced around him irritably and caught Tellie's hand, sending a thrill all the way to her heart. "Come here," he said, drawing her to the car with him.

He put her in the passenger side, closed the door and went around to get in beside her. He reached into the console between the bucket seats and pulled out a gold-wrapped box. He handed it to her.

She took it, her eyes surprised. "For me?"

"For no one else," he drawled, smiling faintly. "Go on. Look."

She tore open the wrapping. It was a jeweler's box, but far too big to be a ring. She opened the box and stared at it blankly.

He frowned. "What's the matter? Don't you like it?"

"It" was a Mickey Mouse watch with a big face and a gaudy red band. She knew what it meant, too. It meant that his secretary, Miss Jarrett, who hated being delegated to buy presents for him, had finally lost her cool. She thought J.B. was buying jewelry for one of his women, and Miss Jarrett was showing him that he'd better get his own gifts from now on.

It hurt Tellie, who knew that J.B. shopped for Marge and the girls himself. He never delegated that chore to underlings. But, then, Tellie wasn't family.

"It's...very nice," she stammered, aware that the silence had gone on a little too long for politeness.

She took the watch out of the box and he saw it for the first time.

Blistering range language burst from his chiseled lips before he could stop himself. Then his high cheekbones went dusky because he couldn't very well admit to Tellie that he hadn't bothered to go himself to get her a present. He'd kill Jarrett, though, he promised himself.

"It's the latest thing," he said with deliberate nonchalance.

"I love it. Really." She put it on her wrist. She did love it, because he'd given it to her. She'd have loved a dead rat in a box if it had come from J.B., because she had no pride.

He pursed his lips, the humor of the situation finally getting through to him. His green eyes twinkled. "You'll be the only graduate on your block to wear one," he pointed out.

She laughed. It changed her face, made her radiant. "Thanks, J.B.," she said.

He tugged her as close as the console would allow, and his eyes shifted to her soft, parted lips. "You can do better than that," he murmured wickedly, and bent.

She lifted her face, closed her eyes, savored the warm, tender pressure of his hard mouth on her soft one.

He stiffened. "No, you don't," he whispered roughly when she kept her lips firmly closed. He caught her cheek in one big, lean hand and pressed, gently, just enough to open her mouth. He bent and caught it, hard, pressing her head back against the padded seat with the force of it.

Tellie went under in a daze, loving the warm, hard insistence of his mouth in the silence of the little car. She sighed and a husky little moan escaped her taut throat.

He lifted his head. Dark green eyes probed her own, narrow and hot and full of frustrated desire.

"And here we are again," he said roughly.

She swallowed. "J.B.…."

He put his thumb against her soft lips to stop the words. "I told you, there's no future in this, Tellie," he said, his voice hard and cold. "I don't want any woman on a permanent basis. Ever. I'm a bachelor, and I mean to stay that way. Understand?"

"But I didn't say anything," she protested.

"The hell you didn't," he bit off. He put her back in her seat and opened his car door.

She went with him back to Marge and the girls, showing off her new watch. "Look, isn't it neat?" she asked.

"I want one, too!" Brandi exclaimed.

"You don't graduate until next year, darling," Marge reminded her daughter.

"Well, I want one then," she repeated stubbornly.

"I'll keep that in mind," J.B. promised. He smiled, but it wasn't in his eyes. "Congratulations again, tidbit," he told Tellie. "I've got to go. I have a hot date tonight."

He was looking straight at Tellie as he said it. She only smiled.

"Thanks for the watch," she told him.

He shrugged. "It does suit you," he remarked enigmatically. "See you, girls."

He got into the sports car and roared away.

"I'd really love one of those," Brandi remarked on a sigh as she watched it leave.

Marge lifted Tellie's wrist and glared at the watch. "That was just mean," she said under her breath.

Tellie smiled sadly. "He sent Jarrett after it. He always has her buy presents for everybody except you and the girls. She obviously thought it was for one of his platinum blondes, and she got this out of spite."

"Yes, I figured that out all by myself," Marge replied, glowering. "But it's you who got hurt, not J.B."

"It's Jarrett who'll get hurt when he goes back to work," Tellie said on a sigh. "Poor old lady."

"She'll have him for breakfast," Marge said. "And she should."

"He does like sharp older women, doesn't he?" Tellie remarked on the way into the house. "He's got Nell at the house, taking care of things there, and she could scorch leather in a temper."

"Nell's a fixture," Marge said, smiling. "I don't know what J.B. and I would have done without her when we were kids. There was just Dad and us. Mom died when we were very young. Dad was never affectionate."

"Is that why J.B.'s such a rounder?" Tellie wondered. As usual, Marge clammed up. "We don't ever talk about that," she said. "It isn't a pretty story, and J.B. hates even the memory."

"Nobody ever told me," Tellie persisted.

Marge gave her a gentle smile. "Nobody ever will, pet, unless it's J.B. himself."

"I know when that will be." Tellie sighed. "When they're wearing overcoats in hell."

"Exactly," Marge agreed warmly.

That night, they were watching a movie on television when the phone rang. Marge answered it. She came back in a few minutes, wincing.

"It's Jarrett," she told Tellie. "She wants to talk to you."

"How bad was it?" Tellie asked.

Marge made a face.

Tellie picked up the phone. "Hello?"

"Tellie? It's Nan Jarrett. I just want to apologize…"

"It's not your fault, Miss Jarrett," Tellie said at once. "It really is a cute watch. I love it."

"But it was your college graduation present," the older woman wailed. "I thought it was for one of those idiot blonde floozies he carts around, and it made me mad that he didn't even care enough about them to buy a present himself." She realized what she'd just said and cleared her throat. "Not that I think he didn't care enough about *you*, of course…!"

"Obviously he doesn't," Tellie said through her teeth.

"Well, you wouldn't be so sure of that if you'd been here when he got back into the office just before quitting time," came the terse reply. "I have never heard such language in my life, even from him!"

"He was just mad that he got caught," Tellie said.

"He said it was one of the most special days of your life and I screwed it up," Miss Jarrett said miserably.

"He'd already done that by not showing up for my graduation," Tellie said, about to mention that none of them had seen him in the stands and thought he hadn't shown up.

"Oh, you know about that?" came the unexpected reply. "He told us all to remember he'd been fighting a fire in case it came up. He had a meeting with an out-of-town cattle buyer and his daughter. He forgot all about the commencement exercises."

Tellie's heart broke in two. "Yes," she said, fighting tears, "well, nobody's going to say anything. None of us, certainly."

"Certainly. He gets away with murder."

"I wish I could," Tellie said under her breath. "Thanks for calling, Miss Jarrett. It was nice of you."

"I just wanted you to know how bad I felt," the older woman said with genuine regret. "I wouldn't have hurt your feelings for the world."

"I know that."

"Well, happy graduation, anyway."

"Thanks."

Tellie hung up. She went back into the living room smiling. She was never going to tell them the truth about her graduation. But she knew that she'd never forget.

CHAPTER TWO

TELLIE HAD LEARNED to hide her deepest feelings over the years, so Marge and the girls didn't notice any change in her. There was one. She was tired of waiting for J.B. to wake up and notice that she was around. She'd finally realized that she meant nothing to him. Well, maybe she was a sort of adopted relative for whom he had an occasional fondness. But his recent behavior had finally drowned her fondest hopes of anything serious. She was going to convince her stupid heart to stop aching for him, if it killed her.

Five days later, on a Monday, she walked into Calhoun and Justin Ballenger's office at their feedlot, ready for work.

Justin, Calhoun's elder brother, gave her a warm welcome. He was tall, whipcord lean, with gray-sprinkled black hair and dark eyes. He and his wife, Shelby—who was a direct descendant of the founder of Jacobsville, old John Jacobs—had three sons. They'd been married for a long time, like Calhoun and Abby. J. D. Langley's wife, Fay, had been working for the Ballengers as Calhoun's secretary, but a rough pregnancy had forced her to give it up temporarily. That was why Tellie was in such demand.

"You'll manage," Justin's secretary, Ellie, assured her with a smile. "We're not so rushed now as we are in the early spring and autumn. It's just nice and routine. I'll introduce you to the men later on. For now, let me show you what you'll be doing."

"Sorry you have to give up your own vacation for this," Justin said apologetically.

"Listen, I can't afford a vacation yet," she assured him with a grin. "I'm a lowly college student. I have to pay my tuition for three more years. I'm the one who's grateful for the job."

Justin shrugged. "You know as much about cattle as Abby and Shelby do," he said, which was high praise, since both were actively involved in the feedlot operation and the local cattlemen's association. "You're welcome here."

"Thanks," she said, and meant it.

"Thank you," he replied, and left them to it.

THE WORK WASN'T that difficult. Most of it dealt with spreadsheets, various programs that kept a daily tally on the number of cattle from each client and the feeding regimen they followed. It was involved and required a lot of concentration, and the phones seemed to ring constantly. It wasn't all clients asking about cattle. Many of the calls were from prospective customers. Others were from buyers who had contracted to take possession of certain lots of cattle when they were fed out. There were also calls from various organizations to which the Ballenger brothers belonged, and even a few from state and federal legislators. A number of them came from overseas, where the brothers had investments. Tellie found it all fascinating.

It took her a few days to get into the routine of things, and to get to know the men who worked at the feedlot. She could identify them all by face, if not by name.

One of them was hard to miss. He was the ex–Green Beret, a big, tall man from El Paso named Grange. If he had a first name, Tellie didn't hear anyone use it. He had straight black hair and dark brown eyes, an olive complexion and a deep, sexy voice. He liked Tellie on sight and made no secret of it. It amused Justin, because Grange hadn't shown any interest in anything in the weeks he'd been working on the place. It was the first spark of life the man had displayed.

He told Tellie, who looked surprised.

"He seems like a friendly man," she stammered.

He lifted a dark eyebrow. "The first day he worked here, one of the boys short-sheeted his bed. He turned on the lights, looked around the room, dumped one of the other men out of a bunk bed and threw him head-first into the yard."

"Was it the right man?" Tellie asked, wide-eyed.

"It was. Nobody knew how he figured it out, and he never said. But the boys walk wide around him. Especially since he threw that big knife he carries at a sidewinder that crawled too close to the bunkhouse. Cag Hart has a reputation for that sort of accuracy with a Bowie, but he used to be the only one. Grange is a mystery."

She was intrigued. "What did he do, before he came here?"

"Nobody knows. Nobody asks, either," he added with a grin.

"Was he stationed overseas, in the army?"

"Nobody knows that, either. The 411 is that he was in the Green Berets, but he's never said he was. Puzzling guy. But he's a hard worker. And he's honest." He pursed his lips and his dark eyes twinkled. "And he never takes a drink. Ever."

She whistled. "Well!"

"Anyway, you'd better not agree to any dates with him until J.B. checks him out," Justin said. "I don't want J.B. on the wrong side of me." He grinned. "We feed out a lot of cattle for him," he added, making it clear that he wasn't afraid of J.B.

"J.B. doesn't tell me who I can date," she said, hurting as she remembered how little she meant to Marge's big brother.

"Just the same, I don't know anything about Grange, and I'm sort of responsible for you while you're here, even though you're legally an adult," Justin said quietly. "Get the picture?"

She grimaced. "I do. Okay, I'll make sure I don't let him bulldoze me into anything."

"That's the spirit," he said with a grin. "I'm not saying he's a bad man, mind you. I just don't know a lot about him. He's always on time, does his job and a bit more, and gets along fairly well with other people. But he mostly keeps to himself when he's not working. He's not a sociable sort."

"I feel somewhat that way, myself," she sighed.

"Join the club. Things going okay for you otherwise? The job's not too much?"

"The job's great," she said, smiling. "I'm really enjoying this."

"Good. We're glad to have you here. Anything you need, let me know."

"Sure thing. Thanks!"

SHE TOLD MARGE and the girls about Grange. They were amused.

"He obviously has good taste," Marge mused, "if he likes you."

Tellie chuckled as she rinsed dishes and put them in the dishwasher. "It's not mutual," she replied. "He's a little scary, in a way."

"What do you mean? Does he seem violent or something?" Brandi wanted to know.

Tellie paused with a dish in her hand and frowned. "I don't know. I'm not afraid of him, really. It's just that he has that sort of effect on people. Kind of like Cash Grier," she added.

"He's calmed down a bit since Tippy Moore came to stay with him after her kidnapping," Marge said. "Rumor is that he may marry her."

"She's really pretty, even with those cuts on her face," Dawn remarked from the kitchen table, where she was arranging cloth for a quilt she meant to make. "They say somebody real mean is after her, and that's why she's here. Mrs. Jewell stays at the house at night. A stickler for convention, is our police chief."

"Good for him," Marge said. "A few people need to be conventional, or society is going to fall."

Brandi looked at her sister and rolled her eyes. "Here we go again with the lecture."

"Uncle J.B. isn't conventional," Dawn reminded her mother. "He had that football team cheerleader staying at his house for almost a month. And his new girlfriend was a runner-up Miss Texas, and she spends weekends with him…"

Tellie's hands were shaking. Dawn grimaced and looked at her mother helplessly.

Dawn got up and hugged Tellie from behind. "I'm sorry, Tellie," she said with obvious remorse.

Tellie patted the hands around her waist. "Just because I'm a hopeless case, doesn't mean you have to walk on eggshells around me," she assured the younger woman. "We all know that J.B. isn't ever going to get married. And even if he did, it would be some beautiful, sophisticated—"

"You hush," Marge broke in. "You're pretty. Besides, it's what's inside that counts. Beauty doesn't last. Character does."

"Her stock phrase," Brandi said with a grin. "But she's right, Tellie. I think you're beautiful."

"Thanks, guys," Tellie murmured.

She went back to her task, and the conversation became general.

THE NEXT DAY Grange came right up to Tellie's desk and stood staring down at her, wordlessly, until she was forced to look up at him.

"They say that you live with J. B. Hammock's sister, Marge," he said.

She was totally confounded by the question. She stared at him blankly. "Excuse me?"

He shrugged, looking uncomfortable. "I didn't come to Jacobsville by accident," he said, glancing around as Justin came out of his office and gave him a faint glower. "Have lunch with me," he added. "It's not a pass. I just want to talk to you."

If it was a line, it was a good one. "Okay," she said.

"I'll pick you up at noon." He tipped his wide-brimmed hat, nodded toward Justin and went back out to the feedlot.

Justin went straight to Tellie. "Trouble?" he asked.

"Well, no," she said. "He wants to talk to me about Marge, apparently."

His eyebrows arched. "That's a new one."

"He was serious. He wants me to have lunch with him." She grinned. "He can't do much to me over a hamburger in town."

"Good point. Okay, but watch your step. Like I said," he added, "he's an unknown quantity."

"I'll do that," she promised.

BARBARA'S CAFÉ IN town was the local hot spot for lunch. Just about everybody ate there when they wanted something home cooked. There were other places, such as the Chinese and Mexican restaurants, and the pizza place. But Barbara's had a sort of Texas atmosphere that appealed even to tourists.

Today it was crowded. Grange got them a table and ordered steak and potatoes for himself, leaving Tellie to get what she wanted. They'd already agreed they were going Dutch. So he must have meant it, about it not being a date.

"My people were all dead, and Marge and J.B. took me in," Tellie said when they'd given their orders to the waitress. She didn't add why. "I've known the Hammocks since I was a child, but I was fourteen when I went to live with Marge and her girls. She was widowed by then."

"Are you and J.B. close?" he queried, placing his hat in an empty chair.

"No," she said flatly. She didn't elaborate. She started to get the feeling that it was not Marge he wanted information on.

His dark eyes narrowed as he studied her. "What do you know about his past?" he asked.

Her heart jumped. "You mean, generally?"

"I mean," he added with flaming eyes, "do you know anything about the woman he tried to marry when he was twenty-one?"

She felt suddenly cold, and didn't know why. "What woman?" she asked, her voice sounded hoarse and choked.

He looked around them to make sure they weren't being overheard. He lifted his coffee cup and held it in his big, lean hands. "His father threatened to cut him off without a cent if he went through with the wedding. He was determined to do it. He withdrew his savings from the bank—he was of legal age, so he could—and he picked her up at her house and they took off to Louisiana. He was going to marry her there. He thought nobody could find them. But his father did."

This was fascinating stuff. Nobody had said anything to her about it, certainly not J.B. "Did they get married?"

His face tautened. "His father waited until J.B. went out to see about the marriage license. He went in and talked to the woman. He told her that if she married J.B., he'd turn in her brother, who was fourteen and had gotten mixed up with a gang that dealt in distribution of crack cocaine. There had been a death involved in a drug deal gone bad. The boy hadn't participated, but he could be implicated as an accessory. J.B.'s father had a private detective document everything. He told the woman her brother would go to prison for twenty years."

She grimaced. "Did J.B. know?"

"I don't know," he said uncomfortably. "I came here to find out."

"But what did she do?"

"What could she do?" he asked curtly. "She loved her brother. He was the only family she had. She loved Hammock. She really loved him."

"But she loved her brother more?"

He nodded. His whole face clenched. "She didn't tell

Hammock what his father had done. She did tell her father."

"Did he do anything?"

"He couldn't. They were poor. There was nothing he
could do. Well, he did get her brother to leave the gang
when she killed herself. It was all that saved him from
prison."

She was hanging on his every word. "What about the
woman?"

"She was already clinically depressed," he said in an
odd monotone, toying with his fork, not looking at her.
He seemed to be far away, in time. "She knew that she
could never be with Hammock, that his father would
make sure of it. She couldn't see any future without him."
His fingers tightened on the fork. "She found the pistol
her brother had hidden in his room. She shot herself. She
died instantly."

The iced tea went all over the tablecloth. Tellie quickly
righted the glass and grabbed at napkins to mop up the
flow. Barbara, seeing the accident, came forward with
a tea cloth.

"There, there, we all spill things," she told Tellie with
a smile. "Right as rain," she added when she'd mopped
the oilcloth-covered table. "I'll bring you a new glass.
Unsweetened?"

Tellie nodded, still reeling from what Grange had told
her. "Yes. Thanks."

"No problem," Barbara said, smiling at them both as
she left.

"You really didn't know, did you?" Grange asked quietly. "I'm sorry. I don't want to hurt you. It's not your
fault."

She swallowed, hard. It all made sense. Why J.B. never

got serious about a woman. Why he refused to think of marriage. He'd had that death on his conscience all his life, when it wasn't even his fault, not really. It was his father's.

"His father must have been a horror," she said unsteadily.

Grange stared at her. "Have been?" he queried.

She nodded. "He died in a nursing home the year I moved in with Marge," she said. "He'd had a stroke and he never fully recovered from it. It left him in a vegetative state. J.B. paid to keep him in the facility."

"And the old man's wife?"

"She died long before I lived with Marge. I don't know how."

He looked odd. "I see."

"How do you know all this?" she wondered.

"Her brother is a friend of mine," he told her. "He was curious about the old man. I needed a job, and this one at the feedlot came available. I like Texas. It was close enough that I could find out about old man Hammock for him."

"Well, now you know," she said, trying not to let the trauma show in her face.

He frowned. His hard face went even harder. He stared down into his coffee cup. "I didn't realize it would have such an impact on you."

"J.B. is like an older brother to me," she told him, lying through her teeth. "But nobody ever told me why he plays the field like he does, why he won't consider ever getting married. I thought he just liked being a bachelor. I guess he blames himself for what happened, don't you think?" she added, surprising an odd look on Grange's face. "Even though it was his father who did the real dam-

age, J.B. surely realized that if he'd never gotten mixed
up with the poor woman, she'd still be alive."

He winced. "You don't pull your punches, do you?"

"It's the truth, isn't it?" she added thoughtfully.

"So he doesn't want to get married," he said after a
minute.

She nodded. "He has lots of girlfriends. The new one
was a runner-up in the Miss Texas pageant."

He didn't even seem to be listening. He finished his
steak and sat back to sip cold coffee.

Barbara came around with Tellie's new glass of tea and
the coffeepot. She warmed Grange's in his cup.

"Thanks," he said absently.

She grinned at him. "No problem. You're new here,
aren't you?"

"I am," he confessed. "I work for Justin and Calhoun,
at the feedlot."

"Lucky you," she said. "They're good people."

He nodded.

She glanced at Tellie. "How's Marge?"

There was something in the question that made Tellie
stare at her. "She's fine. Why?"

Barbara grimaced. "It's nothing, really."

"Tell me," Tellie persisted. It was her day for learning
things about people she thought she knew.

"Well, she had a dizzy spell the last time she ate lunch
here. She fell into one of the tables." She sighed. "I wondered if she ever had a checkup. Just to make sure. I never
knew Marge to have dizzy spells."

"Me, either," Tellie said, frowning. "But I'll find out,"
she promised.

"Don't tell her I told you," Barbara said firmly. "She
can light fires when she's mad, just like J.B."

"I'll ask her gently, I promise," Tellie said, smiling. "She won't get mad."

"If you do, you'll eat burned hamburgers forever," Barbara told her.

"That's just mean," she told the older woman, who grinned and went back to the kitchen.

"Well, it's your day for revelations, apparently," Grange observed.

"I don't think I know anybody anymore," she agreed.

"Listen, don't tell Hammock's sister about any of this," he said suddenly. "I'm not here to cause trouble. I just wanted to find out what became of the old man." His eyes darkened. "I suppose J.B. knew what his father did?"

"I have no way of knowing," she said uneasily.

He put cream into his hot coffee. He drew in a long breath. "I'm sorry if I shattered any illusions."

He had. He'd just put the final nail in the coffin of her dreams. But that wasn't his fault. Tellie always felt that people came into your life for a reason. She forced a smile. "I don't have illusions about J.B.," she told him. "I've seen all his bad character traits firsthand."

He searched her green eyes. "One of the boys said you're in college."

She nodded. "I start master's work in the fall."

"What's your subject?"

"History. My field is Native American studies. I hope to teach at the college level when I finally get my master's degree."

"Why not teach grammar school or middle or high school?" he wondered.

"Because little kids walk all over me," she said flatly. "Marge's girls had me on my ear the first six months I lived with them, because I couldn't say no. I'd make a lousy elementary school teacher."

He smiled faintly. "I'll bet the girls loved you."

She nodded, smiling back. "They're very special."

He finished his coffee. "We'll have to do this again sometime," he began, just as the café door opened and J.B. walked in.

J.B.'s eyes slithered over the patrons until he spotted Tellie. He walked to the table where Tellie and Grange were sitting and stared down at Grange with pure venom. His eyes were blistering hot.

"What are you doing here in Jacobsville?" he asked Grange.

The other man studied him coolly. "Working. Tellie and I are having lunch together."

"That doesn't answer the question," J.B. replied, and he'd never sounded more menacing.

Grange sipped coffee with maddening calm. "So the old man did finally tell you what happened, did he?" he asked with a sudden, piercing glance. "He told you what he said to my sister?"

J.B.'s big fists clenched at his side. He aged in seconds. "Not while he was alive. He left a letter with his will."

"At least you had time to get used to the idea, didn't you?" Grange asked icily. "I found out three weeks ago!" He forced his deep voice back into calmer channels and took a deep breath. "Care to guess how I felt when my father finally told *me*, on his deathbed?"

J.B. seemed to calm down himself. "You didn't know?" he asked.

"No," Grange said harshly. "No, I didn't know! If I had...!"

J.B. seemed suddenly aware of Tellie's rapt interest and he seemed to go pale under his tan. He saw her new knowledge of him in her paleness, in her suddenly averted face. He looked at Grange. "You told her, didn't you?" he demanded.

The other man stood up. He and J.B. were the same height, although Grange seemed huskier, more muscular. J.B. had a range rider's lean physique.

"Secrets are dangerous, Hammock," Grange said, and he didn't back down an inch. "There were things I wanted to know that I'd never have heard from you."

"Such as?" J.B. asked in a curt tone.

Grange looked at him openly, aware that other diners were watching them. His shoulders moved in a curious jerk. "I came here with another whole idea in mind, but your young friend here shot me in the foot. I didn't realize that you were as much a victim as I was. I thought you put your father up to it," he added tautly.

Tellie didn't know what he meant.

J.B. did. "Things would have ended differently if I'd known," he said in a harsh tone.

"If I'd known, too." Grange studied him. "Hell of a shame that we can't go back and do things right, isn't it?"

J.B. nodded.

"I like working at the feedlot, but it's only for a few months," he said. "If it helps, I'm no gossip. I only wanted the truth. Now I've got it." He turned to Tellie. "I shouldn't have involved you. But I enjoyed lunch," he added quietly, and he smiled. It changed his dark eyes, made them deep and hypnotic.

"Me, too," she said, flushing a little. He really was good-looking.

Grange shrugged. "Maybe we can do it again."

She did smile then. "I'd like that."

He nodded at J.B. and left them to go to the counter and pay for his meal. J.B. sat down in the chair Grange had vacated and looked at Tellie with mingled anger and concern.

"Don't worry, J.B., he didn't spill any state secrets," she lied as she sipped tea. "He only said your father had done something to foil a romance years ago, and he wanted to know how to get in touch with the elder Mr. Hammock. He said he wanted to know for a friend of his." She hoped he believed her. She'd die if he realized she knew the wholeterrible secret in his past. She felt sick to her stomach, imagining how he must feel.

He didn't answer her. He glanced at Grange as the younger man left the café, and then caught Barbara's eye and ordered coffee and apple pie.

Tellie was trying not to react at the surprise of having coffee with J.B., who'd never shared a table in a restaurant with her before. Her heart was beating double-time at just the nearness of him. She had to force herself not to stare at him with overt and visible delight.

Barbara brought coffee. He grinned at her and she grinned back. "Dating in shifts these days, huh, Tellie?" she teased.

Tellie didn't answer. She managed a faint smile, embarrassed.

J.B. sipped his coffee. He never added cream or sugar. Her eyes went to his lean, darkly tanned hands. There was a gold cat's-eye ring on his left ring finger, thick and masculine, and a thin expensive watch above it on his wrist. He was wearing a lightweight gray suit with a cream Stetson. He looked expensive and arrogant and seductive.

"I don't like the idea of your going out with that man," J.B. told her curtly.

"It wasn't a date, J.B., it was just lunch," she said.

"It was an interrogation," he corrected. "What else did he want to know?"

She knew she'd never get away with lying. "He wanted to know about your father," she said.

"What about him?"

"If he was still alive. I told him he wasn't. That was all."

"What did he say?"

"Not much," she returned. She searched his green eyes. They were troubled and stormy. "Just that a friend had asked him to find out about your father, over some romance of yours that went bad years ago. He didn't say anything specific," she added without looking at him. He usually could tell when she was lying.

His face tautened as he looked at her. "I never meant anyone to know about what happened except Marge and me," he said tightly.

"Yes, I know, J.B.," she replied, her voice weary and resigned. "You don't share things with outsiders."

He frowned. "You're not an outsider. You're family."

That, somehow, made things even worse. She met his eyes evenly. "You sent Jarrett out to get my graduation present. You'd never do that to Marge or the girls. And you lied about being at the graduation exercises. You were in the office with some businessman and his daughter. I gather that she was a real looker and you couldn't tear yourself away," she added with more bitterness than she realized.

His eyes almost glowed with anger. "Who told you that?"

"I took classes in ESP in college," she drawled facetiously, and with a bite in her voice. "What does it matter how I know? You lied to me!"

His indrawn breath was audible. "Damn it, Tellie!"

"Why can't you be honest with me?" she demanded. "I'm not a kid anymore. You don't have to protect me from the truth."

"You don't know the truth," he said curtly.

"Sure I do. I'm a liability you assumed because I had no family and you felt sorry for me," she replied.

"I felt sorry for you," he conceded. "But I've always included you in family activities, haven't I?"

"Oh, yes," she agreed. "I get to have Christmas and summer vacation and all the other holidays with Marge and the girls, I even get to go on overseas trips with them. I've never doubted that I was part of Marge's family," she said meaningfully.

He frowned. "Marge is part of my family."

"You're not part of mine, J.B.," she replied. Her heart was breaking. "I'm in the same class as your big-boobed blondes, disposable and unimportant. We don't even rate a handpicked present. You just send out the secretary to buy it, and to lie for you when you avoid events you'd rather not be forced to attend."

He glared at her. "You've got the whole thing upside down." He cursed under his breath. "Damn Grange! If he hadn't barged in…!"

Something was fishy here. "You know him!"

His lips made a thin line. "I know him," he admitted reluctantly. "I went to see him at the feedlot when I realized who he was. But I barely had time to say anything to him before Justin showed up. I didn't go back."

"Who is he, J.B.?" she asked, but she was sure that she already knew the answer.

"He's her brother," he said finally. "He's the brother of the woman my father kept me from marrying."

CHAPTER THREE

THE LOOK IN J.B.'s eyes was painful to Tellie, who loved him with all her heart, despite the knowledge that he was never going to be able to love her back. She could almost feel the pain that rippled through him with the words. The woman, the only woman, he'd ever loved had killed herself, because of him. It was a pain he could never escape. And now the woman's brother had shown up in his own town.

"Why is he here, do you think?" she asked.

J.B. sipped coffee. "Revenge, perhaps," he said tautly, "at first."

"Revenge for what?" she asked, because she knew the answer, but she didn't want him to realize how much Grange had told her.

He glanced at her appraisingly. "It's a story that doesn't concern you, Tellie," he said quietly. "It's ancient history."

She finished her own coffee. "Whatever you say, J.B.," she replied. "I have to get back to work."

She stood up. So did he. "How are you going to get back to the feedlot?" he asked abruptly. "Didn't you ride in with Grange?"

She shook her head. "It was Dutch treat."

"Are you coming to the barbecue Saturday?" he added.

It was the end of roundup, one that he gave for the

ranch hands. Marge and the girls, and Tellie, were always invited. It was a comfortable routine.

Tellie had never felt less like a routine. "No, I don't think so," she said abruptly, and was pleased to see his eyelids flicker. "I have other plans."

"What other plans?" he demanded, as if he had the right to know every step she took.

She smiled carelessly. "That's not your business, J.B. See you."

She went to the counter and paid Barbara. When she left, J.B. was sitting there, brooding, his face like steel.

It wasn't until that night Tellie finally had time to digest what she'd learned. She waited until the girls went to bed and then cornered Marge at the kitchen table where she was piecing a quilt.

"Do you know a family named Grange?" she asked Marge.

The older woman blinked, surprised. "Grange? Why?"

That wasn't an innocent look Marge was giving her. Tellie folded her hands on the table. "There's a man named Grange who came to work at the feedlot," she said. "He's tall and dark eyed and dark haired. J.B. was going to marry his sister a long time ago…"

"Him! Here! Dear God!" Marge exclaimed. She put her hands to her mouth. "No!"

"It's all right, Marge," she said at once. "He came looking for your father, not J.B."

Marge's eyes were wide, frightened. "You know?" she asked huskily.

She sighed heavily. "Yes. Grange told me everything. J.B. doesn't know that," she added quickly. "I said that

Grange only mentioned that there was a romance gone bad in the past."

Marge drew her hands over her mouth. "It was much worse than that, Tellie. It was a nightmare," she said heavily. "I've never seen J.B. like that. He went crazy after she died. For three months, he went away and nobody even knew where he was. We couldn't find him. Dad cried…" She took a steadying breath. "I never understood what happened, why she did it. J.B. thought it was because they'd had an argument about her giving up her house to live with us. They parted in anger, and he didn't know what had happened until her best friend called him and gave him the news. He blamed himself. He lived with the guilt, but it ate him alive. Dad was so kind to him afterward," she added. "They'd had problems, like some fathers and sons do. They were both strong willed and domineering." She sighed. "But Dad went out of his way after that to win J.B.'s affection. I think he finally succeeded, before he had the stroke." She looked up. "Did Grange have any idea why she did such a desperate thing?"

Now things were getting sticky. Tellie hesitated. She didn't want to destroy Marge's illusions about her father. And obviously, J.B. hadn't told his sister about his father's interference that had caused the tragedy.

Marge realized that. She smiled sadly. "Tellie, my father never cared one way or the other about me. I was a girl, so I was a disappointment to him. You don't need to spare my feelings. I would like to know what Grange told you."

Tellie took a deep breath. "All right. He said that J.B.'s father came to see the girl and told her that if she married J.B., he had enough evidence to put her fourteen-year-old brother in prison for the rest of his life. The boy was involved in drugs and part of a gang."

She gasped. "So that was it! Did he tell J.B.?"

"Yes," she said. "He did. Apparently Grange only just found out himself. His father only told him when he was dying. I'm sure he was trying to spare Grange. He'll go through his own pain, realizing that he provided your father with the reason to threaten his sister."

"So many secrets," Marge said, her voice thready. "Pain and more pain. It will bring it all back, too. J.B. will relive it."

That was painful. But it wasn't all Grange's fault. "Grange just wanted to know the truth." Tellie defended the stranger. "He thought J.B. put his father up to talking to the woman."

"My brother doesn't have any problem telling people unpleasant things," she replied musingly. "He does his own dirty work."

"He does," Tellie agreed.

She frowned at the younger woman's expression. "What are you not telling me?"

She shrugged. "Jarrett let something slip."

"J.B.'s secretary? Did she? What?" she asked with a lazy smile.

"J.B. wasn't at the graduation exercises, Marge," Tellie said sadly. "He was in a meeting with a businessman and his attractive daughter. He made Jarrett cover up for him. She was really upset about what he said to her. She was more upset when she found out that the present he wanted her to buy was for me, for my graduation."

"Wait a minute," Marge replied, frowning. "He lied about being at the stadium? He actually did that?"

Tellie grimaced. "Yes."

"I'll strangle him!" the older woman said forcefully.

"To what end, Marge?" Tellie asked. She felt old, tired, worn-out. "Can you make him love me? Because that isn't ever going to happen. I thought he was just a carefree playboy who liked variety in his women. But it's not that at all, is it?" She sat back in her chair, her face drawn and sad. "He blames himself because the woman he loved died. He won't risk feeling that way about another woman, setting himself up for another loss. He thinks he doesn't deserve to be happy because she killed herself."

"And all along, it was our father who did the dirty work." Marge's eyes were thoughtful. "I noticed that he seemed haunted sometimes, absolutely haunted. And I'd ask him if anything was wrong. He'd just say that people had to pay for their sins, and he hoped his punishment wouldn't be as bad as he deserved. I didn't know what he was talking about, until today. I suppose he was afraid to tell the truth, because he knew he'd lose J.B. forever."

"You couldn't have blamed him. Whatever he thought of the woman, it was J.B.'s life, and his decision. The old man couldn't live his life for him."

"You didn't know him, honey. He was just like J.B. There's the wrong way, and there's J.B.'s way. That was Dad, too."

"I see."

Marge reached across the table and held her hand. "I'm sorry you had to find it out like this. I told J.B. we should tell you, but he said—" She stopped suddenly. "Anyway, he wouldn't hear of it."

Tellie knew what Marge had avoided saying, that it was none of Tellie's business because she wasn't family. She smiled. "Don't pull your punches. I'm getting tougher by the day since I graduated."

"J.B.'s helped, hasn't he?" she said with a scowl.

"He can't change the way he feels," she said wearily. "If he was going to fall head over heels in love with me, it wouldn't have taken him seven years, Marge. Even now, I'm just a stray that he took in. Well, that *you* took in," she corrected. "J.B. decided that both of you would take care of me, but you'd do the daily work." She laughed. "And it's just like him."

"It is," Marge had to admit. She squeezed Tellie's hand and then let go. "Maybe it isn't a bad thing that you know the truth. It helps explain the way he is, and why there was never much hope for you in the first place."

"Perhaps you're right," Tellie agreed. "But you mustn't ever let J.B. know. Promise me."

"I'll never tell him what you know, Tellie," Marge agreed. She hesitated. "What is Grange like?"

"Mysterious," she replied. "Dangerous. Nobody knows much about him. They say he was in Special Forces."

"Not in the Mafia?" Marge replied dryly, and she wasn't totally kidding.

"He said that his sister's death took him right out of drug use and gang participation, although he told me at first that it was a friend and not himself," she replied. "The tragedy saved him, in fact. He felt guilty, I'm sure, when he realized that she died partially because J.B.'s father threatened to put him in prison. The awful thing is that he didn't know that until three weeks ago. I expect he's hurting as much as J.B. did when he read the letter his father left him."

"That was another bad month, when J.B. got that letter attached to Dad's will," Marge said. "He got extremely drunk." She frowned. "That was the year before you graduated from high school, in fact. You came over and took a gun away from him," she added, shocked at the memory. "I yelled at you, and you wouldn't listen. You went right into his den, poured the bottle of whiskey down the sink with him yelling curses at you, and then you took away the pistol and popped the bullets out on the floor. I screamed…"

"You thought he'd hit me," she agreed, smiling. "But I knew better. J.B. would never hit a woman, not even if he was stinking drunk. Which he was, of course."

"You led him off to bed and stayed with him all night. The next morning he carried you into the living room where I was, and laid you out on the sofa under an afghan. He looked very funny. When I asked him why, he said it was the first time in his life that he'd ever had a woman take care of him. Our mother wasn't domestic," she added quietly. "She was never very nurturing. She was a research chemist and her life was her work. Housekeepers raised J.B. and me. It was almost a relief for Dad, and us, when she died. I did admire her," she added. "She did a socially beneficial job. A dangerous one, too. She was working with a terrible virus strain, looking for a cure. One day in the lab, she stuck a needle, accidentally, into her hand through her rubber glove and died. I was sorry, and I went to the funeral. J.B wouldn't go and neither would Dad. They said she deserted all of us for her job."

"That sounds like him," Tellie agreed.

"J.B. never stopped fussing about the way you took care of him," she recalled on a laugh. "But then he'd lose his temper when you weren't around to do it. He was furious when you spent your summer vacations with those friends at Yellowstone National Park."

"I had a good time. I miss Melody. She and I were wonderful friends, but her parents moved overseas and she had to go with them."

"I don't think I have one friend left in Jacobsville, from my school days," Marge recalled.

"What about Barbara?"

"Oh. Yes. Barbara." She chuckled. "She and that café. When we were girls, it was what she wanted most of all, to own a restaurant."

"It's a good one." Tellie hesitated. "Now, don't get angry, but she's worried about you," she added.

"Me? Why?"

"She said you had a dizzy spell."

Marge frowned. "Yes, I did. I remember. I've had two or three lately. Odd, isn't it? But then, I'm prone to migraine headaches," she added carelessly. "You get all sorts of side effects from them. In fact, I see fireworks and go blind in one eye just before I get one. The doctor calls them vascular headaches."

Tellie frowned. "Why? Does blood pressure cause them?"

Marge laughed. "Not in my case, honey. I have the lowest blood pressure in two counties. No, migraine runs in my family. My mother had them, and so did her mother."

"I'll bet J.B. doesn't have them," Tellie mused.

"That's a fact," came the laughing reply. "No, he doesn't get headaches, but he certainly gives them."

"Amen."

Marge went back to her piecing. "Maybe it's just as well that you know all about J.B. now, Tellie," she said after a minute. "Maybe it will save you any further heart-ache."

"Yes," the younger woman agreed sadly. "Maybe so."

GRANGE DIDN'T ASK her out again, but he did stop by her desk from time to time, just to see how she was. It was as if he knew how badly he'd hurt her with the information about J.B.'s past, and wanted to make amends.

"Listen," she said one day when he gave her a worried look, "I'm not stupid. I knew there was something in J.B.'s past that, well, that caused him to be the way he is. He never cared about me, except as a sort of adopted relative." She smiled. "I've got three years of college to go, you know. No place for a love life."

He studied her quietly. "Don't end up like him," he said suddenly. "Or like me. I don't think I've got it in me to trust another human being."

Her eyes were sympathetic. He was blaming himself for his sister's death. She knew it. "You'll grow old and bitter, all alone," she said.

"I'm already old and bitter," he said, and he didn't smile.

"No gray hairs," she observed.

"They're all on the inside," he shot back.

She grinned. Her whole face lit up.

He gave her an odd look and something in his expression softened, just a little.

"If you really want to look old, you should dye your hair," she pointed out.

He chuckled. "My father still had black hair when he died. He was sixty."

"Good genes," she said.

He shrugged. "Beats me. He never knew who his father was."

"Your mother?"

His face hardened. "I don't talk about her."

"Sorry."

"I didn't mean to growl," he said hesitantly. "I'm not used to women."

"Imagine a man ever admitting that!" she exclaimed with mock surprise.

He cocked an eyebrow. "You're sassy."

"Yes, I am. Nice of you to notice. Now would you mind leaving? Justin's going to come back any minute. He won't like having you flirt with me on his time."

"I don't flirt," he shot back.

"Well, excuse me!"

He shifted. "Maybe I flirt a little. It isn't intentional."

"God forbid! Who'd want to marry you?" she asked curiously.

He scowled. "Look here, I'm not a bad person."

"Well, I wouldn't want to marry you," she persisted.

"Who asked you?" he asked curtly.

"Not you, for sure," she returned. "And don't bother," she added when he started to speak. "I'm such a rare catch that I have men salivating in the yard, wherever I go."

His dark eyes started to twinkle. "Why?"

"Because I can make French pastry," she told him. "With real whipped cream and custard fillings."

He pursed his lips. "Well!"

"See? I'm quite a catch. Too bad you're not in the running."

He frowned. "Even if I were interested, what would I do with a wife?"

"You don't know?" She gave him such an expression of shock and horror that he burst out laughing.

She grinned at him. "See there? You're improving all the time. I'm a good influence, I am!"

"You're a pain in the neck," he returned. "But not bad company." He shrugged. "Like movies?"

"What sort?"

"Science fiction?"

She chuckled. "You bet."

"I'll check and see what's playing at the theater Saturday, if you're game."

Saturday was the barbecue at J.B.'s that she was determined not to attend. Here was her excuse to miss it. She liked Grange. Besides, no way was she going to sit home and eat her heart out over J.B., especially when she'd already told him that she had other plans. "I'm game."

"Your adopted family won't like it," he said slowly.

"Marge won't mind," she said, certain that it was true. "And I don't care what J.B. thinks."

He nodded. "Okay. It's a date. We'll work out the details Friday."

"Fine. Now please go away," she added, glancing at the door, where Justin was just coming inside the building. "Or we may both be out looking for work on Monday!"

He grinned and left her before Justin got the door closed.

MARGE WAS LESS enthusiastic than Tellie had expected. In fact, she seemed disturbed.

"Does the phrase 'rubbing salt on an open wound' ring any chimes?" Marge asked her somberly.

"But Grange didn't do anything," she protested. "He was as much a victim as J.B. was."

Marge hesitated, uneasy. "I understand that. But he's connected with it. J.B. will see it as a personal attack on him, by both of you."

"That's absurd!"

"It isn't, if you remember the way my brother is."

For the first time since Grange had asked her out, Tellie wasn't sure she was doing the right thing. She didn't want to hurt J.B., even if he'd given her reason. On the other hand, it was a test of control, his over hers. If she gave in now, she'd be giving in forever. Marge was her friend, but J.B. was Marge's brother. It was a tangled situation.

Marge put an arm around her. "Don't worry yourself to death, honey," she said gently. "If you really want to go out with him, go ahead. I'm just saying that J.B. is going to take it personally. But you can't let him run your life."

Tellie hugged her back. "Thanks, Marge."

"Why don't you want to go to the barbecue?" the older woman asked.

Tellie grimaced. "Miss runner-up beauty queen will be there, won't she?"

Marge pursed her lips. "So that's it."

"Don't you dare tell him," came the terse reply.

"Never." Marge sighed. "I didn't even think about that. No wonder you're so anxious to stay away."

"She's really gorgeous, isn't she?"

Marge looked old and wise. "She's just like all the other ones before her, Tellie, tall and blonde and stacked. Not much in the way of intelligence. You know," she added thoughtfully, "I don't think J.B. really likes intelligent women much."

"Maybe he feels threatened by us."

"Don't you believe it," Marge scoffed. "He's got a business degree from Yale, you know."

"I'd forgotten."

"No, I think it has to do with our mother," she continued. "She was always running down our father, making him feel like an idiot. She was forever going to conventions with one of her research partners. Later, they had a serious affair. That was just before she died."

"J.B. didn't have a great respect for women, I guess."

"Not in his younger days. Then he got engaged, and tragedy followed." She seemed far away. "I lost my first love to another woman, and then my husband died of an embolism after surgery." She shook her head. "J.B. and I have poor track records with happily-ever-after."

Tellie felt sad for both of them. "I suppose it would make you gun-shy, when it came to love."

"Love?" Marge laughed. "J.B. doesn't believe in it anymore." She gave Tellie a sad, gentle appraisal. "But you should. Maybe Grange will be the best thing that ever happened to you. It wouldn't hurt to show J.B. that you're not dying of a broken heart, either."

"He won't notice," Tellie said with conviction. "He used to complain that I was always underfoot."

"Not recently."

"I've been away at college for four years more or less," she reminded the older woman. That reminded her of graduation, which he hadn't attended. It still stung.

"And going away for three more." Marge smiled. "Live your life, Tellie. You don't have to answer to anybody. Be happy."

"That's easier said than done," Tellie pointed out. She smiled at Marge. "Okay. If you don't mind me dating Grange, J.B. can think what he likes. I don't care."

Which wasn't the truth, exactly.

GRANGE WAS GOOD company when he relaxed and forgot that Tellie was a friend of J.B.'s.

The movie was unforgettable, a film about a misfit crew aboard a space-going freighter who were protecting a girl from some nasty authorities. It was funny and sweet and full of action.

They came out of the theater smiling.

"It's been a good year for science-fiction movies," he remarked.

"It has," Tellie agreed, "but that was the best I've seen so far. I missed the series when it was on television. I guess I'll have to buy the DVD set."

He gave her an amused look. "You're nice to take around," he said on the way to his big gray truck. "If I weren't a confirmed bachelor, you'd be at the top of my list of prospects."

"Why, what a nice thing to say!" she exclaimed. "Do you mind if I quote you frequently?"

He gave her a quick look and relaxed a little when she laughed. "Quote me?" he asked quizzically.

Her shoulders rose and fell. "It's just that nobody ever said I was marriageable before, you see," she told him. "I figure with an endorsement like that, the sky's the limit. I mean, I won't be in college forever. A woman has to think about the future."

Grange stared at her in the light from the parking lot. "I don't think I've ever been around anyone like you. Most women these days are too aggressive for my taste."

Her eyebrows arched. "Like doormats, do we?" she teased.

He shook his head. "It's not that. I like a woman with spirit. But I don't like being seen as a party favor."

"Now you know how women feel," she pointed out.

"I never treated a woman that way," he returned.

"A lot of men have."

"I suppose so," he conceded. He gave her a smile. "I enjoyed tonight."

"Me, too."

"We'll do it again sometime."

She smiled back. "Suits me."

GRANGE DROPPED HER off at Marge's house, but he didn't try to kiss her good-night. He was a gentleman in the best sense of the word. Tellie liked him. But her heart still ached for J.B.

Tellie assumed that Marge and the girls were in bed, because the lights were all off inside. She locked the door behind her and started toward the staircase when a light snapped on in the living room.

She whirled, surprised, and looked right into J. B. Hammock's seething green eyes.

CHAPTER FOUR

"WHAT...ARE YOU DOING HERE?" she blurted out, flushing at the way he was looking at her. "Has something happened to Marge or the girls?" she added at once, uneasy.

"No. They're fine."

She moved into the room, putting her purse and coat on a chair, her slender body in jeans with pink embroidered roses and a pink tank top that matched. Her pale eyes searched his dark green ones curiously. She ran a nervous hand through her wavy dark hair and grimaced. He looked like an approaching storm.

"Then why are you here?" she asked when the silence became oppressive.

His eyes slid over her body in the tight jeans and tank top and narrowed with reluctant appreciation. He was also in jeans, but his were without decoration. A chambray shirt covered his broad, muscular chest and long arms. It was unfastened at the throat. He usually dressed casually for barbecues, and this one didn't seem to be an exception.

"You went to a movie with Grange," he said.

"Yes."

His face tautened. "I don't like you going out with him."

Her thin dark eyebrows arched. "I'm almost twenty-two, J.B."

"Jacobsville is full of eligible bachelors."

"Yes, I know. Grange is one of them."

"Damn it, Tellie!"

She drew in a steadying breath. It was hard not to give in to J.B. She'd spent most of her adolescence doing exactly that. But this was a test of her newfound independence. She couldn't let him walk all over her. Despite his reasons for not wanting her around Grange, she couldn't let him dictate her future. Particularly since he wasn't going to be part of it.

"I'm not marrying him, J.B.," she said quietly. "He's just someone to go out with."

His lean jaw tautened. "He's part of a painful episode in my past," he said flatly. "It's disloyal of you to take his side against me. I'm not pushing the point, but I gave you a home when you needed one."

Her eyes narrowed. "*You* gave me a home? No, J.B., *you* didn't give me a home. You decided that *Marge* would give me a home," she said emphatically.

"Same thing," he bit off.

"It isn't," she replied. "You don't put yourself out for anybody. You make gestures, but somebody else has to do the dirty work."

"That's not how it was, and you know it," he said curtly. "You were fourteen years old. How would it have looked, to have you living with me? Especially with my lifestyle."

She wanted to argue that, but she couldn't. "I suppose you have a point."

He didn't reply. He just watched her.

She moved to the sofa and perched on one of its broad, floral-patterned arms. "I'm very grateful for what your family has done for me," she said gently. "But nobody can say that I haven't pulled my weight. I've cleaned and cooked for Marge and the girls, been a live-in babysitter, helped keep her books— I haven't just parked myself here and taken advantage of the situation."

"I never said you did," he replied.

"You're implying it," she shot back. "I can't remember when I've ever dated anybody around here…!"

"Of course not, you were too busy mooning over me!"

Her face went white. Then it slowly blossomed into red rage. She stood up, eyes blazing. "Yes," she said. "I was, wasn't I? Mooning over you while you indulged yourself with starlet after debutante after Miss Beauty Contest winner! Oh, excuse me, Miss Runner-up Beauty Contest winner," she drawled insolently.

He glared at her. "My love life is none of your business."

"Don't be absurd," she retorted. "It's everybody's business. You were in a tabloid story just last week, something about you and the living fashion doll being involved in some sleazy love triangle in Hollywood…"

"Lies," he shot back, "and I'm suing!"

"Good luck," she said. "My point is, I date a nice man who hasn't hurt anybody…"

He let out a vicious curse, interrupting her, and moved closer, towering over her. "He was Special Forces in Iraq," he told her coldly, "and he was brought up on charges for excessive force during an incursion! He actually slugged his commanding officer and stuffed him in the trunk of a civilian car!"

Her eyes widened. "Did he, really?" she mused, fascinated.

"It isn't funny," he snapped. "The man is a walking time bomb, waiting for the spark to set him off. I don't want him around you when it happens. He was forced out of the army, Tellie, he didn't go willingly! He had the choice of a court-martial or an honorable discharge."

She wondered how he knew so much about the other man, but she didn't pursue it. "It was an honorable discharge, then?" she emphasized.

He took off his white Stetson and ran an irritated hand through his black hair. "I can't make you see it, can I? The man's dangerous."

"He's in good company in Jacobsville, then, isn't he?" she replied. "I mean, we're like a resort for ex-mercs and ex-military, not to mention the number of ex-federal law enforcement people..."

"Grange has enemies," he interrupted.

"So do you, J.B.," she pointed out. "Remember that guy who broke into your house with a .45 automatic and tried to shoot you over a horse deal?"

"He was a lunatic."

"If the bullet hadn't been a dud, you'd be dead," she reminded him.

"Ancient history," he said. "You're avoiding the subject."

"I am not likely to be shot by one of Grange's mythical old enemies while watching a science-fiction film at the local theater!" Her small hands balled at her hips. "The only thing you're mad about is that you can't make me do what you want me to do anymore," she challenged.

A deep, dark sensuality came into his green eyes and one corner of his chiseled mouth turned up. "Can't I, now?" he drawled, moving forward.

She backed up. "Oh, no, you don't," she warded him off. "Go home and thrill your beauty queen, J.B., I'm not on the market."

He lifted an eyebrow at her flush and the faint rustle of her heartbeat against her tank top. "Aren't you?"

She backed up one more step, just in case. "What happened to you was…was tragic, but it was a long time ago, J.B., and Grange wasn't responsible for it," she argued. "He was surely as much a victim as you were, especially when he found out the truth. Can't you imagine how he must have felt, when he knew that his own actions cost him his sister's life?"

He seemed to tauten all over. "He told you all of it?"

She hadn't meant to let that slip. He made her nervous when he came close like this. She couldn't think. "You'd never have told me. Neither would Marge. Okay, it's not my business," she added when he looked threatening, "but I can have an opinion."

"Grange was responsible," he returned coldly. "His own delinquency made it impossible for her to get past my father."

"That's not true," Tellie said, her voice quiet and firm. "If I wanted to marry someone, and his father tried to blackmail me, I'd have gone like a shot to the man and told him…!"

The effect the remark had on him was scary. He seemed to grow taller, and his eyes were terrible. His deep, harsh voice interrupted her. "Stop it."

She did. She didn't have the maturity, or the confidence, to argue the point with him. But she wouldn't have killed herself, she was sure of it. She'd have embarrassed J.B.'s father, shamed him, defied him. She wasn't the sort of person to take blackmail lying down.

"You don't know what you're talking about," he said, his eyes furious. "You'd never sacrifice another human being's life or freedom to save yourself."

"Maybe not," she conceded. "But I wouldn't kill myself, either." She was going to add that it was a cowardly thing to do, but the way J.B. was looking at her kept her quiet.

"She loved me. She was going to have to give me up, and she couldn't bear to go on living that way. In her own mind, she didn't have a choice," he said harshly. He searched her quiet face. "You can't comprehend an emotion that powerful, can you, Tellic? After all, what the hell would you know about love? You're still wrapped up in dreams of happily-ever-after, cotton-candy kisses and hand-holding! You don't know what it is to want someone so badly that it's physically painful to be separated from them. You don't understand the violence of desire." He laughed coldly. "Maybe that's just as well. You couldn't handle an affair!"

"Good, because I don't want one!" she replied angrily. He made her feel small, inadequate. It hurt. "I'm not going to pass myself around like a cigarette to any man who wants me, just to prove how liberated I am! And when I marry, I won't want some oversexed libertine who jumps into bed with any woman who wants him!"

He went very still and quiet. His face was like a drawn cord, his eyes green flames as he glared down at her.

"Sorry," she said uneasily. "That didn't come out the way I meant it. I just don't think that a man, or a woman, who lives that permissively can ever settle down and be faithful. I want a stable marriage that children will fit into, not an endless round of new partners."

"Children," he scoffed.

"Yes, children." Her eyes softened as she thought of them. "A whole house full of them, one day, when I'm through school."

"With Grange as their father?"

She gaped at him. "I just went to a movie with him, J.B.!"

"If you get involved with him, I'll never forgive you," he said in a voice as cold as the grave.

"Well, golly gee whiz, that would be a tragedy, wouldn't it? Just think, I'd never get another present that you sent Jarrett to buy for me!"

His breath was coming quickly through his nose. His lips were flattened. He didn't have a comeback. That seemed to make him angrier. He took another step toward her.

She backed up a step. "You should be happy to have me out of your life," she pointed out uneasily. "I was never more than an afterthought anyway, J.B. Just a pest. All I did was get in your way."

He stopped just in front of her. He looked oddly frustrated. "You're still getting in my way," he said enigmatically. "I know that no matter what Marge may have said, she and the girls were disappointed that you missed the barbecue. It's the first time in seven years that you've done that, and for a man who represents as much hurt to Marge herself as he does to me."

She frowned. "But why? She never knew Grange!"

"You told her what my father did," he said deliberately.

She grimaced. "I didn't mean to!" she confessed. "I didn't want to. But she said it wouldn't matter."

"And you don't know her any better than that, after so long in her house? She was devastated."

She felt worse than ever. "I guess it was rough on you, too, when you found out what he'd done," she said unexpectedly.

His expression was odd. Reserved. Uneasy. "I've never

hated a human being so much in all my life," he said huskily. "And he was dead. There was nothing I could do to him, no way I could pay him back for ruining my life and taking hers. You can't imagine how I felt."

"I'm sure he was sorry about it," she said, having gleaned that from what Marge had said about the way he'd treated J.B. "You know he'd have taken it back if he could have. He must have loved you, very much. Marge said that he would have been afraid of losing you if he'd told the truth. You were his only son."

"Forgiveness comes hard to me," he said.

She knew that. He'd never held any grudges against her, but she knew people in town who'd crossed him years ago, and he still went out of his way to snub them. He didn't forgive, and he never forgot.

"Are you so perfect that you never make mistakes?" she wondered out loud.

"None to date," he replied, and he didn't smile.

"Your day is coming."

His eyes narrowed as he stared down at her. "You won't leave Grange alone. Is that final?"

She swallowed. "Yes. It's final."

He gave her a look as cold as death. His head jerked. "Your choice."

He turned on his heel and stalked out of the room. She watched him go with nervous curiosity. What in the world did he mean?

MARGE WAS VERY quiet at breakfast the next day. Dawn and Brandi kept giving Tellie odd looks, too. They went off to church with friends. Marge wasn't feeling well, so she stayed home and Tellie stayed with her. Something was going on. She wondered what it was.

"Is there something I've done that I need to apologize for?" she asked Marge while they were making lunch in the kitchen.

Marge drew in a slow breath. "No, of course not," she denied gently. "It's just J.B., wanting his own way and making everybody miserable because he can't get it."

"If you want me to stop dating Grange, just say so," Tellie told her. "I won't do it for J.B., but I will do it for you."

Marge smiled at her gently. She reached over and patted Tellie's hand. "You don't have to make any such sacrifices. Let J.B. stew."

"Maybe the man does bring back some terrible memories," she murmured. "J.B. looked upset when he talked about it. He must…he must have loved her very much."

"He was twenty-one," Marge recalled. "Love is more intense at that age, I think. Certainly it was for me. She was J.B.'s first real affair. He wasn't himself the whole time he knew her. I thought she was too old for him, too, but he wouldn't hear a word we said about her. He turned against me, against Dad, against the whole world. He ran off to get married and said he'd never come back. But she argued with him. We never knew exactly why, but when she took her own life, he blamed himself. And then when he learned the truth…well, he was never the same."

"I'm sorry it was like that for him," she said, understanding how he would have felt. She felt like that about J.B. At least, she thought, she wasn't losing him to death—just to legions of other women.

Marge put down the spoon she was using to stir beef stew and turned to Tellie. "I would have told you about her, eventually, even if Grange hadn't shown up," she said quietly. "I knew it would hurt, to know he felt like that about another woman. But at least you'd understand why you couldn't get close to him. You can't fight a ghost, Tellie. She's perfect in his mind, like a living, breathing photograph that never ages, never has faults, never creates problems. No living woman will ever top her in J.B.'s mind. Loving him, while he feels like that about a ghost, would kill your very soul."

"Yes, I understand that now," Tellie said heavily. She stared out the window, seeing nothing. "How little we really know people."

"You can live with someone for years and not know them," Marge agreed. "I just don't want you to waste your life on my brother. You deserve better."

Tellie winced, but she didn't let Marge see. "I'll get married one of these days and have six kids."

"You will," Marge agreed, smiling gently. "And I'll spoil your kids the way you've spoiled mine."

"The girls didn't look too happy this morning," Tellie remarked.

Marge grimaced. "J.B. had them in the kitchen helping prepare canapés," she said. "They didn't even get to dance."

"But, why?"

"They're just kids," Marge said ruefully. "They aren't old enough to notice eligible bachelors. To hear J.B. tell it, at least."

"But that's outrageous! They're sixteen and seventeen years old. They're not kids!"

"To J.B., you all are, Tellie."

She glowered. "Maybe Brandi and Dawn would like to go halves with me on a really mean singing telegram."

"J.B. would slug the singer, and we'd get sued," Marge said blithely. "Let it go, honey. I know things look dark at the moment, but they'll get better. We have to look to the future."

"I guess."

"The girls should be home any minute. I'll start dishing up while you set the table."

Tellie went to do it, her heart around her ankles.

IF SHE'D WONDERED what J.B. meant with his cryptic remark, it became crystal clear in the days that followed. He came to the house to see Marge and pretended that Tellie wasn't there. If he passed her on the street at lunchtime, he didn't see her. For all intents and purposes, she had become the invisible woman. He was paying her back for dating Grange.

Which made her more determined, of course, to go out with the man. She didn't care if J.B. snubbed her forever; he wasn't dictating her life!

Grange discovered J.B.'s new attitude the following Saturday, when he took Tellie to a local community theater presentation of *Arsenic and Old Lace*. J.B. came in with his gorgeous blonde and sat down in the row across from Tellie and Grange. He didn't look their way all night, and when he passed them on the way out, he didn't speak.

"What the hell is wrong with him?" Grange asked her on the way home.

"He's paying me back for dating you," she said simply.

"That's low."

"That's J.B.," she replied.

"Do you want me to stop asking you out, Tellie?" he asked quietly.

"I do not. J.B. isn't telling me what to do," she replied. "He can ignore me all he likes. I'll ignore him back."

Grange was quiet. "I shouldn't have come here."

"You just wanted to know what happened," she defended him. "Nobody could blame you for that. She was your sister."

He pulled up in front of Marge's house and cut off the engine. "Yes, she was. She and Dad were the only family I had, but I was rotten to them. I ran wild when I hit thirteen. I got in with a bad crowd, joined a gang, used drugs—you name it, I did it. I still don't understand why I didn't end up in jail."

"Her death saved you, didn't it?" she asked.

He nodded, his face averted. "I didn't admit it at the time, though. She was such a sweet woman. She always thought of other people before she thought of herself. She was all heart. It must have been a walk in the park for Hammock's father to convince her that she was ruining J.B.'s life."

"Can you imagine how the old man felt," she began slowly, "because he was always afraid that J.B. would find out the truth and know what he'd done. He had to know that he'd have lost J.B.'s respect, maybe even his love, and he had to live with that until he died. I don't imagine he was a very happy person, even if he did what he felt was the right thing."

"He didn't even know my sister, my dad said," Grange replied. "He wouldn't talk to her. He was sure she was a gold digger, just after J.B.'s money."

"How horrible, to think like that," she murmured thoughtfully. "I guess I wouldn't want to be rich. You'd never be sure if people liked you for what you were or what you had."

"The old man seemed to have an overworked sense of his own worth."

"It sounds like it, from what Marge says."

"Did you ever know him?"

"Only by reputation," she replied. "He was in the nursing home when I came to live with Marge."

"What is she like?"

She smiled. "The exact opposite of J.B. She's sweet and kind, and she never knows a stranger. She isn't suspicious or crafty, and she never hurts people deliberately."

"But her brother does?"

"J.B. never pulls his punches," she replied. "I suppose you know where you stand with him. But he's uncomfortable to be around sometimes, when he's in a bad mood."

He studied her curiously. "How long have you been in love with him?"

She laughed nervously. "I don't love J.B.! I hate him!"

"How long," he persisted, softening the question with a smile.

She shrugged. "Since I was fourteen, I suppose. I hero-worshipped him at first, followed him everywhere, baked him cookies, waylaid him when he went riding and tagged along. He was amazingly tolerant, when I was younger. Then I graduated from high school and we became enemies. He likes to rub it in that I'm vulnerable when he's around. I don't understand why."

"Maybe he doesn't understand why, either," he ventured.

"You think?" She smiled across the seat at him. "I'm surprised that J.B. hasn't tried to run you out of town."

"He has."

"What?"

He smiled faintly. "He went to see Justin Ballenger yesterday."

"About you?" she wondered.

He nodded. "He said that I was a bad influence on you, and he wondered if I wouldn't be happier working somewhere else."

"What did Justin say?" she asked.

He chuckled. "That he could run his own feedlot without Hammock's help, and that he wasn't firing a good worker because of Hammock's personal issues."

"Well!"

"I understand that Hammock is pulling his cattle out of the feedlot and having them trucked to Kansas, to a feedlot there for finishing."

"But that's horrible!" Tellie exclaimed.

"Justin said something similar, with a few more curse words attached," Grange replied. "I felt bad to cause such problems for him, but he only laughed. He said Hammock would lose money on the deal, and he didn't care. He wasn't being ordered around by a man ten years his junior."

"That sounds like Justin," she agreed, smiling. "Good for him."

He shrugged. "It doesn't solve the problem, though," he told her. "It's only the first salvo. Hammock won't quit. He wants me out of your life, whatever it takes."

"No, it's not about me," she said sadly. "He doesn't like being reminded of what he lost. Marge said so."

Grange's dark eyes studied her quietly. "He didn't want you to know about my sister," he said after a minute. "I ticked him off that first day we went to lunch, by telling you the family secret."

"Marge said that she would have told me herself eventually."

"Why?"

She smiled. "She thinks I'd wear my heart out on

J.B., and she's right. I would have. He'll never get past his lovely ghost to any sort of relationship with a real woman. I'm not going to waste my life aching for a man I can't have."

"That's sensible," he agreed. "But he's been part of your life for a long time. He's become a habit."

She nodded, her eyes downcast. "That's just what he is. A habit."

He drew in a long breath. "If you want to stop seeing me..."

"I do not," she said at once. "I really enjoy going out with you, Grange."

He smiled, because it was obvious that she meant it. "I like your company, too." He hesitated. "Just friends," he added slowly.

She smiled back. "Just friends."

His eyes were distant. "I'm at a turning point in my life," he confessed. "I'm not sure where I'm headed. But I know I'm not ready for anything serious."

"Neither am I." She leaned her head against the back of the seat and studied him. "Do you think you might stay here, in Jacobsville?"

"I don't know. I've got some problems to work out."

"Join the club," she said, and grinned at him.

He laughed. "I like the way I feel with you. J.B. can go hang. We'll present a united front."

"Just as long as J.B. doesn't go and hang us!" she exclaimed.

CHAPTER FIVE

GRANGE LIKED TO BOWL. Tellie had never tried the sport, but he taught her. She persuaded Marge to let the girls come with them one night. Marge tagged along, but she didn't bowl. She sat at the table sipping coffee and watching her brood fling the big balls down the alley.

"It's fun!" Tellie laughed. She'd left the field to the three experts who were making her look sick with her less-than-perfect bowling.

"That's why you're sitting here with me, is it?" Marge teased.

She shrugged. "I'm a lemon," she confessed. "Nothing I do ever looks good."

"That's not true," Marge disputed. "You cook like an angel and you're great in history. You always make As."

"Two successes out of a hundred false starts," Tellie sighed.

"You're just depressed because J.B.'s ignoring you," Marge said, cutting to the heart of the matter.

"Guilty," Tellie had to admit. "Maybe I should have listened."

"Bull. If you give J.B. the upper hand, he'll walk all over you. The way you used to be, when you were fourteen, I despaired of what would happen if he ever really noticed you. He'd have destroyed your life, Tellie. You'd have become his doormat. He'd have hated that as much as you would."

"Think so? He seems pretty uncomfortable with me when I stand up to him."

"But he respects you for it."

Tellie propped her elbows on the table and rested her chin in her hands. "Does the beauty queen runner-up stand up to him?" she wondered.

"Are you kidding? She won't go to the bathroom without asking J.B. if he thinks it's a good idea!" came the dry response. "She's not giving up all those perks. He gave her a diamond dinner ring last week for her birthday."

That hurt. "I suppose he picked it out himself?"

Marge sighed. "I think she did."

"I can't believe I've wasted four years of my life mooning over that man," Tellie said, wondering aloud at her own stupidity. "I turned down dates with really nice men in college because I was hung up on J.B. Well, never again."

"What sort of nice men?" Marge queried, trying to change the subject.

Tellie grinned. "One was an anthropology major, working on his PhD. He's going to devote his life to a dig in Montana, looking for Paleo-Indian sites."

"Just imagine, Tellie, you could work beside him with a toothbrush..."

"Stop that," Tellie chuckled. "I don't think I'm cut out for dust and dirt and bones."

"What other nice men?"

"There was a friend of one of my professors," she recalled. "He raises purebred Appaloosa stallions when he isn't hunting for meteorites all over the world. He was a character!"

"Why would you hunt meteorites?" Marge wondered.

"Well, he sold one for over a hundred thousand dollars to a collector," the younger woman replied, tongue in cheek.

Marge whistled. "Wow! Maybe I'll get a metal detector and go out searching for them myself!"

That was a real joke, because Marge had inherited half of her father's estate. She lived in a simple house and she never lived high. But she could have, if she'd wanted to. She felt that the girls shouldn't have too much luxury in their formative years. Maybe she was right. Certainly, Brandi and Dawn had turned out very well. They were responsible and kindhearted, and they never felt apart from fellow students.

Tellie glanced at the lanes, where Grange was throwing a ball down the aisle with force and grace. He had a rodeo rider's physique, lean in the hips and wide in the shoulders. Odd, the way he moved, Tellie mused, like a hunter.

"He really is a dish," she murmured, deep in thought.

Marge nodded. "He is unusual," she said. "Imagine a boy on a path that deadly turning his life around."

"J.B. said he was forced out of the military."

Marge gaped at her. "He told you that? How did he know?"

Tellie glowered. "I expect he's had a firm of private detectives on overtime, finding out everything they could about him. J.B. loves to have leverage if he has to go against people."

"He won't bother Grange," Marge said. "He just wants to make sure that the man isn't a threat to you."

"He wants to decide who I marry and how many kids I have," she returned coolly. "But he's not going to."

"That's the spirit, Tellie," Marge chuckled.

"All the same," Tellie replied, "I wish he wouldn't snub me. I'm beginning to feel like a ghost."

"He'll get over it."

"You think so? I wonder."

SATURDAY CAME, AND Grange had something to do for Justin, so Tellie stayed home and helped Marge clean house.

A car drove up out front and two car doors slammed. Tellie was on her hands and knees in the kitchen, scrubbing the tile with a brush while Marge cleaned upstairs. J.B. walked in with a ravishing young blonde woman on his arm. She was tall and beautifully made, with a model-perfect face and teeth, and hair to her waist in back.

"I thought they abolished indentured servitude," J.B. drawled, looking pointedly at Tellie.

She looked up at him with cold eyes, pushing sweaty hair out of her eyes with the back of a dirty hand. "It's called housecleaning, J.B. I'm sure you have no idea what it consists of."

"Nell takes care of all that," he said. "This is Bella Dean," he introduced the blonde, wrapping a long arm around her and smiling at her warmly.

"Nice to meet you," Tellie said, forcing a smile. "I'd shake hands, but I'm sure you'd rather not." She indicated her dirty hands.

Bella didn't answer her. She beamed up at J.B. "Didn't we come to take your sister and your nieces out to eat?" she asked brightly. "I'm sure the kitchen help doesn't need an audience."

Tellie got to her feet, slammed the brush down on the floor and walked right up to the blonde, who actually backed away.

"What would you know about honest work, lady, unless you call lying on your back, work…!"

"Tellie!" J.B. bit off.

The blonde gasped. "Well, I never!"

"I'll bet there's not much you've never," Tellie said coldly. "For your information, I don't work here. Marge gave me a home when my mother died, and I earn my keep. When I'm not scrubbing floors, I go to college to earn a degree, so that I can make a living for myself," she added pointedly. "I'm sure you won't ever have a similar problem, as long as your looks last."

"Tellie!" J.B. repeated.

"I'd rather be pretty than smart," the blonde said carelessly. "Who'd want to give you diamonds?" she scoffed.

Tellie balled a fist.

"Go tell Marge we're here," he demanded, his eyes making cold threats.

"Tell her yourself, J.B.," Tellie replied, eyes flashing. "I'm not anybody's servant."

She turned and left the room, so furious that she was shaking all over.

J.B. followed her right into her bedroom and closed the door behind them.

"What the hell was that all about?" he asked furiously.

"I am not going to be looked down on by any smarmy blonde tart!" she exclaimed.

"You behaved like a child!" he returned.

"She started it," she reminded him.

"She thought you were the housekeeper," he replied. "She didn't know you from a button."

"She'll know me next time, won't she?"

He moved closer, glaring at her. "You're so jealous

you're vibrating with it," he accused, his green eyes narrowing. "You want me."

She drew in a sharp breath and her hands tightened into fists. "I do not," she retorted.

He moved a step closer, so that he was right up against her. His big hand went to her cheek, smoothing over it. His thumb rubbed maddeningly at her lower lip. "You want me," he whispered deeply, bending. "I can feel your heart beating. You ache for me to touch you."

"J.B., if…if you don't…stop," she faltered, fighting his arrogance and her own weakness.

"You don't want me to stop, baby," he murmured, his chiseled mouth poised just over her parted lips. "That's the last thing you want." His thumb tugged her lower lip down and he nibbled softly at the upper one. He heard her breath catch, felt her body shiver. His eyes began to glitter with something like triumph. "I can feel your heart beating. You're waking up. I could do anything I liked to you, whenever I pleased, and we both know it, Tellie."

A husky little moan escaped her tight throat and she moved involuntarily, her body brushing against his, her mouth lifting, pleading, her hands going to his hard upper arms to hold him there. She hated him for doing this to her, but she couldn't resist him.

He knew it. He laughed. He pulled away from her, arrogance in his whole bearing. He smiled, and it wasn't a nice smile at all. "She likes to kiss me, too, Tellie," he said deliberately. "But she's no prude. She likes to take her clothes off, and I don't even have to coax her…"

She slapped him. She was humiliated, hurt, furious. She put the whole weight of her arm behind it, sobbing.

He didn't even react, except to lift an eyebrow and smile even more arrogantly. "Next time I bring her over to see Marge, you'd better be more polite, Tellie," he warned softly, and the deep edge of anger glittered in his green eyes. "Or I'll do this in front of her."

Tellie was horrified at even the thought. Her face went pale. Tears brightened her eyes, but she would have died rather than shed them. "There aren't enough bad words in the English language to describe what you are, J.B.," she said brokenly.

"Oh, you'll think of some eventually, I'm sure. And if you can't, you can always give me another one of those god-awful dragon ties, can't you?"

"I bought boxes of them!" she slung at him.

He only laughed. He gave her a last probing look and went out of the room, leaving the door open behind him.

"Where have you been?" the blonde demanded in a honeyed tone.

"Just having a little overdue discussion. We'd better go. See you, Marge."

THERE WERE MUFFLED VOICES. A door closed. Two car doors slammed. An engine roared.

Marge knocked gently and came into Tellie's room, her whole look apprehensive. She grimaced.

Tellie was as white as a sheet, shaking with rage and humiliation.

"I'll tell him not to bring her here again," Marge said firmly. She put her arms around Tellie and gathered her close. "It's all right."

"He's the devil in a suit," Tellie whispered huskily. "The very devil, Marge. I never, never want to see him again."

The thin arms closed around her and rocked her while she cried. Marge wondered why J.B. had to be so cruel to

a woman who loved him this much. She had a good idea
of what he'd done. It was unfair of him. He didn't want
Tellie. Why couldn't he leave her alone? He'd brought
his latest lover here deliberately. Tellie had refused to
go to the barbecue, avoiding being around the woman,
so J.B. had brought her over to Marge's to rub it in. He
wanted Tellie to see how beautiful the woman was, how
devoted she was to J.B. He was angry that he couldn't
stop her from seeing Grange, not even by snubbing her.
This was low, even for J.B.

"I don't know what's gotten into my brother," Marge
said aloud. "But I'm very sorry, Tellie."

"It's not your fault. We don't get to choose our relatives, more's the pity."

"I wouldn't choose J.B. for a brother, after today."
She drew away, her dark eyes twinkling, mischievous.
"Tellie, the girls wouldn't let J.B. introduce them to his
girlfriend. They gave her vicious looks, glared at J.B.
and went to Dawn's room and locked themselves in. He's
mad at them now, too."

"Good. Maybe he'll stay at his own house."

I wouldn't bet on that, Marge thought, but she didn't
say it aloud. Tellie had stood enough for one day.

GRANGE TOOK TELLIE with him around the feedlot the
next week, explaining how they monitored statistics and
mixed the feed for the various lots of cattle. He'd asked
Justin for permission. The older man was glad to give
it. He liked the strange young man who'd come to work
for him. It was a compliment, because Justin didn't like
many people at all.

Grange propped one big booted foot on the bottom
rail of one of the enclosures, with his arms folded on

the top one. His dark eyes had a faraway look. "This is good country," he said. "I grew up in West Texas. Mostly we've got desert and cactus and mountains over around El Paso. This is green heaven."

"Yes, it is. I love it here," she confessed. "I go to school in Houston. It's green there, too, but the trees are nestled in concrete."

He chuckled. "Do you like college?"

"I do."

"I went myself, in the army."

"What did you study?"

He grinned at her. "Besides weapons and tactics, you mean?" He chuckled. "I studied political science."

She was surprised, and showed it. "That was your major?"

"Part of it. I did a double major, in political science and Arab dialects."

"You mean, you can speak Arabic?"

He nodded. "Farsi, Bedouin, several regional dialects. Well, and the Romance languages."

"All three of them?" she asked, surprised.

"All three." He glanced at her and smiled at her expression. "Languages will get you far in government service and the military. I mustered out as a major."

She tried not to let on that she'd heard about his release from the service. "Did you like the military?" she asked with deliberate carelessness.

He gave her a slow appraisal from dark, narrowed eyes. "Gossip travels fast in small towns, doesn't it?" he wondered aloud. "I expect Hammock had something to do with it."

She sighed. "Probably did," she had to admit. "He did everything he could to keep me from going out with you."

"So he holds grudges," he remarked. "Lucky for him that I don't, or he'd be sleeping with guards at every door and a gun under his pillow. If it hadn't been for him, I'd still have my sister."

"Maybe he thinks that, except for you, and his father, he'd be happily married with kids now."

He shrugged. "Nobody came out of it laughing," he said. He looked down at her, puzzled. "If he wanted you to stop going out with me, why haven't you?"

She smiled sadly. "I got tired of being a carpet," she said.

He cocked his head. "Walked all over you, did he?"

She nodded. "Since I was fourteen. And I let him. I never disagreed with anything he said, even when I didn't think he was right." She traced a pattern on the metal fence. "I saw what I could have become last Saturday. He brought his newest girlfriend over to show me. She thought I was the hired help and treated me accordingly. We had words. Lots of words. Now I'm not speaking to J.B."

He leaned back against the gate. "You may not believe it, but standing up to people is the only way to get through life with your mind intact. Nothing was ever gained by giving in."

"So that's how you left the army, is it?" she mused.

He laughed curtly. "Our commanding officer sent us against an enemy company, understrength, without proper body armor, with weapons that were misfiring. I took exception and he called me a name I didn't like. I decked him, wrapped him up in his blanket and gagged him, and led the attack myself. Tactics brought us all back alive. His way would have wiped us out to the last man. The brass didn't approve of my methods, so I had the choice of being honorably discharged or court-martialed. It was a close decision," he added with cold humor.

She just stared at him. "How could they do that? Send you into battle without proper equipment... That's outrageous!"

"Talk to Congress," he said coolly. "But don't expect them to do anything, unless it's an election year. Improvements cost money. We don't have enough."

She stared out over the distant pasture. "What happened to your commanding officer?"

"Oh, they promoted him," he said. "Called his tactics brilliant, in fact."

"But he didn't go, and they were your tactics!" she exclaimed.

He raised an eyebrow. "That's not what he told the brass."

She glowered. "Somebody should have told them!"

"In fact, just last week one of his execs got drunk enough to spill the beans to a reporter for one of the larger newspaper chains. A court-martial board is convening in the near future, or so I hear."

"Will they call you to testify?" she wondered.

He smiled. "God, I hope so," he replied.

She laughed at his expression. "Revenge is sweet?"

"So they tell me. Being of a naturally sweet and retiring disposition, I rarely ever cause problems...why are you laughing?"

She was almost doubled over. He was the last man she could picture that way.

"Maybe I caused a little trouble, once in a while," he had to admit. He glanced at his watch. "Lunch break's over. Better get back to work, so that Justin doesn't start looking for replacements."

"It was a nice lunch break, even if we didn't eat anything."

"I wasn't hungry. Sorry, I didn't think about food."

She smiled up at him. "Neither did I. We had a big breakfast this morning, and I was stuffed. Wouldn't you like to come over for pizza tonight?"

He hesitated. "I would, but I'm not going to."

"Why?"

"I'm not going to provide any more reasons for Hammock to take out old injuries on you."

"I'm not afraid of J.B."

"Neither am I," he agreed. "But let's give him time to calm down before we start any more trouble."

"I suppose we could," she agreed, but reluctantly. She didn't want J.B. to think she was bowing down to him.

THE WEEKEND WENT SMOOTHLY. J.B. and his blonde appendage were nowhere in sight, and neither was Grange. Tellie played Monopoly with Marge and the girls on Saturday night, and went to church with them on Sunday morning.

Monday morning, Marge didn't get up for breakfast. Tellie took her a tray, worried because she seemed unusually pale and languorous.

"Just a little dizziness and nausea, Tellie," Marge protested with a wan smile. "I'll stay in bed and feel better. Really. The girls are here if I need help."

"You'd better call me if you do," she said firmly.

Marge smiled and nodded. Tellie noticed an odd rhythm in her heartbeat—it was so strong that it was shaking her nightgown. Nausea and an erratic heartbeat were worrisome symptoms. Tellie's grandfather had died of heart trouble, and she remembered the same symptoms in him.

She didn't make a big deal out of it, but she did put aside her hurt pride long enough to drive by J.B.'s office on the way to the feedlot.

He was talking to a visiting cattleman, but when he saw Tellie, he broke off the conversation politely and joined her in the outer office. He looked good in jeans and a chambray shirt and chaps, she thought, even if they were designer clothing. He was working today, not squiring around women.

"Couldn't stand it anymore, I gather?" he asked curtly. "You just had to come and see me and apologize?"

She frowned. "Excuse me?"

"It's about time," he told her. "But I'm busy today. You should have picked a better time."

"J.B., I need to talk to you," she began.

He gave her slender figure in the green pantsuit a curiously intent scrutiny, winding his way back up the modest neckline to her face, with only the lightest touch of makeup, and her wavy hair like a dark cap around her head. "On your way to work?"

"Yes," she said. "J.B., I have to tell you something…"

He took her arm and led her back outside to her car. "Later. I've got a full day. Besides," he added as he opened her car door, "you know I don't like to be chased. I like to do the chasing."

She let out an exasperated breath. "J.B., I'm not chasing you! If you'd just give me a chance to speak…!"

His eyes narrowed. "I don't like treating you like the enemy, but I also don't like the way you spoke to Bella. When you apologize, to her, we'll go from there."

"Apologize?"

His face hardened. "You took too much for granted. You aren't part of my family, and you aren't a lover. You can't treat my women like trespassers in my own sister's house. Maybe we were close, when you were younger, but that's over."

"She started it," she began, riled.

"She belongs with me. You don't." His eyes were hard. "I need more from a woman than a handshake at the end of the evening. That's as much as you're able to give, Tellie. You're completely unawakened."

She wondered what he was talking about. But she didn't have time to ponder enigmas. "Listen, Bella's not what I came here to talk about!"

"I'm not giving up Bella," he continued, as if she hadn't spoken. "And chasing after me like this isn't going to get you anything except the wrong side of my temper. Don't do it again."

"J.B.!"

He closed the door. "Go to work," he said shortly, and turned away.

Of all the arrogant, assuming, overbearing conceited jackasses, she thought as she reversed out of the parking space and took off toward town, he took the cake. She wasn't chasing him, she was trying to tell him about Marge! Well, she could try again later. Next time, she promised herself, she'd make him listen.

She walked in the front door after work, tired and dispirited. Maybe Marge was better, she hoped.

"Tellie, is that you?" Dawn exclaimed from the top of the staircase. "Come on up. Hurry, please!"

Tellie took the steps two at a time. Marge was lying

on her back, gasping for breath, wincing with pain. Her face was a grayish tone, her skin cold and clammy.

"Heart attack," Tellie said at once. She'd seen this all before, with her grandfather. She grabbed the phone and dialed 911.

SHE TRIED TO call J.B., but she couldn't get an answer on his cell phone, or on the phone at the office or his house. She waited until the ambulance loaded up Margc, and the girls went with her, to get into her car and drive to J.B.'s house. If she couldn't find him, she could at least get Nell to relay a message.

She leaped out of the car and ran to the front door. She tried the knob and found it unlocked. This was no time for formality. She opened it and ran down the hall to J.B.'s study. She threw open the door and stopped dead in the doorway.

J.B. looked up, over Bella's bare white shoulders, his face flushed, his mouth swollen, his shirt off.

"What the hell are you doing here?" he demanded furiously.

CHAPTER SIX

TELLIE COULD BARELY get her breath. Worried about Marge, half-sick with fear, she couldn't even manage words. No wonder J.B. couldn't be bothered to answer the phone. He and his beautiful girlfriend were half-naked. Apparently J.B. wasn't much on beds for his sensual adventures. She remembered with heartache that he'd wrestled her down on that very sofa when she was eighteen and kissed her until her mouth hurt. It had been the most heavenly few minutes of her entire life, despite the fact that he'd been furious when he started kissing her. It hadn't ended that way, though...

"Get out!" J.B. threw at her.

She managed to get her wits back. Marge. She had to think about Marge, not about how much her pride was hurting. "J.B., you have to listen..."

"Get out, damn you!" he raged. "I've had it up to here with you chasing after me, pawing me, trying to get close to me! I don't want you, Tellie, how many times do I have to tell you before you realize that I mean it? You're a stray that Marge and I took in, nothing more! I don't want you, and I never will!"

Her heart was bursting with raw pain. She hoped she wouldn't pass out. She knew her face was white. She wanted to move, to leave, but her feet felt frozen to the carpet.

Her tormented expression and lack of response seemed to make him worse. "You skinny, ugly little tomboy," he raged, white hot with fury. "Who'd want something like you for keeps? Get out, I said!"

She gave up. She turned away, slowly, aware of the gloating smile on Bella's face, and closed the door behind her. Her knees barely gave her support as she walked back toward the front door.

Nell was standing by the staircase, drying her hands on her apron, looking shocked. "What in the world is all the yelling about?" she exclaimed. She hesitated when she saw the younger woman's drawn, white face. "Tellie, what's wrong?" she asked gently.

Tellie fought for composure. "Marge...is on her way to the hospital in an ambulance, with the girls. I think it's a heart attack. I couldn't make J.B. listen. He's... I walked in on him and that woman... He yelled at me and said I was chasing him, and called me horrible names...!" She swallowed hard and drew herself erect. "Please tell him we'll all be at the hospital, if he can tear himself loose long enough!"

She turned toward the door.

"Don't you drive that car unless you're all right, Tellie," Nell said firmly. "It's pouring down rain."

"I'm fine," she said in a ghostly tone. She even forced a smile. "Tell him, okay?"

"I'll tell him," Nell said angrily. Her voice softened. "Don't worry, honey. Marge is one tough cookie. She'll be all right. You just drive carefully. You ought to wait and go with him," she added slowly.

"If I got in a car with him right now, I'd kill him," Tellie said through her teeth. Helpless tears were rolling down her pale cheeks. "See you later, Nell."

"Tellie…"

It was too late. Tellie closed the door behind her and went to her car. She was getting soaked and she didn't care. J.B. had said terrible things to her. She knew that she'd never get over them. He wanted her to stop chasing him. She hadn't been, but it must have looked like it. She'd gone to his office this morning, and to the house this afternoon. It was about Marge. He wouldn't believe it, though. He thought Tellie was desperate for him. That was a joke, now. She was sure that she never wanted to see him again as long as she lived.

She started the car and turned it. The tires were slick. She hadn't realized how slick until she almost spun out going down the driveway. She needed to keep her speed down, but she wasn't thinking rationally. She was hearing J.B. yell at her that she was an ugly stray he'd taken in, that he didn't want her. Tears misted her eyes as she tried to concentrate on the road.

There was a hairpin curve just before the ranch road met the highway. It was usually easy to maneuver, but the rain was coming so hard and fast that the little car suddenly hydroplaned. She saw the ditch coming toward her and jerked the wheel as hard as she could. In a daze, she felt the car go over and over and over. Her seat belt broke and something hit her head. Everything went black.

J.B. STORMED OUT of the study just seconds after he heard Tellie's little car scatter gravel as it sped away. His hair was mussed, like his shirt, and he was in a vicious humor. It had been a bad day altogether. He shouldn't have yelled at Tellie. But he wondered why she'd come barging in. He should have asked. It was just that it had shamed him to be seen in such a position with Bella, knowing painfully how Tellie felt about him. He'd hurt her with just the sight of him and Bella, without adding his scathing comments afterward. Tellie wouldn't even realize that shame had put him on the offensive. She had feelings of glass, and he'd shattered them.

Nell was waiting for him at the foot of the staircase. She was visibly seething, and her white hair almost stood on end with bridled rage. "So you finally came out, did you?"

"Tellie was tearing up the driveway as she left," he bit off. "What the hell got into her? Why was she here?" he added reluctantly, because he'd realized, belatedly, that she hadn't looked as if she were pursuing him with amorous intent.

Nell gave him a cold smile. "She couldn't get you on the phone, so she drove over to tell you that Marge has had a heart attack." She nodded curtly when she saw him turn pale. "That's right. She wasn't here chasing you. She wanted you to know about your sister."

"Oh, God," he bit off.

"*He* won't help you," Nell ground out. "Yelling at poor Tellie like that, when she was only trying to do you a good turn…!"

"Shut up," he snapped angrily. "Call the hospital and see…"

"You call them." She took off her apron. "You've got my two weeks' notice, as of right now. I'm sick of watching you torture Tellie. I quit! See if your harpy girlfriend in there can cook your meals and clean your house while she spends you into the poorhouse!"

"Nell," he began furiously.

She held up a hand. "I won't reconsider."

The living room door opened, and Bella slinked into

the hallway, smiling contentedly. "Aren't we going out to eat?" she asked J.B. as she moved to catch him by onc arm.

"I'm going to the hospital," he said. "My sister's had a heart attack."

"Oh, that's too bad," Bella said. "Do you want me to go with you and hold your hand?"

"The girls will love that," Nell said sarcastically. "You'll be such a comfort to them!"

"Nell!" J.B. fumed.

"She's right, I'd be a comfort, like she said," Bella agreed, missing the sarcasm altogether. "You need me, J.B."

"I hope he gets what he really needs one day," Nell said, turning on her heel.

"You're fired!" he yelled after her.

"Too late, I already quit," Nell said pleasantly. "I'm sure Bella can cook you some supper and wash your clothes." She closed the kitchen door behind her with a snap.

"Now, you know I can't cook, J.B.," Bella said irritably. "And I've never washed clothes—I send mine to the laundry. What's the matter with her? It's that silly girl who was here, isn't it? I don't like her at all…"

J.B. reached into his pocket and pulled out two large bills. "Call a cab and go home," he said shortly. "I have to get to the hospital."

"But I should go with you," she argued.

He looked down at her with bridled fury. "Go home."

She shifted restlessly. "Well, all right, J.B., you don't need to yell. Honestly, you're in such a bad mood!"

"My sister has had a heart attack," he repeated.

"Yes, I know, but those things happen, don't they? You can't do anything about it," she added blankly.

It was like talking to a wall, he thought with exasperation. He tucked in his shirt, checked to make sure his car keys were in his pocket, jerked his raincoat and hat from the hall coatrack and went out the door without a backward glance.

DAWN AND BRANDI were pacing the waiting room in the emergency room at Jacobsville General Hospital while Dr. Coltrain examined their mother. They were quiet, somber, with tears pouring down their cheeks in silent misery when J.B. walked in.

They ran to him the instant they saw him, visibly shaken. He gathered them close, feeling like an animal because he hadn't even let Tellie talk when she'd walked in on him. She'd come to tell him that Marge was in the hospital with a heart attack, and he'd sent her running with insults. Probably she'd come to his office that morning because something about Marge had worried her. He'd been no help at all. Now Tellie was hurt and Nell was quitting. He'd never felt so helpless.

"Mama won't die, will she, Uncle J.B.?" Brandi asked tearfully.

"Of course she won't," he assured her in the deep, soft tone he used with little things or hurt children. "She'll be fine."

"Tellie said she was going to tell you about Mama. Why didn't Tellie come with you?" Dawn asked, wiping her eyes.

He stiffened. "Tellie's not here?"

"No. She had to go over to your house, because you

didn't answer your phone," Brandi replied. "I guess the lines were down or something."

"Or something," he said huskily. He'd taken the phone off the hook.

"She may have gone home to get Mama a gown," Dawn suggested. "She always thinks of things like that, when everybody else goes to pieces."

"She'll be here as soon as she can... I know she will," Brandi agreed. "I don't know what we'd do without Tellie."

Which made J.B. feel even smaller than he already did. Tellie must be scared to death. She'd been with her grandfather when he died of a heart attack. She'd loved him more than any other member of her small family, including the mother she'd lost more recently. Marge's heart attack would bring back terrible memories. Worse, when she showed up at the hospital, she'd have to deal with what J.B. had said to her. It wasn't going to be a pleasant reunion.

DR. COLTRAIN CAME OUT, smiling. "Marge is going to be all right," he told them. "We got to her just in time. But she'll have to see a heart specialist, and she's going to be on medication from now on. Did you know that her blood pressure was high?"

"No!" J.B. said at once. "It's always been low!"

Coltrain shook his head. "Not anymore. She's very lucky that it happened like this. It may have saved her life."

"It was a heart attack, then?" J.B. persisted, with the girls standing close at his side.

"Yes. But a mild one. You can see her when we've got her in a room. You'll need to sign her in at the office."

"I'll do that right now."

"But, where's Tellie?" Dawn asked when they were alone.

J.B. wished he knew.

HE WAS ON his way back from the office when he passed the emergency room, just in time to see a worried Grange stalking in beside a gurney that two paramedics were rushing through the door. On the stretcher was Tellie, unconscious and bleeding.

"Tellie!" he exclaimed, rushing to the gurney. She was white as a sheet, and he was more frightened now than he was when he learned about Marge. "What happened?" he shot at Grange.

"I don't know," Grange said curtly. "Her car was off the road in a ditch. She was unconscious, in a couple of inches of water, facedown. If I hadn't come along when I did, she'd have drowned."

J.B. felt sick all the way to his soul. It was his fault. All his fault. "Where was the car?" he asked.

"On the farm road that leads to your house," Grange replied, his eyes narrowed, suspiciously. "Why are you here?"

"My sister just had a heart attack," he said solemnly. "The girls and I have been in the emergency waiting room. She's going to be all right. Tellie came to tell me about it," he added reluctantly.

"Then why in hell didn't she ride in with you?" Grange asked, brown eyes flashing. "She must have been upset— she loves Marge. She shouldn't even have been driving in weather this dangerous."

That was a question J.B. didn't want to touch. He ignored it, following the gurney into one of the examination rooms with Grange right on his heels.

He got one of Tellic's small hands in both of his and held on tight. "Tellie," he said huskily, feeling the pain all the way to his boots. "Tellie, hold on!"

"She shouldn't have been driving," Grange repeated, leaning against the wall nearby. He was obviously upset as well, and the look he gave J.B. would have started a fight under better circumstances.

The entrance of Copper Coltrain interrupted him.

Copper gave J.B. an odd look. "It isn't your day, is it?" he asked, moving to Tellie's side. "What happened?"

"Her car hydroplaned, apparently," Grange said tautly. "I found it overturned. She was lying facedown in a ditch full of water. If I'd been just a little later, she'd have drowned."

"Damn the luck!" Coltrain muttered, checking her pupil reaction with a small penlight. "She's concussed as well as bruised," he murmured. "I'm going to need X-rays and a battery of tests to see how badly she's hurt. But the concussion is the main thing."

J.B. felt sick. One of his men had been kicked in the head by a mean steer and dropped dead of a massive concussion. "Can't you do something now?" he raged at Coltrain.

The physician gave him an odd look. It was notorious gossip locally that Tellie was crazy about J. B. Hammock, and that J.B. paid her as little attention as possible. The white-faced man with blazing green eyes facing him didn't seem disinterested.

"What would you suggest?" he asked J.B. curtly.

"Wake her up!"

Grange made a rough sound in his throat.

"You can shut up," J.B. told him icily. "You're not a doctor."

"Neither are you," Grange returned with the same lack of warmth. "And if you'd given her a lift to the hospital, she wouldn't need one, would she?"

J.B. had already worked that out for himself. His lips compressed furiously.

Tellie groaned.

Both men moved to the examination table at the same time. Coltrain gave them angry looks and bent to examine Tellie.

"Can you hear me?" he asked her softly. "Tellie?"

Her eyes opened, green and dazed. She blinked and winced. "My head hurts."

"I'm not surprised," Coltrain murmured, busy with a stethoscope. "Take a deep breath. Let it out. Again."

She groaned. "My head hurts," she repeated.

"Okay, I'll give you something for it. But we need X-rays and an MRI," Coltrain said quietly. "Anything hurt besides your head?"

"Everything," she replied. "What happened?"

"You wrecked your car," Grange said quietly.

She looked up at him. "You found me?"

He nodded, dark eyes concerned.

She managed a smile. "Thanks." She shivered. "I'm wet!"

"It was pouring rain," Grange said, his voice soft, like his eyes. He brushed back the blood-matted hair from her forehead, disclosing a growing dark bruise. He winced.

"You're concussed, Tellie," Dr. Coltrain said. "We're going to have to keep you for a day or two. Okay?"

"But I'll miss graduation!" she exclaimed, trying to sit up.

He gently pushed her back down. "No, you won't," he said with a quizzical smile.

She blinked, glancing at J.B., who looked very worried. "But it's May. I'm a senior. I have a white gown and cap." She hesitated. "Was I driving Marge's car?"

"No. Your own," J.B. said slowly, apprehensively.

"But I don't have a car, don't you remember, J.B.?" she asked pleasantly. "I have to drive Marge's. She's going to help me buy a car this summer, because I'm going to work at the Sav-A-Lot Grocery Store, remember?"

J.B.'s indrawn breath was audible. Before the other two men could react, he pressed Tellie's small hand closer in his own. "Tellie, how old are you?" he asked.

"I'm seventeen, you know that," she scoffed.

Coltrain whistled. J.B. turned to him, his lips parted in the preliminary to a question.

"We're going to step outside and discuss how to break it to Marge," Coltrain told her gently. "You just rest. I'll send a nurse in with something for your headache, okay?"

"Okay," she agreed. "J.B., you aren't leaving, are you?" she added worriedly.

Coals of fire, he was thinking, as he assured her that he'd be nearby. She relaxed and smiled as she lay back on the examination table.

Coltrain motioned the other two men outside into the hall. "Amnesia," he told J.B. at once. "I'm sure it's temporary," he added quickly. "It isn't uncommon with head injuries. She's very confused, and in some pain. I'll run tests. We'll do an MRI to make sure."

"The head injury would cause it?" Grange asked worriedly.

J.B. had a flush along his high cheekbones. He didn't speak.

Coltrain gave him a curious look. "The brain tends to try to protect itself from trauma, and not only physical trauma. Has she had a shock of some kind?" he asked J.B. pointedly.

J.B. replied with a curt jerk of his head. "We had a… misunderstanding at the house," he admitted.

Grange's dark eyes flashed. "Well, that explains why she wrecked the car!" he accused.

J.B. glared at him. "Like hell it does…!"

Coltrain held up a hand. "Arguing isn't going to do her any good. She's had the wreck, now we have to deal with the consequences. I'm going to admit her and start running tests."

J.B. drew a quick breath. "How are we going to explain this to Tellie?"

Coltrain sighed. "Tell her as little as possible, right now. Once she's stabilized, we'll tell her what we have to. But if she thinks she's seventeen, sending her to Marge's house is going to be traumatic—she'll expect the girls to be four years younger than they are, won't she?"

J.B. was thinking, hard. He saw immediately a way to solve that problem and prevent Nell from escaping at once. "She can stay at the house with Nell and me," he said. "She and Marge and the girls did stay there when she was seventeen for a couple of weeks while Marge's house was being remodeled. We can tell her that Marge and the girls are having a vacation while workmen tend to her house. I'll make it right with Dawn and Brandi."

"You and Tellie were close when she was in her teens, I recall," Coltrain recalled.

"Yes," J.B. said tautly.

Coltrain chuckled, glancing at Grange. "She followed him around like a puppy when she first went to live with

Marge," he told the other man. "You couldn't talk to J.B. without tripping over Tellie. J.B. was her security blanket after she lost her mother."

"She was the same way with Marge," J.B. muttered.

"Not to that extent, she wasn't," Coltrain argued. "She thought the sun rose and set on you…"

"I need to go back and check on Marge," J.B. interrupted, visibly uncomfortable.

"I'll stay with Tellie for a while," Grange said, moving back into the examination room before the other two men could object.

J.B. stared after him with bridled fury, his hands deep in his pockets, his eyes smoldering. "He's got no business in there," he told Coltrain. "He isn't even family!"

"Neither are you," the doctor reminded him.

J.B. glared at him. "Are you sure she'll be all right?"

"As sure as I can be." He studied the other man intently. "You said something to her, something that hurt, didn't you?" he asked, nodding when J.B.'s high cheekbones took on a ruddy color. "She's hiding in the past, when you were less resentful of her. She'll get her memory back, but it's going to be dangerous to rush it. You have to let her move ahead at her own pace."

"I'll do that," J.B. assured him. He drew in a long breath. "Damn. I feel as if my whole life crashed and burned today. First Marge, now Tellie. And Nell quit," he added angrily.

"Nell?" Coltrain exclaimed. "She's been there since you were a boy."

"Well, she wants to leave," J.B. muttered. "But she'll stay if she knows Tellie's coming to the house. I'd better phone her. Then I'll go back to Marge's room." He met Coltrain's eyes. "If she needs anything, *anything*,

I'll take care of it. I don't think she's got any health insurance at all."

"You might stop by the admissions office and set things up," Coltrain suggested. "But I'll do what needs doing, finances notwithstanding. You know that."

"I do. Thanks, Copper."

Coltrain shrugged. "I'm glad she's rallying," he said. "And Marge, too."

"Same here."

J.B. left him to go back to the admissions office and sign Tellie in. He felt guilty. Her wreck was certainly his fault. The least he could do was provide for her treatment. He hated knowing that he'd upset her that much, and for nothing. She was only trying to help. Frustration had taken its toll on him and driven him into Bella's willing arms. The last thing he'd expected was for Tellie to walk in on them. He'd never been quite so ashamed of himself. Which was, of course, no excuse to take his temper out on her. He wished he could take back all the things he'd said. While her memory was gone, at least he had a chance to regain her trust and make up, a little, for what he'd done.

TELLIE FELT DRAINED by the time Coltrain had all the tests he wanted. She was curious about the man who'd told her that he found her in the wrecked car and called the ambulance. He was handsome and friendly and seemed to like her very much, but she didn't know him.

"It was very kind of you to rescue me," she told Grange when she was in a private room.

He shrugged. "My pleasure." He smiled at her, his dark eyes twinkling. "You can save me, next time."

She laughed. Her head cocked to one side as she studied him. "I'm sorry, but I don't remember your name."

"Grange," he said pleasantly.

"Just Grange?" she queried.

He nodded.

"Have I known you a long time?"

He shook his head. "But I've taken you out a few times."

Her eyebrows lifted. "And J.B. let me go with you?" she exclaimed. "That's very strange. I wanted to go hiking with a college boy I knew and he threw a fit. You're older than any college boy."

He chuckled. "I'm twenty-seven," he told her.

"Wow," she mused.

"You're old for your age," he said, evading her eyes. "J.B. and I know each other."

"I see." She didn't, but he was obviously reluctant to talk about it. "Marge hasn't been to see me," she added suddenly. "That's not like her."

Grange recalled what J.B. and Coltrain had discussed. "Her house is being remodeled," he said. "She and the girls are on a vacation trip."

"While school's in session?" she exclaimed.

He thought fast. "It's Spring Break, remember?"

She was confused. Hadn't someone said it was May? Wasn't Spring Break in March? "But graduation is coming up very soon."

"You got your cap and gown early, didn't you?" he improvised.

She was frowning. "That must be what happened. I'm so confused," she murmured, holding her head. "And my head absolutely throbs."

"They'll give you something for that." He checked his watch. "I have to go. Visiting hours are over."

"Will you come back tomorrow?" she asked, feeling descrted.

He smiled. "Of course I will." He hesitated. "It will have to be during my lunch hour, or after work, though."

"Where do you work?"

"At the Ballenger feedlot."

That set off bells in her head, but she couldn't think why. "They're nice, Justin and Calhoun."

"Yes, they are." He stood up, moving the chair back from her bed. "Take care. I'll see you tomorrow."

"Okay. Thanks again."

He looked at her for a long time. "I'm glad it wasn't more serious than it is," he told her. "You were unconscious when I found you."

"It was raining," she recalled hesitantly. "I don't understand why I was driving in the rain. I'm afraid of it, you know."

"Are you?"

She shook her head. "I must have had a reason."

"I'm sure you did." He looked thunderous, but he quickly erased the expression, smiled and left her.

SHE SETTLED BACK into the pillow, feeling bruised and broken. It was such an odd experience, what had happened to her. Everyone seemed to be holding things back from her. She wondered how badly she was damaged. Tomorrow, she promised herself, she'd dig it out of J.B.

CHAPTER SEVEN

TELLIE WOKE UP EARLY, expecting to find herself alone. But J.B. was sprawled in the chair next to the bed, snoring faintly, and he looked as if he'd been there for some time. A nurse was tiptoeing around to get Tellie's vitals, sending amused and interested glances at the long, lean cowboy beside the bed.

"Has he been there long?" Tellie wanted to know.

"Since daybreak," the nurse replied with a smile. She put the electronic thermometer in Tellie's ear, let it beep, checked it and wrote down a figure. She checked her pulse and recorded that, as well. "I understand the nurse on the last shift tried to evict him and the hospital administrator actually came down here in person to tell her to cease and desist." She gave Tellie a speaking glance. "I gather that your visitor is somebody very important."

"He paid for that MRI machine they used on me yesterday."

The nurse pursed her lips. "Well! Aren't you nicely connected?" she mused. "Is he your fiancé?"

Tellie chuckled. "I'm only seventeen," she said.

The nurse looked puzzled. She checked Tellie's chart, made a face and then forced a smile. "Of course. Sorry."

Tellie wondered why she looked so confused. "Can I go home today?" she wondered.

"That depends on what Dr. Coltrain thinks," she replied. "He'll be in to see you when he makes rounds. Breakfast will be up shortly."

"Thanks," Tellie told her.

The nurse smiled, cast another curious and appreciative glance at J.B. and left.

Tellie stared at him with mixed emotions. He was a handsome man, she thought, but at least she was safe from all that masculine charm that he used to such good effect on women he liked. She was far too young to be threatened by J.B.'s sex appeal.

It was easy to see why he had women flocking around him. He had a dynamite physique, hard and lean and sexy, with long, powerful legs and big hands. His face was rugged, but he had fine green eyes under a jutting brow and a mouth that was as hard and sensuous as any movie star's. But it wasn't just his looks that made him attractive. It was his voice, deep and faintly raspy, and the way he had of making a woman feel special. He had beautiful manners when he cared to display them, and a temper that made grown men look for cover. Tellie had rarely seen him fighting mad. Most of the time he had excellent self-control.

She frowned. Why did it sting to think of him losing his temper? He'd rarely lost it at Tellie, and even then it was for her own good. But something about her thoughts made her uneasy.

Just as she was focusing on that, J.B. opened his eyes and looked at her, and she stopped thinking. Her heart jumped. She couldn't imagine why. She was possessive of J.B., she idolized him, but she'd never really considered anything physical between them. Now, her body seemed to know things her mind didn't.

"How do you feel?" he asked quietly.

She blinked. "My head doesn't hurt as much," she said. She searched his eyes. "Why are you here? I'm all right."

He shrugged. "I was worried." He didn't add that he was also guilt ridden about the reason for the wreck and her injury. His conscience had him on the rack. He couldn't sleep for worrying about her. That was new. It was disconcerting. He'd never let a woman get under his skin since his ill-fated romance of years past. Even an unexpected interlude with Tellie on the sofa in his office hadn't made a lot of difference in their turbulent relationship, especially when he realized that Tellie was sexually unawakened. He'd deliberately pushed her out of his life and kept her at arm's length—well, mostly, except for unavoidable lapses when he gave in to the passion riding him. That passion had drawn him to Bella in a moment of weakness.

Then Tellie had walked in on him with Bella, and his whole life had changed. He'd never felt such pain as when Grange had walked into the emergency room with an unconscious Tellie on a gurney. Nothing was ever going to be the same again. The only thing worse than seeing her in such a condition was dreading the day when her memory returned, because she was going to hate J.B.

"I'm going to be fine," she promised, smiling. "Do you think Dr. Coltrain will let me go home today?"

"I'll ask him," he said, sitting up straighter. "Nell's getting a room ready for you. While Marge and the girls are away, you'll stay with Nell and me."

"I wish Marge was here," she said involuntarily.

He sighed. Marge was improving, too, but she was worried about Tellie. Dawn had let it slip that she'd been in a wreck, but J.B. had assured her that Tellie was going to be fine. There was this little problem with her memory, of course, and she'd have to stay at the house with him until it came back.

Marge was reassured, but still concerned. He knew that she'd sensed something was wrong between her brother and Tellie, but she couldn't put it into words. He wasn't about to enlighten her. He had enough on his plate.

"I'll be in the way there," she protested.

"You won't," he replied. "Nell will be glad of the company."

She studied her hands on the sheet. "There's something that bothers me, J.B.," she said without looking at him.

"What?"

She hesitated. "What was I doing at your house, at night, in the rain?"

He sat very still. He hadn't considered that the question would arise so soon. He wasn't sure how to answer it, to protect her from painful memories.

She looked up and met his turbulent green eyes. "You were mad at me, weren't you?"

His heart seemed to stop, then start again. "We had an argument," he began slowly.

She nodded. "I thought so. But I can't remember what it was about."

"Time enough for that when you're back on your feet," he said, rising up from the chair. "Don't borrow trouble. Just get well."

So there was something! She wished she could grasp what it was. J.B. was acting very oddly.

She looked up at him. "You leaving?" she asked.

He nodded. "I've got to get the boys started moving the bulls to summer pasture."

"Not on roundup?"

"Roundup's in March," he said easily.

"Oh." She frowned. It wasn't March. She knew it wasn't. "Is it March?"

He ignored that. "I'll talk to Coltrain on my way out," he said.

"But it's not time for rounds…"

"I met him coming in. He had an emergency surgery. I expect he's through by now," he replied.

"J.B., who is that man Grange?" she asked abruptly. "And why did you let me go out with him? He said he's twenty-seven, and I'm just seventeen. You had a hissy fit when I tried to go hiking with Billy Johns."

He looked indignant. "I don't have hissy fits," he said shortly.

"Well, you raged at me, anyway," she corrected. "Why are you letting me see Grange?"

His teeth set. "You're full of questions this morning."

"Answer a few of them," she invited.

"Later," he said, deliberately checking his watch. "I have to get to work. Want me to bring you anything?"

"A nail file and a ladder," she said with resignation. "Just get me out of here."

"The minute you're fit to leave," he promised. He smiled faintly. "Stay put until I get back."

"If I must," she sighed.

HE WAS GONE and she was left to eat breakfast and while away the next few hours until Dr. Coltrain showed up.

He examined Tellie and pronounced her fit to leave the hospital.

"But you still need to take it easy for a week or two," he told her. "Stay out of crowds, stick to J.B.'s house. No parties, no job, nothing."

She frowned. "I thought it was just a mild concussion," she argued.

"It is." He didn't quite meet her eyes. "We're just not taking chances. You need lots of rest."

She sighed. "Okay, if you say so. Can I go horseback riding, can I swim…?"

"Sure. Just don't leave J.B.'s ranch to do them."

She smiled. "What's going on, Dr. Coltrain?"

He leaned forward. "It's a secret," he told her. "Bear with me. Okay?"

She laughed. "Okay. When do I get to know the secret?"

"All in good time," he added, as inspiration struck him. "Keep an eye on J.B. for me."

Her eyebrows arched. "Is something wrong with him…?" she asked worriedly.

"Nothing specific. Just watch him."

She shook her head. "Okay. If you say so."

"Good girl." He patted her shoulder and left, congratulating himself on the inspiration. While she was focused on J.B., she wouldn't be preoccupied with her own health. Far better if she licked the amnesia all by herself. He didn't want her shocked with the truth of her condition.

J.B.'s HOUSE WAS bigger than Tellie remembered. Nell met them at the door, all smiles and welcome.

"It's so good to have you back," Nell said, hugging the younger woman. "I've got a nice room all ready for you."

"Don't think you're going to get to wait on me," Tellie informed her with a grin. "I'm not an invalid."

"You have a concussion," Nell corrected, and the smile faded. "It can be very dangerous. I remember a cowboy who worked here…"

"Remember us something to eat, instead," J.B. interrupted her, with a meaningful look.

"Oh. Of course." She glared at J.B. "You had a call while you were out. I wrote the information on the pad on your desk."

He read through the lines and assumed it was from Bella. "I'll take care of it."

"Who's bringing Tellie's suitcase?" Nell asked.

J.B. stood still. "What suitcase?"

"I'll have to go over to Marge's and get my things," Tellie began.

"I'll go—!"

"I can do that," J.B. interrupted Nell. "You look after Tellie."

"When haven't I?" Nell wanted to know belligerently.

"You two need to stop arguing, or I'm going to go sit on the front porch," Tellie told both of them.

They glared at each other. J.B. shrugged and went into his den. Tellie's eyes followed him past the big sofa. The sofa... She frowned. Something about that sofa made her uneasy.

"What's wrong?" Nell prompted.

Tellie put a hand to her forehead and laughed faintly. "I don't know. I looked at the sofa and felt funny."

"Let's go right up and get you settled," Nell said abruptly, taking Tellie by the arm. "Then I'll see about some lunch."

It was almost as if Nell knew something about the sofa, too, but that would be ridiculous, Tellie told herself. She was getting mental.

SHE'D WANTED TO watch television, but there wasn't one in the bedroom. Nell told her that there was a problem with the satellite dish and it wasn't working. Odd, Tellie thought, it was almost as if they were trying to keep her from watching the news.

She had to stay in bed, because Nell insisted. Just after she had supper on a tray, J.B. walked in, worn and dusty, still in his working clothes.

Tellie was propped up in bed in pink-striped pajamas that made her look oddly vulnerable.

"How's it going?" he asked.

"I'm okay. Why is the satellite not working?" she added. "I can't watch The Weather Channel."

His eyebrows arched. "Why do you want to?"

"You said it was March, but Nell says it's May," she said. "That's tornado season."

"So it is."

She glowered at him. "Grange said it was March and Marge and the girls were away on Spring Break."

He pursed his lips.

"I know better, so don't bother trying to lie," she told him firmly. "If it's May, where are they?"

He leaned against the doorjamb. "They're around, but you can't see them just yet. Nothing's wrong."

"That's not true, J.B.," she said flatly.

He laughed mirthlessly and twirled his hat through his fingers. "No use trying to fool you, is it? Okay, the concussion did something to your head. You're a little fuzzy about things. We're supposed to let your mind clear without any help."

She frowned. "What's fuzzy about it?"

He jerked away from the door. "Not tonight. I'm going to clean up, then I've got...someplace to go," he amended.

"A date," she translated, grinning.

There was faint jealousy in her expression, but she

was hiding it very well. He felt uncomfortable. He was taking Bella out, and here was Tellie, badly injured on his account and hurting.

"I could postpone it," he began guiltily.

"Whatever for?" she exclaimed.

His eyebrows arched. "Excuse me?"

"I'm seventeen," she pointed out. "Even if I were crazy about you, it's obvious that you're far too old for me."

He felt odd inside. He studied her curiously. "Am I?"

"I still don't understand why you're letting Grange date me," she mused. "He's twenty-seven."

"Is he?" He considered that. Grange was seven years his junior, closer to Tellie's own age than he was. That stung.

"You're hedging, J.B.," she accused.

He checked his watch. "Maybe so. I've got to go. Nell will be here if you need anything."

"I won't."

He turned to go, hesitated, and looked back at her, brooding. If she tried the television sets, she'd discover that they all worked. "Don't wander around the house."

She gaped at him. "Why would I want to?"

"Just don't. I'll see you tomorrow."

She watched him go, curious about his odd behavior.

LATER, SHE TRIED to pump Nell for information, but it was like talking to a wall. "You and J.B. are stonewalling me," she accused.

Nell smiled. "For a good cause. Just relax and enjoy being here, for the time that's left." She picked up the empty iced-tea glass on the bedside table, looking around the room. "Odd that J.B. would put you in here," she said, thinking aloud.

"Is it? Why?"

"It was his grandmother's room," she said with a smile. "She was a wonderful old lady. J.B. adored her. She'd been an actress in Hollywood in her youth. She could tell some stories!"

"Does he talk about her?" Tellie wondered.

"Almost never. She died in a tornado." She nodded, at Tellie's astonished look. "That's right, one of the worst in south Texas history hit here," she recalled. "It lifted the barn off its foundations and twisted it. His grandmother's favorite horse was trapped there, and old Mrs. Hammock put on a raincoat and rushed out to try to save it. Nobody saw her go. The tornado picked her up and put her in the top of an oak tree, dead. They had to get a truck with a cherry picker to get her down, afterward," Nell said softly. "J.B. was watching. He hates tornadoes to this day. It's why we have elaborate storm shelters here and in the bunkhouse, and even under the barn."

"That's why he looked funny, when I mentioned liking to watch The Weather Channel," she said slowly.

"He watches it religiously in the spring and summer," Nell confided. "And he has weather alert systems in the same places he has the shelters. All his men have cell phones with alert capability. He's something of a fanatic about safety."

"Have I ever been in a tornado?" she asked Nell.

Nell looked surprised. "Why do you ask?"

"J.B. said I'm fuzzy about the past," she replied. "I gather that I've lost some memories, is that it?"

Nell came and sat down in the chair beside the bed. "Yes. You have."

"And the doctor doesn't want me remembering too soon?"

"He thinks it's better if you remember all on your own," Nell said. "So we're conspiring to keep you in the dark, so to speak," she added with a gentle smile.

Tellie frowned. "I wish I could remember what I've forgotten."

Nell burst out laughing. "Don't rush it. When you remember, we'll leave together."

Tellie gaped at her. "You're quitting? But you've been here forever!"

"I've been here too long," Nell said curtly, rising. "There are other bosses who don't yell and threaten people."

"You yell and threaten back," Tellie reminded her.

"Remembered that, did you?" she teased.

"Yes. So why are you leaving him?"

"Let's just say that I don't like his methods," she replied. "And that's all you're getting out of me. I'll be in the kitchen. Just use the intercom if you need me, okay?"

"Okay. Thanks, Nell."

Nell smiled at her. "I like having you here."

"Who's he dating this week?" Tellie called after her.

"Another stacked blonde, of course," came the dry reply. "She has the IQ of a lettuce leaf."

Tellie chuckled. "Obviously he doesn't like competition from mere women."

"Someday he'll come a cropper," she said. "I hope I live to see the day."

Tellie watched her close the door with faint misgivings. J.B. did like variety, she seemed to know that. But therewas something about the reference, about a blonde woman, that unsettled her. Why had she and J.B. argued? She wished she could remember.

HER LIGHT WAS still on when he came home. She was reading a particularly interesting book that she'd found in the bookcase, an autobiography by Libbie Custer, the woman who'd married General George Custer of Civil War and Little Bighorn fame. It was a tale of courage in the face of danger, unexpectedly riveting. Mrs. Custer, it seemed, had actually gone with her husband to the battlefield during the Civil War. Tellie had never read of women doing that. Mrs. Custer was something of a renegade for her oppressed generation, a daring and intelligent woman with a keen wit. She liked her.

J.B. opened the door to find her propped up in bed on her pillows with the book resting against her upraised knees under the covers.

"What are you doing up at this hour?" he asked sternly.

She glanced at him, still halfway in the book she was reading. He looked elegant in a dinner jacket and black tie, she thought, although the tie was in his hand and the shirt was open at the throat, over a pelt of dark hair. She frowned. Why did the sight of his bare chest make her heart race?

"I found this book on the shelf and couldn't put it down," she said.

He moved to the bed, stuck the tie in his pocket and sat down beside her. He took the book in a big, lean hand and checked the title. He gave it back, smiling. "Libbie Custer was one of my grandmother's heroines. She actually met her once, when she gave a speech in New York while my grandmother was visiting relatives there as a child. She said that Mrs. Custer was a wonderful speaker. She lived into her nineties."

"She wrote a very interesting book," Tellie said.

"There are three of them altogether," he told her. "I

believe you'll find the other two on the shelf as well, along with several biographies of the Colonel and the one book that he wrote."

"General Custer," she corrected.

He grinned. "That was a brevet promotion, given during the Civil War for outstanding courage under fire. His actual military rank was Colonel, at the time he died."

"You read about him, too?" she asked.

He nodded. "These were some of the first books I was exposed to as a child. My mother was big on reading skills," he said coolly. "Her picks were nonfiction, mostly chemistry and physics. Grandmother's were more palatable."

She noted the play of emotions on his lean, hard face. "Your mother was a scientist," she said suddenly, and wondered where the memory came from.

"Yes." He stared at her intently. "A research chemist. She died when we were young."

"You didn't like her very much, did you?"

"I hated her," he said flatly. "She made my grandmother miserable, making fun of her reading tastes, the way she dressed, her skills as a homemaker. She demeaned her."

"Was your grandmother your mother's mother?"

He shook his head. "My father's mother. In her day, she was an elegant horsewoman. She won trophies. And she was an actress before she married. But that, to my mother's mind, was fluff. She only admired women with Mensa-level IQs and science degrees."

"What about your father, couldn't he stop her from tormenting the old lady?"

He scoffed. "He was never here. He was too involved

with making money to pay much attention to what went on around the house."

Her eyes narrowed. "You must have had an interesting childhood."

He cocked an eyebrow. "There's a Chinese curse—'may you live in interesting times.' That would have been appropriate for it."

She didn't quite know what to say. He looked so alone. "Nell said she died in a tornado. Your grandmother, I mean."

He nodded. "She was trying to save her horse. She'd had him for twenty-five years, ridden him in competition. She loved him more than any other thing here, except maybe me." He grimaced. "I'll never forget watching them bring her down from the treetop. She looked like a broken doll." His eyes closed briefly. "I don't have much luck with women, when it comes to love."

That was a curious thing to say. She felt odd as he said it, as if she knew something more about that, but couldn't quite call it up.

"I guess life is a connected series of hard knocks," she mused.

He glanced at her. "Your own life hasn't been any bed of roses," he commented. "You lost your father when you were born, and your grandfather and your mother only six months apart."

"Did I?" she wondered.

He cursed under his breath. "I shouldn't have said that."

"It didn't trigger any memories," she assured him, managing a smile. "I'm pretty blank about recent events. Well, I remember I'm graduating," she amended, "and

that I borrowed Marge's car to drive to your house…"
She hesitated. "Marge's car…"

"Stop trying to force it," he said, tapping her knee
with a hard finger. "Your memory will come back when
it's ready to."

"Nell said she was quitting. Did you have a row with
her?"

"Did she say that I had?" he asked warily.

"She didn't say much of anything, J.B.," she muttered.
"I can't get a straight answer out of anybody, even that
nice man who was in the emergency room with me." She
hesitated. "Has he come by to see me?"

He shifted restlessly. "Why ask me?" he wondered,
but he wouldn't meet her eyes.

"He did come to see me!" she exclaimed, seeing the
truth in the ruddy color that ran along his high cheekbones. "He came, and you wouldn't let him in!"

CHAPTER EIGHT

J.B. NOT ONLY looked angry, he looked frustrated. "Coltrain said you didn't need visitors for two or three days, at least," he said firmly.

She was still staring at him, with wide pale green eyes. "But why not? Grange won't tell me anything. Every time I asked a question, he pretended to be deaf." Her eyes narrowed. "Just like you, J.B.," she added.

He patted her knee. "We're all trying to spare you any unnecessary pain," he said.

"So you're admitting that it would be painful if I remembered why you and I argued," she said.

He glared. "Life is mostly painful," he pointed out. "You and I have had disagreements before."

"Have we? And you seem like a man with such a sunny, even disposition," she said innocently.

"Ha!" came an unexpected comment from the hall.

They both turned to the doorway, and there stood Nell, in a housecoat with her hair in curlers, glaring at both of them.

"I have an even disposition," he argued.

"Evenly bad," Nell agreed. "She should be asleep," she said, nodding at Tellie.

He got to his feet. "So she should." He took the book away from Tellie and put it on the bedside table. "Go to sleep."

"Can I get you anything before I go to bed, Tellie?" Nell asked.

"No, but thanks."

J.B. pulled the pillows out from under her back and eased her down on the bed. He pulled up the covers, studied her amusedly and suddenly bent and brushed his hard mouth over her forehead. "Sleep tight, little bit." He turned off the lamp.

"I don't need tucking in," she said.

"It never hurts," he mused. He passed Nell. "You going to stand there all night? She needs her sleep."

"You're the one who was keeping her awake!" Nell muttered.

"I was not...!"

Their voices, harsh and curt, came through the closed door after he'd pulled it shut. Tellie sighed and closed her eyes. What an odd pair.

THE NEXT MORNING, there was heavy rain and lightning. Thunder shook the house. Alarmed, Tellie turned on the weather alert console next to her bed and listened to the forecast. There was a tornado watch for Jacobs County, among others in south Texas.

She grimaced, remembering tornadoes in the past. She'd seen one go through when she was a little girl. It hadn't touched down near their house, but she could never forget the color of the clouds that contained it. They were a neon green, like slimy pond algae, enclosed in thick gray swirls. She got to her feet, a little shakily, and went to the window to look out. The clouds were dark and thick, and lightning struck down out of them so unexpectedly and violently, that she jumped.

"Get away from that window!" J.B. snapped from the doorway.

She turned, her heart racing from the double impact of the storm and his temper. "I was just looking," she protested.

He closed the door behind him, striding toward her with single-minded determination. He swung her up in his powerful arms and carried her back to bed.

"Lightning strikes the highest point. There are no trees taller than the house. Get the point?" he asked.

She clung to his strong neck, savoring his strength. "I get it."

He eased her down on the pillow, his green eyes staring straight into hers as he rested his hands beside her head on the bed. "How's your head?"

"Still there," she mused. "It does throb a bit."

"No wonder," he said. He searched her eyes for so long that her heart raced. He looked down at her pajama jacket and his teeth clenched. She looked down, too, but she didn't see anything that would make him frown.

"What's wrong?" she asked.

He drew in a long breath. "You're still a child, Tellie," he said, more for his own benefit than for hers. He stood up. "Ready for breakfast?"

She frowned. "Why did you say that?"

He stuck his hands in his pockets and went to the window to look out.

"You'll get struck by lightning," she chided, throwing his own accusation back at him.

"I won't."

His back was arrow straight. She stared at it longingly. It had been sweet to lie in his arms while he carried her. She felt an odd stirring deep in her belly.

"You really hate storms, don't you?" she said.

"Most people do, if they've ever lived through one."

She remembered what he'd told her about the grandmother he loved so much, and how she'd died in a tornado. "I've only seen one up close."

He turned toward her, his eyes watchful and quiet.

"What are you thinking?" she asked.

"I don't remember you going out on more than two dates the whole time you were in high school."

The reference to the past, luckily, went right over her head. She blinked. "I was always shy around boys," she confessed. "And none of them really appealed to me. Especially not the jocks. I hate sports."

He laughed softly. "Was that why?"

She twisted the hem of the sheet between her fingers and stared at them. "You must have noticed at some point that I'm not overly brainy or especially beautiful."

He frowned. "What does that have to do with dating?"

"Everything, in high school," she reminded him curtly. "Besides all that, most boys these days want girls who don't mind giving out. I did. It got around after I poured a cup of hot chocolate all over Barry Cramer when he slid his hand under my skirt at a party."

"He did what?" he exclaimed, eyes flaming.

The rush to anger surprised her. He'd never shown any particular emotion about her infrequent dates.

"I told him that a hamburger and a movie didn't entitle him to that sort of perk."

"You should have told me," he said curtly. "I'd have decked him!"

Her cheeks colored faintly. "That would have got around, too, and I'd never have had another date."

He moved close to the bed and studied her like an insect on a pin. "I don't suppose you'd have encouraged a boy to touch you like that."

"Whatever for?" she asked curiously.

His jaw clenched, hard. "Tellie, don't you…feel anything…with boys?"

She cocked her head. "Like what?"

"Like an urge to kiss them, to let them touch you."

The color in her cheeks mushroomed. She could barely meet his eyes. "I don't… I don't feel that way."

"Ever?"

She shifted, frowning. "What's gotten into you, J.B.? I'm only seventeen. There's plenty of time for that kind of thing when I'm old enough to think about marriage."

His fist clenched in his pocket. Even at her real age, he'd never seen her get flustered around anything male, not even himself. The one time he'd kissed her with intent, on his own sofa, she'd given in at once, but she'd been reticent and shocked more than aroused. He was beginning to think that she'd never been aroused in her life; not even with him. It stung his pride, in one way, and made him hungry in another. It disturbed him that he couldn't make Tellie want him. God knew, most other women did.

"Is that what you meant, when you called me a kid earlier?" she asked seriously.

He moved to the foot of the bed, with his hands still shoved deep in his pockets, and stared at her. "Yes. That's what I meant. You're completely unawakened. In this modern day and age, it's almost unthinkable for a woman your age to know so little about men."

"Well, gee whiz, I guess I'd better rush right out there and get myself a prescription for the pill and get busy, huh?" she asked rakishly. "Heaven forbid that I should be a throwback to a more conservative age, especially in this house! Didn't you write the book on sexual liberation?"

He felt uncomfortable. "Running with the crowd is the coward's way out. You have to have the courage of your convictions."

"You've just told me to forget them and follow the example of the Romans."

He glowered. "I did not!"

She threw up her hands. "Then why are you complaining?"

"I wasn't complaining!"

"You don't have to yell at me," she muttered. "I'm sick."

"I think I'm going to be," he said under his breath.

"You sure have changed since I was in the wreck," she murmured, staring at him curiously. "I never thought I'd see the day when you'd advise me to go out and get experienced with men. I don't even know any men." She frowned. "Well, that's not completely true. I know Grange." Her eyes brightened. "Maybe I can ask him to give me some pointers. He looks like he's been around!"

J.B. looked more and more like the storm outside. He moved toward the bed and sat down beside her, leaning down with his hands on either side of her face on the pillow. "You don't need lessons from Grange," he said through his teeth. "When you're ready to learn," he added on a deep, husky breath, "I'll teach you."

Ripples of pleasure ran up and down her nerves, leaving chill bumps of excitement all over her arms. Her breath caught at the thought of J.B.'s hard, beautiful mouth on her lips.

His eyes went down to her pajama jacket, and this

time they lingered. For an instant, he looked shocked. Then his eyes began to glitter and he smiled, very slowly.

She looked down again, too, but she couldn't see anything unusual. Well, her nipples were tight and hard, and a little uncomfortable. That was because of her sudden chill. Wasn't it?

Her eyes met his again, with a faint question in them.

"You don't even understand this, do you?" he asked, and suddenly, without warning, he drew the tip of his forefinger right over one distended nipple with the faintest soft brushing motion.

She gasped out loud and her body arched. She looked, and was, shocked out of her mind.

J.B.'s green eyes darkened with sudden hunger. His gaze fell to her parted, full lips, to the pulse throbbing in the hollow of her throat. He ached to open her pajama top and put his mouth right on her breast. Unthinkable pleasures were burning in the back of his mind.

Tellie was frightened, both of what was happening to her body, and of letting him know how vulnerable she was. There was something vaguely unsettling about the way he was looking at her. It brought back a twinge of memory, of J.B. mocking her because she was weak toward him...

She brought up her arms and crossed them over her breasts.

"Spoilsport," he murmured, meeting her shocked eyes.

She fought to breathe normally. "J. B. Hammock, I'm seventeen years old!" she burst out.

He started to contradict her and realized at once that he didn't dare. He scowled and got to his feet abruptly. What the hell was he thinking?

He ran a hand over his hair and turned away. "I've got

to go to town and see a Realtor about a parcel of land that's just come up for sale," he said in a strangely thick tone. "It adjoins my north pasture. I'll send Nell up with breakfast."

"Yes, that would be...that would be nice."

He glanced back at her from the door. He felt frustrated and guilty. But behind all that, he was elated. Tellie was vulnerable to him, and not just in the girlish way she had been for the past few years. She was vulnerable as a woman. It was the first time her body had reacted to his touch in that particular way.

He should have been ashamed of himself. He wasn't. His eyes slid over her body in the pajamas as if she belonged to him already. He couldn't hide the pride of possession that he felt.

It made Tellie shake inside. Surely he wasn't thinking...?

"Don't beat yourself to death over it," he said. "We're all human, Tellie. Even me. See you later."

He went out quickly and closed the door behind him, before his aching body could provoke him into even worse indiscretions than he'd already committed.

NELL BROUGHT BREAKFAST and stared worriedly at Tellie's high color. "You're not having a relapse, are you?" she asked, worried.

Tellie wished she could confide in the housekeeper, or in someone. But she had no close friends, and she couldn't even have told Marge. She couldn't talk to Marge about her brother!

"Nothing's wrong, honest," Tellie said. "I went to look out the window, and a big flash of lightning almost made me jump out of my skin. I'm still reeling."

Nell's face relaxed. "Is that all?" She smiled. "I don't mind storms, but J.B. is always uneasy. Don't forget his grandmother died in a tornado outbreak."

"He told me," she said.

"Did he, now?" Nell exclaimed. "He doesn't talk about the old lady much."

Tellie nodded. "He doesn't talk about much of anything personal," she agreed. She frowned. "I wonder if he confides in his fashion dolls?"

Nell didn't get the point at first, but when she did, she burst out laughing. "That was mean, Tellie."

Tellie just grinned. She was going to forget what J.B. had done in those few tempestuous seconds. She was certain that he'd regretted it.

Sure enough, he didn't come in to see her at all the rest of the day. Next morning, he went out without a word.

About lunchtime, Grange showed up. Since J.B. wasn't there to keep him out, Nell escorted him up to Tellie's room with a conspiratorial grin.

"Company," Nell announced. "He can stay for lunch. I'll bring up a double tray." She went out, but left the door open.

Grange moved toward the bed with his wide-brimmed hat in his hand. He'd had a haircut and a close shave. He smelled nice, very masculine. His dark eyes twinkled as he studied Tellie in her pink pajamas.

She felt self-conscious and pulled the sheet up higher.

He laughed. "Sorry."

She shrugged. "I'm not used to men seeing me in my nightclothes," she told him. It wasn't totally true. He didn't know, and J.B. seemed to constantly forget, that she'd been almost assaulted by a boy in her early teens. It hadn't left immense scars, but she still felt uneasy about her body. She wasn't comfortable with men. She wondered if she should admit that to J.B. It might soften his provocative attitude toward her.

"I'll try not to stare," Grange promised, smiling as he sat down in the chair beside her bed. "How are you feeling?"

"Much better," she said. "I wanted to get up, but Nell won't let me."

"Concussion is tricky," he replied, and he didn't smile. "The first few days are chancy. Better you stay put in bed, just for the time being."

She smiled at him. "I'll bet you've seen your share of injuries, being in the military."

He nodded. "Concussion isn't all that uncommon in war. I've seen some nasty head injuries that looked pretty innocent at first. Better safe than sorry."

"I hate being confined," she confessed. "I want to get out and do things, but Dr. Coltrain said I couldn't. Nell and J.B. are worse than jailers," she added.

He chuckled. "Nell's a character." He hesitated. "Did you know there's a chef in the kitchen, complete with tall white hat and French accent?"

She nodded. "That's Albert," she replied. "He's been here for the past ten years. J.B. likes continental cuisine."

"He seems to be intimidated by Nell," he observed.

"He probably is. Gossip is that when Albert came here, Nell was in possession of the kitchen and unwilling to turn it over to a foreigner. They say," she added in a soft, conspiratorial tone, "that she chased him into the living room with a rolling pin when he refused to make dumplings her way. It took a pay raise and a big-screen TV for his room to keep him here. J.B. and Nell had a real falling out about that, and she threatened to quit. She got a raise, too." She laughed shortly. She'd remembered something from the past! Surely the rest couldn't be far behind now.

Grange chuckled at what she'd told him about Nell. "She seems formidable enough."

"She is. She and J.B. argue most of the time, but it's usually in a good-natured way."

He put his hat on the floor beside his chair and raked a hand through his neatly trimmed straight dark hair. "When they let you out of here, we'll go take in a new science-fiction movie. How about that?"

She smiled. "Sounds like fun." She was curious about him. He didn't seem the sort of man to be vulnerable to women, but it was apparent that he liked Tellie. "Do you have family here in Jacobsville?" she asked in all innocence.

His face hardened. His dark eyes narrowed. "No."

She frowned. She'd struck a nerve. "I'm sorry, is there something else I don't remember—?"

"There's a lot," he cut her off, but gently. "You're bound to wander into a few thickets before you find the right path. Don't worry about it."

She drew in a long breath. "I feel like I'm walking around in a fog. Everybody's hiding things from me."

"It's necessary. Just for a week or so," he promised.

"You know about me, don't you? Can't you tell me?"

He held up a hand and laughed. "I'd just as soon not get on the wrong side of Hammock while you're living under his roof. I'd lose visiting privileges. I may lose them anyway, if Nell spills the beans that I've been here while he was out."

"Doesn't he like you?"

"He doesn't like most people," he agreed. "Especially me, at the moment."

"What did you do to him?"

"It's a long story, and it doesn't concern you right now," he said quietly.

She flushed. His voice had been very curt.

"Don't look like that," he said, feeling guilty "I don't want to hurt you. J.B. and I have an unfortunate history, that's all."

She blinked. "It sounds unpleasant."

"It was," he confessed. "But it happened a long time ago. Right now, our only concern is to get you well again."

Footsteps sounded on the staircase and a minute later, Nell walked in with a tray holding two plates, two glasses of iced tea and a vase full of yellow roses.

"Never thought I'd get up the stairs with everything intact," she laughed as Grange got up and took the tray from her, setting it down gently on the mahogany side table by the bed.

"The roses," Tellie exclaimed. "They're beautiful!"

"Glad you like them," Grange said easily, and with a smile. "We do live in Texas, after all."

"'The Yellow Rose of Texas,'" she recalled the song. She reached over and plucked one of the stems out of the vase to smell it. There was a delicate, sweet scent. "I don't think I've ever had a bouquet of flowers in my life," she added, confused.

"You haven't," Nell replied for her. She sounded irritated. "Nice of Grange to remember that sick people usually like flowers."

She smiled at him. "Wasn't it?" she laughed. "I'll enjoy them. Thank you."

"My pleasure," he replied, and his voice was soft.

Nell stuck a plate in his hands and then put Tellie's

on her lap. "Eat, before the bread molds," she told them. "That's homemade chicken salad, and I put up those dill pickles myself last summer."

"Looks delicious," Grange said. "You didn't have to do this, Nell."

"I enjoy making a few things on my own," she said. She grimaced. "I had to lock Albert in the closet, of course. His idea of a sandwich involves shrimp and sauce and a lettuce leaf on a single piece of toasted rye bread." She looked disgusted.

"That's not my idea of one," Grange had to admit.

"This is really good," Tellie exclaimed after she bit into her sandwich.

"Yes, it is," Grange seconded. "I didn't have time for breakfast this morning."

"Enjoy," Nell said, smiling. "I'll be back up for the tray later."

They both nodded, too involved with chewing to answer.

GRANGE ENTERTAINED HER with stories from his childhood. She loved the one about the cowboy, notorious for his incredible nicotine habit, who drove his employer's Land Rover out into the desert on a drunken joyride, forgetting to take along a shovel or bottled water or even a flashlight. He ran out of gas halfway back and when they found him the next morning, almost dead of dehydration, the first thing he asked for was a cigarette.

"What happened to him?" she asked, laughing.

"After he got over the experience, the boss put him on permanent barn duty, cleaning out the horse stalls. The cowboy couldn't get a job anywhere else locally because of that smoking habit, so he was pretty much stuck."

"He couldn't quit?"

"He wouldn't quit," he elaborated. "Then he met this waitress and fell head over heels for her. He quit smoking, stopped drinking and married her. He owns a ranch of his own now and they've got two kids." His dark eyes twinkled. "Just goes to show that the love of a good woman can save a bad man."

She pursed her lips. "I'll keep that in mind."

He laughed. "I'm not a bad man," he pointed out. "I just have a few rough edges and a problem with authority figures."

"Is that why you don't get along with J.B.?"

He shook his head. "That's because we're too much alike in temperament," he said. He checked his watch. "I've got to run," he said, swooping up his hat as he got to his feet. "Can't afford to tick off my boss!"

"Will you come again?" she asked.

"The minute the coast is clear," he promised, laughing. "If Nell doesn't sell us out."

"She won't. She's furious at J.B. I don't know why, nobody tells me anything, but I overheard her say that she'd quit and had to come back to take care of me. Apparently she and J.B. had a major blowup before I got hurt. I wish I knew why."

"One of these days, I'm sure you'll find out. Keep getting better."

"I'll do my best. Thanks again. For the roses, and for coming to see me."

"I enjoyed it. Thanks for lunch."

She grinned. "I'll cook next time."

"Something to look forward to," he teased, winking at her.

J.B. CAME IN LATE. Apparently he'd been out with which-ever girlfriend he was dating, because he was dressed up and a faint hint of perfume clung to his shirt as he sat down in the chair beside Tellie's bed. But he looked more worried than weary, and he wasn't smiling.

She eyed him warily. "Is something wrong?" she asked.

He leaned back in the chair, one long leg crossed over the other. She noted how shiny his hand-tooled black boots were, how well his slacks fit those powerful legs. She shook herself mentally. She didn't need to notice such things about him.

"Nothing much," he said. Actually he was worried about Marge. She was in the early stages of treatment for high blood pressure, and she'd had a bad dizzy spell this afternoon. The girls had called him at work, and he'd gone right over. He'd phoned Coltrain, only to be re-assured that some dizziness was most likely a side effect of the drug. She was having a hard time coping, and she missed Tellie, as well as being worried about her health. J.B. had assured Marge that Tellie was going to be fine, but his sister wanted to see Tellie. He couldn't manage that. Not yet.

He drew in a long breath, wondering how to avoid the subject. That was when he looked at her bedside table carelessly and saw the huge bouquet of yellow roses. His green eyes began to glitter as he stared at her.

"And just where," he asked with soft fury, "did you get a bouquet of roses?"

CHAPTER NINE

"They were a present," Tellie said quickly.

"Were they?" he asked curtly. "From whom?"

She didn't want to say it. There was going to be a terrible explosion when she admitted that she'd had a visitor. It didn't take mind-reading skills to realize that J.B. didn't like Grange.

She swallowed. "Grange brought them to me."

The green eyes were really glittering now. "When?"

"He stopped by on his lunch hour," she said. She glared up at him. "Listen, there's nothing wrong with having company when you're sick!"

"You're in your damned pajamas!" he shot back.

"So?" she asked belligerently. "You're looking at me in them, aren't you?"

"I don't count."

"Oh. I see." She didn't, but it was best not to argue with a madman, which is how he looked at the moment.

His lips made a thin line. "I'm family."

She might have believed that before yesterday, she thought, when he'd touched her so intimately.

The memory colored her cheeks. He saw it, and a slow, possessive smile tugged up his firm, chiseled lips. That made the blush worse.

"You don't think of me as family?" he asked softly.

She wanted to dive under the covers. It wasn't fair that he could reduce her to this sort of mindless hunger.

He leaned over her, the anger gone, replaced by open curiosity and something else, less definable.

His fingers speared through her dark hair, holding her head inches from the pillow behind her. His chest rose and fell quickly, like her own. His free hand went to her soft mouth and traced lazily around the upper lip, and then the lower one, with a sensuality that made her feel extremely odd.

"I'm...seventeen," she choked, grasping for a way to save herself.

His dark green gaze fell to her parted lips. "You're not," he said huskily, and the hand in her hair contracted. "It can't hurt for you to know your real age. You're almost twenty-two. Fair game," he added under his breath, and all at once his hard, sensuous mouth came down on her lips with firm purpose.

She gasped in surprise, and her hand went to his chest. That was a mistake, because it was unbuttoned in front and her fingers were enmeshed in thick, curling dark hair that covered the powerful muscles.

His head lifted, as if the contact affected him. His eyes narrowed. His heart, under her fingertips, beat strongly and a little fast.

"You shouldn't..." she began, frightened of what was happening to her.

"I've waited a long time for this," he said enigmatically. He bent to her mouth again. "There's nothing to be afraid of, Tellie," he whispered into her lips. "Nothing at all..."

The pressure increased little by little. Her fingers dug

into his chest as odd sensations worked themselves down her body, and she shivered.

He smiled against her parted lips. "It's about time," he murmured, and his mouth grew insistent.

She felt his body slowly move closer, so that they were lying breast to breast on the soft mattress. One lean hand slid under the pajama top, against her rib cage, warm and teasing. She should grab his wrist and stop him, her mind was saying, because this wasn't right. He was a notorious womanizer and she was like his ward. She was far too young to be exposed to such experienced ardor. She was…but he'd said she was almost twenty-two years old. Why hadn't she remembered her age?

His hand contracted in her soft hair. "Stop thinking," he bit off against her mouth. "Kiss me, Tellie," he breathed, and his hand suddenly moved up and cupped her soft, firm breast. His head lifted, to watch her stunned, delighted reaction.

For an instant, she stiffened. But then his thumb rubbed tenderly over the swollen nipple, and a ripple of ardent desire raged in her veins. She drew in a shivery, shaking breath. The pressure increased, just enough to be arousing. She arched involuntarily, and moaned.

"Yes," he said, as though she'd spoken.

His hand swallowed her whole, and his mouth moved gently onto her parted lips, teasing, exploring, demanding. All her defenses were down. There was no tomorrow. She had J.B. in her arms, wanting her. Whether it was wrong or not, she couldn't resist him. She'd never known that her body could experience anything so passionately satisfying. She felt swollen. She wanted to pull him closer. She wanted to touch him, as he was touching her. She wanted…everything!

Her arms slid up around his neck and she arched into the warm pressure of his hand on her body.

His mouth increased its pressure, until he broke open her mouth and his tongue moved inside, in slow, insistent thrusts that made her moan loudly. She'd never been kissed in such an intimate way. She'd never wanted to be. But this was delicious. It was the most delicious taste of a man she'd ever had. She wanted more.

He hadn't meant to let things get so far out of control, but he went under just as quickly as she did. His hand left her breast to flick open the buttons of her pajama jacket. She whispered something, but he didn't hear it. He was blind, deaf, dumb to anything except the taste and feel of her innocence.

He kissed her again, ardently, and while she followed his mouth, he stripped her out of the pajama top and opened the rest of the buttons over his broad chest. He gathered her hungrily to him, dragging his chest against hers so that the rasp of hair only accentuated the pleasure she was feeling.

When his lean, hard body moved over hers, she was beyond any sort of protest. Her long legs parted eagerly to admit the intimacy of his body. She shivered when she felt him against her. She hadn't realized how it would feel, when a man was aroused, although she'd read enough about it in her life. Other women were vocal about their own affairs, and Tellie had learned from listening to them talk. She'd been sure that she would never be vulnerable to a man like this, that she'd never be tempted to give in with no thought beyond satisfaction. What she was feeling now put the lie to her overconfidence. She was as helpless as any woman in love.

Even knowing that J.B. was involved more with his

body than his mind didn't help her resist him. Whatever
he wanted, he could have. She just didn't want him to
stop. She was drowning in sensation, pulsating with the
sweetest, sharpest hunger she'd ever known.

"I've waited so long, Tellie," he groaned into her
mouth. His hand went under her hips and lifted her closer
into a much more intimate position that made her shudder all over. "God, baby, I'm on fire!"

So was she, but she couldn't manage words. She
arched up toward him, barely aware that he was looking
down at her bare breasts. He bent and put his mouth on
them, savoring their firm softness, their eager response
to his ardor.

Her nails bit into his shoulders. She rocked with him,
feeling the slow spiral of satisfaction that was just beginning, like a flash of light that obliterated reason, thought,
hope. She only wanted him never to stop.

His lean hand went to the snap that held her pajama
bottoms in place, just as loud footsteps sounded on the
staircase, accompanied by muttering that was all too familiar.

J.B. lifted his head. He looked as shocked as Tellie felt.
He looked down at her breasts and ruddy color flamed
over his high cheekbones. Then he looked toward the
hall and realized belatedly that the door was standing
wide open.

With a furious curse, he moved away from her and got
to his feet, slinging the cover over her only a minute before Nell walked in with a tray. Luckily for both of them,
she was too concerned over not dumping milk and cookies all over the floor to notice how flushed they were.

J.B. had time to fasten his shirt. Tellie had the sheet

up to her neck, covering the open pajama jacket she'd pulled on.

"Thought you might like a snack," Nell said, smiling as she put the tray down next to the vase of roses.

"I would. Thanks, Nell," Tellie said in an oddly husky tone.

J.B. kept his back to Nell as he went toward the door. "I've got a phone call to make. Sleep tight, Tellie."

"You, too, J.B.," she said, amazed at her acting ability, and his.

When he was gone, Nell moved the roses a little farther onto the table. "Aren't they beautiful, though?" she asked Tellie as she sniffed them. "Grange has good taste."

"Yes, he does," Tellie said, forcing a smile.

Nell glanced at her curiously. "You look very flushed. You're not running a fever, are you?" she asked worriedly.

Tellie bit her lower lip and tasted J.B. there. She looked at Nell innocently. "J.B. and I had words," she lied.

Nell frowned. "Over what?"

"The roses," Tellie replied. "He didn't like the idea that Grange was here."

Nell sighed, falling for the ruse. "I was afraid he wouldn't."

"Do you know why he dislikes him so much?" Tellie asked. "I mean, he agreed that I could go out with Grange, apparently. It seems odd that he wouldn't have stopped me."

"He couldn't," Nell said. "After all, you're of age…" She stopped and put her hand over her mouth, looking guilty.

"I'm almost twenty-two," Tellie said, avoiding Nell's gaze. "I…remembered."

"Well, that's progress!"

It wasn't, but Tellie wasn't about to admit to Nell that she'd had a heavy petting session with J.B. in her own bed and learned about her age that way. She could still hardly believe what had happened. If Nell hadn't walked up the staircase just at that moment... It didn't bear thinking about. What had she done? She knew J.B. was a womanizer. He didn't love women; she knew that even though she couldn't remember why. She'd given him liberties that he wasn't entitled to. Why?

"You look tired," Nell said. "Drink up that milk and eat those cookies. Leave the tray. I'll get it in the morning. Can I bring you anything else?"

A good psychiatrist, Tellie thought, but didn't dare say. She smiled. "No. Thanks a lot, Nell."

"You're very welcome. Sleep well."

She'd never sleep again, she imagined. "You, too."

The door closed behind her. Tellie sat up and started to rebutton her jacket. Her breasts had faint marks on them from J.B.'s insistent mouth. She looked at them and got aroused all over again. What was happening? She knew, she just knew, that J.B. had never touched her like that before. Why had he done it?

She lay awake long into the night, worrying the question.

THE NEXT MORNING, Nell told her that J.B. had suddenly had to fly to a meeting in Las Vegas, a cattlemen's seminar of some sort.

Tellie wasn't really surprised. Perhaps J.B. was a little embarrassed, as she was, about what they'd done together.

"He didn't take his girlfriend with him, either," Nell said. "That's so strange. He takes her everywhere else."

Tellie felt her heart stop beating. "His girlfriend?" she prompted.

"Sorry. I keep forgetting that your memory's limping. Bella," she added. "She's a beauty contestant. J.B.'s been dating her for several weeks."

Tellie stared at her hands. "Is he serious about her?"

"He's never serious about women," Nell replied. "But that doesn't mean he won't have them around. Bella travels with him, mostly, and she spends the occasional weekend in the guest room."

"This room?" Tellie asked, horrified, looking around her.

"No, of course not," Nell said, not noticing Tellie's look of horror. "She stays in that frilly pink room that we usually put women guests in. Looks like a fashion-doll box inside," she added with a chuckle. "You'd be as out of place there as I would."

The implication made her uneasy. J.B. was intimate with the beauty contestant, if she was spending weekends with him. The pain rippled down her spine as she considered how easily she'd given in to him the night before. He was used to women falling all over him, wasn't he? And Tellie wasn't immune. She wasn't even respected, or he'd never have touched her when she was a guest in his house. The more she thought about it, the angrier she got. He was involved with another woman, and making passes at Tellie. What was wrong with him?

On the other hand, what was wrong with her? She only wished she knew.

SHE GOT OUT of bed and started helping Nell around the house, despite her protests.

"I can't stay in bed my whole life, Nell," Tellie argued. "I'll never get better that way."

"I suppose not," the older woman admitted. "But you do have to take it easy."

"I will." She pushed the lightweight electric broom into the living room. The sofa caught her attention again, as it had when she'd come home from the hospital. She moved to its back and ran her hand over the smooth cloth fabric, frowning. Why did this sofa make her uneasy? What had happened in this room in the past that upset her?

She turned to Nell. "What did J.B. and I argue about?" she asked.

Nell stopped dead and stared. She was obviously hesitating while she tried to find an answer that would be safe.

"Was it over a woman?" Tellie persisted.

Nell didn't reply, but she flushed.

So that was it, Tellie thought. She must have been jealous of the mysterious Bella and said something to J.B. that hit him wrong. But, why would she have been jealous? She was almost certain that J.B. had never touched her intimately in their past.

"Honey, don't try so hard to remember," Nell cautioned. "Enjoy these few days and don't try to think about the past."

"Was it bad?" she wondered aloud.

Nell grimaced. "In a way, yes, it was," she replied. "But I can't tell you any more. I'll get in trouble. It might damage you, to know too much too soon. Dr. Coltrain was very specific."

Tellie gnawed her lower lip. "I've already graduated from high school, haven't I?" she asked.

Nell nodded, reluctantly.

"Do I have a job?"

"You had a summer job, at the Ballenger Brothers feedlot. That's where you met Grange."

She felt a twinge of memory trying to come back. There was something between J.B. and Grange, something about a woman. Not the beauty contestant, but some other woman. There was a painful secret...

She caught her head and held it, feeling it throb.

Nell moved forward and took her by the shoulders. "Stop trying to force the memories," she cautioned. "Take it one day at a time. Right now, let's do some vacuuming. Then we'll make a cake. You can invite Grange over to supper, if you like," she added, inspired. "J.B. won't be around to protest."

Tellie smiled. "I'd enjoy that."

"So would I. We'll call him at the feedlot, when we're through cleaning."

"Okay."

THEY DID THE necessary housekeeping and then made a huge chocolate pound cake. Grange was enthusiastic about coming for a meal, and Tellie was surprised at the warm feeling he evoked in her. It was friendly, though, not the tempestuous surging of her heart that she felt when she remembered the touch of J.B.'s hard lips on her mouth.

She had a suitcase that she didn't remember packing. Inside was a pretty pink striped dress. She wore that, and light makeup, for the meal. Grange showed up on time, wearing a sports jacket with dress slacks, a white shirt and a tie. He paid for dressing. He was very good-looking.

"You look nice," Tellie told him warmly as he followed her into the dining room, where the table was already set.

"So do you," he replied, producing another bouquet of flowers from behind his back, and presenting them with a grin.

"Thanks!" she exclaimed. "You shouldn't have!"

"You love flowers," he said. "I didn't think you had enough."

She gave him a wary look. "Is that the whole truth?" she asked suspiciously and with a mischievous grin, "or did you think you'd irritate J.B. if I had more flowers in my room?"

He chuckled. "Can't put anything past you, can I?" he asked.

"Thanks anyway," she told him. "I'll just put them in water. Sit down! Nell and I chased Albert out of the kitchen and did everything ourselves. I understand he's down at the goldfish pond slitting his wrists…"

"He is not!" Nell exclaimed. "You stop that!"

Tellie grinned. "Sorry. Couldn't resist it. He seems to think he owns the kitchen."

"Well, he doesn't," Nell said. "Not until I leave for good."

Leave. Leave. Tellie frowned, staring into space. Nell had quit. Tellie had been crying. Nell was shouting. J.B. was shouting back. It was raining…

Grange caught her as she fell and carried her into the living room. He put her down on the sofa. Nell ran for a wet cloth.

Tellie groaned as she opened her eyes. "I remembered an argument," she said huskily. "You and J.B. were yelling at each other…"

Nell frowned. "You couldn't have heard us," she said. "You'd already run out the door, into the rain."

Tellie could see the road, blinded by rain, feel the tires giving way, feel the car going into the ditch...!

She gasped. "I wrecked the car. I saw it!"

Nell sat down beside her and put an arm around her. "Grange saved you," she told the younger woman. "He came along in time to stop you from drowning. The ditch the car went into was full of water."

Tellie held the cloth to her forehead. She swallowed, and then swallowed again. There were odd, disturbing flashes. J.B.'s furious face. A blonde woman, staring at her. There were harsh words, but she couldn't remember what they were. She didn't want to remember!

"Did I thank you for saving me?" she asked Grange, trying to ward off the memories.

He smiled worriedly. "Of course you did. How do you feel now?"

"Silly," she said sheepishly as she sat up. "I'm sorry. There were some really odd flashbacks. I don't understand them at all."

"Don't try to," Nell said firmly. "Come on in here and eat. Let time take care of the rest."

She got up, holding on to Grange's arm for support. She drew in a long, slow breath. "One way and another, it's been a rough few days," she said.

"You don't know the half," Nell said under her breath, but she didn't let Tellie hear her.

THE NEXT DAY was Saturday. Tellie went out to the barn to see the sick calf that was being kept there while it was being treated. In another stall was a huge, black stallion. He didn't like company. He pawed and snorted as Tellie walked past him. He was J.B.'s. She knew, without re-membering or being told. She moved to another stall, where a beautiful palomino mare was eating from a feed trough. The horse perked up when she saw Tellie, and left her food to come to the front of the stall and nose Tellie's outstretched hand.

"Sand," Tellie murmured. She laughed. "That's your name. Sand! J.B. lets me ride you!"

The horse nudged her hand again. She smoothed the white blaze between the mare's eyes lazily. She was be-ginning to recover some memories. The rest, she was sure, would come in time.

She wandered past the goldfish pond on the patio and stared down at the pretty red and gold and white fish swimming around water lilies and lotus plants. The fa-cade was stacked yellow bricks, and there were huge flat limestone slabs all around it, making an endless seat for people to watch the fish. There were small trees nearby and a white wrought-iron furniture set with a patio um-brella. In fair weather, it must be heavenly to sit there. She heard a car drive up and wondered who it was. Not J.B., she was sure. It was too soon for him to be back. Monday, Nell said, was the earliest they could expect him. Perhaps it was one of the cowboys.

It was a dreary day, not good exploring weather. She wondered how Marge and the girls were, and wanted to see them. She dreaded seeing J.B. again. Things had changed between them. She was uneasy when she con-sidered that J.B. had left town so quickly afterward, as if his conscience bothered him. Or was it that he was afraid Tellie would start thinking about something serious? She knew so little about relationships...

She walked back through the side door into the living room and stopped suddenly. There was a beautiful blonde woman standing in the doorway to J.B.'s office. She was wearing a yellow dress that fit her like a second skin. She had long, wavy, beautiful hair and a perfectly made-up face. She was svelte and sophisticated, and she was giving Tellie a look that could have boiled water.

"So you're the reason I've had to be kept away from the house," the woman said haughtily.

That blonde was familiar, Tellie thought suddenly, and she wanted to run. She didn't want to talk to this person, to be around her. She was a threat.

The woman sensed Tellie's discomfort and smiled coldly. "Don't tell me you've forgotten me?" she drawled. "Not after you walked right in and interrupted me and J.B. on that very sofa?"

Sofa. J.B. Two people on the sofa, both half-naked. J.B. furious and yelling. Nell rushing to see why Tellie was crying.

Tellie put her hands to her mouth as the memories began to rush at her, like daggers. It was all coming back. J.B. had called her ugly. A stray. He could never love her. He didn't want her. He'd said that!

There was more. He'd missed her graduation from college and lied about it. He'd had his secretary buy Tellie a graduation present—he hadn't even cared enough to do it himself. He'd accused Tellie of panting after him like a pet dog. He'd said he was sick of her...pawing him... trying to touch him.

She felt the rise of nausea in her throat like a living thing. She brushed past the blonde and ran for the hall bathroom, slamming the door behind her. She barely made it to the sink before she lost her breakfast.

"TELLIE?"

The door opened. Nell came in, worried. "Are you all right? Oh, for goodness sake…!"

She grabbed a washcloth from the linen closet and wet it, bathing Tellie's white face. "Come on. Let's get you back to bed."

"That woman…" Tellie choked.

"I showed her the door," Nell said coldly. "She won't come back in a hurry, I guarantee!"

"But I recognized her," Tellie said unsteadily. "She and J.B. were on the sofa together, half-naked. He yelled at me. He accused me of trying to paw him. He said he was sick of the way I followed him around. He said…" She swallowed the pain. "He said I was nothing but an ugly stray that he'd taken in, and that he could never want me." Tears rolled down her cheek. "He said he never… wanted to see me again!"

"Tellie," Nell began miserably, not knowing what to say.

"Why did he bring me here, after that?" she asked tearfully.

"He felt guilty," Nell said gently. "It was his fault that you wrecked the car. You would have died, if Grange hadn't found you."

Tellie wiped her eyes with the wet washcloth. "I knew there was something," she choked. "Some reason that he wasn't giving me. Guilt. Just guilt." Was that why he'd kissed her so hungrily, too? Was he trying to make amends for what he'd said? But it was only the truth. He didn't want her. He found her repulsive…

The tears poured down her face. She wanted to climb into a hole. That beautiful blonde was J.B.'s woman. She'd come to Marge's house with J.B., and she'd insulted Tellie. They'd argued, and J.B. had shown Tellie what a hold he had over her, using her weakness for him as a punishment. She closed her eyes. How could he have treated her so horribly?

"I want to go back to Marge's house," Tellie said shakily. "Before he comes home." She looked into Nell's eyes. "And then I never want to see him again, as long as I live!"

CHAPTER TEN

NELL COULDN'T TALK Tellie into staying at the house, not even when she assured her that J.B. wouldn't be back until Monday. Tellie had remembered that Marge had a heart attack, and she was frantic until Nell assured her that Marge was going to be all right. It was even lucky that they'd found the high blood pressure before it killed her.

Now that Tellie remembered everything, there were no more barriers to her going to Marge. She remembered her job at the feedlot, as well, and hoped she still had it. But she phoned Justin at home and he assured her that her job would be waiting when she was recovered. That was a load off her mind.

She didn't dare think about J.B. It was too terrible, remembering the hurtful things he'd said to her. She knew she'd never forgive him for the way he'd reacted when she'd tried to tell him about Marge, much less for his ardor when he knew there was no future in it. He'd taunted her with her feelings one time too many. She wondered what sort of cruel game he'd been playing in her bedroom at his house.

Marge and the girls met her at the door, hugging her warmly. Nell had driven her there, and she was carrying two suitcases.

"Are you sure about this?" Nell asked worriedly.

Marge nodded, smiling warmly. "You know you're welcome here. None of us will yell at you, and we'll all be grateful that we don't have to depend on Dawn's cooking for…"

"Mother!" Dawn exclaimed.

"Sorry," Marge said, hugging her daughter. "I love you, baby, but you know you're terrible in the kitchen, even if you can sing like an angel. Nobody's perfect."

"J.B. thinks he is," Nell muttered.

Marge laughed. "Not anymore, I'll bet. I hope you left him a note, at least."

"I did," Nell confessed. "Brief, and to the point. I hope that blonde fashion doll of his can cook and clean."

"That isn't likely," Tellie said coolly. "But they can always get takeout."

"Are you sure you're okay?" Marge asked Tellie, moving to hug her, too. "Your color's bad."

"So is yours, worrywart," Tellie said with warm affection, returning the hug. "But I reckon the two of us will manage somehow, with a little help."

"Between us," Marge sighed, "we barely make one well person."

"I'll fatten you both up with healthy, non-salty fare," Nell promised. "Dawn and Brandi can see me to my room and help me unpack. Right?"

The girls grinned. "You bet!" they chorused, delighted to see the end of meal preparation and housework. Nell was the best in town at housekeeping.

They marched up the staircase together, the girls helping with the luggage.

Marge studied Tellie closely, her sharp eyes missing nothing. "You wouldn't be here unless something major had happened. What was it?"

"My memory came back," Tellie said, perching on the arm of the sofa.

"Did it have any help?" the older woman asked shrewdly.

Tellie grimaced, her eyes lowering to the sea-blue carpet. "Bella kindly filled me in on a few things."

Marge cursed under her breath as forcefully as J.B. ever had. "That woman is a menace!" she raged. "Copper Coltrain said it would be dangerous for us to force-feed you facts about the past until you remembered them naturally!"

"I'm sure she only wanted J.B. to herself again, and thought she was helping him get me out of the way. I don't mind," Tellie added at once. "J.B. raised hell when Grange came and brought me roses. At least you're not likely to mind that."

Marge smiled. "No, I'm not. I like your friend Grange."

Tellie's eyes were sad and wise. "He's been a wonderful friend. Who'd have thought he'd turn out to be pleasant company, with his background?"

"Not anyone locally, that's for sure." Marge sat down on the sofa, too. She was still pale. "Nothing wrong," she assured Tellie, who was watching her closely. "The medicine still makes me a little dizzy, but it's perfectly natural. Otherwise, I'm seeing an improvement all around. I think it's going to work."

"Goodness, I hope so," Tellie said gently. She smiled. "We can't lose you."

"You aren't going to. Nice of you to bring Nell with you," she added wryly. "Housework and cooking was really getting to us, without you here. Did she come willingly?"

"She met me at the front door with her suitcase," she

replied. "She was furious at what Bella had done. She thinks maybe J.B. put her up to it."

Marge scowled. "That isn't likely. Whatever his faults, J.B. has a big heart. He was really concerned about you."

"He felt guilty," Tellie translated, "because he felt responsible for the wreck. He yelled at me and said some terrible things," she added, without elaborating. Her sad eyes were evidence enough of the pain he'd caused Tellie. "I couldn't stay under his roof, when I remembered them."

Marge picked at a fingernail. "That bad?"

Tellie nodded, averting her eyes.

"Then I suppose it's just as well for you to stay here."

"I don't want to see him," she told Marge. "Not ever again. He's had one too many free shots at me. I'll finish out the week at Ballenger's when I get back on my feet, and then I'm going to ask my alma mater for an adjunct position teaching history for night students. I can teach at night and go to classes during the day. The semester starts very soon."

"Is it wise, to run away from a problem?" the other woman queried.

"In this case, it's the better part of valor," she replied grimly. "J.B. didn't just say unpleasant things to me, Marge, he actually taunted me with the way I felt about him. That's hitting below the belt, even for J.B."

"He did that?" Marge exclaimed.

"Yes. And that's why I'm leaving." She got up. She smiled at Marge. "Not to worry, you'll have Nell to take over here for me, and pamper all three of you. I won't have to be nervous about leaving you. Nell will make sure you do what the doctor says, and she'll cook healthy meals for you."

"J.B. is going to be furious when he gets home and finds you both gone," Marge predicted. She was glad she wasn't going to have to be the one to tell him.

IT WAS DARK and raining when J.B. climbed out of the limo he'd hired to take him to and from the airport. He signed the charge slip, tipped the driver with two big bills and carried his flight bag and attaché case up the driveway to the house.

It was oddly quiet when he used his key to open the front door. Usually there was a television going in Nell's room, which could be heard faintly coming down the staircase. There were no lights on upstairs, and no smells of cooking.

He frowned. Odd, that. He put down his suitcase and attaché case, and opened the living room door.

Bella was stretched out on the sofa wearing a pink gown and negligee and a come-hither smile.

"Welcome home, darling," she purred. "I knew you wouldn't mind if I moved into my old room."

He was worn-out and half out of humor. Bella's mood didn't help. What in the world must Tellie be thinking of this new development, despite her lack of memory.

"What did you tell Tellie?" he asked.

Her eyebrows arched. "I only reminded her of how she found us together the night your sister had to go to the hospital," she drawled. "She remembered everything else just fine, after that, and she went to your sister's." She smiled seductively. "We've got the whole night to ourselves! I'm cooking TV dinners. They'll be ready in about ten minutes. Then we can have champagne and go to bed…"

"You told her that?" he burst out, horrified.

She glowered, moving to sit up. "Now, J.B., you know she was getting on your nerves. You never go to those stupid seminars, you just wanted to get away from her."

"That isn't true," he shot back. And it wasn't. He'd gone to give Tellie, and himself, breathing space. Her ardent response had left his head spinning. For the first time in their relationship, Tellie had responded to him as a woman would, with passion and hunger. He hadn't slept an entire night since, reliving the delicious interlude time after time. He'd had to leave, to make sure he didn't press Tellie too hard when she was fragile, make sure he didn't force memories she wasn't ready for. He'd hoped to have time to show her how tender he could be, before she remembered how cruel he'd been. Now the chance was gone forever, and the source of his failure was sprawled on his sofa in a negligee planning to replace Tellie. He felt a surge of pure revulsion as he looked at Bella.

"Nell!" he called loudly.

"Oh, she went with the girl to your sister's," Bella said, yawning. "She left a note on your desk."

He went to his study to retrieve it, feeling cold and dead inside. The note was scribbled on a memo pad. It just said that Nell was going to work for Marge, and that she hoped Bella was domesticated.

He threw it down on the desk, overwhelmed with frustration. Bella came up behind him and slid her arms around him.

"I'll check on the TV dinners," she whispered. "Then we can have some fun…"

He jerked away from her, his green eyes blazing. "Get dressed and go home," he said shortly. He took out his wallet and stuffed some bills into her hand.

"Where are you going?" she exclaimed when he walked toward the front door.

"To get Nell and Tellie back," he said shortly, and kept walking.

Bella actually screamed. But it didn't do any good. He didn't even turn his head.

MARGE MET HIM at the door. She didn't invite him in.

"I'm sorry," she said, stepping onto the porch with him. "But Tellie's been through enough today. She doesn't want to see you."

He shoved his hands into his pockets, staring at her. "I leave town for two days and the world caves in on me," he bit off.

"You can thank yourself for that," his sister replied. Her dark eyes narrowed. "Was it necessary to use Tellie's weakness for you against her like a weapon?"

He paled a little. "She told you?" he asked slowly.

"The bare bones, nothing more. It was low, J.B., even for you. Just lately, you're someone I don't know."

His broad shoulders lifted and fell. "Grange brought back some painful memories."

"Tellie wasn't responsible for them," she reminded him bluntly.

He drew in a sharp breath. "She won't give up Grange. It's disloyal."

"They're friends. Not that you'd recognize the reference. You don't have friends, J.B., you have hot dates," she pointed out. "Albert phoned and said your current heartthrob was preparing dinner for you. Frozen dinners, I believe…?"

"I didn't ask Bella to move in while I was away!" he

shot back. "And I sure as hell didn't authorize her to fill Tellie in on the past!"

"I'm sure she thought she was doing you a favor, and removing the opposition at the same time," Marge said, folding her arms across her chest. "I love you, J.B., but I'm your sister and I can afford to. You're hard on women, especially on Tellie. Lately it's like you're punishing her for having feelings for you."

His high cheekbones went ruddy. He looked away from Marge. "I didn't want anything permanent, at first."

"Then you should never have encouraged Tellie, in any way."

He sighed roughly. He couldn't explain. It flattered him, softened him, that Tellie thought the world revolved around him. She made him feel special, just by caring for him. But she hadn't been able to give him passion, and he was afraid to take a chance on her without it. For years, he'd given up passionate love, he was afraid of it. When Tellie left for college he didn't want her to be hurt, but he didn't want to be hurt himself. He loved too deeply, too intensely. He couldn't live with losing another woman, the way he'd lost his late fiancée. But now Tellie was a woman, and he felt differently. How was he going to explain that to Tellie if he couldn't get near her?

"Tellie's changed in the past few weeks. So have I." He shifted. "It's hard to put it into words."

Marge knew that he had a difficult time talking about feelings. She and J.B. weren't twins, but they'd always been close. She moved toward him and put a gentle hand on his arm. "Tellie's going back to Houston in a week," she said quietly. "Do her a favor, and leave her alone while she finishes out her notice at the feedlot. Let her get used to being herself. Then maybe you can talk to her, and she'll listen. She's just hurt, J.B."

"She wasn't going back to school until fall semester," he said shortly. "She's been through a lot. She shouldn't start putting pressure on herself this soon."

"She doesn't see it that way. She's going to teach adult education at her college at night and attend classes during the day during summer semester." She lowered her eyes to his chest. "I want her to be happy. She's never going to be able to cope with the future until you're out of her life. I know you're fond of her, J.B., but it would be kinder to let her go."

He knew that. But he couldn't let her go, now that he knew what he wanted. He couldn't! His face reflected his inner struggle.

Her hand closed hard on his forearm. "Listen to me," she said firmly, "you of all people should know how painful it is to love someone you can't have. Everyone knows you don't want marriage or children, you just want a good time. Bella's your sort of woman. You couldn't hurt her if you hit her in the head with a brickbat, she's so thick. Just enjoy what you've got, J.B., and let Tellie heal."

He met her eyes. His were turbulent with frustrated need and worry. "I wanted to try to make it up to her," he bit off.

"Make what up to her?"

He looked away. "So much," he said absently. "I've never given her anything except pain, but I want to make her happy."

"You can't do that," his sister said quietly. "Not unless you want her for keeps."

His eyes narrowed in pain. He *did* want her for keeps. But he was afraid.

"Don't try to make her into a casual lover," Marge cautioned. "You'd destroy her."

"Don't you think I know?" he asked curtly. He turned away. "Maybe you're right, Marge," he said finally, defeated. "It would be kinder to let go for the time being. It's just that she cared for me, and I gave her nothing but mockery and indifference."

"You can't help that. You can't love people just because they want you to," Marge said wisely. "Tellie's going to make some lucky man a wonderful wife," she added gently. "She'll be the best mother a child could want. Don't rob her of that potential by giving her false hope."

Tellie, with a child. The anguish he felt was shocking. Tellie, married to another man, having children with another man, growing old with another man. He'd never considered the possibility that Tellie could turn her affections to someone else. He'd assumed that she'd always worship him. He'd given her the best reason on earth to hate him, by mocking her love for him.

"I've been taking a long look at myself," he said quietly. "I didn't like what I saw. I've been so busy protecting myself from pain that I've inflicted it on Tellie continuously. I didn't mean to. It was self-defense."

"It was cruel," Marge agreed. "Throwing Bella up to her, parading the woman here in Tellie's home, taunting her for wanting to take care of you." She shook her head. "I'm amazed that she was strong enough to take it all these years. I couldn't have."

"What about Grange?" he asked bitterly.

"What about him?" she replied. "She's very fond of him, and vice versa. But he isn't really in the running right now. He's a man with a past, a rebel who isn't comfortable in domestic surroundings. He likes having some-one to take to the movies, but he's years away from being comfortable with even the idea of marriage."

That made J.B. feel somewhat better. Not a lot. He was thinking how miserable Tellie must be, having been force-fed the most horrible memories of her recent life. Coltrain said that her mind had been hiding from the trauma of the past. He didn't know that J.B. was respon-sible for it. He kept seeing Tellie on the gurney as she came into the emergency room, bruised and bleeding, and unconscious. If Grange hadn't shown up, Tellie would have drowned. He'd have had two dead women on his conscience, when one had always been too many.

The thought of Tellie, dead, was nauseating. She'd looked up to him since her early teens, followed him around, ached to just have him look at her. He'd deni-grated those tender feelings and made her look like a lovesick fool. That, too, had been frustration, because he wanted a woman's passion from Tellie and she hadn't been able to give it to him. Not until now. He was sorry he'd been cruel to her in his anguish. But he couldn't go back and do it over again. He had to find some way back to Tellie. Some way to make up for what he'd done to her. Some way to convince her that he wanted a fu-ture with her.

"Tell her that I'm sorry," he said through his teeth. "She won't believe it, I know, but tell her anyway."

"Sorry for what?"

He met her eyes. "For everything."

"She'll be all right," Marge told him. "Really she will. She's stronger than I ever imagined."

"She's had so little love in her life," he recalled bitterly. "Her mother didn't really care much for her. She lost her grandfather at the time she needed him most. I shoved her off onto you and took it for granted that she'd spend her life looking up to me like some sort of hero." He drew in a long breath. "She was assaulted, you know, when she was fourteen. I've pushed that to the back of my mind and neither of us insisted that she go on with therapy after a few short sessions. Maybe those memories had her on the rack, and she couldn't even talk about them."

Marge chuckled. "Think so? Tellie beat the stuffing out of the little creep and testified against him, as well. He never even got to touch her inappropriately. No, she's over that, honestly."

"Even if she is, I made her suffer for having the gall to develop a crush on me."

He sounded disgusted with himself. Marge could have told him that it was no crush that lasted for years and years and took all sorts of punishment for the privilege of idolizing him. But he probably knew already.

He looked up at the darkening sky. "I know how it must look, that I've had Bella staying at the house, and taken her on trips with me. But I've never slept with her," he added with brutal honesty.

Marge's eyebrows arched. That was an odd admission, from a rounder like her brother. "It can't be from lack of encouragement," she pointed out.

"No," he agreed. "It couldn't."

She felt inadequate to the task at hand. She wondered if she was doing the right thing by asking him not to approach Tellie. But she didn't really know what else there was to do. She felt sorry for both of them, especially for her brother who'd apparently discovered feelings for Tellie too late.

"I don't want a wife right now," he said, but without the old conviction. "She knows that, anyway."

"Sure she does," his sister agreed.

He turned and looked down at her with soft affection. "You doing okay?"

She nodded, smiling. "Nell's going to be a treasure. I can't do a lot of the stuff I used to, and the girls hate cooking and housework. With Tellie gone, it's up to us to manage. Nell will make my life so much easier. I can probably even go back to work when the medicine takes hold."

"Do you want to?" he asked curiously.

"Yes," she said. "I'm not the sort of person who enjoys staying at home with nothing intellectually challenging to do. I'd at least like to work on committees or help with community projects. Money isn't enough. Happiness takes more than a padded bank account."

"I'm finding that out," J.B. agreed, smiling. "You take care of yourself. If you need me, I'm just at the other end of the phone."

"I know that. I love you," she said, hugging him warmly.

He cleared his throat. "Yeah. Me, too." Expressing emotion was hard for him. She knew it.

She pulled away. "Go home and eat your frozen dinner."

He grimaced. "I sent Bella home in a cab. It's probably carbon by now."

"Albert will fix you something."

"When he finds out why Tellie's gone, I wouldn't bet on having anything edible in the near future."

"There are good restaurants all over Jacobsville," she pointed out.

He laughed good-naturedly. "I suppose I'll find one. Take care."

"You, too. Good night."

She closed the door and went back inside. Tellie's light was off when she went upstairs. The younger woman was probably worn completely out from the day's turmoil. She wished Tellie had never spent any time with J.B. at all. Maybe then she'd have been spared so much heartache.

TELLIE WAS HARD at work on her last day at the feedlot. It was a sweltering hot Friday, and storm clouds were gathering on the horizon. The wind was moving at a clip fast enough to stand the state flag out from its flagpole. When she went to lunch, sand blew right into her face as she climbed into Marge's car to drive home and eat.

The wind pushed the little car all over the road. It wasn't raining yet, but it looked as if it might rain buckets full.

She turned on the radio. There was a weather bulletin, noting that a tornado watch was in effect for Jacobsville and surrounding counties until late that afternoon. Tellie was afraid of tornadoes. She hoped she never had to contend with one as long as she lived.

She ate a quick lunch, surrounded by Marge and Nell and the girls, since it was a teacher workday and they weren't in school. But when she was ready to leave, the skies were suddenly jet-black and the wind was roaring like a lion outside.

"Don't you dare get in that car," Marge threatened.

"Look at the color of those clouds," Nell added, looking past them out the door.

The clouds were a neon green, and there was a strange

shape growing in them, emphasized by the increasing volume and force of the wind.

While they stood on the porch with the doors open, the sound of a siren broke into the dull rumble of thunder.

"Is that an ambulance?" Dawn asked curiously.

"No," Nell said at once. "It's the tornado alert, it's the siren on top of the courthouse." She ran for the weather radio, and found it ringing its batteries off. There was a steady red light on the console. Even before it blared out the words *tornado warning*, Nell knew what was coming.

"We have to get into the basement, right now!" Nell said, rushing to the hall staircase. "Come on!"

They piled after her, down the carpeted stairs and into the basement, into the room that had been especially built in case of tornadoes. It was steel-reinforced, with battery-powered lights and radio, water, provisions and spare batteries. The wind was audible even down there, now.

They closed themselves into the sheltered room and sat down on the carpeted floor to wait it out. Nell turned on the battery-powered scanner and instead of the weather, she turned to the fire and police frequencies.

Sharp orders in deep voices heralded the first of the damage. One fire and rescue unit was already on its way out to Caldwell Road from a report of a trailer being de-molished. There came other reports, one after another. A roof was off this building, a barn collapsed, there were trees down in the road, trees down on power lines, trees falling on cars. It was the worst damage Tellie had heard about in her young life.

She thought about J.B., alone in his house with memo-ries of his grandmother dying in such a storm. She wished she could stop caring about what happened to him. She couldn't. He was too much a part of her life, regardless of the treatment he'd handed out to her.

"I hope J.B.'s all right," Tellie murmured as the overhead light flickered and went out on the heels of a violent burst of thunder.

"So do I," Marge replied. "But he's got a shelter of his own. I'm sure he's in it."

The violence outside escalated. Tellie hid her head in her crossed arms and prayed that nobody would be killed.

SEVERAL MINUTES LATER, Nell eased the door open and listened for a minute before she went up the staircase. She was back shortly.

"It's over," she called to the others. "There's a little thunder, but it's far away, and you can see some blue sky. There are two big oak trees down in the front yard, though."

"I hope nobody got hurt," Marge mumbled as they went up the staircase.

"Call the house," Tellie pleaded with Nell. "Make sure J.B.'s all right."

Nell grimaced, but she did it. Argue they might, but she was fond of her old boss. The others stared at Nell while she listened. She winced and put down the receiver with a sad face.

"The lines are down," she said worriedly.

"We could drive over there and see," Dawn suggested.

Tellie recalled painfully the last time she'd driven over to J.B.'s place to tell him about a disaster. She couldn't bear to do it again.

"We can't get out of the driveway," Marge said uneasily. "One of the oaks is blocking the whole driveway."

"Give me your cell phone," Nell told Marge. "I'll call

my cousin at the police department and get him to have someone check."

The joy of small-town life, Tellie was thinking. Surely the police could find out for them if J.B. was safe. Tellie prayed silently while Nell waited for her cousin to come to the phone.

She listened, spoke into the phone, and then listened again, grimacing. She thanked her cousin and put down the phone, facing the others with obvious reluctance.

"The tornado hit J.B.'s house and took off the corner where his office was. He's been taken to the hospital. My cousin doesn't know how bad he's hurt. There were some fatalities," she added, wincing when she saw their faces go white. Arguments and disagreements aside, J.B. was precious to everyone in the room.

Tellie spoke for all of them. "I'm going to the hospital," she said, "if I have to walk the whole five miles!"

CHAPTER ELEVEN

As IT HAPPENED, they managed to get around the tree in their raincoats and walk out to the main highway. It was still raining, but the storm was over. Marge got on her cell phone and called her friend Barbara, who phoned one of the local firemen, an off-duty officer who agreed to pick them up and take them to the hospital.

When they got there, J.B. was in the emergency room sitting on an examination table, grinning. He had a cut across his forehead and a bruise on his bare shoulder, but his spirit seemed perfectly unstoppable.

Tellie almost ran to him. Almost. But just as she tensed to do it, a blond head came into view under J.B.'s other arm. Bella, in tears, sobbing, as she clung to J.B.'s bare chest mumbling how happy she was that he wasn't badly hurt.

She drew back and Marge and Nell and the girls joined her, out of sight of J.B. and Bella.

"You go ahead," she told them. "But…don't tell him I was here. Okay?"

Marge nodded, the others agreed. They understood without a word of explanation. "Go on out front, honey," Marge said gently. "We'll find you there when we're through."

"Okay. Thanks," Tellie said huskily, with a forced smile. Her heart was breaking all over again.

As Marge and the girls moved into the cubicle, Tellie walked back to the front entrance where there were chairs and a sofa around the information desk. She couldn't bring herself to walk into that room. J.B. hadn't looked as if he disliked Bella, despite what Marge had told her about his anger that Bella had spilled the beans about Tellie's past. He looked amazingly content, and his arm had been firm and close around Bella's shoulders.

Why, Tellie asked herself, did she continually bash her stupid head against brick walls? Love was such a painful emotion. Someday, she promised herself, she was going to learn how to turn it off. At least, as far as J. B. Hammock was concerned!

She didn't see Bella walk past the waiting room. She hardly looked up until Marge and the girls came back.

"He's going to be all right," Marge told her, hugging her gently. "Just a few cuts and bruises, nothing else. Let's go home."

Tellie smiled back, but only with her eyes.

J.B. BUTTONED HIS shirt while Bella stood waiting with his tie. He felt empty. Tellie hadn't even bothered to come and see about him. Nothing in recent years had hurt so much. She'd finally given up on him for good.

"We can get Albert to fix you something nice for breakfast," Bella said brightly.

"I'm not hungry." He took the tie and put it in place. "At least Marge and the girls cared enough to brave the storm to see me. Tellie couldn't be bothered, I guess," he said bitterly.

"She was in the waiting room," Bella said blankly.

He scowled. "Doing what?"

Bella shrugged one thin shoulder. "Crying."

Crying. She'd come to see about him after all, but she hadn't come into the room? Then he remembered that when Marge and the girls came in, he had Bella in his arms. He winced mentally. No wonder Tellie had taken off like that. She thought…

He looked down at Bella shrewdly. "I'm going to have to let Albert go," he said with calculated sadness. "With all the damage the storm did to the house and barn, I'm going to go in the hole for sure. It's been a bad year for cattle ranchers anyway."

Bella was very still. "You mean, you might lose everything?"

He nodded. "Well, I don't mind hard work. It's a challenge to start from scratch. You can move in with me, Bella, and take over the housekeeping and cooking…"

"I, uh, I have an invitation from my aunt in the Bahamas to come stay the summer with her," Bella said at once. "I'm really sorry, J.B., but I'm not the pioneering type, and I hate housework." She smiled. "It was fun while it lasted."

"Yes," he said, hiding a smile. "It was."

THE NEXT DAY was taken up finding insurance adjusters and contractors to repair the damage at the ranch. He'd lost several head of livestock to injuries from falling trees and flying debris. The barn would have to be rebuilt, and the front part of the house would need some repair, as well. He wasn't worried, though. He could well afford what needed doing. He smiled at his subterfuge with Bella. As he'd suspected, she'd only wanted him for as long as she thought he was rich and could take her to five-star restaurants and buy her expensive presents.

When he had the repairs in hand, he put on a gray

vested business suit, polished boots and his best creamy Stetson, and went over to Marge's to have a showdown with Tellie.

Nell opened the door, her eyes guilty and welcoming all at once. "Glad you're okay, boss," she said stiffly.

"Me, too," he agreed. "Where is everybody?"

"In the kitchen. We're just having lunch. There's plenty," she added.

He slipped an arm around her shoulders and kissed her wrinkled forehead with genuine affection. "I've missed you," he said simply, and walked her into the kitchen.

Marge and the girls looked up, smiling happily. They all rushed to hug him and fuss over him.

"Nell made minestrone," Marge said. "Sit down and have a bowl with us."

"It smells delicious," he remarked, putting his hat on the counter. He sat down, looking around curiously. "Where's Tellie?"

There was a long silence. Marge put down her spoon. "She's gone."

"Gone?" he exclaimed. "Where?"

"To Houston," Marge replied sadly. "She phoned some classmates and found an apartment she could share, then she phoned the dean at home and arranged to teach as an adjunct for night classes. Orientation was today, so she was able to sign up for her master's classes."

J.B. looked at his bowl with blind eyes. Tellie had gone away. She'd seen him with Bella, decided that he didn't want her, cut her losses and run for the border. Added to what she'd remembered, the painful things he'd said to her the day of the wreck, he couldn't blame her for that. She didn't know how drastically he'd changed toward her.

Now he'd have to find a way back into her life. It wasn't going to be easy. She'd never fully trust him again.

But he wasn't giving up before he'd started, he told himself firmly. He'd never really tried to court Tellie. If she still cared at all, she wouldn't be able to resist him—any more than he could resist her.

TELLIE WAS FINDING her new routine wearing. She taught a night class in history for four hours, two nights a week, and she went to classes three other days during the week. She was young and strong, and she knew she could cope. But she didn't sleep well, remembering Bella curled close in J.B.'s arm the night of the tornado. He wouldn't marry the beautiful woman, she knew that. He wouldn't marry anyone. But he had nothing to offer Tellie, and she knew, and suffered for it.

One of her classmates, John, who'd helped her find a room the night before she came back to Houston, paused by her table in the college coffeehouse.

"Tellie, can you cover for me in anthropology?" he asked. "I've got to work tomorrow morning."

She grinned up at him. John, like her, was doing master's work, although his was in anthropology. Tellie was taking the course as an elective. "I'll make sure I take good notes. How about covering for me in literature? I'll have a test to grade in my night-school course."

"No problem," he said. He grinned down at her, with a hand on the back of her chair. "Sure you don't want to go out to dinner with me Friday night?"

He was good-looking, and sweet, but he liked to drink and Tellie didn't. She was searching for a reply when she turned her gaze to the door.

Her heart jumped up into her throat. J.B. was stand-

ing just inside the door of the crowded café, searching.
He spotted her and came right on, his eyes never leaving
her as he wound through the crowd.

He stopped at her table. He spared John a brief glance
that made veiled threats.

"I'd better run," John said abruptly. "See you later,
Tellie."

"Sure thing."

J.B. pulled out a chair and sat down, tossing his hat
idly onto the chair beside hers. He didn't smile. His eyes
were intent, curiously warm.

"You ran, Tellie."

She couldn't pretend not to know what he was talking
about. She pushed back her wavy hair and picked up her
coffee cup. "It seemed sensible."

"Did it?"

She sipped coffee. "Did the tornado do much damage at the ranch?"

He shrugged. "Enough to keep me busy for several
days, or I'd have been here sooner," he told her. He paused
as the waitress came by, to order himself a cup of cappuccino. He glanced at Tellie and grinned. "Make that
two cups," he told the waitress. She smiled and went to
fill the order, while J.B. watched Tellie's face. "You can't
afford it on your budget," he said knowingly. "My treat."

"Thanks," she murmured.

He leaned back in his chair and looked at her, intently,
unsmiling. "Heard from Grange?"

She shook her head. "He phoned before I left Jacobsville to say he was going back to Washington, DC. Apparently he was subpoenaed to testify against his former
commanding officer, who's being court-martialed."

He nodded. "Cag Hart told me. He and Blake Kemp

and Grange served in the same division in Iraq. He said Grange's commanding officer had him thrown out of the army and took credit for a successful incursion that was Grange's idea."

"He told me," she replied.

The waitress came back with steaming cappuccinos for both of them. J.B. picked his up and sipped it. Tellie sniffed hers with her eyes closed, smiling. She loved the rich brew.

After a minute J.B. met her eyes again. "Tellie, is this what you really want?" he asked, indicating the coffeehouse and the college campus.

The question startled her. She toyed with the handle of her cup. "Of course it is," she lied. "When I get my doctorate, I can teach at college level."

"And that's all you want from life?" he asked. "A career?"

She couldn't look at him. "We both know I'll never get very far any other way. I have plenty of friends who cry on my shoulder about their girlfriends or ask me to take notes for them in class, or keep their cats when they go on holiday." She shrugged. "I'm not the sort of woman that men want for keeps."

He closed his eyes on a wave of guilt. He'd said such horrible things to her. She already had a low self-image. He'd lowered it more, in a fit of bad temper.

"Beauty alone isn't worth much," he said after a minute. "Neither is wealth. After I got out of the emergency room, I went home to an empty house, Tellie," he said sadly. "I stood there in the vestibule, with crystal chandeliers and Italian marble all around me, mahogany staircases, Persian rugs…and suddenly it felt like being alone in a tomb. You know what, Tellie? Wealth isn't enough.

In fact, it's nothing, unless you have someone to share it with."

"You've got Bella," she said with more bitterness than she knew.

He laughed. "I told her I was in the hole and likely to lose everything," he commented amusedly. "She suddenly remembered an invitation to spend the summer in the sun with her aunt."

Tellie's eyes lifted to his. She was afraid to hope.

He reached across the table and curled her fingers into his. "Finish your cappuccino," he said gently. "I want to talk to you."

She was hardly aware of what she was doing. This must be a dream, J.B. sitting here with her, holding her hand. She was going to wake up any minute. Meanwhile, she might as well enjoy the fantasy. She smiled at him and sipped her cappuccino.

He took her out to his car and put her in the passenger side. When he was seated behind the wheel, he reached back and brought out a shopping bag with colored paper tastefully arranged in it. "Open it," he said.

She reached in and pulled out a beautiful lacy black mantilla with red roses embroidered across it. She caught her breath. She collected the beautiful things. This was the prettiest one she'd ever seen. She looked at him with a question in her eyes.

"I picked it out myself," he told her quietly. "I didn't send Jarrett shopping this time. Don't stop. There's more, in the bottom of the bag."

Puzzled, she reached down and her fingers closed around a velvety box with a bow on it. She pulled it out and stared at it curiously. Another watch? she wondered.

"Go on. Open it."

She took off the bow and opened the box. Inside was...
another box. Frowning, she opened that one, too, and
found a very small square box. She opened that one, too,
and caught her breath. It was a diamond. Not too big, not
too small, but of perfect quality in what looked like expensive yellow gold. Next to it was an equally elegant
band studded with diamonds that matched the solitaire.

J.B. was holding his breath, although it didn't show.

She met his searching gaze. "I...don't understand."

He took the box from her, lifted out the solitaire and
slid it gently onto her ring finger. "Now, do you understand?"

She was afraid to try. Surely it was still part of the
dream. If not, it was a cruel joke.

"You don't want me," she said bitterly. "I'm ugly, and
you can't bear me to touch you...!"

He pulled her across into his arms and kissed her with
unabashed passion, cradling her against his broad chest
while his mouth proceeded to wear down all her protests.
When she was clinging to him, breathless, he folded her
in his arms and rocked her hungrily.

"I was ashamed that you found me like that with
Bella," he said through his teeth. "It was like getting
caught red-handed in an adulterous relationship. For
God's sake, don't you have any idea how I feel about
you, Tellie?" he groaned. "I was frustrated and impatient, and Bella was handy. But I've never slept with her,"
he added firmly. "And I never would have. You have to
believe that."

She was reeling mentally. She let her head slide back
on his shoulder so that she could see his face. "But...why
were you so cruel...?"

His lean hand pressed against her cheek caressingly.

"Do you remember when you were eighteen?" he asked huskily. "And I made love to you on the couch in the study?"

She flushed. "Yes."

"You loved being kissed. But when I started touching you, I felt you draw back. You liked kissing me, but you weren't comfortable with anything more intimate than that. You didn't feel anything approaching passion, Tellie. You were like a child." He sucked in a harsh breath. "And I was burning, aching, to have you. I knew you were too young. It was unfair of me to push you into a relationship you weren't nearly ready for." He studied her shocked face. "So I drew back and waited. And waited. I grew bitter from the waiting. It made me cruel."

Her eyes were wide, shocked, delighted, as she realized what had been going on. She hadn't dreamed that he might feel something this powerful for her, and for so long.

"Yes, now you see it, don't you?" he breathed, lowering his mouth to hers again, savoring its shy response. "I was at the end of my rope, and you seemed just the same. Desperation made me cruel. Then," he whispered, "you lost your memory and I had you in my house. I touched you…and you wanted me." He kissed her hungrily, roughly. "I was over the moon, Tellie. You'd forgotten, temporarily, all the terrible things I said to you when you caught me with Bella. But it ended, all too soon. Your memory came back." He buried his face in her neck, rocking her. "You hated me. I didn't know what to do. So I waited some more. And hoped. I might still be waiting, except that Bella told me she saw you crying in the emergency room when I thought you hadn't even come to see about me after the tornado hit." He kissed her again, hungrily, and felt with a sense of wonder her arms clinging to him, her mouth answering the passion of his own.

"You brought that awful woman to Marge's house and let her insult me," she complained hotly.

He kissed her, laughing. "You were jealous," he replied, unashamedly happy. "It gave me hope. I dangled Bella to make you jealous. It worked almost too well."

"You vicious man," she accused, but she was smiling.

"Look who's talking," he chided. "Grange gave me some bad moments."

"I like him very much, but I didn't love him," she replied quietly.

"No. You love me," he whispered. His eyes ate her face. "And I love you, Tellie," he whispered as he bent again to her mouth. "I love you with all my heart!"

She closed her eyes and gave in to his ardor, blind to the fact that they were sitting in a parked car on a college campus.

She felt some disturbance around her and looked up. In front of the car were three students with quickly printed squares of poster paper. One said "9," and two said "10." They were grading J.B. on his technique. He followed her amused gaze and burst out laughing.

He drew her up closer. "Don't protest," he murmured as his head bent. "I'm going for a perfect score…"

He took her back to his hotel. His intentions were honorable, of course, but it was inevitable that once they were alone, he'd kiss her. He did, and all at once the raging fever he'd contained for so many years broke its bonds with glorious abandon.

"J.B.," she protested weakly as he picked her up and

carried her into one of the bedrooms in his suite, closing the door firmly behind them.

"You can't stop an avalanche, honey," he ground out against her mouth. "I'm sorry. I love you. I can't wait any longer…!"

She was flat on her back, her jeans on the floor, swiftly joined by her blouse and everything underneath. He looked down at her with a harsh, heartfelt groan. "I knew you'd be perfect, Tellie," he whispered as he bent to touch his mouth reverently to her breasts.

There was hardly any sane answer to that sort of rapt delight. She felt faintly apprehensive, but she was wearing an engagement ring and it was apparent that it wasn't a sham, or a dream. She came straight up off the bed as his mouth increased its warm pressure on her breast and began to taste it with his tongue.

"Like that, do you?" he whispered huskily. "It's only the beginning."

As he spoke, he sat up and quickly removed every bit of fabric that would have separated them.

Shyly she looked at his hard, muscular body with eyes that showed equal parts of awe and apprehension.

"People have been doing this for millennia," he whispered as he lowered his body against hers. "If it didn't feel good, nobody would indulge."

"Well, yes, but…" she began.

His lean hand smoothed over her belly. "You have to trust me," he said softly. "I won't hurt you. I swear it."

Her body relaxed a little. "I've heard stories," she began.

"I'm not in them," he replied easily, smiling. "If I were less modest, I'd tell you that women used to write my telephone number on bathroom walls."

That tickled her and she laughed. "Don't you dare brag about your conquests," she muttered.

He laughed. "Practice," he said against her mouth. "I was practicing, while I waited for you. And this is what I learned, Tellie," he added as his body slid against hers.

She felt his hands and his mouth all over her. The lights were on and she couldn't have cared less. Sensation upon sensation rippled through her untried body. She saw J.B.'s face harden, his dark green eyes glitter as he increased the pressure of his powerful legs to part hers, as his mouth swallowed one small, firm breast and drew his tongue against it in a sweet, harsh rhythm.

He was touching her in ways she'd only read about. She gasped and moaned and, finally, begged. She hadn't dreamed that her body could feel such things, could react in this headlong, demanding, insistent way to a man's slow, insistent ardor.

The slow thrust of his body widened her eyes alarmingly and she tensed, but he whispered to her, kissed her eyes closed and never stopped for an instant. He found the place, and the pressure, that made her begin to sob and dig her nails into his hips. Then he smiled as he increased the rhythm and heard her cry out again and again with helpless delight.

It seemed hours before he finally gave in to his own need and shuddered against her in a culmination that exceeded his wildest dreams of fulfillment. He held her close, intimately joined to him, and fought to get enough air to breathe.

"Cataclysmic," he whispered into her throat. "That's what it was."

She was shivering, too, having experienced what the

self-help articles referred to as "multiple culminations of pleasure."

"I never dreamed…!" she exclaimed breathlessly.

"Neither did I, sweetheart," he said heavily. "Neither did I."

He moved and rolled over, drawing her close against his side. They were both damp with sweat and pulsating in the aftermath of explosive satisfaction.

"Marge would kill us both," she began.

He chuckled. "Not likely. She's been busy on our behalf."

"Doing what?" she asked.

He ruffled her dark hair. "Sending out emailed invitations, calling caterers, ordering stuff. Which reminds me, I hope you're free Saturday. We're getting married at the ranch."

She sat up, gasping. "We're what?"

"Getting married," he replied slowly. "Why do you think I bought two rings?"

"But you've been swearing for years that you'd never get married!" Then she remembered why and her eyes went sad. "Because of that woman, the one you were going to marry," she said worriedly.

He drew her down beside him and looked at her solemnly. "When I was twenty-one, I fell in love. She was my exact opposite, and because my father opposed the marriage, I rebelled and ran headlong into it. She took the easy way out, rather than fighting him. You were right about that, although it hurt me to acknowledge it," he said quietly. "You'd have marched right up to my father and told him to do his worst." He smiled. "It's one of the things I love about you, that stubborn determination. She wasn't strong enough to stand up to him. So she killed

herself. It would have been a disaster, if she hadn't," he
added. "I'd have walked all over her, and she'd have been
miserable. As things worked out, she saved her brother
from prison and both of us from a bitter life together. I'm
sorry it happened that way. I think she was mentally un-
stable. She was unhappy and she couldn't see a future
without me. If she'd been able to talk to anyone about it,
I don't think she'd have done it. I'll always regret what
my father did, but he paid for it, in his way. So did I, un-
fortunately. Until you came along, and shook up my life,
I didn't have much interest in living."

She felt happier, knowing that. She was sad for his
fiancée, but she couldn't be sad that she'd ended up with
J.B.

He traced her eyebrows, exploring her face, her soft
body, with slow, tender tracings. "I never knew what
love was, until you were eighteen. It was too soon, but
I'd have married you then, if you'd been able to return
what I felt for you."

Her arms closed around him. "It was too soon. I have
a degree and I've had independence."

"And now?" he asked. "What about college?"

She drew in a slow, lazy breath. "You can always go
back to college," she murmured. "I'd like to be with you
for a few years. We might have a baby together and I'll
be needed at home for a while. I can teach adult education at our community college if I get the urge. I only
need a BA for that, and I've got it."

"We might have a baby together?" he teased, smiling.
"How would that happen?"

She drew up one long leg and slid it gently over one
of his. "We could do a lot more of what we've just done,"

she suggested, moving closer to him. "If we do it enough, who knows what might happen?"

He pursed his lips and moved between her legs. "More of this, you mean?" he drawled, easing down.

"Definitely…more of this," she whispered unsteadily. She closed her eyes and tugged his mouth down over hers. Then she didn't speak again for a long, long time.

CHAPTER TWELVE

NELL WAS OVERCOME with delight when Tellie walked into Marge's house with J.B.'s arm around her. "You're back," she exclaimed to Tellie. "But what...how...why?"

J.B. lifted Tellie's left hand and extended it, with the diamond solitaire winking on her ring finger.

"Oh, my goodness!" Nell exclaimed, and hugged both of them with tearful enthusiasm. "Have you told Marge and the girls?" she asked.

"Marge is making all the arrangements for us," J.B. said with an ear-to-ear grin. "I'm sure she's told the girls. But it looks as if she was saving it as a surprise for you!"

"I can't believe it," Nell repeated, dabbing at her wet eyes. "I've never been so happy for anyone in my life! Have you had lunch?"

"Not yet," J.B. replied. "I thought we might have it with you, if that's all right?" he added with unexpected courtesy.

Nell's eyebrows went up. "Well! That's the first time you've ever treated me with any sort of courtesy."

"She's been working on me," he said, nodding toward Tellie.

"To good effect, apparently, too," Nell agreed. "I'm just floored!"

"Cook while you're getting adjusted," J.B. suggested.

"I'm going to get Tellie's bag from her room and put it in the car. Marge packed it for her."

"Thanks," she said shyly, and not without a smile.

"How did you do it?" Nell asked when he was out of sight.

Tellie shook her head. "I have no idea. He showed up at the café where I was having coffee, and the next thing I knew, I was engaged. I thought he was involved with Bella."

"So did I," Nell agreed.

"But he wasn't," she replied, with a happy smile. "I went away thinking my life was over. Now look at me."

"I couldn't be happier for you," Nell said. "For both of you."

"So am I," Tellie told her. "In fact, I'm over the moon!"

LATER, MARGE AND the girls came home, and all of them spent the evening going over wedding plans, because there wasn't much time.

J.B. drove Tellie to his house and installed her in the same guest bedroom he'd given her when she stayed with him during her bout of amnesia. They'd already decided that they'd abstain from any more sensual adventures until after the wedding, however old-fashioned it sounded.

The next day, J.B. bounced Tellie out of bed early. "Get up, get up," he teased, lifting her free of the covers to kiss her with pure delight. "We're going shopping."

"You and me?" she asked, breathless.

He nodded, smiling. "You look pretty first thing in the morning."

"But I'm all rumpled and my hair isn't brushed."

He kissed her again, tenderly. "You're the most beautiful thing in my house, and in my heart," he whispered against her lips.

She kissed him back, sighing contentedly. She had the world in her arms, she thought. The whole world!

ALBERT FIXED THEM croissants and strong coffee for breakfast, and J.B. privately lamented the lack of bacon and eggs and biscuits that Nell had always provided. Albert considered such a breakfast too heavy for normal people.

After breakfast, J.B. drove Tellie to a boutique in San Antonio to shop for a wedding gown.

"But you can't see it!" she insisted.

He glowered at her. "That's an old superstition!"

"Whether it is or not, you aren't looking," she said firmly. "Go get a cup of coffee and come back in an hour. Okay?"

He sighed irritably. "All right."

She reached up and kissed him sweetly. "I love you. Humor me."

He stopped glowering and smiled. "Headache," he accused.

"I'll make it all up to you. I promise."

He bent and brushed his mouth over her closed eyelids. "You already have. Everything!"

She hugged him close. "Go away."

He laughed, winking as he left her to go down the street toward a nearby Starbucks.

The owner of the boutique gave her a wicked grin. "You manage him very well."

"I do, don't I? But he doesn't know I'm doing it, and we're not going to tell him. Deal?"

"Deal! Now let me show you what I've got in your size…"

TELLIE ENDED UP with a gloriously embroidered gown with
cap sleeves, a tight waist, a vee neckline and an exquisite
long train, also embroidered. The veil was held in place
by jeweled combs and fell to the waist in front. It was
the most beautiful gown she'd ever seen, and it suited
her nice tan.

"I love it," Tellie told the owner. "It's a dream of a
wedding gown."

"It looks lovely on you," came the satisfied reply.
"Now for the accessories!"

BY THE TIME J.B. came back, the gown and accessories
were all neatly boxed and ready to carry out.

"Did you get something pretty?" he asked.

"Something beautiful," Tellie told him, smiling.

"I wish you'd let me pay for it," he said as they drove
home. "I'd have taken you to Neiman Marcus."

"What I got is lovely," she said, "and one of a kind.
The owner of the boutique is a designer in her own right.
You'll see. It's going to make a stir."

He clasped her hand tight in his own. "You'll make
the stir, sweetheart. You're lovely."

She gave him an odd look, and his jaw tautened.

"I didn't mean it, Tellie," he said quietly. "I was
ashamed and frustrated and I took it all out on you. I
wanted you so much. I thought you'd never be able to
feel desire for me. It made me cruel."

"Maybe if you'd tried a little harder," she pointed out,
"it wouldn't have taken me so long."

He sighed. "Leave it to you to put your finger on a
nerve and push," he said philosophically. "Yes, I should
have.But I was still living in the past, afraid of being devastated again by love. It wasn't until Grange came along,

and cauterized the wound, that I realized I was using the past as an excuse. Maybe I sensed that it was going to be different with you."

"I can see why you were reluctant," she said. Her hand tightened in his. "But I'd never hurt you, J.B. I love you too much."

"Thank God for that," he said, sighing contentedly. He smiled. "You'll never get away from me, Tellie."

"I'll never want to." She meant it, too.

THE WEDDING WAS a small, private one, but two reporters with cameramen showed up, and so did Grange, resplendent in a blue vested suit. He looked very different from the cowboy Tellie had dated. The Ballengers were there, also, with their wives, and of course Marge and Dawn and Brandi and Nell. Even Albert put on a suit and gave Tellie away.

Tellie couldn't see much of J.B. as she walked down the aisle with her veil neatly in place. But when she got to the altar, she was shocked, delighted and amused to see what he was wearing with his suit. It was one of the ties—the gaudy, green-and-gold dragon tie that she'd given him for every single birthday and Christmas for years. She had to force herself not to laugh. But she didn't miss his wink.

When the minister pronounced them man and wife, he turned and lifted her veil, and the look on his face was the most profound she'd ever seen. He smiled, tenderly, and bent and kissed her with soft, sweet reverence.

Nell and Marge cried. The girls sighed. Tellie pressed close into J.B.'s arms and just hugged him, feeling radiant and happier than she'd ever been in her life. He hugged her back, sighing contentedly.

"I suppose the best man won," Grange mused at the reception Albert and the caterers had prepared in the ballroom at the ranch.

"I guess he did," J.B. replied, with a forced smile.

"She's very special," the other man said quietly. "But it was always you, and I always knew it. I'm a bad marriage risk."

"I thought I was, too," J.B. replied. He looked toward Tellie with his heart in his eyes. "But maybe I'm not."

Grange just laughed, and lifted his champagne glass in a toast.

"How'd you come out at the court-martial?" J.B. asked.

Grange grinned. "He got five years. I got a commendation and the offer of reinstatement."

"Are you going to take them up on it?"

Grange shrugged. "I don't know yet. I'll have to think about it. I've had another offer. I'm thinking it over."

"One that involves staying here?" J.B. asked shrewdly.

"Yes." He met the other man's gaze. "Is that going to be a problem?"

J.B. smiled wryly. "Not now that Tellie's married to me," he drawled.

Grange laughed. "Just checking."

J.B. sipped champagne. "The past is over," he said. "We can't change it. All we can do is live with it. I loved your sister. I'm sorry things worked out the way they did."

"She was a sad person," the other man replied solemnly. "It wasn't the first time she'd thought about taking her own life. There were two other times, both connected with men she thought didn't want her."

J.B. looked shocked.

Grange grimaced. "Sorry. Maybe I shouldn't have said anything. But in the long run, you're better off with the truth. She was emotionally shattered, since childhood. She went to a psychiatrist when she was in high school for counseling, because she slashed her wrists."

"I didn't know," J.B. ground out.

"Neither did I until my father was dying, and told me everything. He said my mother had always worried that suicide would end my sister's life. She couldn't handle stress at all. It's nothing against her. Some people are born not being able to cope with life."

"I suppose they are," J.B. said, and he was remembering Tellie, and how she would have handled the same opposition from his father.

Grange clapped J.B. on the shoulder. "Go dance with your wife. Let the past bury itself. Life goes on. I hope both of you will be very happy. And I mean that."

J.B. shook his hand. "Thanks. You can come to dinner sometimes. As long as you don't bring roses," he added dryly.

Grange burst out laughing.

THAT NIGHT, ALBERT went to see his brother for the weekend, and Tellie and J.B. spent lazy, delicious hours trying out new ways to express their love for each other in his big king-size bed.

She was shivering and pouring sweat and gasping when they finally stopped long enough to sip cold champagne.

"I just didn't read enough books," she said breathlessly.

He grinned. "Good thing I did."

She laughed, curling close to his hairy chest. "Don't brag."

"I don't need to. Will you be able to walk tomorrow?"

"Hobble, maybe," she murmured sleepily. "I'm so tired...!"

He bent and kissed her eyelids shut. "You're magnificent."

"So are you," she said, kissing his chest.

He took the champagne glass away, put it on the table along with his own and stroked her hair. "Tellie?"

"Hmm?"

"I hope you want kids right away."

"Hmm."

He drew in a lazy breath and closed his eyes. "That had better be a yes, because we forgot to think about precautions."

She didn't answer. He didn't worry. She'd already made her stand on children very clear. He figured he'd get used to fatherhood. It would be as natural as making love to Tellie. And *that* he seemed to do to perfection, he thought, as he glanced down at her satisfied, dreamy expression.

"It's just indecent, that's what it is," Marge groaned as she and Tellie went shopping at the mall outside Jacobsville. She glowered at the younger woman. "I mean, honestly, J.B. didn't have to be so impatient!"

"It was a mutual impatience," Tellie pointed out with a grin, "and I'm happier than I ever dreamed I could be."

"Yes, but Tellie, you've just been married two weeks!"

"I noticed."

Marge shook her head. "J.B.'s strutting already. You shouldn't let him send you on errands like this. I mean, things do go wrong, sometimes..."

"They won't this time," Tellie said dreamily. "I'm as

sure of it as I've ever been of anything. Besides," she added with a grin, "tell me you aren't excited."

Marge grimaced. "Well, I am, but..."

"No buts," Tellie said firmly. "We just take one day at a time and enjoy it. Hi, Chief!" she broke off to greet their police chief. "How's it going?"

"Life is beautiful," Cash Grier said with a grin.

"We heard that Tippy laid a frying pan across the skull of her would-be assassin," Marge said, digging gently.

"She did. And have you seen the tabloid story about it, by any chance?" he asked them, and his dark eyes twinkled.

"The one that says you're getting married soon?" Tellie teased.

"That's the one. In fact, we're getting married tomorrow." He chuckled. "I'm not going to let her get away now!"

"Congratulations," Tellie told him. "I hope you'll both be as happy as J.B. and I are."

"We're going to be," he said with assurance. "I expect to grow old fighting what little crime I can dig up here in Jacobsville. In between, Tippy may make a movie or two before we start our family."

Tellie put a hand on her belly. "J.B. and I already have started," she said, smiling from ear to ear. "The blood test came back positive just yesterday."

He whistled. "You two don't waste time, do you? You've only been married two weeks!"

"We were sort of in a hurry," Tellie chuckled.

"A flaming rush," Marge added. "And now we're out prematurely buying maternity clothes, do you believe it?"

"That's the spirit," Cash said. "If you've got it, flaunt it, I always say."

He went on toward his squad car, and Tellie dragged Marge into the maternity shop.

THREE MONTHS LATER, J.B. came in looking like two miles of rough road. He was wet and muddy and his chaps were as caked as his shirt. But when he saw Tellie in her maternity pants and blouse, all the weariness went out of his face.

He chuckled, catching her by the waist. "I love the way that looks," he said, and bent to kiss her. "I'm all muddy," he murmured when she tried to move closer. "We don't want to mess up that pretty outfit. Tell you what, I'll clean up and we'll call Marge and the girls and go out for a nice supper. How about that?"

She hesitated, looking guilty. "Well…"

His eyebrows arched. "Is something wrong?" he asked, suddenly worried.

"It's not that."

"Then, what?"

"So you're finally home!" came a stringent voice from the direction of the kitchen. Nell came out, wearing a dirty apron and carrying a big spoon. "I made you chicken and dumplings, homemade rolls and a congealed fruit salad," she announced with a smile.

J.B. drew in a sharp breath. "You're back? For good?" he asked hopefully.

"For good," she said. "I have to take care of Tellie and make sure she eats right. Marge is getting some help of her own, so it isn't as if I'm leaving her in the lurch. And I gave her Albert. Is that okay?" she added worriedly.

"Thank God!" he exclaimed. "I didn't have the heart to let him go, but I'm damned tired of French cooking! All I want is meat and potatoes. And apple pie," he added.

"I made one," Nell said. "Albert likes Marge, and the girls love his cooking. They're of an age to like parties. So, all our problems are solved. Right?"

He grinned. "Most of them, anyway. I'll get cleaned up and we'll have a romantic dinner for…"

"Six," Nell informed him.

"Six?" he exclaimed.

Tellie moved close to him and reached up to kiss his dirt-smudged cheek. "I invited Marge and the girls over for chicken and dumplings. It will be romantic, though, I promise. We'll have lots of candles."

He laughed, shaking his head. "Okay. An intimate little romantic dinner for six." He kissed her back. "I love you," he said.

She smiled. "I love you back."

He went upstairs and Nell sighed. "I never thought I'd see the boss look like that," she told Tellie. "What a change!"

"I inspire him," Tellie mused. "And while I'm inspiring, I'd really like to remodel that frilly pink bedroom and make a nursery out of it."

Nell wriggled her eyebrows. "Count on me as a co-conspirator. I'll be in the kitchen."

Tellie watched her go. She looked toward the staircase, where J.B. had disappeared. So much pain, she thought, had led to so much pleasure. Perhaps life did balance the two after all. She knew that she'd been so happy. J.B. and a baby, too. Only a few months before, she'd been agonizing over a lonely, cold future. Now she was married, and pregnant, and her husband loved her obsessively. It was a dream come true.

She turned and followed Nell into the kitchen. Life, she thought dreamily, was sweet.

Later, she spared a thought for that poor young woman who'd died so tragically years ago, and for Grange, who'd paid a high price for his illegal activities. She hoped Grange would find his own happiness one day. He'd gone to DC, but was planning to come back and do something a little more adventurous than working for the Ballengers, but he didn't mention what it was. He'd sent her a postcard telling her that, with his new address. J.B. had seen the card, and murmured that he hoped Tellie wasn't planning any future contact with Grange. She assured him that she hadn't any such plans, and kissed him so enthusiastically that very soon he forgot Grange altogether.

Marge and the girls were happy about the baby, and Marge was finally in the best of health on her new medicines. Tellie was relieved that she continued to improve.

That night, while J.B. slept, Tellie sat and watched his lean, hard face, wiped clean of expression, and thought how very lucky she was. He wasn't perfect, but he was certainly Tellie's dream of perfection. She bent and very softly kissed his chiseled mouth.

His dark eyes slid open and twinkled. "Don't waste kisses, sweetheart," he whispered, and reached up to draw her down into his warm, strong arms. "They're precious."

"Yours certainly are," she whispered back, and she smiled contentedly against his mouth.

"Yours, too," he murmured.

She closed her eyes and thought of a happy future, where they'd be surrounded by children and, later, grandchildren. They'd grow old together, safe in the cocoon of their love for each other, with a lifetime of memories to share. And this, Tellie thought with delight, was only the beginning of it all! Her arms tightened around J.B. Life was sweeter than her dreams had ever been. Sweeter than them all.

* * * * *